Jodi Perry was born in Sydney, Australia, and has lived there her whole life. Under the name J.L. Perry, her last four novels were all number one bestsellers in ebook. Jodi travels annually to the UK and US to promote her books and to meet her many fans.

Nineteen Letters is the first novel to be published under the name Jodi Perry.

Jodi would love to hear from you

f /JodiLPerryAuthor

🐦 @JLPerryAuthor

JODI PERRY

Nineteen Letters

sphere

SPHERE

Published in Australia and New Zealand in 2017 by Hachette Australia
(an imprint of Hachette Australia Pty Limited)
First published in Great Britain in epub by Sphere in 2017
This paperback edition published by Sphere in 2018

13 5 7 9 10 8 6 4 2

A CIP catalogue record for this book
is available from the British Library.

ISBN 978-0-7515-7183-7

Printed and bound in Great Britain by
Clays Ltd, St Ives plc

Papers used by Sphere are from well-managed forests
and other responsible sources.

Sphere
An imprint of
Little, Brown Book Group
Carmelite House
50 Victoria Embankment
London EC4Y 0DZ

An Hachette UK Company
www.hachette.co.uk

www.littlebrown.co.uk

This book is dedicated to
Rebecca Saunders.

Thank you for taking a chance on me.

If you love someone, set them free.
If they come back, they're yours;
if they don't, they never were.

—RICHARD BACH

Nineteen. There's something about that number; it not only brought us together, bonding us forever, it also played a hand in tearing us apart.

The nineteenth of January 1996. I'll never forget it. It was the day we met. I was seven and she was six. It was the day she moved in next door, and the day I developed my first crush on a girl.

Exactly nineteen years later, all my dreams came true when she became my wife. She was the love of my life. My soul mate. My everything. The reason I looked forward to waking up every morning.

Then tragedy struck. Nineteen days after we married, she was in an accident that would change our lives forever. When she woke from her coma, she had no memory of me, of us, of the love we shared.

I was crushed. She was my air, and without her I couldn't breathe.

The sparkle that once glistened in her eyes when she looked at me was gone. To her, now, I was a stranger. I had not only lost my wife, I had lost my best friend.

But I refused to let this tragedy be the end of us. That's when I started to write her letters, stories of our life. Of when we met. About the happier times, and everything we had experienced together.

What we had is far too beautiful to be forgotten.

This is our story . . .

ONE

Jemma

It's a wet and dreary morning is the first thing I hear when the radio booms to life, alerting me to the fact it's time to get up.

Dreary doesn't even come close. The thought of no longer being able to spend every waking minute with my gorgeous husband has already put a dampener on my day. I can't believe our time off together has come to an end. I hate that I have to go back to work this morning, and leave the little bubble Braxton and I have been living in for the past four weeks.

Right up until the wedding, things were so busy with our careers, building our dream house and organising our special day. Everything combined seemed to take away from us being together. This one-on-one time we've had since tying the knot was just what we both needed.

'Morning, Mrs Spencer.'

He rolls onto his side, pulling me further into his warm, luscious body. It has been exactly nineteen days since we exchanged wedding vows, and I'm still floating.

'Morning, Mr Spencer.' I lean my forehead against his. 'I'm not ready to go back to work. I can't stand the thought of spending the entire day without you.'

He chuckles as his teeth nip at my pouting lip. 'I feel exactly the same way, babe. Our time off has gone way too quick. We should have taken two months off, instead of one.'

Despite him being a constant figure in my daily life, for the past nineteen years, I still get a rush when I think about what our future together holds.

I met Braxton when my parents and I moved in next door. We were just kids, but we've been inseparable ever since. He's my one and only. He always has been, and always will be. He's not only the love of my life; he's my best friend, my soul mate, my forever boy.

He's incredibly dreamy, with his movie-star looks. I run my fingers through his sandy blond hair as my eyes roam over his perfectly sculpted face; his big blue eyes pop against his tanned skin. He has a smile that makes my knees weak. His front tooth turns in ever so slightly, but it takes nothing away from his Colgate-worthy smile.

When he realises I'm checking him out, the sexy grin that I adore appears on his face. It highlights the cute dimple in his left cheek. To this day, he still manages to turn my insides to mush, but it's his inner beauty that affects me the most.

'I could always call in sick,' I say, perking up for a moment, but in reality I know it's not possible. I have a big client coming in first thing Monday morning, and I need to prepare.

'If I didn't have this damn meeting later this morning, I'd say do it,' he replies, smiling.

'I'm going to miss you.'

'I'm going to miss you too, Jem. The past four weeks have been my kind of heaven.'

I sigh. 'I'd give anything to be back in Kauai right now.'

My fingers move from his hair and skim down the side of his face as I speak. The beach has always been our favourite place. That's why we built our dream home overlooking the ocean. The soothing sound of the waves crashing against the shore as I drift off to sleep every night, and the sweet smell of sea air first thing in the morning . . . it's cathartic. It's also one of the reasons we chose Hawaii—a beautiful villa on the majestic shores of Tunnels Beach—as the place to spend the first two weeks of our married life.

'Me too.' He gives me a wistful look. 'I'll take you back there over the Christmas break, I promise.'

'I'd like that.' My fingertips dance over his collarbone, before moving across his shoulder. When I run a path down his strong back, he groans.

I sigh again when I think that Christmas is ten months away, but I guess we have the rest of our lives together to create the kind of memories we did in Hawaii.

Untangling my legs from his, I pause briefly. I don't want to leave him. I exhale a drawn-out breath. 'I suppose I better jump in the shower.'

'Would you like some company?'

Reaching for me, he rolls onto his back, taking me with him. I laugh when he wiggles his eyebrows. I straddle his waist before covering his mouth with mine. My shower can wait. Making love to my man is much more important.

Sliding forward, I line myself up. His strong hands grip my hips, and we moan in unison as I sink down onto him.

My eyes lock with his as I slowly rock my body against him. 'I love you, Brax.'

'I love you too, Jem. So much.'

He reaches for my hands, lacing his fingers through mine. We've always had such a strong bond, but when we're connected like this, we become one. I'll never tire of these feelings he evokes in me.

There are times I feel guilty because together, we're perfect. None of our friends have the kind of relationship Braxton and I do. What we have is unbreakable. Sometimes my feelings for him overwhelm me. I'm not sure how either of us would survive without the other.

—

As I rush around putting the finishing touches on my make-up, I catch a glimpse of Braxton in the mirror. He's leaning up against the doorframe watching me get ready. He's shirtless and wearing a pair of grey sweats that hang low on his hips. My pulse quickens as my eyes rake over his bare chest, and each delicious muscle that defines his torso, from the perfect V just above the waistband, right up to his washboard abs. One of my favourite things to do is watch him work out on the small home gym he set up in the garage. I don't think he even realises how sexy he is. Growing up, he didn't notice the way all the girls swooned over him. But I did.

My eyes move back to his, and the adoring look on his face sends my heart into a flutter. The sheer love I feel for this man consumes every fibre of my being. It's euphoric.

'How long have you been standing there?' I ask as my mouth curves into a smile.

'I'm just admiring my beautiful wife.' I love hearing him call me his wife.

He pushes off the doorframe and stalks towards me. When his arms encircle my waist, he pulls me back into him. A soft moan falls from my mouth as his lips trail a path up my neck. I tilt my head to the side, allowing him better access.

'I'm already running late,' I breathe.

'I wish you didn't have to go.' His warm breath on my skin leaves goosebumps in its wake.

'Me either.'

'The next eight hours are going to feel like an eternity.'

I sigh in agreement. 'I know.'

His tongue glides over the sensitive spot behind my ear, sending shivers down my spine. He did that on purpose.

'Don't make any plans for tonight, because I'm taking you out to dinner.'

'You're taking me out? Where?'

'The Sea Shanty.' He groans as he sucks my earlobe into his mouth.

'What's the special occasion?'

'Our anniversary.'

My eyes fly open to meet his in the mirror. 'Our what?' My mind starts to race. *What anniversary?*

He turns me in his arms so I'm facing him, and pulls a small black box from his pocket. 'I was going to give this to you tonight, but I want you to have it now. Happy nineteenth anniversary, sweetheart.'

My hands tremble slightly as I take hold of the box. That's when I remember that today we have been married for nineteen days, and a huge smile breaks out on my face. The number nineteen has always held special significance for us.

Tears of happiness pool in my eyes as I open the lid. Inside I find a white-gold necklace that's holding a diamond-encrusted number-nineteen pendant.

'Oh Braxton, it's beautiful. I love it . . . I love you.'

He smiles as he tucks a lock of hair behind my ear. 'I can't wait to spend the rest of my life with you, Jem.'

'Same.'

A lump forms in my throat and I feel like I'm choking back tears. I use my hand to fan my eyes; I don't have time to redo my make-up.

Taking the box out of my hand, he removes the necklace. 'Turn around, and hold up your hair.' I do as he asks, gathering my long brown hair on top of my head so he can fasten the necklace. 'Perfect,' he says, planting a soft kiss on my skin at the base of my neck.

My fingertips glide over the pendant as I admire it in the mirror. 'Thank you . . . I'll treasure it.'

Sliding his arms around my waist again, he rests his chin on my shoulder, and his eyes meet mine in the mirror. 'You know, I've been thinking . . .'

'That could be dangerous.'

I laugh when he pokes my side.

'I want you to stop taking the pill.'

I feel my heartbeat accelerate as I swing around to face him. 'You do?'

'Yes. It's time we gave it another try, Jem. I want to see our baby growing inside you.'

I swipe my finger under my eye to catch the stray tear that has fallen. 'I want that too, but what about my job? We just took out a second mortgage to build this house . . . we need the money.'

He exhales before continuing. 'I know how much your career means to you, but you're giving so much of yourself to that bastard, Andrew. We both know he doesn't appreciate you. Why don't you think about setting up your own interior-design business from home? That way you'd be here to look after our son, and still be able to do what you love.'

'Or our daughter,' I say with a smile.

'As long as our baby is healthy, I don't care what sex it is.'

I bow my head as memories of that day flood my mind. I want this so badly, but I'm scared.

'Can we talk more about it tonight over dinner? Andrew's going to chew me out if I don't get to the office soon.'

'He better not!'

I run my finger over his forehead, trying to flatten out the crinkles of his frown. I love how protective he is. He hates the way my boss treats me, but he'd never interfere because he knows how much I love what I do.

The rain has eased by the time I'm ready to leave, but Braxton still insists on walking me out so I don't get wet. 'Bye,' I say reluctantly, when we come to a stop beside my car.

'Don't let Andrew keep you any later than needed.'

'I won't,' I say, placing my lips against his. 'Good luck with your meeting. They're going to love the new design.'

'I hope so.' He opens the driver's-side door, and moves the umbrella closer to shield me from the rain. 'Be careful on the roads, they'll be slippery.'

'I will. Stop worrying.'

'I'll always worry where you're concerned, Jem. It's my job to look after you.'

I smile up at him once I'm seated. 'I love how much you love me.'

'That'll never change,' he says, winking, as he closes my car door.

My heart feels heavy as I blow him a kiss and reverse out of the driveway . . . I miss him already.

⟶

I'm driving cautiously but still faster than usual on my way to work. I know I shouldn't, considering the roads are slippery from all the rain, but the backlog of work I'm going to face from being on holidays for a month is making my stomach knot. Just the thought of facing Andrew in one of his moods this morning is quickly undoing all the calm I've felt while being away from him. Braxton's idea of starting my own business is sounding better by the second.

I smile to myself as I replay his words in my head. My fingertips lightly skim over my stomach. I'd like nothing more than to have his baby growing inside me again.

'Shit,' I mumble to myself when the heavens open up. I turn the wiper speed up to full, but visibility is still poor. I can barely see the car in front of me now. I jump when my phone starts to ring. I grip the wheel tightly with my right hand as I reach across the passenger seat, my hand blindly fumbling in my bag as I try to find it.

I just know that it's Andrew wondering where I am; I should have been there fifteen minutes ago. My chest tightens just thinking about it.

My eyes leave the road for a split second as I glance down at the screen. I was right, it's him. As I attempt to accept the call, I hear the loud sound of an angry horn, and the screech of tyres. My head snaps to the left as my body is thrown violently sidewards. The sickening crunching sound of metal is almost deafening.

Images of Braxton and our life together flash through my mind as a crushing sensation consumes the right side of my body. My head connects with the driver's-side window, and the sound of shattering glass fills my ears.

Oh god. I don't want to die.

'Braxton . . . Braaaax,' I cry out as the world around me stills, and I succumb to the darkness.

TWO

Braxton

I take a sip of strong black coffee as I stare out of the floor-to-ceiling windows that adorn the back of our house. I'm drinking out of my favourite mug. Jem bought it for me on our first official Valentine's Day together, eight years ago. The inscription on the front still brings a smile to my face. *You're cute, can I keep you?*

The interior of the cup is now stained from all the coffee I've consumed in it, and part of the heart on the front has worn away over time, but I adore this mug and everything it represents. Nowhere near as much as I adore my wife, though.

The ocean is less than forty metres away from where I'm standing, but the rain is pelting down so hard that I can't even see it. An uneasy feeling settles in the pit of my stomach, and I have no idea why. I'm not anxious about the meeting I have this morning; I'm confident the deal is in the bag. But still, something feels off.

It might be that the thought of Jemma being out there in this weather doesn't sit well with me. I know she feels like I smother her sometimes, but it's only because I love her. I've never loved anyone, or anything, as deeply as I do her. She's like the missing part of my soul.

Removing my phone from my pocket, I search through my contacts for her number. She would have got a bit of traffic on the way to work this morning, especially with this rain, but surely she'd be there by now.

I'm not concerned when it goes straight to voicemail. Her boss is a pompous arse, so she probably turned her phone off to avoid getting into trouble. I'd love nothing more than to wring his neck for the way he speaks to her sometimes, but I know Jem wouldn't want that. She loves her job, and all I want is for her to be happy.

Opening my messages, I shoot her a text.

Just checking in to make sure you arrived at work safely. Is it wrong that I miss you already? Because I do. I can't wait for our date tonight. Hope you have a great day. Call me when you get a chance.

It will ease my mind to know she's okay. My head needs to be in the game this morning. This deal means everything to me, and to my business partner, Lucas—it's the break we need to catapult our company to the next level.

I know that the roads are going to be chaotic, so I head into the kitchen and pour the remainder of my coffee into a travel mug before grabbing my briefcase and the plans for the new shopping centre we've designed, from my office. This is the first time Lucas and I have branched out from our usual portfolio of designing houses and office blocks. If we pull this off it will be the biggest deal we've ever landed and will launch our small architectural firm into the big league.

Lucas and I are still young, and have long careers ahead of us, but that doesn't stop us from yearning for that big break. It's what we've always strived for. We met at university eight years ago, and clicked straightaway. He's not only my business partner, he's like a brother to me. Our ideas are fresh, and we're not afraid to push boundaries. It's what gives us the edge over our competition—we're visionaries, you could say. There are exciting times ahead for L&B Architectural Designs, I can feel it in my bones.

If we seal this deal today, Jemma won't need to work anymore if she doesn't want to. She loves what she does, though. She has an exceptional eye for detail, and is already forging her place among some of the top interior designers in the country.

Is it crazy that even our careers go hand in hand? I design houses for a living, and Jemma creates the interiors. It's not something we planned, it's just another reason we're perfect for each other.

When my phone rings, I slide it out of my pocket. I'm expecting to see Jem's number on the screen, but instead it's Lucas.

'Hey, buddy,' I say when I place the phone to my ear. 'I'm just getting ready to leave now.'

'That's why I'm calling. I left five minutes ago. The traffic is horrendous. There's been a bad accident at the Main and Riley intersection. It must be pretty serious because the roads are closed in both directions. Traffic is being diverted all over the place.'

The uneasy feeling in my gut intensifies. That's the route Jemma takes to work. But I force my voice to sound normal as I reply.

'I'll leave now. Hopefully one of us gets there in time.'

I redial Jemma, but again it goes to voicemail, so this time I leave her a message. *Jem, it's me. Call me as soon as you get this. I need to know you're okay.*

I try not to sound panicked, but I'm pretty sure I fail. I've always been protective of her, and that will never change.

Sliding my phone back into my suit jacket, I pick up my briefcase and tuck the blueprints cylinder under my arm, before reaching for my travel mug. I was up until late last night going over the final draft, ensuring it was *perfect*. I know our clients are going to love the amendments I made to the original design.

I look down at my watch as I head towards the door. *Jemma left an hour and twenty minutes ago.* I tell myself that I'm overreacting, that she's probably safe and sound at work.

Then why is my stomach in knots?

The rain has eased to a light sprinkle as I walk across the front lawn. Placing the travel mug on the roof of the car, I fish in my pocket for the keys. Once I've stowed the blueprints and my briefcase on the back seat, I reach for my coffee as I close the back door.

I pause when a car pulls into the driveway behind me. It's not just any car, it's a police car. Fear grips me as images of my wife flash through my mind, and I internally freak the hell out. My brain is telling me to calm down, not to panic until I have reason to, but my heart already knows this isn't good news.

'Mr Spencer?' the officer asks as he exits his vehicle and approaches me. He already knows my name, which does nothing to calm me. I open my mouth to speak, but nothing comes out. My heart is thumping hard against my ribcage, and there's a part of me that wants to flee so I don't have to hear what he's going to say. Inhaling a large breath, I hold it as he comes to a stop a few feet in front of me. 'Are you Braxton Spencer?'

Words again fail me, but this time I manage to nod my head.

'I'm Officer Martin. I'm sorry to be the one to inform you,' he says, reaching out and placing his hand on my shoulder. Every ounce of air leaves my body as I wait for him to continue. 'Your wife's been in an accident.'

I swear I feel all the colour drain from my face as my legs threaten to give way underneath me. Lucas's words swim around in my head. *It must be pretty serious because the roads are closed in both directions.*

The travel mug in my hand drops to the driveway below with a thud. I vaguely feel the sting of the hot liquid as it soaks into the fabric of my trousers. The world around me appears to be moving in slow motion as the officer grabs hold of my arm in an attempt to steady me.

'Is ... is she okay?' I'm not sure I even want to hear his reply, but I need to know.

'She was transported to the local hospital by ambulance.'

'I need to get to her. Are her injuries serious? Is she ... alive?' I'm rambling.

'Only the doctors can answer that, Mr Spencer. All I can tell you is the car she was travelling in was T-boned after driving through a stop sign. She had to be cut out of the vehicle, but yes she was alive.'

I scrub my trembling hands over my face as my stomach churns. I think I'm going to be sick.

'I'm sorry, Mr Spencer. This is the part of my job that I hate the most. If you like, I can take you to her.'

'Please.'

This can't be happening. Less than two hours ago, I was making love to my wife and looking forward to not only our evening together, but our future. We were going to start a family. But now, in the blink of an eye, every hope and every dream we've shared seems uncertain.

My eyelids close as I rest my head against the seat in the back of the police car. I've never been the praying type, but that's exactly what I'm doing in this moment. I'd do anything to save my girl. *Anything.*

I feel numb.

Please God, let her be okay. Just let her be okay.

⌒

'Braxton,' I hear as I pace in the small room I was shoved into when I arrived at the hospital. I feel like I'm going out of my mind as I wait for answers, for news, for anything. My head snaps up as Jemma's mother, Christine, comes barrelling into the room. 'Oh, Braxton,' she cries as she collapses into my arms and sobs hysterically against my chest.

Jemma is her only child, so of course she is distressed, but I'm trying so hard to hold myself together here, and this is not helping.

I don't even remember the drive to the hospital. It's like I'm in limbo, and I can't seem to get my thoughts straight. I vaguely remember the officer asking me if there was anyone I should contact when we arrived. 'Her parents,' I'd mumbled. Apart from me, they're all she has.

The universe couldn't be so cruel as to take her away from me when our life together as husband and wife has only just begun. Could it?

'Is there any news?' Christine asks as she pulls away from me. 'They won't tell me anything.'

'I've had no news yet.' After the nurse guided me into this room, she said the doctor would be in to see me shortly, but since then there's been nothing. Not a damn word.

I check my watch and see it has only been twenty minutes, but it feels like an eternity. In this moment, everything I hold dear is hanging by a thread.

Minutes later, the door flies open again. My heartbeat climbs to a dangerous level. I don't know if I'm ready. As much as I need to know how she is, I cling to the premise that no news is good news.

I'm flooded with relief when I see Jemma's father, Stephen, standing near the doorway looking sombre and breathless.

'What are you doing here?' Christine snaps as her eyes narrow.

These two once had a marriage I envied; now they can't stand to be in the same room. Well, Christine can't stand to be in the same room as Stephen. We had to sit them at opposite sides of the room at our wedding reception. Jemma's mother threatened not to attend if she was seated anywhere near him. It's hard seeing what this animosity does to Jem; she loves her parents and hates being brought into the middle of their drama. It's ludicrous. Stephen messed up, but he's remorseful for what he did. He's a good man. I've always liked him. I'm not condoning what he did—he made a mistake, a huge one—but Christine played a hand in it as well, and it's not fair that she's making us all suffer. Especially now; now is the time to focus on Jem.

'She's my daughter too, Chris. I have a right to be here.'

'Huh,' she huffs.

Stepping back from Jemma's mother, I walk towards her father and shake his hand. 'No word yet. Hopefully the doctor will be able to tell us something soon.'

He bows his head. 'She's my little girl . . . my pumpkin,' he whispers.

I have to fight back my own tears as I watch him. *She has to be okay.* I can't even fathom any other outcome right now.

THREE

Braxton

'I can't stand this,' I mumble under my breath as I push through the doors and head out into the corridor to find a nurse, or a doctor—anyone who can give me answers. I also need a break from those two. Christine is slumped in a chair, crying. Stephen tried to comfort her at one stage, but the daggers she shot him had him retreating to the corner of the room. She's hurting—we all are. None of us know what condition Jemma's in, but I do know she's going to need all our love and support. She hates what has become of her once tightknit family, and their constant bickering would just upset her.

I head straight for the nurses' counter, and force out a small smile when the nurse looks up from the computer screen in front of her. 'Hi. My wife, Jemma Spencer, was brought in earlier. She was in a car accident. Is there any news on her condition? I'd be grateful if you could help me, we've been waiting for almost half an hour. Anything, please.'

She gives me a sympathetic look before typing something into the keyboard. 'She's being looked at by the trauma team at the moment. I'll see if someone can come and talk to you.'

Trauma team. Those words are like a knife plunging straight into my heart. 'Is there any way I can see her?' She's probably frightened, and I know she would want me there. And I need to be with her.

'Not at the moment, Mr Spencer. I'm sorry. I'll have someone come and give you an update ASAP.'

The desperate part of me wants to scream at the nurse and demand she take me to Jemma. Thankfully, the logical side of me wins out. She's only doing her job.

'Thank you.'

Turning, I pinch the bridge of my nose as I walk back towards that cramped room of torture; the thought of going back in there has me feeling stifled. Stopping, I take a moment and roll my shoulders a few times. I feel lost, and completely alone. Jemma has always been my rock; we have always faced everything together. I'm craving her comfort, which is ironic—I'm not the one who was in a car accident, the one who is somewhere in this godforsaken hospital being worked on by the trauma team.

I feel even more helpless when I meet the hopeful eyes of Jemma's parents. 'No news yet, I'm afraid.'

Christine just buries her face in her hands and continues to cry.

'What's taking so long?' her father asks.

I wish I knew. In my heart I know her injuries are serious, but I refuse to let my mind go there. I'm not sure how much more I can take, or how long I can hold it together.

Fifteen excruciating minutes pass before the doctor finally enters the room. *Please let this be good news*. I know I'm grasping at straws; if things weren't serious we wouldn't be in the hospital.

'Hi. I'm Doctor Bolton. I'm in charge of the trauma team looking after Jemma,' he says as he looks at each of us.

'I'm Braxton Spencer, Jemma's husband.' I reach for his extended hand. 'How is she?'

'Her injuries are serious.' His words have my heart dropping into the pit of my stomach, but at least that means she's still alive. I have to grab onto anything positive; it's the only way I'm going to get through this. 'Why don't you take a seat?'

'I'm Stephen, Jemma's father,' he says, stepping forward. After shaking the doctor's hand, he gestures towards Christine. 'And this is my wife, Christine.'

'Ex-wife,' Christine snaps.

My eyes briefly meet hers—I don't bother to hide my anger—shaking my head as I take a seat. 'I'm sorry, Braxton,' she says, placing her hand on my leg. 'I'm sorry.'

I tune her out as I focus my attention on the doctor. 'We've managed to stabilise her,' he says.

I run my hands nervously down the front of my trousers. That doesn't sound good, but in this moment I honestly don't care what condition I get her back in. I just need her back.

'What do you mean by "stabilise her"?' Stephen asks. 'How bad are her injuries?'

'They're serious,' he replies. 'She's been in and out of consciousness since she arrived. There appears to be some swelling on her brain, some internal bleeding, lesions and multiple broken bones. She's been sedated and we're taking her down for some scans now.'

'Christ.' The glimmer of hope I've been clinging to since the officer arrived at my house is dwindling at a rapid pace. 'She's going to pull through, right?'

He gives me a sympathetic look. 'It's touch and go. The next forty-eight hours are going to be critical, but I assure you we're doing everything possible to save your wife.'

I cannot bring myself to reply as the doctor's words sink in. Forty-eight hours? I can't wait that long. The last forty minutes nearly killed me. Sheer panic consumes me. I can't lose her, I just can't. I rub my hand over the tightness that has now settled in my chest. I can't breathe without her. She's my air.

She's got to pull through this. She just has to.

———

An hour passes and we're still waiting for another update. How long does a scan take? I can't seem to settle, and haven't stopped pacing since the doctor left. I'm going to wear a path in the linoleum floor pretty soon.

I'm pulled from my internal turmoil when my phone rings in my pocket. Glancing down at the screen I see Andrew's name. Presumably he's wondering why Jemma hasn't arrived at work. It's unlike him to call me—the last time he did, it wasn't pretty. Jemma had left for the day, and when he couldn't find something in the office he called her; when she didn't answer her phone, he contacted me. He had the audacity to tell me if she wasn't back there within the hour to find it, he would fire her. He was just being unreasonable as usual, and I took great satisfaction in finally speaking my mind. He was lucky to have someone like her working for him, and he knew it, and it was the first and last time he ever spoke about her like that in front of me.

I have a good mind to ignore his call, but I know Jem wouldn't want that. 'Andrew,' I say in a clipped tone when I answer. I don't even give him a chance to reply. 'Jemma was in a car accident on the way to work. She won't be coming in today.'

'I need her here,' he snaps. When he lets out an exasperated breath, I feel my temper rise.

'Well, it's not possible.'

'Can I expect her on Monday?'

'No, she won't be in on Monday either.' At this stage, I want to hang up on him, but again, I hold my temper for Jemma's sake. 'It's serious. We're at the hospital. I'm not sure when she'll be back.' With that, I end the call. That's all the explanation he needs.

As I go to place my phone back in the pocket of my suit jacket, it rings again. My thumb moves to press the decline button, thinking it's him again, but I see Lucas's number on the screen instead. *Christ, our meeting.*

'Where the hell are you?' he screeches into the phone. 'I've been trying to call you for nearly an hour. Please don't tell me you're still stuck in traffic. I've been stalling for as long as I can. We need those plans.'

'Lucas.' I'm so glad to hear his voice, even if he's shouting at me. I need to draw on his strength because I'm about to crumble. Pushing through the door, I step into the corridor. 'I'm sorry, mate. I should've called . . . it slipped my mind.'

'Jesus, Brax. *Slipped your mind?* What's going on?'

'I'm at the hospital.'

'What?' He pauses briefly. 'Why?'

'That accident,' I say, my voice cracking. 'It was Jemma.'

'Bullshit . . . no way.'

The line goes quiet, and the shock I felt when I first got word comes crashing back down. Saying it aloud makes it too real, and I know how badly Lucas will take the news. He not only adores Jemma, he cares about me. Growing up, it was always just Jem and me, and then I went away to university, leaving her behind. It was the first time we'd ever been separated, and it was hard. We spoke every day, and drove back and forth to be together each weekend, but it wasn't the same. I struggled without her. I was lost—and Lucas saved me. Jemma was the other half of me, but I never realised how much I needed a bro, a best mate, until I found him.

'What hospital are you at? I'm coming to you now.'

A small smile tugs at my lips. In the eight years we've been friends, he has never let me down. 'Don't. Finish the meeting, it's important. There's nothing you can do here. We're still waiting for news from the doctor.'

'I can be there for you. I know what she means to you. She's your life.'

'She is,' I whisper, as tears sting my eyes, but I flat out refuse to cry. I need to stay strong for her. 'Lucas, I don't think I can survive without her.'

'Hang in there, buddy. Jem's a fighter. She'll pull through this.'

He has no idea how much I needed to hear those words. 'God, I hope so.'

FOUR

Braxton

I'm gripped with fear as I follow the nurse down the corridor towards the intensive-care unit. Jemma's parents are close behind. We're finally able to see her, but only one person at a time. I'm thankful they didn't protest when I said I wanted to be the first.

I'm trying to prepare myself for the worst. I'm not sure what I'm going to find when I walk into that room, but I know it won't be pretty. My beautiful wife who left me this morning with a smile and a kiss won't be the same person I'm about to see.

When the doctor finally came back to update us on her condition we learned that due to the swelling on her brain, she has been placed in an induced coma. I asked the doctor a million questions, but there wasn't much he could say, except that the next few days will be a waiting game, and Jemma will be closely monitored in the ICU.

Her injuries are extensive. The surgeon managed to stitch her open wounds, but they won't be able to operate until the swelling subsides. She's going to need pins in her right arm and leg, as well as a hip replacement because the bones are shattered. As much as I hate that my girl is so broken and battered, we can deal with that. She's alive, and bones heal. For now, our primary concern is getting her through the next few days. As the doctor said, she's healthy, and she's strong. I know she'll fight. She has to.

The nurse stops walking and turns to face me when we reach Jemma's room. My heart is beating so fast I can hear the thumping in my ears. There's a sympathetic smile on her face. 'This is your wife's room, Mr Spencer.'

'Thank you.'

I turn and nod to Jemma's parents. No words would be enough to comfort any of us in this moment. Christine's sad eyes meet mine, and she manages to force a smile as she reaches out to rub her hand down my arm. This is the caring and nurturing woman I love, and miss.

'Good luck,' she says. 'We'll be out here waiting if you need us.'

I pause in the doorway and steady myself. *I can do this.* Willing my legs to move, I take a step forward, followed by another. I take a sharp breath the moment my eyes land on Jemma. My knees threaten to give way underneath me as I approach the bed. The person lying before me doesn't even resemble my wife.

I'm not sure what I expected to see when I walked in here, but it certainly wasn't this. The white sterile sheets are pulled up under her chin, so I can only see her bruised and battered face. She's hooked up to several machines, and a large white tube protrudes from her mouth.

I stand and stare for the longest time, afraid to go closer. It's a surreal feeling. Never in my life did I think I'd have to face anything like this. The right side of her face and forehead are heavily bandaged. I immediately divert my eyes away from the dried blood I see caked in her hair. I can't bear it. Her face is so swollen. I can't even describe how much it hurts to see her like this.

There's a chair sitting by the wall. I make my way towards it and drag it to Jemma's bedside. The left side is still perfect, still her. Tears rise to my eyes as I gently run the tip of my fingers down the left side of her face.

I promised myself before coming in here that I would remain strong for her, but I'm so overcome with sadness I no longer can. I'm so scared. Leaning forward, I place my lips softly on her cheek. She's so lifeless, so pale, and her skin feels cold against my mouth. Sliding my hand under the blanket, I fold her hand in mine.

I want to wrap her in my arms and beg her to get better, but I'm too afraid to touch her. I don't want to hurt her any more than she's already hurting. I've spent my entire life caring for and protecting her, but the one time she needed me most, I wasn't there. Logically, I know there's nothing I could have done to avoid this. None of us could have seen it coming, but it doesn't lessen the guilt that I'm feeling.

The officer's words from this morning echo in my mind. *All I can tell you is the car she was travelling in was T-boned after driving through a stop sign.*

'Jem,' I whisper against her skin. 'I need you, baby. Don't leave me.' I can taste the saltiness of my tears. 'Fight for us . . . fight for you. Just *fight*.'

My heart aches as I rest my face against hers for the longest time. Even this simple contact gives me strength, and I can only hope it gives Jem strength too.

I'm startled when I feel a hand rest on my shoulder. I look up to find the nurse beside me. 'Mrs Spencer's parents would like to come in and see their daughter now.'

'Okay,' I say, leaning back into my chair and wiping the tears from my face.

'You can come back in once they've seen her.'

I wait until she leaves the room, then I lean forward in my chair again. 'Your parents are here to see you,' I whisper.

'I'll be right outside. I'm not going anywhere.' I brush my lips against her cheek once more before standing. 'I love you.'

My heart feels shattered as I leave the room. I pass Christine in the doorway. She reaches for my arm, but I shrug her off.

'How is she?' she asks. I shake my head in reply. I'm numb. I have no words for how she is. Christine will see for herself in a minute.

Stephen pats my back as I pass him. I know that the grim look on his face is reflected in my own. I feel bad for what they're about to see. Jemma has always been their little girl. Seeing her in this condition won't be easy.

'Braxton.' I glance over my shoulder as I walk towards the line of chairs positioned along the wall. *Lucas*. No words are spoken as he comes to a stop in front of me and pulls me into his arms, holding me tight. He has never hugged me like this before, but I'm too grateful to feel awkward. I need something, anything, to hold me together right now. 'She's going to pull through this, buddy.'

I'm so glad he's here.

I pull out my phone when I feel it vibrate in my pocket. I see it's a text from Jemma's friend Rachel. She's on her way here from New York. 'Why don't you go home for a few hours and get some rest,' Stephen says, placing his hand on my shoulder. 'You look like crap.'

'Geez, thanks.'

Three days have passed since the accident, and I haven't left my wife's side. I'll go home when I can take her with me, and not before. Although it's apparently against hospital policy, the nurse let me have a shower this morning. It made me feel somewhat human again. Lucas went to our place and brought back some toiletries and fresh clothes. He's been calling in to the hospital on his way to work, and again in the evenings on his way home. There's not much he can do here, but I'm grateful he's keeping things moving at the office, even though I'm struggling to focus on anything other than Jem at this moment.

'You know what I mean, son,' Stephen says. 'Jemma's going to need you when she wakes, and you won't be able to function if you keep this up.' He's right. I've barely slept and I'm not really eating, but I can't leave. The truth is, I won't be able to breathe easy until I know for certain she's going to be okay.

'I'm not leaving her.'

She survived the first forty-eight hours, and with every passing day my confidence grows. She's still in an induced coma, but the doctor did some more scans this morning, and they showed that the swelling is subsiding. I know she's going to have a long road to recovery once she's conscious, but she'll never be alone. Me, her parents, Lucas, and her best friend, Rachel—we will all help her, every step of the way.

'You need some rest,' Stephen persists.

None of us are really functioning properly at the moment. Stephen and Christine are here from early morning until late at night, but unlike me, they go home to sleep.

'For god's sake,' Christine snaps. 'His wife is lying in the hospital. Why would he want to leave her? He's committed to the woman he loves. Unlike you, he'll honour his wedding vows.'

Burying my face in my hands, I will myself to bite my tongue. I'm at my wit's end with the snarky remarks she's thrown at Stephen over the past few days. I get it, I do: she'd worshipped the ground he walked on, until he broke her heart. But what we're facing at the moment is proof that life is short. None of us knows what lies around the corner. And Jemma is their only child; surely if anything could bring them closer, it's their shared pain and love for their daughter. Christine needs to move forward and somehow try to forgive. The hate and resentment she's carrying around is making a once compassionate and loving person bitter and resentful. I barely recognise the woman who was so kind to me when I lost my own mum.

I feel for them both. It's evident they still love each other; any fool could see that. But it appears Christine is going to make him pay for his mistake for the rest of his life. It's so sad; the love they once shared is far too precious to waste.

'I'm going to get a coffee,' Stephen snaps as he stalks towards the door. I think he's just hanging on by a thread as well. This is the closest his wife has let him get to her since they split two years ago.

'You really should cut him some slack,' I say, turning towards Christine. I've tried to stay out of this for the past few years, but right now it's almost impossible. I even managed to refrain from speaking my mind during the whole wedding fiasco. What Christine failed—or refused—to realise then, was that Jemma's father was going to be present at our wedding and give his little girl away whether Christine wanted him there or not. The pressure nearly tore Jemma apart—on more than one occasion I held her in my arms while she cried tears of frustration brought on by her mother—but I know how much she loves both her parents, so I kept quiet. But not now.

'This shit really needs to stop,' I say. 'I won't stand by and let you upset Jemma during her recovery.'

Christine's eyes narrow slightly and her mouth opens to speak, but then she pauses. I see her whole body deflate, and I know she knows I'm right. Our priority right now needs to be Jemma.

'You're right,' she replies, exhaling loudly. 'I've tried to let go of the hurt, but I can't.'

Rising from the chair, I make my way towards her. 'I know this isn't easy for you, Christine, but tell me this: does constantly beating him down make *you* feel any better?'

'No,' she whispers. 'No, it doesn't.'

This isn't her. Not the real Christine, the mother figure I loved growing up. When my own mother passed away, Christine stepped in and cared for me like I was her own, and I'll always be grateful. She has been wonderful to me and my father over the years. She and Stephen both.

'Just try to be a little bit nicer,' I say, placing my hand on her shoulder. 'Jemma's going to need all of us to be united when she wakes.'

'I know.' The remorseful look on her face tells me she's at least going to try.

———

I open my eyes just as the night nurse is leaving the room. Apart from the thin strip of light coming from behind Jemma's bed, the room is bathed in darkness. I crick my neck from side to side as I sit forward in the reclining lounge that has become a makeshift bed. I long for the day that I can again sleep in my own comfortable bed, with my wife wrapped in my arms. My watch shows it's just after two in the morning.

Rising, I drag the chair closer to Jemma's bed. I need to be nearer. If she wasn't hooked up to so many machines, I wouldn't hesitate to climb into bed beside her and hold her. I miss so much about her—her smile, her laugh, her touch, her love—but more than anything I miss waking up with her. She's been my life for as long as I can remember, so having her here but not present makes my heart ache.

Bending down, I place my lips on her forehead. 'Please come back to me soon.' I lie back down on the recliner and slide my hand under the blanket that's covering her. I need the contact. Maybe this might help me sleep; I need to be at my strongest when she wakes. 'I love you,' I whisper as my fingers wrap around hers. We have never gone to sleep without saying these words.

FIVE

Braxton

I pace back and forth in the corridor. Today's the day. The doctor and two nurses are in with my wife now. The swelling on her brain has subsided, so they're going to start the process of bringing her out of the coma. They'll also take her off the machines that have been helping to keep her alive. I should be feeling relieved, but I'm not—I'm extremely anxious. As positive as I'm trying to remain, there's still no guarantee she will pull through.

Christine, Stephen and Lucas are all sitting down watching me. I'm sure I'm making them feel uneasy, but I can't stay still. My stomach is in knots.

'Braxton!' I look up and see Rachel, Jemma's best friend, running towards me. Rachel moved to New York for work just over a year ago, but there was no doubt in my mind that she would come home once she found out about the accident. They're as close as sisters. That's why I waited until the day after the accident to call her. I didn't want her flying back here unnecessarily. She was only here three weeks ago, to be Jemma's maid of honour.

My heart hurts when I think back to us picking her up from the airport when she arrived for our wedding. She and

Jemma Skype each week but they hadn't seen each other for nearly a year. The moment Rachel emerged from Customs, Jemma had dropped my hand to run to her. They held each other and cried for the longest time.

Arriving this time must have been hard for her, for such a different reason and with nobody to greet her. But my mind has been clouded with worry and I just didn't think to organise somebody to collect her.

No words are spoken as she collapses into my arms and sobs. I can feel her body trembling, or maybe it's mine, I'm not sure. All I know in this moment is that I'm exhausted, frightened and struggling to keep it together.

'How is she?' she asks looking up at me through her tears. She has been texting me over the past few days for updates during her travel. My reply was always the same: *No change. Critical yet stable.* That's all I could tell her. It has been a waiting game for all of us.

'The doctor's with her now,' I tell her. 'The swelling's gone down, so they're going to bring her out of the coma.'

The doctor spoke to me at length before he went in. They're going to stop the drugs that they've been using to keep her comatose, but will continue with the fluids, and the pain medication to help keep her comfortable. It could take anywhere from twelve to seventy-two hours for her to fully wake.

I just want this nightmare to be over.

―――

Many hours have passed and there's still no sign of her waking. At least the tube that was helping her breathe has been removed from her mouth. The bruising and swelling on the right side of her face has gone down. Although she looks far from the Jemma I know, I'm grateful that I can already see an improvement.

Over the past four days I was asked to leave the room while they dressed her wounds, so I'm yet to see what lies underneath all those bandages. I'm not sure I want to.

Apart from that, I haven't left her side. Christine has been trying her best not to antagonise Stephen, but in my opinion she could try harder. They've been alternating their time spent in the room with Lucas and Rachel. The rules are different in the ICU. They don't usually allow more than one person in the room at a time, but they have made an exception for us. Christine has paired up with Rachel, and Lucas with Stephen. I'm somewhat relieved that Jemma's parents have been split up; it's just easier for everyone.

When evening falls, I encourage them all to go home and get some rest. I'm not leaving, though. I can't. Christine protests at first, but Rachel eventually convinces her it's for the best. She will stay with Christine while she's here. Christine loves Rachel like a daughter, so I'm happy they will have each other for support. Having Rachel here will free me up so I can put my efforts into getting my wife well again. Christine doesn't drive, so when Stephen moved out of the family home, running her around was always left to Jem and me.

I'm sitting by the bed with Jemma's hand wrapped in mine when one of the night nurses enters the room. 'Mr Spencer,' she says with a nod. 'I'm surprised to see you're still awake.'

I give her a half-hearted smile. There's no denying that I'm tired; I'm struggling to keep my eyes open, but I don't want to go to sleep in case Jemma regains consciousness. She'll be confused and scared, wondering where she is and how she got here. I need to be here to put her mind at ease.

'It could take a few days.'

'I know,' is my only reply.

'You're a good man, Mr Spencer. Your wife's lucky to have you.'

'I feel like I'm the lucky one.'

'Is there anything I can get you before I leave?'

'No. I'm fine, thank you.'

'Try to get some rest, Mr Spencer. I'll be checking on your wife every hour, so if there's any change in her condition, I'll wake you.'

'Thank you.'

It's fifteen minutes past midnight when she leaves. That means it has been almost fourteen hours since the doctors stopped the drugs that were keeping her unconscious. I can't sleep now. It might take days, but there's also the possibility that she'll wake at any moment.

I'm jolted from my sleep when I feel someone squeeze my hand. My eyes are heavy and my mind is in a haze. I'm still sitting in the chair beside Jemma's bed. I look down at my watch and see that it's just after 5am. Then the realisation hits me. Someone squeezed my hand.

'Jemma,' I say, sitting upright in my chair. 'Jemma, baby.' I lean my body closer to her as I lightly squeeze the hand that's still wrapped in mine, but there's nothing. No movement. I must have imagined it.

I exhale a large breath as I rest my forehead on her shoulder. 'Wake up, babe. Please.' My voice cracks as I try to hold my emotions in. I'm not sure how much more of this I can take. 'Please, Jem,' I whisper. 'I need you.'

Minutes pass. I continue to rest my head on her, all the time struggling to hold back the tears. I feel like I'm losing my mind, but it's probably just the sleep deprivation. I'm mentally and physically spent. I lean back in my chair and rub my free hand over my face, scratching against the whiskers. I've never gone this long without shaving.

I have to admit to myself that a warm shower and a shave might revitalise me. Jem's never been a fan of beards. She thought my occasional stubble was sexy, but that was her limit.

I gently unravel my fingers from hers and stand up to stretch. I arch my back and raise my hands high in the air, trying to relieve the ache that seems to have taken permanent residence in my weary muscles. I usually try to work out most days, but I can't do that while I'm here.

It's now a little after seven. The nurse has just left after checking Jem's vitals; there's still no change. She told me the doctor would be in shortly, when he starts his rounds. I'm on edge. I pace back and forth for a few minutes, before coming to a stop beside the bed.

'Jem, baby. Can you hear me?' Leaning forward, I run my fingers down the side of her face. 'I need you to wake up.' There's desperation in my voice as I speak. 'Please.'

My gaze is fixed on her as I stand to full height. This waiting game is really messing with my head. Then I see movement. Well, I think I do; maybe I'm just imagining it like I did with the hand squeeze. I rub my eyes before focusing on her again. This time I know I'm not seeing things. Her eyelids flutter slightly, before a soft groan falls from her lips. My heart rate picks up as I lean over her again. 'Open your eyes, Jem,' I beg as I reach for her hand under the blanket, folding it in mine.

I can't explain how joyous I feel when she does as I ask. She looks me straight in the eye with a vacant stare. Considering everything she's been through, that doesn't surprise me.

A huge smile forms on my face.

'Welcome back,' I whisper as my eyes cloud with tears.

Her gaze moves from me to her surroundings. I can only imagine how confused she must be feeling. I'm trying hard to hold it together, but I'm so overcome with emotion my resolve is slipping with each passing second.

I gently run my hand down the left side of her face when her gaze moves back to me. I hate that the familiar sparkle is gone, but I know it will come back. Leaning forward, I rest my forehead against hers as tears stream from my eyes.

I haven't cried like this since my mum died. But these tears are different. They're tears of joy, not heartache. Tears of gratitude and relief, not guilt. All the uncertainty I've been feeling the past few days vanishes in an instant. She's back. She's alive. I can finally breathe again.

'I've missed you so much, Jem.'

'Stop.' Her speech is raspy, and sounds nothing like *my* Jemma. 'Get off me,' she pleads, weakly pushing against my chest.

She's never spoken so harshly to me before, and my first instinct is that I've hurt her somehow. 'Jem.' I pull back in confusion.

'Who are you?' she asks in a frightened voice.

My heart drops. 'It's me, Braxton . . . your husband.'

She doesn't say another word, and she doesn't need to. The fear I see in her eyes says it all. The relief I felt moments ago is quickly replaced by panic.

She doesn't remember me.

She doesn't know who I am.

SIX

Braxton

I rest my forehead against the steering wheel after turning off the ignition, saying a silent prayer that today is the day my wife's memory returns. After the horrors of her waking up and not remembering me—or anybody, for that matter, not even her parents—things have been on a downward spiral.

I've been forced to return home each night without her. I swore I wouldn't go back to the house unless she was with me, but that's the thing—she doesn't want me around. For the interim, anyway.

She practically had me forcefully removed from her room the first night. To her I'm now a stranger, and that's exactly how she's been treating me. I'm pretty sure if Jemma had her way she'd even stop me from coming here during the day. I alternate between utter bleakness and determination; it hurts like hell, but I refuse to accept that this is the end for us.

She may no longer remember the love we share, or every-thing we've been through together, but I do. Every moment . . . every second. I carry enough love for both of us.

Christine and Stephen are completely devastated by Jemma's memory loss and, like me, are struggling to adjust. It's a huge blow for them, in their already fractured lives. You can't help but feel for them.

Jemma's doctor spoke with me at length last night, before I left the hospital. He referred to Jemma's condition as retrograde amnesia. He said it's not uncommon for a patient to suffer some form of memory loss after sustaining a head injury. But unfortunately, there's no magic cure. For now, it's yet another waiting game. Her memory loss may be temporary, but there's a chance—and this is my greatest fear—that her memory will never return.

Either way, I'm not giving up on us. *Never.* Optimism is all I have right now. We belong together, and in time I'm sure she'll come to realise that as well. My heart belongs to her, like hers belongs to me.

When the accident happened, I worried she would never wake up, and I would lose her. Not once did I contemplate the possibility that she would wake up and I would lose her anyway.

It's only 7am as I walk the long, familiar corridor of the hospital towards her room, so there's not much activity. I make sure I'm here every morning when her breakfast arrives so I can cut up her food. She's incapable of doing it herself, with only one functioning arm. She hates it, I can tell, but she needs to eat. The old Jemma was always strong-willed and independent. It's something I love and admire about her, so I'm glad that's a trait she hasn't lost. She's still in there somewhere, I just need to find a way to bring her back out.

'Morning, Mr Spencer,' one of the nurses says as I pass.

'Morning.' I've become a regular fixture around here. Jemma was moved out of the ICU four days ago, and into a normal ward. They kept her in intensive care long enough for her to have the hip replacement, and the pins inserted into her broken bones. The operation was successful, and they had her up and walking—albeit slowly and with help—within twenty-four hours.

My stomach tightens the closer I get. The love I used to see in her eyes when she looked at me has been replaced by a blank stare; that's if I can get her to look in my direction. She spends most of her time pretending to be asleep so she doesn't have to talk to us. She's giving everyone the cold shoulder, including her parents. It breaks my heart, and not just for Christine and Stephen and me; I can only imagine how scared, confused and alone Jemma must be feeling.

'Morning,' I say, when I enter her room. She's awake and staring at the ceiling. I hate that her face no longer lights up when she sees me. I hate that she no longer smiles that beautiful smile.

Her eyes dart to me briefly before fixing back on the ceiling. 'Hi,' she replies in a voice so soft it's barely audible. Nevertheless, I force out a smile. I can't let her see how much this is affecting me—I need to be her strength. I want to pull her into my arms and tell her to hang in there, and that everything is going to work out, but I know better than to do that. My hopes may be dwindling, but I refuse to believe that this is what our future holds.

'Breakfast is late this morning,' I say, taking a seat near her bed, trying not to let this new awkwardness overwhelm me.

'I told them I didn't want any.' She's still refusing to look at me.

Sliding my chair forward I reach for her hand, but I'm not surprised when she jerks her arm away. 'You've got to eat. You need it to help regain your strength. I'm sure you don't want to stay in this place forever.' Her gaze moves to me, but she doesn't speak. 'Aren't you itching to get home?' Because I know I'm itching to have her back there.

'Home? What home? I don't have a home. How could I possibly be itching to go to a place I don't even remember?'

I'm stung by the bitterness in her voice and I go to reach for her hand again, but think better of it. 'Your home is with me, Jem.' The blank stare she gives me has me diverting my gaze to the floor as silence falls over us. The air is so thick in this room you could cut it with a knife.

'Don't you have somewhere else to be, like a job or something?' she eventually says. She doesn't even wait for my reply before rolling onto her side, facing her back to me.

⸺

'Let me help you,' I offer as she moves to rise from the bed. Today she's leaving the hospital ward and checking into the rehabilitation centre. She has some intensive therapy ahead of her, but it means she's one step closer to coming home. I'm still holding onto hope that this whole ordeal will soon be behind us, and we can move towards getting back to what we had before the accident. Without hope, a man has nothing. I'd even settle for something remotely close to that.

'I'm not an invalid!' she snaps, snatching her arm out of my grasp.

'I'm sorry,' I whisper, stepping back. I shove my hands into the pockets of my trousers so I'm not tempted to reach out for her again.

Once she finally manages to stand, she turns to face me. I hear her sigh before she speaks. 'No, *I'm* sorry,' she says, bowing her head. 'You've been nothing but kind to me. I'm sorry for the way I've been treating you, it's uncalled for.'

'It's okay,' I say, taking a step forward. I'm hurting for her. This is hell for me, so I can't even imagine what she is going through.

'I just feel so . . .' Her focus is still planted on the floor, but I don't miss the crack in her voice as she speaks. I place my finger under her chin, to gently bring her gaze up to meet mine. A lump rises to my throat when I see tears pooling in her beautiful eyes. 'I feel so lost.'

'Oh Jem.' Instinctively I pull her into my arms. This is the first time she has allowed me to hold her since the accident, and I'm so grateful she doesn't pull away. I need this just as much as she does. I feel like we're both drowning and neither of us knows how to come up for air.

'What time does your flight leave tomorrow?' I ask Rachel as we take a seat in the hospital cafeteria. I'm thankful to have her and Jemma's parents here to lean on. They've been a godsend. This is where we usually hang out while Jemma undergoes physiotherapy. The food isn't great and the coffee is mediocre at best, but that's all they have on offer. I'm not leaving the hospital just to find something better. Being near Jemma is far more important, so for the interim this home away from home is our reality.

I spend my entire day here, from sun up to sun down. I'd be here twenty-four-seven if Jemma would allow it. I promised to love her during sickness and health, and that's exactly what I plan to do.

'The flight leaves at three,' Rachel replies as her gaze moves down to the table. She falls silent and I watch as she nervously picks at the napkin in front of her. I know that leaving isn't easy for her, she's also hurting that Jemma doesn't remember their friendship. Reaching across the table, I place my hand on hers.

'Don't feel guilty for leaving, Rach. You know I'll take care of her. You have a life in New York; Jemma knows how much your career means to you.' I pause briefly. Well, Jemma used to know. 'She wouldn't want you to stay and risk everything you've worked so hard for.'

'She needs me, she needs you, she needs all of us,' Rachel says as she covers her face and starts to cry. 'She may not know it, but she needs us.' I stand quickly and move around to her side of the table, pulling her into my arms. 'If it was me lying in that hospital bed, she'd be right by my side.'

'Go,' I say firmly. 'Everything will work itself out in the end.'

It has to. I'm not sure who I'm trying to convince more. Rachel wraps her arms tightly around my waist, but doesn't reply.

We are jolted apart when we hear a loud cough from beside us. The angry glare I see in Lucas's eyes as they move between me and Rachel shocks me.

'Am I interrupting something?' His eyes lock on Rachel as he speaks. Her hands drop by her sides, and she looks at the floor. I don't know what is going on with these two, but something has happened. They used to be close, to the point that Jemma and I hoped one day they'd get together. They're our best friends, and the four of us have done so much together over the years, including trips away, both here and abroad. The animosity that has become ever present when these two are in the same room doesn't make sense.

Rachel doesn't make eye contact with either of us as she reaches for her handbag. 'I'm going to go and see if Jemma is back in the room.'

'Don't leave on my account,' Lucas snaps as she walks around us, heading for the exit.

'What in the hell was that all about?' I ask Lucas when Rachel is out of hearing range.

'You need to watch her,' he says, flicking his head in her direction. The hate, or maybe just the anger he's feeling towards her, is rolling off him. These two were tight, right up until our wedding. They seemed fine on the day; they even danced together.

'Watch Rachel? Why?'

'Just be careful,' he replies, undoing the buttons on his suit jacket and taking a seat at the table.

'What happened with you two? Seriously, man, talk to me.'

'There's nothing to talk about,' he says, brushing me off and signalling the waitress over to the table.

There's a lot more to this than either of them is letting on, but I give him the reprieve he so clearly needs. 'How's business?' I ask. 'I feel bad I've lumped you with all of it.'

'Don't even think about it. The contracts are being drawn up as we speak.'

'Great,' I say, smiling. Even if my heart's not completely in it, I'm truly happy for us; we've worked hard to get to where we are, to signing this big deal. If things were different we'd be out celebrating—the three of us: me, Jem and Lucas. 'I'm sorry you're left to deal with it all on your own.'

'Stop saying that. You're where you need to be. I'm pretty much the brains of our company anyway.' He says it with a straight face, but I know he's just trying to rile me up like he always does.

'Whatever, arsehole,' I snap.

He throws back his head and laughs, because I always bite. *Always.*

SEVEN

Braxton

ONE MONTH LATER . . .

There's definitely a spring in my step as I carry the last of the groceries into the house. I was up early this morning and heading to the shops to stock up on all of Jem's favourite foods. Well, she used to love them. Her memory still hasn't shown any sign of returning, so nothing has changed between us; our relationship is still strained, to say the least. I'm not even sure she would class me as a friend, but I refuse to let my mind go there. It hurts too much.

Today marks Jemma's last day of full-time live-in rehab. She's finally coming home. This is her dream house, the one I built for her. She loves it here. I desperately hope being home will be just what she needs to spark her memory.

Rachel came over yesterday to help me get the house in order. To my surprise, she returned from New York last week. Apparently her company has granted her special leave. I suspect there's more to it, but I'm so grateful to have her here. She has really helped me keep my head above water.

I want everything to be perfect for Jem's return. The house is exactly the way it was the last time she left, though I have made up the spare room for her. She belongs in our bed, next to me, but I know that's not going to happen right away. I miss her . . . no, I crave her, but if she needs time, that's what I'll give her. I'm just over the moon to have her home again.

Once the groceries are packed away, I search in the cupboard under the sink for vases. I went to three different florists on the way home to buy Jemma's favourite flowers, every stem I could find. They're the same flowers I gave her on our first date, and every date since—and they're what she chose for her wedding bouquet. She has always loved the vivid contrast in colours between the rich yellow roses and the bright purple irises.

As desperate as I am for her to remember those times, that's not why I'm doing this. I'm doing it because I want to see her reaction, for her face to light up just like it used to. That look; *Christ. I miss that look.* It's exquisite, one of pure beauty. The happiness I see on her face is infectious.

I close my eyes and remember. I need to cling to these memories to help get me through. One day she will love me again, I truly believe that. The alternative is unimaginable.

As I walk through the automatic doors of the rehabilitation centre I'm as nervous as hell—but I'm still smiling. 'Good morning,' I say to Olivia, the young receptionist behind the front desk.

'Good morning, Mr Spencer.'

The staff, just like those at the hospital, have been wonderful with Jemma. I couldn't have asked for better people to care for my wife.

I'm still getting used to the feelings that run through me every time I see her now: a mixture of love, elation and gripping fear. After the accident I told myself I would be grateful to have her back in any condition, and I am, but I wasn't prepared for this. How can she so easily forget the bond we shared? How can she not feel it, when I still do? For me, it's stronger than ever. How could she forget how much she loves me? Because I know she loved me just as much as I love her. I felt her love every day of my life. How can that just vanish overnight?

'Good morning, ladies,' I say as I enter Jemma's room. My eyes briefly skim past Christine and Rachel, before landing on Jem, and the smile I'm wearing immediately drops from my face when my eyes take in her expression. Turning my head slightly, my gaze moves back to Christine, then Rachel. They're each wearing the exact same sombre face. My heart sinks. Something's going on. Are they not letting Jemma come home?

'Is everything okay?' I ask Jemma as I step towards the bed. 'Has something happened?'

She bows her head, and I hate that she can't look at me. 'We need to talk.' She says it in a voice so soft I barely hear her.

'Sure,' I reply, even though my gut tells me I'm not going to like what she has to say. Talking was something we were always good at. We rarely fought. In nineteen years, I can probably count on one hand the number of arguments we've had.

'We'll give you two a few minutes,' Rachel says, ushering Christine towards the door I just entered through. The sympathetic look Rachel gives me as she leaves only heightens my concern.

I watch as Jemma slowly manoeuvres her legs over the side of the bed and sits. The plaster cast has been removed and replaced with a plastic splint. She's still limping when she walks, but the doctors say it will improve in time as her leg strengthens. She will come here five mornings a week as an outpatient. I hope to return to work next week, but I have agreed with Lucas that I'll just work in the afternoons so I can bring her to her appointments.

'Come, sit,' she says, tapping the mattress beside her. Her asking me to sit next to her should have me smiling, but it doesn't. I know her better than she knows herself, and what she's about to say isn't something pleasant.

The moment I'm seated, she reaches for my hand. Although I'm bracing myself for what's to come, I still manage to close my eyes briefly so I can savour her touch.

She sighs deeply before lifting her eyes to meet mine. 'I can't thank you enough for everything you've done for me over the past six weeks. I know I haven't been the most gracious or accommodating patient.' She takes another breath, and I can tell she's apprehensive about saying whatever it is she needs to say. 'I hadn't really given it any thought until Rachel mentioned it, but she said you were eager to have me home.' She pauses briefly before continuing. 'That's not my home anymore, Braxton. I don't even know where I belong.' And there it is. I feel something crumple inside me when the meaning behind her words sinks in. 'I won't be coming home with you today. I, umm . . .' Her gaze moves back down to the bed before she continues. 'I think, under the circumstances, it's best if I go to my mother's house.'

I swear I feel my heart tear in two. *She's not coming home.*

Standing from the bed, I rub my hand over my chest as that crushing ache returns. I feel like I'm struggling to breathe. 'I'm so sorry, Braxton.' It's obvious by the tone of her voice she's hurting as well. Maybe not as much as I'm hurting, but it's there.

'It's okay.' It's not okay, but I can't bring myself to hurt her further. Nothing about this is okay.

I pack the last of her clothes into a suitcase and zip it up. She wouldn't even come to the house to gather some of her things. She sent Rachel here instead. It's just another blow to my heart.

45

My eyes scan the room as I pick the suitcase up from the bed. I might be taking a few of her possessions out of this room, but she will still be here, in this room, in this house. There are pieces of her everywhere.

My legs are heavy as I descend the stairs to the living room, where Rachel is waiting. I can't help but feel like I'm giving up, like I'm allowing this to happen by handing over this suitcase. But on the other hand, what can I do? I can't force her to love me.

I find Rachel with her back to me, staring at the flowers I bought for Jemma's homecoming. I strategically placed a number of vases throughout the house; I wanted her to smile no matter which room she entered. But that's not going to happen since she refuses to even step inside this house.

'Here's her things,' I say, placing the suitcase down in front of me. It holds clothes, shoes, underwear, toiletries and her make-up. They're not even mine to keep, yet I'm hesitant to let Rachel take them. They're material things and in the grand scheme of things they're insignificant, but it doesn't stop me from feeling like I'm losing another piece of my wife. It's only a matter of time before she asks for more. Before I know it, I'll be left with nothing. Nothing but memories and a shattered heart.

Rachel turns to face me, and the sadness in her eyes is visible from here. I think she can sense this is the beginning of the end for Jemma and me, but neither of us can bring ourselves to say it out loud.

'The flowers are beautiful. She would have loved them.' The haunted tone of her voice sends a chill down my spine, intensifying the desperation I'm feeling inside. There's still a tiny light within me. Although it has diminished considerably, it's still there. I'm hanging onto that tiny piece of hope with everything I have.

I bow my head and run my hand through my hair. The old Jemma would indeed have loved those flowers—this new version, I'm not so sure. The old Jem would have been busting to get home. She would have hated being separated from me, and struggling just like I am. How could life be so cruel? It has taken the one thing that meant the most to both of us: our love for each other.

'Oh, Braxton,' Rachel says, crossing the room and coming to a stop in front of me. A strangled sob escapes from deep in the back of my throat when I hear her crying. When she wraps me tightly in her arms, all my strength vanishes as I completely break down. I weep for Jemma . . . for me . . . for us.

Is this really the end?

I feel stupid when I pull away and wipe my eyes with the back of my hand. I'm not one to show weakness, to anyone. Not even Jemma. We all have demons we hide from the rest of the world.

I turn away from Rachel's tear-stained face, as she stares at me. I hate the pity I see in her eyes. I need a drink; anything to dull this ache.

I head into the kitchen and grab the first bottle I find, reaching for a glass on the top shelf. Rachel doesn't move from where she stands, but her eyes never leave me. I fill the glass almost to the top. I already know it won't be enough. The entire bottle won't be.

Tilting my head back, I down the liquid in two large gulps. It burns on its way down, but I welcome it. I don't hesitate in pouring myself a refill, but before I get a chance to bring it to my lips, Rachel appears beside me and wraps her hand around my wrist. 'Don't. This isn't the answer.'

I want to snatch my wrist from her hold and tell her to mind her own business, but I don't. I know she's suffering as well. This isn't easy for any of us. She may have lost her friend, but my loss is far greater. I've lost my life, *my everything*.

'Please don't tell me you're giving up on her, Braxton.'

All I can do is breathe out. I have no words. In this moment I'm desperate and dipping into self-pity, but deep down I know I haven't given up. I could never give up on us. If it takes me the rest of my life to win her back, then so be it. I'm in this for the long haul.

'You've got to fight for this, Brax.'

I place the glass down. 'How can I fight for something she doesn't even remember?'

'Make her remember.'

I chuckle sarcastically at her response. If only it were that easy.

'I'm serious, Braxton. Talk to her. Remind her of everything you shared.'

'She won't talk to me.' I think that's what hurts the most—that she can't even talk to me. We've never been at a loss for words, until now. We'd talk about anything and everything, until now. We were completely invested in each other's lives, until now.

'Make her listen,' Rachel presses. 'Remind her of what you had together. Write her a damn letter if you have to. Just don't give up. You two are meant for each other.'

'*Were* meant for each other,' I say quietly.

'No, you're wrong, you still *are*! You two share a love like no other.'

I pause and ponder her words. Maybe she's right. If Jemma won't listen to my spoken words, she might at least read my written ones. She needs to know what our lives were once like. What we had is far too beautiful to be forgotten.

EIGHT

Jemma

The persistent knocking on my bedroom door has me begrudgingly rising from the bed. I thought if I ignored her long enough she would go away. I don't know much about this woman who claims to be my mother, but one thing for sure is she's unrelenting.

My leg is still in this ridiculous splint, so I move at a slow pace. I'm beginning to enjoy the hydrotherapy my doctor has me doing to strengthen my leg, only because it means I'm free of this dreaded thing, if only temporarily. The downside to my therapy is being forced to spend time with Braxton. That's not because he's a hard person to be around; quite the opposite, he's always friendly and nice. It's what I see on his face when we're together that's hard. The pleading, almost desperate look in his eyes. Like he's silently begging me to remember him. It weighs me down with guilt.

I'll never forget the look on his face when I told him I wasn't going home. His devastation tore at my heart. I could feel him breaking apart in front of me without a sound, or a single tear. It was a terrible thing to witness, especially knowing I was the cause of it. It's something I hope to never see, or feel, again.

He has been so good to me. So tolerant. The last thing I want to do is hurt him, but he needs to put himself in my shoes. I don't know him. Yes, he's become somewhat familiar over the past weeks and, yes, he seems like a wonderful guy— sweet, caring and loyal—but that's just not enough.

I've been suddenly thrust into a world I don't know, don't remember, and it's scary as hell. I'm surrounded by strange people loving me and fussing over me but I feel nothing for them in return. It's extremely daunting. I don't know anyone, but worst of all, I don't even know myself.

What's my favourite colour, or my favourite food? I'd settle for favourite anything right about now. Just a glimmer of the person I once was. Am I a nice person? Or am I a bitch? Even though these people come back day after day with smiles on their faces, and love in their hearts, I can't help but lean towards the *bitch* side. I haven't exactly reciprocated the affection that's been showered upon me. Does that mean I'm uncaring, or am I just empty inside? I certainly feel empty.

'Oh good, you're awake,' Christine says with a smile, when I open my bedroom door. I have an urge to roll my eyes at her statement. Even if I hadn't been, she wouldn't have stopped knocking until I was.

'I was just resting.' Hiding from her more like it, but she doesn't need to hear that. She's been nothing but kind since I got here. She's been giving me the space I need, and isn't trying to push too much onto me at once. Like Braxton, she seems unsure how to treat me.

I think I made the right decision coming here. I had to do what was best for me . . . what was safe. I have no idea what the real Braxton Spencer is like behind closed doors. My gut tells me he's a good guy. The side I see when we're together doesn't appear to be forced or fake, but the truth is I don't know if that's the real him. I don't know anything about him.

'These just arrived for you,' she says, holding up an exquisite arrangement of yellow and purple flowers. Without knowing what kind of flowers they are, or even who they're from, they make my breath catch in my throat. I can't explain it, but they make me feel . . . something. But what, I have no idea.

'It's so nice to see you smiling,' my mother says. 'I've missed your pretty smile.'

My gaze moves from the flowers to her, and I'm surprised to find her eyes brimming with tears. Am I smiling? I wasn't aware that I was. And why is she crying? I study her face trying to find the answer, but all I see is sadness. Is she thinking about the old me? The daughter I once was, not the shell she's now left with.

'They're beautiful,' I state, trying to push the thought that I'm hurting everyone from my mind.

'They are.'

I sense there's more behind her words, that these particular flowers hold significance and I should know that. Or maybe I'm just reading too much into it.

'They're from Braxton.'

The smile drops from my face and the anxiety kicks back in. This is a more familiar feeling. Other than numbness, I haven't experienced much emotion since waking from my coma, but this anxiousness I cannot bear.

'The card says, *I hope you're settling in*.' She points to it. 'He's such a good man, he's always been so thoughtful.'

'It was very nice of him,' I reply, reaching for the bouquet. She hasn't said much about my previous relationship with Braxton, but I don't miss her subtle hints. She obviously adores him.

'You really loved him, you know?' Sometimes she's not so subtle.

'Really? And how do you know that? Could you feel what I was feeling inside?'

Her eyes widen slightly. 'No, Jemma. I could see it. Everyone could see it.' With that she turns and leaves. I immediately feel bad for being so aggressive towards her.

Closing my door and locking it, I walk towards the window. I'm not sure why I want these flowers near me, but I do. I find myself smiling again as I place them down in the centre of the dresser. I'll be able to admire them from my bed.

My eyes move down to the small rectangular card pinned to the silver ribbon that adorns the white ceramic vase. There's something about the writing that seems familiar, which is crazy. I presume it's Braxton's since the flowers are from him. Is it even possible that I remember his handwriting, but not him?

—

'How's it taste?' Christine asks with a hopeful expression. I cut off a small piece of crumbed chicken and hesitantly place it in my mouth. I've been living here for almost a week and nothing much has changed. I'm still feeling lost . . . just like my memory.

Christine patiently waits for my answer as I slowly chew the food. It actually tastes good. *Really good.* I presume I've eaten this before. Christine seemed almost excited when she announced we were having chicken schnitzel for dinner. Everything is an experiment of some sort, as I'm forced into experiencing what life has to offer all over again. Tastes, smells, sights, sounds and feelings. So much of life seems foreign to me now.

'Nice,' I reply, finally swallowing. She continues to watch me like she's waiting for me to elaborate, but I don't. Instead I shove a forkful of mashed potato in my mouth.

'It's your favourite! I always made it for you on special occasions, like your birthday, or when you were feeling down.'

That statement does nothing to cheer me up, it only helps to remind me of everything I've lost. When is my birthday?

I know she's trying, but I wish she'd stop. Nothing she can do will help—certainly not a piece of crumbed chicken. I've practically given up on my memory returning. Surely there would have been at least a minor breakthrough by now. I feel like I'm falling deeper and deeper into this black abyss that has become my existence.

Silence falls over us as we continue to eat. It's for the best. Especially if she wants me to digest this food.

'Oh, I almost forgot,' she says, rising from her chair at the end of the meal. 'A package arrived for you.' My eyes follow her as she walks across the room to retrieve it. I have no idea why anyone would send me a package. 'It came while you were lying down. I didn't want to disturb you.'

That's the excuse I use to lock myself away from everybody. *I'm tired, I'm going to lie down.* My reluctance to be around anyone isn't helping matters. I even managed to drive Rachel away. She stayed here for the first three nights before packing her things and moving to a hotel. She assured me she wasn't running away from me, that it was only to give me the space she thought I needed. Maybe that was the case. I don't understand why these people give so much, for so little in return.

'Here,' my mother says, placing a large cream parcel in front of me. 'Are you done?'

She points down to my plate, and I nod before answering. 'Yes, thanks.'

My eyes scan the writing across the front of the parcel. It's the same writing that was on the card, so I know it's from Braxton. I find it ironic that despite losing my memory I can still read. I have no recollection of who taught me how, or even which school I attended.

I can't comprehend why that part of my brain is okay, yet people, places and all the important moments from my past have been completely wiped. I've had to undergo numerous tests, and the doctor couldn't find any evidence of permanent brain injury, but it's obvious there is.

I turn the parcel over, feeling suddenly uneasy. I saw him this morning, when he drove me to rehab. He didn't mention the package, but I suppose I didn't give him a chance to engage in any sort of conversation. It's just easier that way. Easier for everyone. I don't want to give him false hope, when there's no hope to give.

Looking up, I find my mother eyeing me sceptically from the other side of the kitchen. I wish she'd stop watching me the way she does. It's unnerving. She might remember me as her daughter, someone she has raised and loved, but she is nothing to me. The person they loved is gone. I may look like the Jemma they once knew, but she's no more.

'I'm going to lie down,' I say, rising from the chair.

'Okay, sweetheart.' She forces out a smile, just like she does every time I disappear upstairs.

My past, my parents, my husband, my friends, my enemies, my first kiss, my achievements and failures, my likes and dislikes . . . the list of things I don't remember is endless. I should feel grateful for surviving the accident, but I don't. I have no idea where I belong. I would never voice this out loud, but there's a huge part of me that wishes I didn't wake up. That might sound selfish, but that's exactly how I feel. There's no light at the end of the tunnel, only darkness.

After locking my bedroom door, I walk across the room and slump on my bed. This is apparently the room I grew up in. Christine said she left it just the way it was when I moved away for university. There are little trinkets of my past everywhere. Trophies, medals, photos, banners, stuffed toys. None of it is familiar.

Instead of comforting me, they haunt me. It's a past I can't remember. Things that probably once held great significance, now mean nothing. I hate it in here, but at the same time, it's the only place I truly feel safe. I can lock myself away from everyone and just be numb. I don't have to pretend I'm okay, or that I'm coping, because I'm not. I feel like I'm drowning in a sea of nothingness, which is ironic. How can you drown in nothing?

I stare at the parcel on my lap for the longest time. I'm curious to know what's inside, but I'm apprehensive as well. According to Christine, Braxton was the love of my life. Once upon a time he may have been, but when I look at him now, I feel nothing. Which I find strange. If I loved him as much as everyone says I did, wouldn't my heart still feel it?

I wait till my stomach settles before I finally find the courage to open it. As desperate as I am to remember, it's frightening when people tell me or show me things from my past. I feel like I'm hurting everyone by not remembering. Don't they realise how much I wish things were different?

I hold my breath as I tear through the top of the parcel and slowly remove the contents, laying them out on the bed beside me. There's a long red rectangular box with a card attached, as well as another, smaller envelope. The card on the box has *Open me first* written on the front, so I pick it up.

Enclosed you'll find a memory bracelet. For now it's empty, but over time you'll understand why I've called it this. Since you're not comfortable talking to me, I've decided to write to you instead. I hope you take the time to read my letters when you're ready. They're letters about our past, and of the happier times we've spent together. Memories of your life through my eyes. It's my way of trying to give you back a piece of what you've lost. Whether or not these letters lead you back to me, you need to know what we once shared, and what our life was like for us.

Closing the card, I ponder his words. I'm touched that he has gone to these lengths, but I can't see how a few letters are going to help. How he can show up here day after day with a smile on his face when I treat him the way I do. He's a better person than I am; I would have given up on me weeks ago.

My fingers hover over the lid, and then I take a breath and open it. I run my fingertips over the white-gold chain. He wasn't lying when he said the memory bracelet was empty. Just like me.

I continue to run my fingers over the links. Deep inside I know this is my way of stalling. I'm afraid to read the letter. I don't want to be freaked out by things I can't remember, yet there's a part of me that yearns to read what he has to say.

LETTER ONE . . .

Dearest Jemma,

The nineteenth of January 1996 was an important day from our past. I'll never forget it. It was the day we met, and the day that changed my life forever.

For you to get a clearer picture of the impact this day had on me, I should start by telling you what my life was like before we met.

Like you, I'm an only child. My father, John Spencer, owned and managed the local hardware store. It's something he inherited when his father died. Hardware was never his thing, but he wanted to keep my grandfather's dream alive, and gave up his own aspirations in life to do just that. He's a good man, my father; one of the best.

There wasn't a lot of money in hardware, so things were pretty tight. Apart from two casual employees, he ran the store on his own, which meant long hours away from his home and family. What I remember most when I think of him is his absence, but I understand why it had to be that way.

He would leave for the store before I woke, and some nights I was already in bed when he returned. Once I started school, my mother, Grace, took a job as a receptionist to help make ends meet. I heard my dad telling my mum one night that we were in danger of losing our house.

I had a great childhood nevertheless. I was happy enough, but when I think back to the times before you moved in next door, what I remember most is the loneliness. With both parents working, I was home on my own a lot. There were no other children living in our street. I used to look forward to going to school so I could play with the other kids. Then you came along, and everything changed.

I still remember that day vividly. It was a hot summer Friday afternoon. Unlike most kids, I didn't look forward to the weekends. Sure, I got to watch cartoons on a Saturday morning, but once they were finished there wasn't much to do. My father was at the store, and my mother used that time to catch up on housework, laundry and preparing meals for the coming week. My days were spent riding my bike up and down the street, or kicking a ball around the yard on my own.

Sunday afternoon was my favourite. My mum would cook a roast dinner every Sunday, and it was also the one day my father closed the store early. It was our family night. If the weather was good, he'd kick the ball around with me in the backyard, until Mum called us inside for dinner.

When I close my eyes I can still remember the delicious aromas that filled the house as the roast cooked in the oven. After dinner, we'd play board games. I miss those times.

It was school holidays, so I was bored out of my brain. I was lying on the sofa watching television when I heard the loud rumble of an engine coming from outside. I jumped up, and through the window I saw a large truck parked in the driveway next door. I can't remember the name of the company—I was only seven—but I do remember the large, bold, blue letters and the word REMOVALIST down the side.

The fact that we were getting new neighbours should have excited me, but it didn't. I missed the old couple, Mr and Mrs Gardener, who used to live next door. She used to bake chocolate-chip cookies every weekend and would bring me over a special batch with extra chocolate chips. To this day, I still miss those cookies.

I didn't want new neighbours. All I could think about were the cookies I would never get to eat again. Cookies are important to seven-year-olds.

My shoulders were slumped and I'm pretty sure my feet were dragging as I headed into the kitchen to pour myself a glass of milk. Thinking about those cookies made me thirsty.

I'd only managed to take a sip when the phone rang. I climbed onto the countertop and reached for the receiver that hung on the wall. I already knew it would be either my mum or dad. They always called numerous times throughout the day to make sure I was okay. My parents hated that I was left alone so much, but we needed the money that their jobs provided.

'There's new people moving in next door,' I told my dad.

'Oh yes, Joe mentioned it.' Joe Pentecost was the local real estate agent, and a friend of my father's. 'I believe they have a daughter who's about your age.'

Those words instantly got my attention, and gave me the pick-me-up I needed. Having someone my age living next door far outweighed my need for chocolate-chip cookies.

The moment I was off the phone, I gulped down my milk and grabbed my bike from the back shed. I was desperate to get a glimpse of you as I pushed my bike down the driveway. I wasn't even disappointed that you were a girl. I was just excited by the prospect of a new friend.

I hovered around the front yard waiting, but there was no sign of you. That's when I climbed on my bike and moved to the street. I rode around in circles waiting for you to come out of *the house, but your father and the removal guys were the only people I saw.*

A lot of time passed and I was ready to give up and go inside, but for some reason my eyes were drawn to one of the windows on the upper floor. I think my heart actually skipped a beat when I saw you leaning against the glass windowpane, looking down at me.

A smile exploded onto your face, and I immediately reciprocated. I still remember the way my heart raced. I was so focused on you that I hadn't noticed how close I'd come to the gutter until it was too late. Before I knew what was happening, I'd been flung over the handlebars and landed with a thud on the asphalt.

I lay there for a short time. I wasn't going to cry, no matter how much my fall had hurt. I'd already embarrassed myself enough.

I finally found the strength to move, and flinched. It took every bit of strength I had not to cry. As I tried to stand, a shadow fell over me. When my gaze snapped up to you, I swear you looked like an angel with the sun forming a bright halo around your pretty face.

'Are you okay?' you asked, crouching down to my level. I wasn't okay, but I forced out a tight smile, trying to brush it off. 'Oh my god, you're bleeding,' you said quickly.

Looking down at my grazed knee, and the blood that was now trickling down my leg, made the milk I'd drunk earlier rise to the back of my throat. I kept telling myself not to throw up in front of you. I'd already made a horrible first impression; if I could have had a re-do, I would have chucked a really cool wheelie instead of stacking it.

'Come, can you stand?' You held out your hand and helped me to my feet, and then you picked my buckled bike off the road as I hobbled towards my house. 'Let me help you up the stairs.'

'I'm fine,' I said, trying my best to remain brave. I wasn't fine. I was in pain . . . and humiliated. You rushed ahead of me,

banging on the front door. I had to grab onto the rail to help propel me up the stairs. 'What are you doing?' I asked.

'Getting your mum. You're hurt bad.'

My parents didn't like me telling people I was home alone, but I told you anyway. 'My mum's not home . . . she's at work.'

I could tell by your widening eyes that you were shocked, but it didn't deter you from opening the door and waltzing straight into my house. Even then I knew that it was extremely careless of you to enter a stranger's house like that, but your actions made me smile. In that moment, I knew we were going to be great friends.

After you got me seated on a chair in the kitchen and placed a wet cloth on my bleeding knee, you ran next door to get your mum.

Your mum wasn't impressed that I was left alone at such a young age, and she made sure to let my mum know when she met her later that afternoon.

Your mother placed the first-aid kit she'd brought with her on the table and proceeded to clean up my wounds. She was very sweet to me that day, just like you were.

'This is going to sting,' she said as she poured some antiseptic onto a cotton ball.

She wasn't lying; it hurt like hell. It felt like she was dabbing my knee with a burning hot coal, not a soft cotton ball. The more she dabbed, the more it stung. The tears I'd managed to keep at bay until now threatened to fall.

You were standing beside me, and out of the corner of my eye I could see you watching me, but I refused to look at you. The moment my vision became blurry, I clenched my eyes closed. I wasn't going to let you see me cry.

When a tear leaked from the corner of my eye, I quickly turned my head away from you. I wasn't expecting you to reach for my hand, but that's exactly what you did. I've never told you this, but it helped. It really did. So, thank you.

You didn't let go until your mum had finished. 'You were so brave,' you said as your mum packed everything away.

Those words made me feel so much better. 'I'm Braxton,' I said, holding out my hand to you. 'Braxton Spencer.' If we were going to be best friends, you needed to know my name.

'Jemma . . . Jemma Isabella Rosalie Robinson,' you stated proudly.

'That's a pretty name.'

I felt my face flush the moment those words left my mouth. It was a ridiculous thing for a seven-year-old to say, but it was the truth. Your name was almost as pretty as you were.

'If your leg is better tomorrow, do you want to come over and play?'

'Yes,' I answered without hesitation.

You gave me a beautiful toothless smile, and my heart started to race for the second time that day. I'm going to marry this girl one day, was the first thought that entered my mind.

That thought only grew stronger in the years that followed. What we had is far too beautiful to be forgotten.

Yours always,

Braxton

A tight feeling forms in the back of my throat as I look down at the tiny bike charm in my hand. It was inside the letter along with a photo of us as kids sitting on our bikes. The memory bracelet now makes sense.

A small smile creeps onto my lips when I pick up the photo and study it. My two front teeth are missing and the toothless smile he mentioned in the letter is present. We look so happy. I swallow hard, but the lump that's formed doesn't go away. This small gesture has me feeling somewhat surprised and strangely overwhelmed. He was right: in a way it has given me a tiny piece of my life back. A tiny yet significant moment from my past.

I've been anything but nice to Braxton since the moment I woke from my coma, yet his commitment has never wavered despite me constantly pushing him away. I've been so wrapped up in my own sense of loss that I haven't really considered how much this has affected him.

Pulling the letter towards me, I clutch it tightly against my chest as I make a silent promise to myself. Tomorrow when I see him, I will make more of an effort.

NINE

Braxton

I knock on the door twice before turning the handle and entering. I pray that he's having a good day, I really need a lift.

'Hi,' I say with a smile when my eyes land on the elderly man sitting in a chair by the window. I can't believe how much he has aged over the past two years. He'll always be the same man to me, but he looks well beyond his actual age of fifty-two. Sadly, this illness has really knocked him for six.

'Hello, young man.' His green eyes light up as he stands slowly, extending his hand to greet me. He usually calls me 'son' when he remembers who I am, so I already know today is not one of his good days. I've struggled to come to terms with this, but even more so since Jemma's accident. I am now a stranger to the two most important people in my life. It's ironic and heartbreaking in equal measure.

I wrap my hand around his when I come to a stop in front of him, and I get a pang in my heart at the weak handshake he gives me in return. I hate what's become of my father. The once strong and virile man he was, is no more.

He was diagnosed with early-stage Alzheimer's almost three years ago, and it has progressed rapidly since. I used to think it was an old person's disease, but I've learned that even people as young as me can be struck by it. That's how my father eventually ended up here. It almost broke me to put him in a nursing home, but I was left with no choice.

In the beginning we tried to convince him to move in with us, but he didn't want to leave his house, the home he had shared with my mother, and I couldn't blame him for that. I arranged for nurses to visit him, but when he started to wander off at all hours of the day and night, it became unsafe. He needed full-time care, which neither Jemma nor I could provide.

When the inevitable finally came, Jem and I looked at a dozen different homes before we eventually decided on this one. It was important to know he was getting the best care available; I wouldn't have been able to go through with it otherwise.

'Sit,' he says, gesturing to the chair opposite his. It astounds me that he has no idea who I am yet he's so welcoming. I'm grateful that his illness hasn't stolen that special trait. He has always been loved for his down-to-earth, friendly nature.

'You have a lovely view here,' I say, glancing out the large bay window beside us. His room overlooks the well-maintained gardens. Jemma had insisted on him having a room with a view of the native trees that are dotted throughout the landscape. The flowers attract the native birds and that's what he loves. One of the downfalls of this home was a strict no-pet policy, but it was a small price to pay for all the other benefits this place offered.

His beloved rainbow lorikeet, Samson, came to live with Jemma and me. It took a lot of patience and persistence from Jem to get Samson to eat in those first few days, but since then he has become part of our home.

'Yes,' he says as a smile brightens his face. 'The birds come and visit often, I really like them.' He lifts his arm and points in the direction of the garden. 'See that hollowed log over there?'

'Yes,' I reply following his gaze.

'There's a large blue-tongue lizard living in it. He's a beauty,' he says, holding his hands in front of him to show me roughly what size it is. 'I sit here for hours watching him bake in the sun.'

'That's great.' I feel my lips curve into a smile as I watch him. He seems happy here and that helps ease the guilt somewhat.

I feel mixed emotions as I pull up outside Jemma's mother's house. Although Jem is now living here, I will never refer to it as her home. Her home is with me.

The letter should have arrived by now, but I have no idea how she would've reacted to it, or if she even read it. I pray that she did. I'm so lost without her; it's a day-to-day struggle I won't ever get used to. A huge part of me is missing and I feel like I'm mourning her, yet she's still alive.

With the persistence of Lucas and Rachel—separately; they still won't speak to each other—I have finally gone back to work. I've been starting around midday so I can visit my dad and take Jemma to her daily physio appointments at the rehabilitation centre, and then I make up for my late start by working long into the night. There's nobody waiting for me at home, and I haven't been sleeping well anyway. I designed every inch of that house for Jem with love and care, and now I hate being in it without her. At least while I'm working I'm not wallowing in the living hell that my life has become.

I stay seated in the car for a few minutes. I'm usually itching to see her, even if the sentiment isn't mutual, but today I'm hesitant. These letters may be my last hope and I'm not sure I'm ready for another setback.

Eventually I step out of the car. I'm never going to get the answers I seek by sitting out here. One thing's for sure, though: whatever the outcome, I'm not giving up.

As I round the front of the car, I'm surprised when I see the front door open and Jemma step out. The doctor issued her with a walking stick, but she's stubborn and refuses to use it. The limp is still visible when she walks, but she's getting around a lot better now and improves each time I see her.

'Good morning,' I say, walking towards her. I offer my hand when she reaches the steps. I can tell that she doesn't like me doing this, but I can't bring myself to stop being there for her.

'Morning,' she replies, reaching for my hand for the first time. Her touch is brief but I savour it, and a smile comes to my lips. Any kind of contact, no matter how brief, is welcome.

I open the passenger-side door for her, and she makes eye contact with me before smiling and thanking me. Something is different about her today. Could it possibly be the letter? My gaze moves down to her wrist when she reaches for the seatbelt, and I try not to be disappointed to see that she's not wearing the bracelet I sent.

I'm curious to know if she's read the letter, but the fact that she's not wearing the bracelet has me biting my tongue. No point setting myself up for more heartache.

Usually she avoids looking at me, but today her eyes follow my every move as I seat myself in the driver's side, again leaving me to wonder what's going on.

'Which house did you live in?' she asks as I back out of the driveway.

She read the letter.

Her words spark a ray of hope inside me. She could've asked her mother that question, but she saved it for me. It's the first one she's asked since she woke from her coma. It's been as if there is a part of her that doesn't want to remember, or be reminded. She has shut all of us down every time we have mentioned her past, but it seems today is the beginning of . . . something.

'That one there,' I say, leaning forward and pointing to the two-storey red-brick house next door. It pained me greatly when I had to sell it to pay for my father's room at the nursing home, and I still get a sick feeling in my gut every time I see it. Some of my best, and my worst, moments happened in that house, but selling it was the only way to guarantee that my father would get the care he needed.

'Do your parents still live there?'

I glance at her briefly before focusing back on the road. 'No. No they don't.' I hope she's satisfied with that answer because I don't feel like elaborating. It's too depressing. There was no happy ending for my family.

Looking out the passenger-side window, she studies the house as we pass. It still looks exactly the same as it did when I lived there. Does it seem familiar to her? 'Did we go to the same school? Was it around here?'

'Yes, and yes,' I say as a smile forms on my face. 'We can drive past on our way home if you like.'

'I'd like that.'

I close my eyes briefly and chant a silent thank you. My letter has ignited something within her, I'm sure of it. That spark of hope is growing. I'm eager to write to her again. I've only just touched on the beauty we once were.

TEN

Braxton

'**S**hit!'
 I screw up another piece of paper. The first letter came easily—it made sense to start at the very beginning—but now that I know she's actually going to read them, my approach has changed. I want to cram as much as I can into this one. There's so much I yearn to say.

Resting my elbows on the desk in front of me, I bury my face in my hands. I can't rush this.

With that in mind I put pen to paper. Her interest was piqued when we stopped off at the primary school we both attended. She even got out of the car and walked around the perimeter of the school. It's odd yet sad to know she's seeing these old, familiar things through fresh eyes.

LETTER TWO . . .

Dearest Jemma,

The seventeenth of March 1997 was a pinnacle time in our young lives. We'd been neighbours for over a year at this stage, and our friendship was growing stronger with each passing day.

The fact that I was a year older than you meant we were in different grades, and we never played together at school. I'd smile whenever we passed each other, though, because just seeing you made me happy.

In the playground, you hung around the girls in your grade, and I played with my mates. In the beginning I was scared to tell my friends about you. To them, any girl was a germ-infested no-go zone. You were never like that to me; from that very first day I found you different. You were funny, easy to get along with, and incredibly sweet.

Now that your mother knew I was home alone in the afternoons, she insisted that I stay at your house until my mum got back from work. I looked forward to that hour or so each day because you were all mine. You seemed just as happy to be around me.

In those moments I didn't have to pretend not to like you, because I did. A lot. It would have been impossible for me not to. I was at an impressionable age, and to an eight-year-old boy reputation is everything.

Little did we know that year would be a game changer for us. One incident in the school playground changed everything. It was a moment that put my entire reputation on the line.

It was a Monday. I only remember that because I'd spent the entire Sunday with you and your parents at the beach. I was still on a high from it, and sought you out in the playground. On the down-low, of course.

I steered my mates around to the grassed area at the back of the school when the lunch bell sounded, because I knew that's where you played elastics, or skipped rope with your friends. It was a risky move on my part, but a risk I was willing to take. I just needed a glimpse of you to get me through to the end of the day. It sounds silly when I say it like that, but that's exactly how you made me feel ... how you still make me feel.

When there was no sign of you, I started to worry. Call it a sixth sense, but I knew something was off. I didn't hesitate to leave my friends to go in search of you. I looked high and low—the front playground, the library, I even checked the sick bay in the office in case you'd been hurt. But, nothing, and now I was getting desperate.

I ran back to your friends to ask them if they'd seen you. One of them said you'd gone back to the classroom because you'd forgotten to bring your lunch down to the playground, so I headed in that direction. I remember bounding up the stairs two at a time.

As soon as I hit the landing I heard you. You were crying. I called your name as I broke into a run. The moment you stepped out from behind the partition wall I was filled with a mixture of relief and confusion. It was the first time I'd ever seen you cry. 'What's wrong?' I asked, placing my hands on your shoulders.

'Larry . . . Larry Wilson.' When you buried your face in my chest, I wrapped you in my arms. No other words were needed. 'The Looter' was what everyone called Larry Wilson behind his back. He was the school bully, and ruled the playground with his iron fist. He was in grade five, and although only ten, he was enormous. Even the sixth graders were frightened of him. He was notorious for preying on the weak and taking whatever he wanted. In this case, your lunch.

I'd never experienced anger like I did in that moment. I had no idea how, but Larry Wilson was going to pay for what he'd done to you.

Manoeuvring you over to the large bench seat by the wall, I sat you down. 'Do you like ham, cheese and lettuce?' I asked you.

'Yes,' you sniffled, wiping the tears from your face.

After unwrapping my sandwich, I passed half to you. You were lucky it was a Monday; my mum always bought meat from the deli on Sundays. It usually only lasted until midweek, so the rest of the days were boring old Vegemite.

Once we'd finished eating, I walked you back to your friends before going in search of The Looter. I was running on pure adrenaline. A clear-thinking Braxton wouldn't have even entertained the idea of taking on the school giant, but that's what seeing you upset did to me.

I briefly rethought my plan the moment I was standing in front of him. He was almost as wide as he was tall, and towered over me. But then I remembered your tear-stained face and that was enough to give me the courage to take him on.

I squared my shoulders and took a deep breath before I spoke. 'Why did you steal Jemma's lunch?'

He laughed and pushed me in the chest, making me stumble. 'Get out of my face, loser,' he'd growled, and something inside me snapped.

Lunging at him, I threw my arms around his waist, ramming my shoulder into his stomach. The adrenaline coursing through my veins made me feel invincible.

I heard the loud gasps from the other students when Larry landed on the muddy ground with a thud. I was now on top of him. A few kids started to chant—'Fight! Fight! Fight!'—and it didn't take long for a large crowd to gather.

My eyes briefly locked with his, and the anger I could see reflecting back at me only spurred me on further. He was probably going to eat me up just like he had your lunch, but I wasn't going down without a fight.

When he tried to wriggle out from underneath I pulled him into a headlock, I was surprised by my own strength. 'You like stealing food from little girls?' I said as I reached for a handful of mud. The moment he opened his mouth to speak, I shoved the mud into his gob. The more he tried to protest, the more mud I managed to force into his mouth.

'Get off me,' he said in a muffled cry, as tears leaked from his eyes. He wasn't so tough now.

'Not until you swallow it.'

I'd never done anything so mean before, but he had this coming.

The crowd started to point and laugh as The Looter struggled to swallow the mud in his mouth. A part of me actually felt sorry for him, but the pain he had inflicted on the other students far outweighed what was happening to him in that moment. I always knew it would only be a matter of time before he pushed someone too far. I just never thought that someone would be me.

'Hey, break this up.' The teacher on playground duty grabbed hold of the back of my shirt, pulling me to my feet. 'Go to the principal's office immediately!'

I knew I was in big trouble, but it was worth it. To this day, I still remember the awe on people's faces as I stood tall and walked away from the scene, ready to receive my punishment. For those few minutes, I felt like the king of the world.

Because this was a first offence for me, the school didn't contact my parents. I did, however, receive lunchtime detention for the rest of the week. It was a small price to pay. After that day he never picked on you again.

I'll never forget how I felt when I left the classroom after my first day of detention. I found you in the corridor just outside my lunchtime prison, sitting on the floor by the wall with your legs crossed. You looked so lost and sad.

'What are you doing here?' I asked as I helped you to your feet.

'It's my fault you're in trouble.'

'No it's not, Jem. You didn't make him eat mud.'

'Yes it is.'

'Is that why you're here?'

'Yes. I started all of this, it's only fair that I do the detention too.' You took a step towards me, getting up on the tips of your toes to plant a soft kiss on my cheek. 'I'll never forget what you did for me.'

I'm pretty sure that's the exact moment I fell in love with you. It was evident that you cared about me, and you have no

idea how much I needed someone like you in my life. It was
comforting to know that you had my back, just like I had yours.

We became inseparable after that day. I had only taken the
risk to protect you, and had no idea I would come out the other
end as the school legend. I would've done it again in a heartbeat
for you, Jem. There's nothing I wouldn't do for you.

That day our bond was cemented in stone forever.

What we had is far too beautiful to be forgotten.

Yours always,

Braxton

Just because she doesn't remember our bond, doesn't mean it's not there. All those old feelings are buried somewhere deep inside her, I know it. You can't love someone so completely one day, and feel nothing for them the next. It's not possible. It's just going to take time to coax those feelings back to the surface.

I read over the letter before folding it in half and sliding it into the envelope. Reaching for the tiny sandwich charm sitting on my desk, I lay it in the palm of my hand. I feel myself smiling as I think back to that day.

These letters were supposed to help Jem get back pieces of her past, but they're helping me as well. She may be lost to me for now, but reliving all these precious memories I've made with her over the years will keep me going until I have her back.

ELEVEN

Braxton

The questions start the moment Jemma is seated in my car. 'Did you really make Larry Wilson eat mud?' Without even looking at her I can hear the amusement in her voice.

'I did. He spent the rest of the day in the sick bay. Rumour has it he vomited on the principal's shoes.'

'Oh my god,' she says, covering her mouth with her hand to muffle her giggle. Just hearing her laugh again makes me happier than I have felt in weeks.

'Did he stop bullying after that?'

'For a while,' I say, glancing in her direction. 'Old habits die hard, I guess. He left you alone, though, which was all that mattered to me.'

A sweet smile forms on her face as she looks over at me from the passenger seat. 'Thank you for sticking up for me, and for sharing your sandwich.'

'I'll always be here for you, Jem, no matter what.'

I love that the letters are opening up a line of communication for us. I think in her own small way she's starting to come to terms with what has happened. It may not be as fast as I'd like, but I hope these letters will help her to eventually get back to where she once was.

She goes quiet for a while, and I'm relieved when she finally speaks again. 'Did we go to the beach much when we were kids?'

'Yes,' I answer as I steer the car into a parking spot at the rehab centre. 'It was one of your favourite places to go. Your parents took us often when we were kids, and once we were old enough we'd go on our own. That's why we built our house near the beach. You ran along the sand every morning.'

'Really?' she says, turning her head in my direction. When I see her brow furrow, I know she's trying to remember.

As much as I would like to show her our place, I'm not sure if she's ready for that. I can already see the tiny shift she's made since I started writing her the letters, and I don't want to do anything that might jeopardise her progress.

'I can drive you past your favourite beach on the way home if you like. It's not that far out of our way.'

'I'd like that,' she replies with a smile.

She reaches for the door handle. 'Let me get that for you.' Pulling the keys out of the ignition, I step out of the car.

Opening the passenger-side door, I extend my hand to her. She smiles up at me as her dainty fingers wrap around mine. Seeing her smile has always been my undoing. In this split second, everything seems perfect, just the way it used to be. So much so that I actually forget that things aren't.

'I love you, Jem,' I say without thinking. They're words that have come naturally for me—for us both—for so long.

I don't even realise what I've said until her face drops, and she pulls her hand from mine. With just three little words I undo all the progress we've made over the past week.

⸻

'Hey,' Lucas says as he enters my office and takes the chair in front of me. 'You okay, bro? You don't seem yourself today.'

'I haven't been myself since Jemma's accident,' I reply dryly, slumping back in my chair.

'I know. How are things going with you two?'

I shrug. 'It's all over the place. Every time we manage to make a bit of progress, something happens and we end up right back where we started.'

The air feels thick as I silently berate myself. Things had shifted dramatically after those three words. She withdrew back into herself and became cold and aloof.

'You know what?' Lucas says, slapping the palm of his hand down onto my desk, startling me from my thoughts.

'What?' My eyes move back to him.

'We're shutting shop early today. I'm taking you out for a few drinks, and if you're lucky I might even buy you dinner.'

I appreciate what he's trying to do, but going out is the last thing I want. 'I can't—'

He cuts me off before I get a chance to tell him how far behind I am. I've barely accomplished anything today.

'No excuses.' He looks down at his watch as he rises from his chair. 'Finish up what you're working on, we're leaving in ten.' I open my mouth to protest again, but he raises his hand to stop me. 'Tonight's happening, no ifs or buts. I miss my friend. Besides, we never got a chance to celebrate our big deal. We worked our arses off to land that contract.'

I can't argue with that. He's right on all counts. 'Okay.'

'Good. You need this just as much as I do.' He gives me a satisfied nod before he turns to leave.

'Lucas,' I say when he reaches the doorway. 'Thank you.'

'A bottle of your finest scotch, and two glasses,' Lucas says to the bartender before gesturing for me to take a seat on one of the black leather stools that line the long white granite bar.

This is my first time here, so my eyes are everywhere. The floor-to-ceiling bright yellow splashback behind the bar, paired with the lines of the black boxed shelves that adorn the wall, is striking. The perfectly positioned down lights make it all pop.

My first thought is that Jem would love this place, and that I must bring her here. Then reality hits. I used to love watching her eyes light up when we walked into somewhere new. She would have a notepad at the ready so she could sketch or take down notes of things that caught her eye. She was so passionate about her work and everything to do with design.

'How'd you find this place?' I ask Lucas.

It's a huge step up from where we usually go for drinks. It makes me wonder if he purposely avoided our usual haunt because of the memories it holds; or perhaps he chose this place because it's more fitting for such a momentous celebration.

We'd dreamed of this moment for so long, and our hard work had finally paid off. Our relatively small architectural firm has suddenly been catapulted into the big time. It's a shame that even now as I think of what this means for us, and for our company, the excitement is lost on me. The axis of my world is no longer aligned, and until that's rectified everything is going to feel out of kilter.

'One of our clients brought me here. It was when . . .' He flicks his hand to dismiss whatever he was going to say. 'Never mind.' I know whatever it was it had something to do with Jemma. I don't blame him for not wanting to go there tonight. It's been hard on all of us.

'We have a nice twenty-five-year-old bottle of Chivas Regal,' the bartender says, placing it down in front of us. 'It's six hundred dollars.' Lucas doesn't even flinch. He wasn't wrong when he said the good stuff. We splurged on a bottle that was a fraction of that price the day we opened our company, but we were just starting out then, so there wasn't a lot of cash. We'd thrown everything we had into getting it up and running.

The bottle went four ways because Jemma and Rachel were both there to help us celebrate. I chuckle to myself when I think of that night. Jemma is such a lightweight, and after two glasses she was drunk. She's been by my side for every celebration, every milestone since we were kids. It seems unjust not having her here.

Lucas passes the bartender our company credit card and pours a small amount into each glass. 'To our continued success,' he says, holding his glass in the air.

I raise my glass and clink it with his before chugging down the smooth, ridiculously expensive amber liquid. Maybe a few more of these will help me get in the celebratory mood because right now it's the last thing I feel like doing.

A few scotches in and I feel myself starting to relax, but my faux pas with Jemma is still at the forefront of my mind.

'So, tell me,' Lucas says, refilling my glass again, 'what's got you so down? Apart from the obvious, of course.'

I shrug, bringing the glass to my mouth so I don't have to answer him. I don't want to burden him with my worries. He's got enough on his plate trying to single-handedly run our company.

'Hey, this is me,' he says, placing his hand on my shoulder. 'There's nothing you can't say to me. I know how hard this is, and I'm worried about you. If you keep going on like this . . .' His words drift off, but I already know what he was going to say, *It's only a matter of time before you break.*

If I allowed myself to give in to the darkness that's crying out to me from deep within, then yes, I would; but that's the thing—I won't let it take over. I refuse to let this beat me. To beat us.

I throw back my scotch before placing the glass back down on the bar. The truth is, I need to talk to someone. I'm struggling trying to be the strong one. I can't be that person tonight. I feel like everything I hold dear is slipping through my fingers: my wife, my dad. My world is crumbling around me and I don't know how to make it stop.

'I've been writing Jem letters.'

I half expect him to laugh, but he doesn't. He's always given me a hard time about the depth of love I have for that woman. He doesn't understand, not yet. One day someone's going to come along and bring him to his knees. He won't know what hit him.

'What kind of letters? Like, love letters? Don't you think that's coming on pretty strong under the circumstances?'

'They're not really love letters. Well, they kind of are. They're letters about our life. How we met. That kind of thing.'

'Did she read them?'

'I've only written her two so far, but yes she has.'

'And? I feel like I'm missing something here. That's a good thing, right?'

'Yes, and I think they're helping. She was starting to open up to me.' I exhale a long breath before continuing. 'But this morning I screwed up. I told her I loved her. And I think it freaked her out.'

'Oh.'

'"Oh" is right. She withdrew again after that. After her physio she said she was tired and wanted to go straight home. She didn't say a word the whole way, she just stared out the window like she used to do.'

Lucas stares down into his drink, taking it all in before speaking again. 'I get that it's hard for you to hold back when you still feel so much, but put yourself in her shoes. She probably just felt awkward. What did you expect her to do, tell you she loved you too?'

'No . . . Yes . . . I don't know. I just want things to be the way they used to be.'

'I know you do, you poor bastard. I want that for you too, but things may never be that way again. I hate to be the bad guy here, but you need to prepare yourself for that.' I feel my shoulders slump as my gaze moves to the floorboards. Logically I know he's right, but it's still like a kick to the guts. I want to believe that one day everything will be the way it used to be. I have to believe that. 'You just need to find your new normal.'

I want the old normal, I ache for it.

'What if I don't ever get her back? How am I supposed to deal with that?'

'You'll deal with it the same way you always have. Just like you did when your mum died, or when your father got sick, or when Jem first had her accident. You just will. You're not a quitter, Spencer. You know that just as much as I do. You'll never give up.'

TWELVE

Jemma

'You girls stacked the dishwasher, so let me do the rest of it,' Christine says, gesturing with her hand for us to leave the kitchen. This place is still a long way from feeling like home, but I'm beginning to feel comfortable here.

'You cooked us a lovely dinner, so it's only fair that we clean up,' Rachel replies. 'It's a few pots . . . Jemma and I can do them.'

I'm grateful that she's always pushing me. Everyone else walks on eggshells when they're around me, but not Rachel. Although she is no longer staying here at the house, she has been coming over daily.

She arrives early afternoon because she knows I have rehab in the mornings and a lie-down after lunch. She uses that time to catch up on her work, and then Christine always insists she stay for dinner. I'm starting to like having her around. I enjoy her company, and I can easily see how we were once friends.

'I insist. Now go and watch some TV or something. You heard me, shoo.' We both laugh when Christine flicks the tea towel at us. I've learned that there's no point arguing with Christine when her mind is made up. I'll never win. She's as stubborn as all hell.

'Do you want to go up to my room?'

'Your room?' Rachel's eyes widen. 'Of course.' The pure elation I see on her face from a simple invitation to come and hang out in my bedroom has that ever-present guilt stirring inside me. I glance over my shoulder at Christine as we leave the kitchen, and find her smiling after us. I think in our own way, we're all adjusting to this as best we can. 'You seem to be managing these stairs well now.'

The first day I got here, Rachel and Christine had to practically carry me up to my room. Christine had initially wanted to set up a temporary bed for me in the lounge room, but I craved the sanctuary of my own room.

'The physio and hydrotherapy have really helped.'

'I'm glad.'

She follows me into my room, and I gesture for her to sit on my bed. There's nowhere else. The lounge room probably would have been a better option, but I have my reasons for inviting her up here. I need someone to talk to, and Christine is too emotionally invested to give the kind of advice I need.

Rachel, on the other hand, seems like a straight shooter, and I'm yearning for an unbiased opinion on this awkward situation. I don't know how to handle this without hurting Braxton more than I already have.

'Braxton told me he loves me today,' I say as we take a seat.

A sad expression crosses her face. 'Really? And that made you feel . . .'

'Uncomfortable.'

'Poor guy. Oh, don't get me wrong,' she says, holding her hands up in front of her, 'I feel for you as well . . . for both of you. I can understand how it would make you feel uncomfortable, but you've got to remember that those feelings are still well and truly alive for him. You were his life.'

'I know.' My gaze moves down to my lap. 'Everything's such a mess. Hopefully one day we'll both find some normality again.'

'You may not want to hear this, but you loved him just as deeply once. I envied what you guys had. I'm pretty sure everyone who knows you did. Together you were . . . spectacular.' She ends her sentence with a sigh, which only enhances her words.

We fall quiet. I have no reply, and she probably doesn't know what else to say.

'Do you have a boyfriend?' I ask, trying to divert the conversation away from me. She's supposed to be my best friend, so it feels weird that I don't know that already.

'Nope. I don't have time for relationships.' My eyes scan her dark hair, her face; her almond-shaped hazel eyes, her delicate facial features, her flawless skin. I mean I really study it. I've done the same thing with Braxton, and my parents. I'm always on the lookout for a sign, a flicker . . . anything. Each time I experienced exactly what I'm feeling now: absolutely nothing. It's like looking at a stranger, someone I might not even recognise if I passed them on the street. Will they ever feel familiar to me again?

'That's silly,' I say with amusement in my voice. 'You spend your days sitting around here, it's not like you're time poor.'

'When I'm in New York working, I am. My job is demanding and doesn't really allow time for a personal life.'

'That's sad. Braxton mentioned you worked overseas. What is it you do again?'

I see sadness and disappointment flash through her eyes before her gaze moves down to the comforter on my bed. I study her hands as she traces a figure-eight pattern with her finger. It's the same look I get from everyone when I simply can't remember. 'I'm a fashion designer. We used to joke that when we were finished uni you would make the interior of people's homes beautiful, and I was going to do the same for the occupants . . .'

Her words drift off when she realises that the joke is now lost on me.

'Tell me about us—about our friendship. How did we meet?'

Her gloomy expression is quickly replaced with a smile. If I can't remember these people, maybe it's time I let them remind me.

'We met through the university. We'd both applied for off-campus accommodation, and we were assigned as roommates. We clicked from day one . . .'

———

Just because I've been stand-offish with Braxton the past few days doesn't mean I haven't been eager to ask him more questions, or enthusiastic to receive another letter. I really hope there's one on its way. They've sparked a curiosity in me. A thirst for knowledge. I wasn't sure I would like being reminded of my past, but the more I find out, the more I need to know. Who is the real me? What was I like? All I know is the shell I've become.

Things have been off with Braxton. He's still his sweet, gentlemanly self, but he has pulled back from me. It's funny, because there were times in the beginning that I wished he would stop trying to communicate with me, but now that he's not, I don't like it. I miss his meaningless chatter.

'Your splint?' I bet the smile I see on Braxton's face is mirrored in my own. He stands from where he was seated in the reception area, and closes the distance between us. My slight limp is still present, but the physio said in time it should go.

'I'm so glad to be rid of it,' I say as I look down at my feet. I've been carrying my spare sandal in my handbag all week, hoping each time I come here it would be the day I was rid of that damn thing for good.

My right leg appears to be slightly thinner than my left one, or maybe it just looks that way because it's lighter in colour. I'm glad the dress I'm wearing is long enough to cover the hideous scars. My body is riddled with them. My arm, my hip . . . the side of my face. They're a constant reminder of the accident. An accident I don't even remember having.

I can deal with those, though. It's the scars on the inside that I'm not sure about.

'He said my leg has healed well, so I don't need it anymore. I'll still need ongoing physio, but it feels good to be finally free of it.'

'That's great news.' His arms reach towards me before pausing mid-air. When he takes a step back and shoves his hands into the pockets of his jeans, I know he was about to hug me but thought better of it.

'I was wondering,' I say as we walk towards his car, 'does your offer to show me the beach still stand? I'd love to go when you have time.'

'Really?'

'Yes.'

The happiness I see on his face makes my heart smile. I don't want things to be so weird between us. The last thing I want to do is hurt him. I'd like to work at being friends, but that's all I can offer him at this stage.

'Do you feel up to going now?'

'Yes! I'd love to.'

When I see the sand dunes between some of the properties we pass, I feel a tinge of excitement, knowing we're so close.

'All the houses on your side of the street back onto the ocean,' he says, like he just read my train of thought.

'They're beautiful.'

He slows down and I use the opportunity to eye off each property as we pass. I can tell by the sheer size of some of the houses that it would cost a pretty penny to live in this area.

They feel too fancy for my taste, which is ridiculous because I don't even know what my taste is.

Further down the street, a white two-storey weatherboard house catches my eye. It's not as opulent as some of the other houses in the street, but I've already decided it's my favourite so far. It has character and an old-world charm, but a modern feel to it as well. The contrast of the white weatherboard and the sky-blue shutters and trim around the windowpanes suits the beach location beautifully, and the whole thing is topped off by a white picket fence along the front of the property.

All thoughts of that house are soon forgotten when Braxton pulls over to the side of the road in front of a small wooded area.

'There's a narrow track through the bush that leads to the beach. That's how we used to get down there when we were kids. Do you want to check it out?'

My seatbelt is off and my fingers are already wrapped around the door handle before he's finished speaking. 'Yes.'

'Let me get the door for you,' he says, quickly removing his own seatbelt. I'm quite capable of opening my own door, but at the same time I find it sweet that he always insists on doing it. I've noticed he does it for Christine when she's in the car as well.

My eyes follow him as he walks around the front of the vehicle. Dare I say he really is handsome? His good looks stood out to me the moment I opened my eyes in the hospital. There is something about his big blue eyes, and the way he looks at me that's just . . . *comforting*.

I grab hold of his hand as he helps me out of the car. I like the way my hand fits inside his; it feels safe.

His mood has lifted since I suggested coming here, and that pleases me. 'This way,' he says. He lets go of my hand and gestures towards the walking track that has been worn into the grassy dune. I'll admit, I felt a twinge of disappointment the moment he let go.

We walk quietly beside each other; the only sounds are the crunch of the dry leaves under the weight of our shoes, and the distant echo of the ocean. I use this time to take a deep breath, inhaling the salty freshness in the air. I look up to watch the green foliage of the trees above, as the leaves dance in the breeze. I can already feel myself relaxing.

The ground becomes softer, and the track widens slightly as we reach the end. The sudden brightness from the sun reflecting off the sand has me squinting.

We come to a stop and I give my vision a moment to adjust to the wide open space now before us. 'Here we go,' Braxton says.

I find myself holding my breath as my gaze travels across the sand towards the crashing waves. An unfamiliar warm feeling bubbles up inside me as my eyes take it all in. 'It's beautiful,' I whisper. I'm not even sure if beautiful does it justice, but I already know I love this place.

I'm not sure how long I stand there and stare, mesmerised, out at the horizon but it's a while. Eventually I manage to tear my eyes away from the beauty before me and seek out Braxton. There's a huge smile on his face as he watches me. 'Why are you looking at me like that?'

He opens his mouth to say something, but then closes it again. 'No reason,' he says with a shrug. My eyes focus on the cute dimple that forms on his left cheek when he gives me a nervous grin. 'It's just nice to see you smile.'

I know there was more to that look, but I don't push it. The last thing I want is to make things awkward between us again.

'Can we walk down towards the water?'

He usually goes to work after he drops me back at Christine's, but I'm not ready to leave this place yet. I like how it makes me feel.

'Of course.' He lifts one leg up and slides the shoe from his foot, followed by his sock. I can't help but notice that he has lovely feet. He goes about removing his other shoe and sock, so I slowly lower myself until I'm sitting on the sand. I'm grinning as I pull my leg back towards my chest. It shows how far I've come since the accident. I couldn't do this a month ago.

Once I've removed my sandals, I place them beside me and wriggle my toes in the sand. Braxton bends over and rolls up the bottom of his jeans before helping me to my feet.

'Thank you.' I go to retrieve my shoes, but he stops me.

'Just leave them there. We can collect them on our way back to the car.'

We make our way down to the water and I gasp when a small wave rolls in and the cold water laps over my feet. I love how the wet sand feels squished between my toes.

'Do you feel up to a walk along the beach?'

'Yes,' I reply eagerly. I want to drag out my time here as long as I can. For a woman who doesn't know where she belongs, a part of me feels at home here.

'Great. There's a rock pool a little further down that I'd love to show you.'

'Lead the way.'

We walk in silence, but it's in no way uncomfortable. In fact, it feels totally natural to be here with him.

I watch as he reaches down and picks up a stick from the sand. A few seconds later he tosses it out into the water. 'I'm thinking of getting a dog,' he says. 'It gets lonely in the house on my own. I think it'll be good company for me.'

'That's a great idea.' I don't know what else I can say. I feel sad for him, but I can't live with him. Not now.

'I thought a dog would be better than a cat. I don't think Samson would be pleased if I brought home a feline.'

'Samson?'

'Our bird. He's a rainbow lorikeet. We inherited him.'

'Oh.'

He stops walking, and faces me. 'I don't want to, but I need to accept that there's a chance you may never come back home.'

I smile at him sympathetically. 'I don't think any of us can predict what lies ahead, Braxton.'

I can't give him hope when there's no hope to give.

THIRTEEN

Jemma

I lie on my bed and stare at the shell Braxton found for me at the rock pool. I've put it on my bedside table because I wanted it close. I reach for it and run my fingertip over the smooth porcelain surface.

Closing my eyes, I bring it to my ear. I feel my lips curve up as I listen to the sound of the ocean trapped inside. My smile widens as I think back to that moment on the beach. I wasn't sure what to expect but I was surprised to see that the rock pool was brimming with sea life. My favourites were a small starfish and a crab no bigger than my thumbnail—I was enthralled when it ran sideways on its journey back to the sea.

I watched on as Braxton headed towards a small sandy patch nestled between the rocks. The area was littered with remnants of the sea. He picked up a few things and brushed them over with his fingertips. 'Nope,' he said as he discarded each one. 'Nup, has a chip in it.' I'm pretty sure he was talking to himself, and it was amusing to watch him. 'Yes . . . perfect.' He climbed back up to where I stood and opened the palm of his hand to reveal a shell.

'For me?' I asked as he moved his hand towards me.

'Yes.'

'Thank you. It's so pretty.' I took the white cone-shaped shell and studied it.

'Hold it to your ear,' he said. 'You'll be able to hear the ocean inside.'

By the time we got back to the car, my cheeks ached from all the smiling. I clutched the shell in my hand all the way home. It was my very first treasured memory. Not only did I have the shell to keep, I got to experience this memory firsthand. Every beautiful second of it.

I paid special attention on our drive back to Christine's. I wanted to be able to remember how to get there again. I even memorised some of the street names, and wrote them down as soon as I got home. I'm not sure how I'll get back there, but I'll find a way.

I'm pulled from my thoughts when there's a knock on my bedroom door. 'It's me, sweetheart,' Christine calls out. 'A delivery just arrived for you.'

I sit up so fast I feel dizzy, so I wait until my head stops spinning before I stand.

'Coming.'

I think I startle Christine with how eagerly I open the door. 'Hi.'

'Hi. This just arrived,' she says smiling as she holds out a parcel. It's a lot larger than the last one, at least ten times the size of the one that held my memory bracelet. But that's not what excites me. It's the letter I see attached to it. *He wrote me another letter.* 'Someone's getting spoilt.'

'I am,' I reply, taking it from her.

'It's nice to see you smiling again, sweetheart. Braxton was the only boy to ever make you smile like that. I'm glad that hasn't changed.'

'I'm going to open this,' I say, lifting the box.

'Of course.'

'Thank you for bringing it up to me.'

'You're welcome. Rachel should be here soon, and I've made a cake for our afternoon tea. It's your grandmother's recipe. It was always one of your favourites.'

'Sounds nice. I'll be down soon.'

I wait until she starts to descend the stairs before I close my bedroom door and rush towards the bed. Unlike the caution I showed opening the first two letters, I tear straight into this one. This time I don't search for the charm inside. It's the written words I crave.

My hands tremble slightly with anticipation as I carefully unfold the letter.

LETTER THREE . . .

Dearest Jemma,

The twenty-first of December 1998. I remember the date only because it was the day after my tenth birthday. It was a stinking hot day. Your father and my parents were all working, so you'd begged your mum to take us to the beach.

The three of us caught the bus, and you were that excited you practically bounced the whole way. I used to get a kick out of watching you. Unlike you, I grew up with water, so it wasn't a big deal to me. You, on the other hand, were a country girl. The first six years of your life were spent on a farm. Your family only moved to the city because your father had been offered a promotion through the bank he worked for, to come and manage our local branch. Your parents were hesitant to leave the country life behind and head to the big smoke, but they knew it was a great opportunity.

When we arrived, we stripped down to our bathers and laid our towels out on the sand under your mum's big red umbrella, before running down to the shore.

It was a hot day, so the beach was crowded. You weren't a strong swimmer back then, so you were only allowed to splash around in the shallows. I was okay with that. Sometimes we'd sit near the water's edge and build sandcastles, or dig large holes in the sand and bury ourselves until only our heads were visible. On Boxing Day we built snowmen out of sand. We always had fun no matter what we were doing.

After lunch, your mum bought us ice-creams. She told us we'd be leaving to go home soon, so we used this time to walk further down the beach towards the rock pools. It's where all the good shells were. It was our thing. On your first ever trip to the beach I had found a pretty shell that had been washed up on the shore, and gave it to you. You loved it so much I made it my mission to collect one for you every time we visited the beach. Even back then there was nothing I wouldn't do to see you smile.

I stepped up onto the rocks first, then reached for your hand. 'Be careful, the rocks can be slippery,' I warned. I'm pretty sure I said that to you every time. I'd slipped on some moss one day when I was rock-fishing with my dad, and the jagged edges had cut deep into my arm resulting in numerous stitches. I didn't want the same fate for you.

You squatted down and poked around in the rock pool with a small stick, while I headed over to the sandy patch to find you a shell.

'Come and look at this, Brax. It's so blue and so pretty.'

Shoving the shell I'd just found into my pocket, I headed towards you. 'Don't—' I called out as soon as I saw what you were doing, but before I got a chance to finish, you moved your hand through the water and scooped the pretty blue thing into your palm. It wasn't pretty. It was a bluebottle.

Your scream was high-pitched as you dropped the bluebottle onto the rocks below. I'd seen it happen before with others, so I knew you'd be okay, but I hated the thought of you being in pain.

I tried to steer you back towards your mum, but you were so upset. I remember trying to lift you, but I think I only made it about two steps before I had to put you down. I'd turned ten the day before, but it would be another few years before I had a growth spurt. So instead, I sat you down on the edge of a rock and ran to get your mum.

'Jemma's been stung by a bluebottle,' I blurted out as soon as I reached her. 'I'm going to run up to the surf club and get one of the lifeguards.'

'Where is she?' your mother asked in a panic as she dropped the book she was reading and stood.

'On the rocks.' I turned and pointed in your direction.

I was out of breath by the time I arrived at the watch-tower, but relieved when the guy radioed to one of the lifeguards on patrol. Once I knew help was on the way I bolted back down the beach. But my knees turned to jelly when I got close enough to hear your mother calling out in a panicked voice, 'Somebody help me, please . . . my daughter can't breathe.'

We hadn't known you were severely allergic to jellyfish, and you were experiencing an anaphylactic reaction.

I held your hand while your mother encouraged you to breathe. The terrified look in your eyes and the blue tinge around your lips is a sight I will never forget.

It felt like a lifetime had passed before help finally reached you. They moved everyone back so they could assess you. I sat on a rock a few metres away and buried my head in my hands when they placed an oxygen mask over your face. I'd never been so frightened; it took all my strength not to cry. I was petrified I was going to lose you.

My body was trembling by the time they lifted you onto a stretcher and rushed you across the sand towards the waiting ambulance. You'd been given a shot of adrenaline, so by the time we arrived at the hospital there was a marked improvement, but it did nothing to ease my worry, or stop me from feeling responsible.

The hospital admitted you, and you stayed for a number of hours for observation. You slept for most of the time. I sat on a chair in the corner, while your parents hovered over your bed.

Your father had rushed straight to the hospital when he got word. The worry that was etched on their faces as they watched you made me feel sick in the stomach.

My parents called by to pick me up a few hours later, but I refused to leave. I broke down in my mother's arms the moment she got there. I'd stayed strong for you for as long as I could, but my mum's hug was my undoing. She gave the best hugs. After begging them not to take me home, they let me stay. I couldn't leave you ... I just couldn't.

When you finally woke, the first thing you asked your parents was, 'Where's Braxton?' You have no idea how happy that made me. Even more so when I reached your bedside and saw your face light up.

When you got home your mum wouldn't let you leave the house, so we just lay around your place talking and watching television for the next few days.

—

The twenty-fifth of December 1998. Christmas morning arrived, and I was barely out of bed when you bashed on my front door.

'Merry Christmas, sweet girl,' my mum had said to you as she embraced you in a hug. She always called you that. I think she saw you as the daughter she never had.

'Merry Christmas, Mrs Spencer.'

I was so excited to give you your Christmas present. Usually we just exchanged handmade cards, but that year I'd made you something special.

The week before, your family had spent a few days at your grandparents' place. I'd spent that time with my dad, at his hardware store where he helped me make your gift.

'Merry Christmas, Jem,' I said, grabbing the large wrapped gift from under our tree and passing it to you.

'You bought me a present?'

I was beaming when your eyes widened.

'No, I made it,' I replied proudly. My eyes briefly met my father's across the room, and he winked at me. As much as I had missed you in those few days you were away, I'd enjoyed my special time with my dad. There was never enough of it. He was such a kind and patient man and I always loved being around him.

I held my breath as you tore into the wrapping paper.

'Braxton,' you whispered as you looked down at the wooden box I'd made you. I'd carved JEM'S TREASURES into the lid.

'It's a box to put your shells in.'

'I love it,' you said, throwing your arms around me and squeezing me tight. 'I love it so much.'

When you let go of me, I saw tears brimming in your eyes. I was so pleased you loved your gift. I was so proud of it.

'I only have a card for you,' you said.

You looked sad as you passed it to me.

'That's okay.' I honestly didn't mind. I loved the cards you made for me. I still have them. Every single one.

This particular one had a large green Christmas tree on the front, with colourful balls all over it. MERRY CHRISTMAS was written in multicolour underneath, and the large yellow star on top had way too many points. Drawing stars wasn't your forte, but I thought it was spectacular. This card will always hold a special meaning to me because that year you wrote something different inside.

'To my best friend Braxton,

I love you.

From your best friend Jemma.'

You even signed it with three kisses.

Your words far outweighed any gift you could've given me. 'I love it, Jem. Thank you.'

You smiled when I said that.

I already knew I loved you too, but I wasn't good at expressing my feelings. Actions speak louder than words, my mother always

said. Many more years would pass before you heard those three
magic words from me.

What we had is far too beautiful to be forgotten.
Yours always,
Braxton

I sit for the longest time trying to digest his words. I love his descriptive writing; it holds just enough detail that if I close my eyes I can almost picture these scenes in my mind.

When I eventually place the letter down, I pick up the envelope in search of my charm. I'm surprised when I find two—a heart-shaped one that says *Best Friends*, and a tiny clam-shaped shell. I clench them both in the palm of my hand as a smile spreads across my face.

I feel equally nervous and excited as I remove the paper from the large parcel. I gasp the moment the contents are revealed. The first thing I see are the words *JEM'S TREASURES*. It's the box he made me all those years ago. Tears fill my eyes when I lift the lid and see hundreds, possibly a thousand, shells inside, in a variety of shapes, colours and sizes. All together, that's exactly what they look like . . . *treasure.*

I remove a few shells from the top and study them. It's not until I go to put them back that I find something sitting just below the surface. It's wrapped in plain white paper. When I unravel it, I find a small pink shell inside. There's writing on the inside of the paper, so I flatten it out with my hand so I can read it.

This is the shell I picked out for you the day you were stung by
the bluebottle. I found it in my pocket that night when I got home
from the hospital, and I've kept it all these years. I never ended
up giving it to you because at the time this was a moment I didn't
want you to remember. I see things differently now. I'm learning

to appreciate every second, because you never know when it can be taken away from you. Good or bad, it was a chapter in your life, so it's meaningful. x

He's wrong. His words are just as beautiful as his actions.

FOURTEEN

Jemma

'I'm glad to see your appetite is returning,' Christine says as she places a plate of eggs down in front of me. 'You always loved your food.'

I bet if Rachel were here she would have made me make them myself. It's not that I'm not willing to try new things. I can feel my confidence growing. I still have a long way to go, but for now I have hope that I'll find some sort of normality. I'd love to be able to go back to work one day, but doing what, who knows. I'm no longer sure if design is my thing.

I look up at Christine and smile. 'Thank you.'

She rests her hand on my shoulder and leans down to place a soft kiss on the top of my head. It's the first time she's ever done anything like that, yet it's an action that seems so natural.

I scoop some egg onto my fork as I slide the newspaper towards me. The sudden ringing from the phone startles me. My eyes follow Christine's every move as she wipes her hands on a tea towel before reaching for the receiver mounted on the wall.

'Hello,' she says as her eyes meet mine. I give her a brief smile before scooping more egg into my mouth. 'Braxton.' The mere mention of his name has me on full alert. She falls silent and listens to whatever he's saying. I find myself wishing I could hear as well. 'Oh sweetheart.' My stomach churns when I see her expression turn grim. 'I'm so sorry to hear that. Is he going to be okay?' She goes quiet again and I have a strange compulsion to snatch the phone from her hands. 'Let me know if there's anything I can do.' She pauses again, so I grab my plate and rise from the table. 'Sure, I'll put her on.' She holds the receiver out in front her. 'It's Braxton. He wants to talk to you.'

'Okay.' Placing my plate on the countertop I take the phone out of her hand. 'Hello.'

'Hey, Jem. I'm sorry, but I'm not going to be able to take you to rehab today.'

'Oh. Okay.' I'm surprised by how disappointed I feel. I had so many things I wanted to ask him today. 'Do you want me to see if I can make the appointment for later this afternoon?'

'I'm not going to be able to make it later either. I've organised a taxi to take you. It should be there in around fifteen minutes. The driver's going to give you a card when you're dropped off. The fare is already taken care of. All you need to do is give the card to Olivia at the front desk, and she'll call him when you're done so he can take you back home.'

'Is everything okay, Braxton? You sound . . . stressed out.'

I hear him sigh through the phone. 'I'm at the hospital with my dad. He had a fall this morning and hit his head.'

'Your dad?' He has mentioned his parents in his letters, but other than that I know nothing about them. 'I'm sorry to hear that. Is he okay?' I wonder why I haven't met them. They never came to the hospital. Do they hate me? That thought doesn't sit well with me.

'He's as well as can be expected under the circumstances. Are you going to be all right on your own? I feel dreadful for letting you down, but my dad needs me. I'm all he has.'

'I'll be fine, honestly,' I say, having no idea if I will be, but I want to ease his mind.

'How about I call your father instead? I know he's at work already, but he might be able to duck away.'

'Don't be silly, I'll be fine.'

The line goes quiet briefly. 'Will you at least take the phone I bought you? Did you charge it?'

'Yes. I've never used it, but it's charged. If it will make you feel better, I'll take it.'

'It will. You remember how to make a call, right?'

'Yes.'

Well, I think I do. It seemed easy enough when he walked me through it.

'Call me if there's a problem. I mean it, Jem.'

'Okay.' I already know I won't. I'm an adult, and like Rachel continually reminds me, I need to start living like one. 'I hope your father's going to be okay.'

'Thank you, so do I.'

'Bye.'

'Bye, Jem. Good luck today.'

Christine takes the phone from my hand, hanging it back on the wall. 'Braxton's really having a rough time lately. I feel for him, and poor John. He was always such a lovely man. Life hasn't been very kind to him.'

I know the rough time she mentioned includes what I'm putting him through. I'm sure she didn't say that to hurt me, but her comment stings nevertheless.

'I'm going to run up to my room and get my phone. Braxton said the taxi will be here soon.'

'Okay, sweetheart. I'll just finish packing the dishwasher. It will only take me a few minutes to change.'

'Why do you need to change?'

'I'm not wearing this old thing to your appointment.'

'You don't have to come with me.'

'I'm not letting you go on your own.'

'Braxton said the taxi will drop me off and pick me back up. I'll be fine. I'm not a child.'

I'm not a hundred per cent comfortable with the idea of doing this on my own, but there's also a part of me that wants to try. It's the push I need. It's time I started to stand on my own two feet. I can't keep relying on everyone else for the rest of my life. I've disrupted their lives enough.

'Are you ready for your taxi, Mrs Spencer?' Olivia asks when I re-enter the reception area. 'Your husband has already called twice. It's sweet how much he cares about you.'

I smile courteously instead of replying. I'm not going to correct her; my personal business is my own. Technically he is my husband, on paper anyway. She must presume we're still a couple because he's here with me every day.

But she's right, he is sweet. Braxton, Christine, Stephen and Rachel have all been wonderful. Although I haven't seen Stephen since I moved in with Christine. It's clear my parents aren't very fond of each other, and I'm curious to know why.

I glance towards the exit. Despite my initial misgivings, I've enjoyed the independence today has brought, and I want to make the most of the limited freedom I have. It took all my strength to talk Christine out of coming with me. She can be very persistent. It's not that I didn't want her with me, it's more that I wanted to challenge myself. I know Rachel will be proud of me for going it alone.

'Umm . . . I think I might have a look around town while I'm here. Is that okay?'

'Of course. Just come back when you're ready and I'll organise the taxi for you.'

'Thank you, Olivia.'

'It's no problem, Mrs Spencer. Marcy's Boutique has a great little sale on at the moment.'

I nod and smile at her as I sling my handbag over my shoulder. I feel a mixture of excitement and nerves as I walk through the automatic doors and out onto the street. The curious side of me has wanted to explore this area, I'm not even sure why. I guess every new experience is a discovery and a step towards finding the new me. The way I look at it, I have two choices: I can wallow away in self-pity, or I can start to live again. I choose to live. I'm scared for what my future holds, but I've been through too much to just give up.

I let the heat of the midday sun hit my skin. It's an exquisite autumn day, and I suddenly feel grateful to be alive. That in itself says so much. It wasn't that long ago I wished I had perished in that accident. Those first few weeks were a dark time for me, but now I'm finally starting to see the light.

I feel my lips curve into a smile as I inhale deeply, filling my lungs with air. Today would be a perfect day to sit on the beach, but it's on the other side of town, and though my leg is improving every day, I'm in no shape to walk such a long distance. I'm confident that I will be in time.

When I round the corner to the main street, I mill in with the rest of the crowd. It doesn't take long for the sea of faces heading towards me to get my blood pumping to the point that I have to keep telling myself not to panic, that I can do this. *I have to do this.*

I walk another ten or so metres before it almost becomes too much. What if I pass someone I should know but no longer do? What if they stop me? What do I say? All these questions and more swim around in my head. I thought I was ready to tackle this head-on, but I'm obviously not.

I weave through the mass of people until I emerge into a small clearing. Leaning my back against a wall, I take a few deep breaths. I was stupid to think that I could jump in head first. What I need is a plan of attack.

I dig through my bag, looking for my phone. After turning it on, I stare at the screen as I wait for it to come alive. When it does, I see it's 12.17pm. On cue my stomach growls. All the hydrotherapy I do certainly works up my appetite, and Christine usually has a sandwich waiting for me when I arrive back from the physio. Ham, cheese and lettuce has been my sandwich of choice ever since I read Braxton's letter.

My gaze moves to the left as I scope out the shops ahead. I see a small alfresco dining area further down, so I head in that direction. Christine stuffed a fifty-dollar note into my pocket before I left the house. *Just in case of an emergency*, she'd said.

Like Braxton, she's very good to me. I might not remember my life with them but I do appreciate the care they've shown me. I know how lucky I am to have them. I'd hate to think where I'd be without their support.

When I reach the restaurant, I read the neon sign above the entryway: *Callaghan's Burger and Grill*. I can't remember what a burger even tastes like, or whether I even like them, but the delicious aroma coming from inside is enough to make my stomach growl again.

With that in mind, I make a conscious decision to go in. Today is a day of discovery, so I'm going to try a burger and find out for myself.

Once inside, I scan the décor. This place isn't fancy, but it appears to be clean. The bright lime-green walls are the first thing to draw my attention. It's not the greatest colour, but with the large strategically placed black-and-white prints, and the black wooden tables and chairs, it works well.

The uncertainty creeps in again as I look around the restaurant for some kind of clue as to what to do. There are some people already seated, but there's also a woman and a young couple standing in front of the counter. Relief floods me when I spot a sign that says, *Please order and pay before being seated.*

Moving forward, I come to a stop behind the couple ordering. The menu board stretches across the back wall, and the vast array of choices overwhelms me. I'm so engrossed in making a decision, I don't notice when the couple pay for their order and take a seat at one of the tables.

'Next,' the male server says in an abrupt tone. My eyes meet his briefly as I step towards the counter, and I'm surprised by the annoyance I see on his face. When my gaze fixes on the menu once more, the panic I felt earlier rushes back and grows as I desperately try to make a decision. When he impatiently clears his throat, my eyes dart back to him.

'Umm . . .'

'Come on, lady, I don't have all day.'

'Can I . . . umm . . . get . . .' My words drift off.

'Can you . . . umm . . . get *what*?' he repeats mockingly. His rudeness has me on the verge of tears. I open my mouth to tell him I've changed my mind about placing an order, when an elderly gentleman approaches. The friendly smile on his face has a slight calming effect on me.

'Is there a problem here, Mr Wilson?' The mention of that name sparks something within me, and now I find myself staring at the man before me.

'Nope, no problem,' the server replies with a smile. This must be his boss, because his bad attitude instantly vanishes.

The elderly gentleman nods his head in approval and smiles at me once more before walking away. I want to call out that everything isn't okay, and his employee is a complete jerk, but I don't. Instead I focus again on Mr Wilson. That name is so familiar. Why? And then it hits me. Larry *'The Looter'* Wilson. It couldn't be. I seek out the name badge on his shirt and can't help but stare when I see the name LARRY engraved in bold black letters.

My eyes scan his face as my mind races. How many twenty-something Larry Wilsons with a bad attitude can there be? He's tall, just like Braxton had said, and around my age; *it has to be him.* That thought has my pulse racing. I see nothing recognisable as I study his chubby face. His receding hairline only makes his face look even rounder.

He opens his mouth to speak and I notice his teeth are stained brown and appear to be rotting. This guy has nothing going for him in the looks department, and his personality certainly leaves a lot to be desired.

Braxton's story gives me the courage to lean forward into Larry's space. It may be around twenty years too late, but I presume I never got the chance to wreak my revenge for what he did to me, and for the trouble he caused Braxton. I feel compelled to put him in his place.

I raise my hand towards my mouth and glide my fingertip over my front teeth. 'You have some mud stuck in between your teeth,' I whisper, trying my hardest to remain serious. His eyes narrow as he looks hard at me, clearly confused. 'Just there.' I run my finger over my teeth once more. 'Mud . . . in your teeth.'

His eyes widen, and his face turns a bright shade of red. 'It's not mud,' he snaps.

I stop fighting my smile now. It's funny, a few minutes ago I was on the verge of tears and now I'm struggling to contain my laughter. If it wasn't for the letters from Braxton I never would have known the significance of this moment. Words can't even express how grateful I am for that, or how satisfying this moment feels.

'Crazy bitch,' he mumbles under his breath as I turn and head towards the exit. His nasty comment doesn't get under my skin, even though that word—*crazy*—is pretty close to home for me right now.

Instead I feel *enlightened*, and extremely proud of myself. It's clear the hate Larry Wilson carried around when he was a kid has followed him into adulthood. It's sad, but in a way it's a huge wake-up call for me. It only reiterates everything I've been feeling lately. I need to let go of this anger and resentment I'm carrying around. I don't want it to destroy me.

I may have lost my past, but that doesn't mean I don't have a wonderful future. I have the power to not only reinvent myself, but to write my own ending.

FIFTEEN

Braxton

'Son,' my father says when he opens his eyes and sees me sitting beside his bed. As crappy as I'm feeling right now, that one word has me smiling. *He remembers me.* Even if they only last a few minutes, I treasure these moments. As time wears on they seem less frequent, which saddens me more than I care to admit, especially with what's going on with Jem.

'Hi, Pop. How are you feeling?'

'A little sore.'

When he tries to sit up, I quickly stand from my seat and help him. The ugly bruising on his forehead has darkened over the course of the day, and the swelling has yet to subside.

'That's understandable,' I say as I straighten his pillow. 'You had a fall and hit your head.'

'Did I?' I hate the confused look he gets on his face when he can't remember the things I tell him.

'You did. The doctors ran some tests earlier, and apart from a few stitches and some bruising, you're going to be fine.'

'I've got stitches?' He lifts his shaky hand and runs it over his bandaged forehead.

'Just a few.'

I check my watch and see that it's just after four. He had his last lot of pain medication just before midday. 'I'm going to grab the nurse and get you something for the pain.'

The X-rays show his skull isn't fractured, which is such a relief. He does have a nasty concussion, though, as well as a large lump and six stitches in his forehead. The staff at the nursing home told me he'd tripped in the community dining room and hit his head on the table on his way down. I feel guilty for not being there, even though I know there's nothing I could have done.

'You're a good boy,' he says, softly patting my hand. 'You were always such a good boy.'

I find myself smiling again as I walk towards the nurses' station. I'd give anything to have him back the way he was, but like Jemma, I'll take him any way I can have him. He's here, and for that I'm thankful.

Things were tough in the first few years after my mother's death. I was only eleven when she died, but I tried to be there for my dad as much as I could. Seeing him so broken only intensified the guilt I felt. We never talked about what happened. At the time I was grateful, but there's always been a part of me that wished we had. He never blamed me for my actions the night she died, but a part of me has always yearned for him to voice his forgiveness anyway. I know that's never going to come now, so I'm left with never-ending regret.

—

It's around six when I leave the hospital. I hung around to make sure my father ate some of his dinner, but now that he's fallen back to sleep, I quietly duck away.

I will spend the night at the hospital. The irony isn't lost on me. It was only a few short months ago that I was doing this for Jem.

I need to head home to shower and change. But more importantly, I need to see Jemma. Even though Christine alerted me the moment she returned home safely from rehab, like I'd asked her to, I still have to see her with my own eyes. I feel like I let her down by not being there for her today.

'Hey, buddy,' I say as I place a fresh bowl of water inside Samson's cage. Jumping down from his perch, he nibbles the tip of my finger. 'I'm sorry I haven't been around much lately.' He bobs up and down when I lightly scratch between the feathers at the back of his neck. He has barely spoken a word over the past few weeks, and I know it's because he's missing Jemma. She became his lifeline when my father had to give him up. 'I'm going to see *pretty girl*.' I taught him to call her that when we first got him.

'Pretty girl,' he repeats, bobbing up and down. Just mentioning her name perks him up. We both know that this place is not the same without her.

As I climb the front steps to Christine's house, my stomach is a combination of nerves and excitement. I never know how I'm going to be received when I knock on the front door.

'I'll get it,' Jemma calls from the other side. Just hearing her voice calms me. Her face lights up when she opens the front door and sees me standing on the porch, and this in turn has me grinning like a fool. I haven't seen that reaction in a while. 'Braxton.'

'Hey. I'm on my way back to the hospital, but I just wanted to check you were okay.'

'How's your dad?'

'He's doing okay.'

'I'm glad,' she says. 'Are you coming in?'

'I can't stay long, but sure, if you want me to.' I'm not going to pass up a chance to spend time with her.

'Of course I want you to come in, silly.'

I feel breathless when a playful smile forms on her lips. That smile has always been my weakness.

'I'm sorry I wasn't able to take you to your appointment this morning. How did it go?'

'Don't be. It did me good to stand on my own two feet for a change. I had an interesting day.' She briefly glances at me over her shoulder as I follow her down the hallway towards the kitchen.

'I should be able to take you tomorrow.'

'Oh.' She stops walking and turns to face me.

'What?' I ask, when her brow furrows. 'Don't you want me to?' The happiness I felt a few moments ago quickly evaporates.

'It's just that Stephen called earlier and I've organised to go with him. I haven't seen him since leaving rehab.'

'Sure, okay. I'm happy to hear you're going to spend some time with your dad.' I force out a smile, trying to hide my disappointment. Taking her to rehab was my one guarantee of being able to see her.

'He's only dropping me off. You can pick me up if you like.'

And just like that my elation returns. I'm not sure what's happened to bring about this change in her, but I like it.

'I'd love to.'

'Great.'

'Look who's here,' she says to Christine when we enter, and the tone of her voice makes my heart sing. *She really is pleased to have me here*. 'Sit, and I'll make you coffee. You like coffee, right? I can make you tea if you don't.'

'Coffee's fine,' I chuckle.

My gaze moves to Christine as she approaches me. She winks when my eyes widen in amazement. 'She's been like that all afternoon,' she whispers as I bend down slightly to kiss her cheek. I'm not sure what has happened in the past twenty-four hours, but I'm certainly not complaining. This is a small glimpse of my old Jem. 'How's your father?'

'He's okay.'

Christine watches me for a moment and smiles softly; she understands that I don't want to get into this right now. 'Let me know if there's anything I can do.'

'Thank you,' I say.

Christine is the closest thing I have to a mother. She really stepped up and cared for me after my mum died. She has *always* been there for me, and I truly love her for that.

I take a seat at the kitchen table I have sat at thousands of times over the years. 'Oh my god, you'll never guess who I ran into today!' Jemma says with excitement as she places the coffee in front of me before taking the seat beside me. I prefer my coffee black, but there's no way I will complain about the milk she put in it.

I'm momentarily stunned by the enthusiasm I hear in her voice. This is *my* Jem, the happy-go-lucky, chatty, full-of-life woman I fell hopelessly in love with all those years ago. Just watching her has my heart racing. It's moments like these that make me truly believe the real her is buried in there somewhere.

'Who?'

'The Looter,' she laughs. 'Larry Wilson.'

'No way,' I say, sitting forward in my chair. 'Where?'

'He works at the burger place in town. Callaghan's. He hasn't changed much. He's still as rude as ever.'

I stare at her. 'You remember him?'

'Only from your letters,' she replies. 'He's still fat, and he's going bald.'

'Jemma,' Christine scolds. She looks at her mother briefly before focusing her attention back on me.

'I don't remember what his teeth were like at school, but they're all rotten now. There's horrible dark brown lines between each tooth,' she says, leaning forward in her seat, bringing her body closer. 'You're never going to believe what I said to him.'

I smile again when she places her hand over her mouth to muffle her laugh.

'What did you say?' I take a sip of my milky coffee, trying to mask my own amusement.

'I told him he had mud in between his teeth,' she whispers.

I throw my head back and roar with laughter. That's something I haven't done in a very long time. It feels good.

—

'How's your dad?' Jemma asks as I help her into the car.

'He's a little better today. He's improved enough that the doctors are talking about discharging him tomorrow.'

My night was spent by his bedside, and it was deja vu at its worst. It was only recently that I did the same thing with Jem. It really messed with my head . . . my world is slipping through my fingers and I'm powerless to stop it.

'How come I've never met your parents?' she asks as soon as I'm seated in the driver's side. 'When did they move?'

'The house was sold a few years ago.'

'Oh.'

I hope that's enough to quell her curiosity because I'm tired and pretty much frazzled with everything that's going on. No good can come from dredging this up.

'Where did they move to?' she asks innocently. 'Is it far away?'

I breathe out slowly as I reverse out of my parking spot at the rehab centre. I guess we're going to dredge it all up. 'My mum died when I was eleven.'

I keep my eyes trained on the road ahead, as I put on my indicator and turn into the street. It's times like this that I need my old Jem the most. She always knew the right thing to say to comfort me. I never felt alone with her by my side because we faced everything together.

'Oh, Braxton,' she says, briefly placing her hand on my thigh. 'I'm sorry to hear that.'

'Thank you.'

I lean forward and turn up the volume on the radio. She takes the hint because she falls silent, but I can sense her eyes on me as we drive.

As we near Christine's place Jemma finally speaks again. 'What do you know about my time in the country? Did I ever go back there?'

Reaching over, I turn down the radio, relieved and keen to re-engage with her. 'Yes, you went back often. Your grandparents lived in the same town up until they passed away. Your grandfather was a farmer. They owned an apple orchard.'

'My grandparents died?' she asks in a shocked tone.

'Yes.'

Suddenly I have to think about where this conversation might lead. It was such a dark period in all our lives. Her grandparents were great people, and a huge part of my life growing up. Their sudden deaths were a shock to us all. Part of me is glad that Jemma doesn't remember. She took their deaths hard, but not as hard as Christine. This was a turning point for her, which created a huge domino effect in her life. Things were never the same after that.

SIXTEEN

Jemma

My head is spinning by the time I get out of Braxton's car. The questions I asked only seem to create more questions. He is usually the one initiating the conversation, but not today. Well, I hope that's all it is. We seemed to be in a good place when he left last night, but there was definitely a shift in him this morning.

I'm feeling somewhat flat when I enter the kitchen. Maybe Christine can answer some of the questions I have. What happened to his mum? And what about my grandparents?

'I'm back,' I say, when I see her bent over retrieving something out of the fridge.

Straightening, she stands to full height. The moment she turns to face me, I can tell that something is off with her as well. The smile that usually greets me is gone.

'I didn't know your father was taking you to your appointment today.'

I'm confused, is this an issue? 'He called me yesterday,' I start, but then pause when I see the frown working its way across her face. 'I . . . umm . . . mentioned I'd caught a taxi, so he offered to drop me off today.'

'Huh,' she scoffs. 'Well, I'd appreciate it if you didn't invite him to come to this house. He's not welcome here.'

I'm taken aback by the venom in her voice. It's obvious they have had problems, they're no longer together, but I have no idea why. Stephen seems like a lovely man. I really like him. He's gentle and kind, though he did look a bit sad when he asked how Christine was this morning.

'Okay.' I've seen her go through ups and downs since I've been living here, but this is the first time she's ever been angry with me. Yesterday was a good day, and I felt better than I have since waking from my coma, but now I feel downright shitty.

We usually sit down and eat lunch together, but I've suddenly lost my appetite. 'I'll be up in my room if you need me,' I say, turning and heading towards the staircase. I wish I knew why she dislikes Stephen so much, but on the other hand maybe it's better that I don't.

———

I've been locked away in my room for the better part of the day. My head is pounding as I lie on my bed and stare up at the ceiling. I think it's a combination of stress and hunger, but I can't seem to find the courage to venture downstairs to get something to eat. Logically I know I can't stay up here forever; I've got to eat sooner or later. I just hope Christine has calmed down by then.

I'm pulled from my thoughts by a knock on the door. 'Jemma, it's me.' Her tone is softer than before. 'Can I come in?'

'Yes,' I reply, slowly sitting up. Part of me feels bad for walking away like I did. There's obviously more to this situation than I know, but I'm yet to find the courage to ask her what happened.

She opens my bedroom door and I'm relieved when I see a smile on her face. 'I thought you might be hungry since you missed lunch. I'm sorry about earlier.' She approaches the bed and passes me a plate with a sandwich on it. 'A lot went on between me and your father.' I shift over slightly when she sits down beside me. 'I shouldn't have got angry at you. I know you don't remember any of it.'

'It's okay,' I say, placing my hand on her leg. 'I'm sorry. I wouldn't have brought him here if I knew it was going to upset you. What happened between you two? You obviously loved each other once.'

Her whole body seems to shrink at my question, and sadness washes over me. 'Your father was the love of my life . . . I thought I was his as well.'

'What happened to change that?' I ask tentatively.

'He broke my heart.' I see tears rise to her eyes before she turns her face away.

'I'm sorry he did that to you.'

I have so many more questions, but I feel like now is not the time to ask them.

'Eat your sandwich,' she says, rising from the bed. 'You must be starving.' She pauses when she gets to the doorway. 'Oh, I almost forgot, this just arrived for you.'

A smile tugs at my lips when she removes a letter from the pocket of her trousers.

LETTER FOUR . . .

Dearest Jemma,

The first portion of this letter is more of a confession than a memory. This is something I've never spoken about, not even to you. It's a burden I've carried for almost fifteen years, and maybe it's time I come clean.

The eighteenth of July 2000. I don't remember a lot of what had gone on during that day, but I do remember my mum hadn't been feeling well. When she tucked me into bed that night, she bent over to kiss me.

'Sweet dreams,' she whispered as she ran her hand over my forehead. It was something she said to me every night.

'Night, Mumma,' I replied. 'I love you.'

'I love you too, sweet boy.'

She smiled briefly, but then her face screwed up like she was in pain. I quickly sat up when she placed her hand on her lower abdomen.

'What's wrong?' I asked. 'Are you okay?'

'It's just a little pain,' she replied, brushing it off. 'I'm fine, sweetheart.'

Her words were enough to ease my worry and I quickly drifted off to sleep. It was just after midnight when my father came into my room to wake me.

'Braxton,' he said. 'You need to get up, son.' I was so tired and sleepy; I groaned and rolled over onto my side. 'Braxton,' he repeated, a little sterner this time. 'Your mother isn't well. I'm going to take her to the hospital.'

'I don't want to get up,' I whined. 'I'm tired.'

'Please, son. Your mother's in a lot of pain.' My father was a very patient man, and rarely lost his temper with me. 'If you don't want to come to the hospital, I can phone the Robinsons and see if they'll watch you until we return. Come downstairs once you're dressed.'

He left the room and I did something incredibly selfish: I fell back to sleep. I'm not sure how much time had passed, but this time I was woken by my father screaming. 'Braxton, get out of bed now!' He threw back the covers and tugged on my arm. 'I told you to get up and get dressed. Your poor mother's in agony.'

This time I didn't hesitate. I could tell by the tone of my father's voice that he was very concerned for my mother.

When I got downstairs I found her doubled over in pain. She was moaning loudly, and that's when the panic set in. I'd never seen her like this before.

'Mumma!' I cried as I ran over to her at the front door. 'Are you okay?'

'I'll be fine, baby,' she replied breathlessly, forcing out a smile. But the terrified look in her eyes told me she was far from fine. It was the middle of winter, but her blonde curls were glued to her forehead from the perspiration.

'Come, Grace,' my father said sweetly, placing his arm around her. 'Let me get you in the car.' She only made it down the first step when a blood-curdling moan ripped from her mouth. 'Oh dear god,' my father muttered as he scooped her into his arms and dashed towards the car. 'Go next door, son; the Robinsons are expecting you. They'll take care of you until we get home.'

Just as my father said that, the porch light came on at your house. Your father emerged wearing a striped robe over his pyjamas, but I just stood there, paralysed with fear.

The next few minutes were a blur.

'I love you, Mumma!' I called out, as my father bundled her into the car.

'She's going to be okay,' your father said from beside me, placing his hand on my shoulder. It startled me because I hadn't realised he was standing there. My eyes were fixed on the car as my dad screeched out of the driveway and sped down the street. I remember I was fighting back the tears as your father led me towards your house. 'Christine is making you up a bed on the couch.'

I wasn't able to fall back to sleep, I'd been too worried about my mum. I was watching the time on the VCR tick over to 3.56am when I heard my father's car pull up next door. Although I had been awaiting his return, I felt sick inside. It's like a part of me knew that my life was about to change forever.

The hall light came on a few seconds after he knocked on your front door, and I just lay there, too afraid to move. I saw your father sliding his arms into his robe as he entered the hallway, your mother following closely behind.

'How's Grace?' she asked the moment they let my dad in. I had a clear line of sight from where I lay, and the blank stare on his face when he came into view is one I'll never forget.

He shook his head before he spoke, and I saw your mother's hand fly up to cover her mouth. 'Her appendix ruptured before we arrived at the hospital. They rushed her into theatre, but she didn't make it . . . she died on the operating table.'

I heard your mother's loud gasp moments before my father fell to his knees. My own tears silently fell as he covered his face with his hands and started to sob. It was the first and only time I have ever seen him cry.

This is the reason I turned up the radio this morning. This is a time in my life that's too painful to revisit. If only I had got out of bed when my father had first asked me, they might have made it to the hospital in time, and maybe she'd still be alive today.

To this day, just thinking about her hurts. I miss her so much. She was only thirty-three; far too young and beautiful to die.

There are another two pages of the letter, but at this stage I have to put it down. I can no longer see the words through my own tears. My heart breaks for the little boy he once was, and for what his family went through. The fact that he has carried around this guilt for all these years makes me feel incredibly sad. Leaning over, I pluck two tissues out of the box on my bedside table.

I wipe my eyes and move to the white desk that sits underneath the window. My fingers grip the back of the chair as I stare at the house next door; the place where he and his family used to live. I find myself wondering about his father and why he doesn't live there anymore. Did he remarry after his wife's death?

I grab my handbag and rummage through it, looking for my phone. I have so many questions and so much I want to say to Braxton in this moment. I press the button on the side of the handset, bringing it to life. Opening the messages app, I find only one text in the list, from Braxton. It says, *Test*; he sent it when he was giving me a rundown on how the phone works. Clicking on that, I type a reply. *I'm so sorry about what happened to your mum.*

I press send. I don't know what else to say to him, but I want him to know that I am sorry. Truly sorry. I wish I could find words deep enough to ease his pain.

I'm startled a few seconds later when my phone dings with a reply. *Thank you. I shouldn't burden you with my problems, and I'm ashamed that it has taken me so long to come clean. I feel somewhat lighter for finally speaking the truth.*

I respond quickly, without having to think much about my reply; it's just how I feel. *I'm thankful you chose to share it with me, it took a lot of courage. You shouldn't hold yourself responsible for her death. It was just one of those unfortunate things. You were just a kid, Braxton.*

His message comes through seconds later. *It means a lot that you'd say that.*

It's the truth. I really want to hug you right now.

There is silence for nearly a minute before my phone beeps. *You do?*

Yes. And it's true.

I could really go one of your hugs, he writes. *You give the best kind. I'm in the middle of an important meeting at work, and then I'm heading back to the hospital, but can I get a raincheck for the morning?*

I find myself grinning at his reply, and I'm actually looking forward to tomorrow so I can hug him. I want to ask him what he does for work, but he's in a meeting, so I don't. I feel selfish for not knowing these things about him.

I'm sorry to bother you at work. Enjoy the rest of your day. I'm going to go and finish reading the rest of your letter.

He writes back immediately. *You could never be a bother. Hearing from you has made my day. I'm sitting here in the boardroom with a ridiculous smile on my face, and Lucas is giving me a strange look. Message me any time of the day or night. I'll always be available for you, Jem. Always.*

My smile widens. *Thank you. I appreciate you saying that. I'll see you tomorrow.*

I'm looking forward to it, and my hug.

Although I can't see my own face, I'm pretty sure I'm wearing the same ridiculous smile.

I walk back towards my bed, placing my phone down on the bedside table. There's a fluttery feeling in my stomach that I've never experienced before.

I eat my sandwich before reading the rest of the letter. I'm famished, and I need a few minutes to compose myself.

The death of my mother, and the long hours my father worked, meant I spent a lot more time at your house. Your mother had offered to help my dad out wherever she could. In the months that followed, he pretty much fell apart, and seeing him like that only intensified my guilt.

That's where your mother stepped in. She basically took care of me like I was her own. There was many a night that she sat up late with me and held me while I cried. She went above and beyond, and I'll forever love her for that. Your parents had always been fantastic with me, but in the years that followed you all became my family. I'm not sure how my father and I would have survived without your family's support.

The third of January 2002. It was summer and we were on school holidays. I'd met your grandparents when they came to the city to visit your family, but this was my first time staying on their farm in the country. Ma and Pa was what you called them, and eventually I did too.

Your grandparents, Albert and Isabella Griggs, were two of the nicest, most genuine people I've ever met. I grew to love them very much over the years.

You adored them, as they did you. You were their only grandchild and were affectionately known as their little Jem-Jem. Pa used to say that you were the apple of his eye, which used to make us laugh because he was an apple farmer. He had more than two hundred apple trees in his orchard. He would hire pickers around harvest time, but he used to pay us a few dollars each to pick up the apples that had fallen from the trees. With the money we earned we would ride our bikes to the corner shop in town and buy ice-creams and lollies.

You'd beg Pa to let us climb the ladders like the other workers, but he wouldn't hear of it. It was rare for him to say no to you, especially when you'd pout your bottom lip and stare up at him with your big brown eyes, but he wouldn't budge on this. You weren't happy about that, but he only said no because he didn't want us to get hurt. I on the other hand was relieved.

Since it appears I'm confessing my deepest darkest secrets to you in this letter, I might as well tell you I'm afraid of heights. Petrified would be a better word. It's unmanly, I know, and I hope you don't think less of me because of it, but it's the truth. Give me spiders, snakes, scary rides (as long as they're close to the ground) and even fast cars, but not heights; never heights. It's ironic considering what I do for a living, but being high up is something I've never been comfortable with. Maybe if I'd told you this sooner, I wouldn't have had to suffer through all the terrifying things you've made me do over the years.

Our time on the farm was always fun. Especially for a city boy like me. It's such a different lifestyle in the country. You used to love Pa's tractor rides. He would often fill the trailer with bales of hay and take us for joyrides around his hundred-acre property.

I remember watching you as he drove us around—your beautiful long brown hair would fly around in the wind, but it was the pure joy on your face that I loved the most. You have the most breathtaking smile. It's one of my favourite things in the world.

There was never a shortage of things to do, and my times spent there were some of the happiest moments of my life.

Another one of your favourite things was going down to the river. It ran through the back of the property, and we would often have picnics down by the water. Ma was one of the best cooks I've ever known. She would make us delicious sandwiches on the bread she baked that morning, and add slices of cake or pieces of her homemade apple pie—it was to die for—into the basket as a special treat. Pa even built us a swing out of an old tyre, and hung it from the huge willow tree that sat on the banks of the river. We spent hours swinging from the tree and jumping into the water during summer.

In the colder months, we fished for trout or took out Pa's small row boat. I usually did the rowing because, frankly, you sucked at it. No matter how hard you tried, you could never get the boat to go in the direction you wanted it to.

On your twelfth birthday, your grandparents bought you a beautiful chestnut mare that had belonged to a friend of Pa's. You named her Tilly-Girl, and you loved her so much. You would double me around on her for hours. She was four years old when you got her, and she had such a gentle nature, just like you.

You two had a special bond. Each time we arrived at the farm, you ran over to the paddock and called out, 'Tilly-Girl!' at the top of your lungs. She came bolting towards you from wherever she was, and would do this funny bouncing dance as soon as she saw you. Then, when she calmed down she would approach you and rub her face against the side of yours. The connection you two had was simply beautiful.

Late one afternoon we emerged from the river after our swim. You walked over to the tree to untie Tilly-Girl's reins from a *branch, while I gathered the blanket and picnic basket. I looked up just in time to see Tilly-Girl rear up on her hind legs, knocking you to the ground.*

I stood in shock for a moment—it was so out of character for her—but then I dropped the basket and ran to your side. That's when I noticed the large eastern brown snake lying in the grass ready to pounce. Its body was coiled into a circle, and its head was raised and aimed straight at you. It's the second most venomous snake in the world, with the potential to kill a human within minutes.

'Don't move, Jem,' I whispered. 'Stay completely still.'

Your eyes widened when I pointed to the snake, less than a metre away. I'll never forget the look of sheer terror on your face.

I knew I had to act fast, and to say my adrenaline was pumping as my eyes scanned the surrounding foliage is an understatement. I spotted a small boulder a few metres away and, slowly and precisely, I moved towards it. It was heavy, but I managed to pick it up.

'I'm going to count to three,' I said to you once I was in place. 'On three I want you to stand up and run as fast as you can towards the river. Okay?' You were too frightened to even speak, so you blinked your eyes a few times instead.

Using all my strength, I lifted the boulder high in the air. 'One. Two. Three!' The moment I saw you move out of the corner of my eye, I dropped the boulder. Thank god my aim was spot on because the snake lunged towards you just as the rock came down hard, landing on its head.

When I ran over to you, you fell into my arms and began to weep. 'You saved my life,' you said.

I did what I needed to do to protect you, but you made me feel like a hero.

Ma and Pa were upset when we told them what happened, but Ma gave me an extra slice of apple pie that night as a reward

*for my bravery. Tilly-Girl got an apple for the part she'd played,
by knocking you out of the way before you stepped on the snake.*

*We slept in bunk beds in the spare room when we stayed
at your grandparents' place. That night as I was drifting off to
sleep I heard you whisper into the darkness. 'I love you, Braxton
Spencer.' It was the first time you'd ever said those words out loud.*

*I pretended to be asleep so I didn't have to reply, but let's just
say that night I fell asleep with a huge smile on my face.*

What we had is far too beautiful to be forgotten.

Yours always,

Braxton

I read the letter one more time before eagerly searching
inside the bottom of the envelope for my charms. I smile
broadly when I find a tiny apple, as well as a beautiful horse.

I wonder what ever happened to my Tilly-Girl.

SEVENTEEN

Braxton

I wait until the doctor does his morning rounds, checking on my dad, before I duck home to shower and change. I'm eager to get to Christine's house to see my girl. She promised me a hug today, and although I don't hold out high hopes that I'll actually get one, the texts she sent me yesterday were enough to boost my spirits.

I remain relatively calm on my drive over there. I'm trying not to expect too much; I've had enough letdowns in the past few months to last me a lifetime. But I'm grateful she still wants me in her life.

'Morning,' I say as I get out of the car and walk towards the house.

'Morning,' she replies as she descends the front steps. There's a sweet smile on her face that warms my heart. I don't seem to hurt as much now when I look at her, because she seems happier. The sadness she carried after the accident was hard for me to see. That's all I've ever wanted for her: happiness.

I offer my hand to her when she reaches the last step, and she takes it willingly.

'How are you feeling today?'

'Good. I'm feeling really good.' Her gaze moves down to the path below as she comes to a stop beside me. 'I believe I owe you a hug.' She looks unsure as her big brown eyes finally lift to meet mine.

'You don't have to hug me if it makes you feel uncomfortable, Jem.'

'But I want to. I want to for so many reasons. I want to hug you for the loss of your mother. I want to hug you for saving me from the snake. I want to hug you for everything you've given me since the accident. In the weeks that followed my coma . . . there was no hope. I can't even put into words how I felt back then. There were times I even wished I hadn't survived.'

'Jem,' I say as a lump rises to my throat. I knew she was down, with good reason, but never once did I think things were that desperate.

'Then you started writing the letters.' Although there are tears brimming in her eyes, there's a smile on her face as she speaks. 'You have no idea what those letters have done for me. They've given me hope where there was none.'

Her words have me smiling. 'I'm glad they're helping.'

'They are.' A blush creeps across her face as her expression turns hopeful. 'So, can I hug you?'

'Hug away,' I say, opening my arms wide.

She giggles nervously as her hands slide around my waist, her touch awakening all my nerve endings.

Folding her in my arms, I pull her in tight against me. 'You never need to ask permission to hug me, Jem. Never. Consider me your own personal hugging machine.'

A sweet laugh falls from her lips as she buries her face in my chest. 'Mmm. You smell so good.'

My smile widens. The old Jemma used to say that all the time.

Everything in me wants to bury my face in her hair and inhale deeply. She's always had the most intoxicating scent, but I don't want to freak her out. Instead I close my eyes and savour the feeling of having her in my arms again.

'Is my grandparents' farm a long drive from here?' she asks as soon as we're seated in the car.

'A couple of hours,' I reply. 'My father's being discharged from hospital today, so I won't have time to take you, but we can go for a drive up there on the weekend if you like.'

When I glance in her direction I find her grinning. 'I'd love that, and I'm pleased to hear your father's doing better. I'd love to meet him.'

'Whenever you're ready, just say the word.'

'I know technically I've already met him, but . . .'

'You could come to the hospital with me after your physio if you're feeling up to it?'

'Okay. I'd like that.'

And so would I.

———

'I need to warn you,' I say to Jemma as we walk down the long corridor towards my father's room, 'he might not remember you, so don't be disillusioned if he doesn't.' I guess it works both ways, she won't remember him either.

'Why wouldn't he remember me?'

'He has Alzheimer's.'

'Oh Braxton,' she says in a sympathetic tone. 'I'm so sorry.'

I force a tight smile instead of replying. I'm sorry too. I feel helpless not being able to stop this disease from progressing, but mostly my heart aches for him. It's just so unfair.

When we enter his room, I find him sitting up in bed drinking a cup of tea. 'Hi, Pop,' I say as we approach his bed.

'Hi there,' he replies, but I can already tell by the dazed look in his eyes that he doesn't know who we are.

'You're checking out of this joint today.' I hold up the

small bag in my hand that contains his clothes. 'I brought you some clothes.'

I see his gaze drift towards Jemma, and when I look at her, she's staring at him intently. 'And who is this pretty little thing?' my father asks.

'This is Jemma.'

'It's lovely to meet you, Mr Spencer,' she says, extending her hand to him.

'Likewise, young lady.'

I pull up a chair for Jem, and she just sits there and studies him.

When he's finished his cup of tea, I help him from the bed and lead him into the bathroom so he can change. I'm paranoid he's going to fall again. The sad part is that his body is still reasonably fit and strong for his age. It's only his mind that's failing him.

I walk behind Jemma and my father when we reach the home. She has her arm hooked through his as they chatter away. It reminds me of the good old times, when they adored each other.

I once took everything I had for granted, but not anymore. I would give anything for things to be the way they were.

'Your father's really sweet,' Jemma says as I back out of the parking space.

The staff at the home love him; he never gives them any trouble. Two nurses were fussing over him when we left, and he was smiling. I think he likes all the attention, which always makes it easier for me to leave him here.

'He's a good man. You two were very close once.'

'I really like him. Has he been sick for long?'

'He was diagnosed almost three years ago. At first he would forget little things, like where he'd put his glasses, or if he'd taken his medication. When he started to ask the same question numerous times, or constantly repeat himself, we knew there was a problem. The medication the doctor gave him seemed to help for a while, but his illness has progressed rapidly since then.'

'That's so sad.'

'It is. It almost killed me to put him in here, but it's the best place for him. I have to try to remember that.'

'I can imagine how hard that decision would have been for you.'

'It was. You were a great support, though. You always knew how to make me feel better. I don't think I could have gone through with it without you.'

My eyes briefly leave the road, moving to her. God, I miss my wife so much. I know she's still very much here, but on the other hand she isn't. Things are nothing like they used to be, and I don't know if they ever will be again.

We're silent for the majority of the drive home, and then she speaks softly.

'Braxton?'

'Yes.'

'Are you really afraid of heights?'

I clear my throat, as I turn into Christine's street.

I can't believe I even confessed that after all this time. 'Yes.' I shift in my seat slightly. I don't know why I feel like less of a man because of this, but I do.

'You should have told me. I'm sure I would have understood.' She's right, she probably would have, but it was my own insecurity that stopped me from admitting my deepest fears to her. I could do no wrong in her eyes. She always made me feel like her hero, when in reality I was anything but. 'I hope I didn't make you suffer too much.'

Her response makes me chuckle. If only she knew. When I think about all the things I've forced myself to do with her over the years because I was too scared to tell her the truth, it's kind of ridiculous.

'Are we still on for the weekend? We can head to the country Saturday morning if you like,' I ask, keen for a change of subject.

'That sounds perfect.'

'Great.'

When I pull into Christine's driveway, she picks up her handbag from the floor by her feet.

'Thanks for coming with me to see my dad,' I say, when she reaches for the door handle.

'Thanks for taking me.' She pauses briefly before speaking again. 'Would it be okay if I came with you to visit him sometimes?'

'I'd like that, and I think my dad would too. It's funny, he doesn't remember us, yet I still get the feeling he knows we belong to him.'

She smiles before opening the door. 'I'll see you tomorrow.'

It's not lost on me that she didn't elaborate on what I just said. My father's situation and hers are very similar, but I don't think she feels like she belongs to us anymore.

'Let me get the door for you.'

'It's okay, I've got it.'

I lean back into my chair and read over the letter in my hand.

LETTER FIVE . . .

Dearest Jemma,

The ninth of August 2002. It was your thirteenth birthday, and because it was such an important one, your mum had organised something special—a high tea with all of your girlfriends from school. It was going to be a grand affair. The invitations were handmade and looked like something you'd receive for a wedding, not for a teenage girl's birthday party.

She bought you a pretty pink party dress—it was all satin, frills, bows and lace. She'd put up a large white marquee in the backyard, and bunches of pink helium balloons adorned the tables.

Your grandmother was coming down to help with the food preparation. The menu consisted of tiny quiches, bite-size jam tarts, fancy cupcakes and cucumber sandwiches cut into dainty finger-size portions. They were brought out on multi-layer stands. It was all very posh.

Your mum had even booked you in at the local beautician that morning to have your hair done and your fingernails painted. Thirteen meant you were becoming a young lady, and she wanted it to be celebrated in style.

You weren't a tomboy, but nor were you a girly girl, so let's just say you were pretty pissed off with all her plans.

'I don't want a stupid high tea!' you told me. 'I don't even drink tea. You should see the ridiculous dress she wants me to wear, Brax.' I struggled not to laugh when you stuck your finger in your mouth and pretended to gag. 'I'm going to look like that ugly crochet doll that Ma has sitting over her spare roll of toilet paper.' I had to agree that doll was hideous and creeped me the hell out, but I also knew it was impossible for you to look ugly. 'I want to wear jeans and a T-shirt and go to McDonald's with you and eat cheeseburgers until I puke, and have ice-cream cake. Lots and lots of ice-cream cake.'

I felt bad for you. You always looked forward to your birthday. Every year on the first of January your countdown began. I had to wait until December, so I never bothered counting down to mine.

'I'm sure it's not going to be that bad,' I told you. I had no idea what a high tea even involved, but I knew that your mother always went above and beyond for you, so whatever she'd planned would be special. She also always made a big fuss of me on my birthday after my mother died. She was wonderful like that.

'I know this isn't your thing, pumpkin,' your father had said a while later when he came searching for you. He always called you pumpkin. 'But your mum has put a lot of effort into this party. She's been planning it for months. Can't you just go along with it? It's just for a few hours. It would make her so happy.' When he wrapped you in his arms and kissed the top of your head, I knew by the grim look on your face, this party was going ahead.

Your mum invited all the girls from your class. Of course I was invited as well, but I was the only boy. There was no way I was going to sit there and sip on pink lemonade and eat cucumber sandwiches with a bunch of life-sized girls who resembled Ma's toilet-paper doll. For a nearly fourteen-year-old boy, that's the stuff of nightmares. Luckily your dad felt the same—though he hadn't dared suggest not holding the party; he would do anything for you but the love he felt for your mum was something else—so we came up with a plan for us to be the waiters for the day. Your mum even hired us tuxedos so we looked the part.

I'd been doing odd jobs around my house for months to earn extra pocket money so I could buy you a present. I bought you a kite. You used to love playing with mine when we'd go to the beach. Yours was multi-coloured like a rainbow, in the shape of a butterfly.

I was out in the backyard helping your father fill up a drink tub with ice when you came through the back sliding doors onto the patio.

'Braxton, you're getting ice everywhere,' he said, but his words didn't register. I was completely mesmerised by you. There was never a moment that I hadn't thought you were beautiful, but this was the first time you'd stolen all my air and left me completely breathless. There'd be so many more moments like this over the years, but the first time is always the one that stands out the most.

Your long brown hair was down, just the way I liked it. The hairdresser had put soft curls in it, and a pretty pink bow to match your dress. You looked nothing like a toilet-paper doll. You were the most beautiful thing I'd ever seen, and so grown up. It was *in that moment my true feelings for you were confirmed. I didn't just love you, I was completely in love with you.*

'You can close your mouth now, son,' your father said in an amused tone.

His statement was enough to snap me back into reality. That's when I realised the plastic bag in my hand was now empty, and its contents, the ice, had piled into a small mountain around my feet.

The party was going well, and you even seemed to be having a good time. Well, you were until Sonia Mitchell set her sights on me. She was the mean girl in your class, and you never really liked her.

I was over by the bar refilling the glasses of pink lemonade and placing them on a tray, trying my best to ignore her. It was rude of me, but she'd been following me around for over an hour and it was starting to get on my nerves. There was only one girl at that party I was interested in, and that was you.

A few minutes later you approached us, grabbing one of the drinks from the tray. I was both pleased and relieved when you came to stand beside me. You casually stared down Sonia, as you sipped on your pink lemonade. It did nothing to stop her advances, though.

'You must get bored hanging out with Jemma all the time,' she said in a bitchy tone as she looked you up and down. I heard you gasp from beside me, but I bit my tongue. I didn't want to say or do anything that was going to ruin your party. It was your special day, and your mother had gone to so much trouble.

My reply came without hesitation. 'Never! Hanging out with Jem is my favourite thing to do.'

'Huh,' she scoffed, narrowing her eyes at you before focusing her attention back on me. Smiling, she innocently twisted her long blonde hair around her finger, which was ironic; she was anything but sweet and didn't fool me for a second. 'You should come to Daddy's restaurant sometime, Brax. We could make you our special guest.'

Her eyes narrowed again when they moved back to you, and I was struggling to keep my cool. 'You want to come with me, Jem?' I asked.

'I meant just you . . . alone,' Sonia snapped. To say I wasn't expecting you to react like you did would be an understatement. You lunged forward, faking a trip, which was pretty much an impossibility since you were standing still.

'Oh gosh, I'm so sorry, Sonia,' you said as the pink lemonade from your glass soaked into her white silk party dress.

'Ahh! You did that on purpose,' she screamed as she turned and ran into the house crying.

I tried not to laugh, honestly I did, but the moment my gaze moved to you and I saw you fighting back a smile, I lost it. It was one of the funniest things I'd ever seen. It was about time someone put Sonia Mitchell in her place.

She had her daddy come to pick her up ten minutes later. The party only seemed to improve once she left. Sonia never really spoke to you after that day, but that didn't seem to bother you in the slightest.

The following morning you knocked on my door early. I was still in my pyjamas, eating Coco Pops while I watched television.

'Can you help me put my kite together?' you asked excitedly. 'Dad offered to help, but I want you to do it.'

You were given jewellery, clothes, perfume and an array of girly things for your birthday that year, but you told me the kite was your favourite present. You have no idea how happy that made me.

We put it together in no time, and you sat on my sofa impatiently waiting while I ran upstairs to change.

It was a dreary, overcast winter day, but there was enough breeze to launch that baby into the air. I watched as you ran laps around your backyard, the kite flying behind you. Seeing you happy always made my heart smile. To this day, it still has the same effect on me.

Things were going perfectly until a big gust of wind came and blew the kite towards the large tree in your backyard, snagging it on one of the branches. I tried over and over to untangle it for you, but it was no use.

Your bottom lip started to quiver as you fought back the tears, and my heart suddenly hurt. The only way that kite was coming down was if someone went up there to get it. It was so high up, and I prayed that someone wasn't going to be me.

'I'll go and see if your dad can help us,' I said and ran inside. You can imagine how I felt when your mum told me he had gone for a walk to get the Sunday paper.

My feet dragged as I headed back outside to break the bad news to you.

'I'm going to climb up and get it,' you said.

'No, Jem. It's too high.' I grabbed hold of your elbow to try to stop you.

'Let me go,' you snapped, snatching your arm out of my grip. 'I'm going up there.' You were so stubborn, and as much as the thought of climbing that tree terrified me, I didn't really have a choice. There was no way I was letting you do it.

'Fine. I'll go up and get it.'

I felt sick as I climbed onto the first branch. Don't look down . . . don't look down, I chanted in my head as I made my way up.

'Be careful, Brax,' you called out from below.

I swear my whole body was trembling when I lifted my leg and pulled my body up onto the last branch. I sat there for the longest time, paralysed by fear. Don't look down . . . don't look down, I continued to say over and over in my head.

'Are you okay?' you called out.

'I'm fine.' I wasn't, but there was no way I was admitting that to you.

Reaching into my back pocket, I pulled out my Swiss Army knife. It had belonged to my grandfather. He gave it to my dad on his thirteenth birthday, and he'd carried on the tradition by giving it to me. I took it everywhere, except to school.

'What are you doing?'

I was stalling, that's what I was doing. In that moment, I couldn't find the courage to move. 'I'm carving my name into the tree.'

I lied. I was carving my heart into that trunk. My deepest, darkest secret—my fear of losing you was what stopped me from ever telling you.

In reality it was probably only ten minutes, but to me it felt like a lifetime had passed. And you were growing impatient. 'Come on, Brax. I want my kite.'

'Okay.' I folded my knife away and slipped it back into my pocket. Then I took a deep breath and willed myself to move, as I lay face down onto the branch. Don't look down . . . don't look down.

I'd only made it about a metre along when I heard the first crack. My heart was beating so fast I could hear it thumping in my ears.

'Please be careful,' you called out again.

I could hear the fear in your voice and it only intensified my panic. I took another deep breath and continued to snake forward, one terrifying inch at a time. I was only about five metres off the ground, but it felt more like a hundred.

I heard another crack, followed closely by another. My grip on the branch tightened and before I even realised what was happening, I was falling. 'Braaaaax!' I heard you scream moments before I hit the ground hard.

I don't remember much after that.

My father was at work, but your parents rushed me to the hospital. My injuries weren't serious, but my arm was broken in two places. On a positive note, your kite had come down with me in the fall.

The hospital kept me in for a few hours for observation because I'd also hit my head in the fall. You sat by my bed in emergency, and held my hand while they plastered my arm. I lost count of how many times you apologised.

My dad closed his store and came straight to my bedside when your parents called him. I felt bad when I saw the anguish on his face. You refused to leave with your parents, just like I had years earlier when you'd been stung by that bluebottle. You remained by my side the entire time.

As soon as we arrived home, my father ordered me to go and lie down. Apart from the dull ache in my arm, I felt fine, but I did as I was told. I could tell he was angry with me for recklessly climbing the tree, but also incredibly relieved I was okay. I understand it more now; with everything that had happened with my mum, I was all he had left.

You followed us up to my room and when my father suggested you go home so I could rest, you refused. I was grateful he let you stay. You sat on the edge of my bed while my father fussed over me, but the moment he left the room, you pulled back my covers and climbed into bed beside me. You'd never done anything like that before.

'I'm so sorry, Brax,' you said for the hundred-millionth time as you slid your arm around my waist and snuggled into my chest. When I heard you sniffle I knew you were crying, so I pulled your body closer to mine.

'Stop apologising, Jem. It's not your fault, it was an accident.'

'When you fell from that tree . . . I . . . I . . . I thought I was going to lose you,' you sobbed. 'I've never been so scared in my life.'

'Don't cry.' I ran my hand up and down your back in an attempt to soothe you.

'I couldn't imagine my life without you in it, Braxton Spencer,' you whispered.

I couldn't imagine my life without you either, I still can't. You're my life, Jem.

I held you tightly until you were sound asleep. It was the first time you'd ever slept in my arms. Before I closed my eyes, I planted a soft kiss on your hair, and only then did I dare say the words I'd never before been able to voice out loud, 'I love you with all my heart, Jemma Isabella Rosalie Robinson.'

What we had is far too beautiful to be forgotten.

Yours always,

Braxton

I fold the letter and place it in the envelope, adding the tiny tree charm. I tried to get her a kite as well, but the jeweller didn't have any in stock.

It's almost midnight when I log off from my laptop and grab my briefcase from beside my desk, turning off the lights as I leave the office. The thought of going home to an empty house, without Jem there waiting for me, is something I don't think I'll ever get used to.

I'm almost home when I decide to take a detour. I know she'll already be in bed, but the urge I have to be near her is overwhelming.

I place the letter inside the letterbox, then stand back and look up at Jemma's bedroom window. I'm not sure how long I stand on the footpath outside Christine's house, but it's a while.

Even though my heart is heavy, I smile as I think back to that very first day I saw her pressed up against the glass watching me. In that moment, I never could have predicted how close we would become in the coming years.

I would give anything to be up there sleeping beside her, and holding her in my arms.

Anything.

EIGHTEEN

Braxton

I can't contain my excitement as I jog up the front steps to Christine's front door. I've been awake since 5am, wandering aimlessly around the house just waiting for it to be time to leave. I even skipped my usual morning workout and coffee on the back deck because I couldn't seem to sit still long enough.

'Good morning, Christine,' I say, leaning forward to kiss her cheek when she answers the door.

'Good morning,' she replies beaming. 'The happiness I see on my little girl's face seems to be infectious.'

'I'm spending the day with her. You have no idea how happy that makes me.'

'I think I do,' she replies, rubbing her hand affectionately down my arm. 'I'm glad you two seem to be working things out.'

'We still have a way to go, but we're getting there slowly.'

She smiles as she moves aside to let me enter.

'Jemma!' she calls out from the bottom of the stairs. 'Braxton's here.'

'Coming!' Jemma yells.

I try to stand still as I eagerly wait to see her. A few seconds later I inhale a sharp breath when she appears at the top of the staircase. The first thing I notice is that she has changed her hair. Her dark brown locks are now shorter, and sit just above her shoulders. It's different from how it has always been, but I like it.

A beautiful yet unsure smile graces her face as she descends the stairs. She's wearing a pretty white sundress, which accentuates her lean body and tanned skin. My fingers are itching to reach out and touch her. She's always had a bronzed glow—especially in summer when we spend so much time at the beach—but months have passed since she's been in the sun.

I extend my hand to her when she's within reach. 'You look beautiful,' I say. 'And I love your hair.'

'You do?' she asks as a pink tinge fills her cheeks. I find her bashfulness, something new I have learned about her, endearing.

'I do.'

She tucks a strand behind her ear as the smile on her face grows.

My eyes land on the jagged red scars that are now visible along her hairline. It takes nothing away from her beauty, but I get a pang in my heart nevertheless. They will serve as a constant reminder of everything we've lost.

'I had it cut yesterday while I was out. I bought this as well,' she says, fanning out the skirt of her dress.

'It's lovely.'

'Thank you.'

I had no idea she went out yesterday, but I don't really know what she gets up to during the day, apart from our daily trips to rehab. Christine told me she spends most of her time in her room, which saddens me. She was always an outdoorsy person, and hated being locked away.

'I caught the bus into town.'

'Wow. That's great.' As much as I wish it was me she was spending her time with, I'm glad she's starting to get out of the house, starting to live again. 'I'm proud of you.'

'I wanted to go back to that beach you took me to.'

'Ah, that explains your tan.'

'I didn't go in the water, just sat in the sun watching the waves. I really love it there,' she says, in a breathy kind of sigh.

'It was always your favourite place to be.'

'I wish you'd have something to eat before you leave, Jemma,' Christine says when we walk into the kitchen. 'I don't like the idea of you going out with an empty stomach.'

'I'm fine,' Jemma says, placing a kiss on her mother's cheek before scooping a basket off the kitchen table. 'We have this, remember?' Her gaze moves to me. 'I packed us a picnic lunch. Like we used to have by the river at Ma and Pa's farm.'

I'm grinning as I take the basket out of her hands. Today already feels like old times.

'This place is beautiful,' Jemma says as we pass through the small town and head towards the rolling green hills of the countryside. It hasn't changed in the past few years. 'It's so green . . . so picturesque. I can see why my grandparents chose to never leave.'

'They loved it here. This is where your grandfather grew up. Ma moved here after they were married.'

'Tell me about them, Braxton. I only know what you've told me in the letters. Christine never talks about them.'

'They were amazing people . . . truly amazing. I don't know how they met, but I'm sure your mother can fill you in on that story. I do know that Ma was a city girl before she married. She loved her life here with Pa.'

'I wish I could remember them.' I wish she could as well. I wish she could remember me, and how much we loved each other. 'What happened to them? How long ago did they die?'

I knew that question would come up today. There's no good way to answer it.

'Your Pa died first,' I say, glancing her way. 'It was unexpected, and very sudden.'

She's hesitant with her reply. 'How?'

'He had a heart attack in the orchard. When he didn't come up to the house for lunch Ma went searching for him, and found him lying beneath one of the apple trees. She tried to resuscitate him. The coroner said he'd been dead for over an hour by the time she found him.'

I see her hand come up to cover her mouth, as her head turns away from me. 'Poor Ma,' I hear her whisper. Poor Ma is right. Pa's death broke her, and what happened in the days that followed proved that.

The tyres crunch as I turn off the main road and head down the long gravel driveway that leads to the farmhouse. The branches of the large jacaranda trees that line both sides of the driveway overlap in the middle forming a kind of archway. It's such a shame they aren't in bloom; the sea of purple flowers that cover the trees when they are, and the blanket they create on the ground when the flowers fall, really is a sight to see. Jemma loved that so much. I hope I get the chance to bring her back in spring so she can experience it again.

When we reach the end of the driveway, the farmhouse comes into view. It's been three years since I've been back here, but the place hasn't changed much. The gardens aren't as colourful and lush as they once were, but just being here makes me smile. Ma loved her garden, and would potter around out here for hours while Pa was working the land out back. This place holds so many wonderful memories for me, as it once did for Jemma.

'Are you okay?' I ask, placing my hand on Jemma's leg as I turn off the ignition.

'Yes,' she replies, turning her face towards me. She smiles, but I can tell it's forced.

'It was a terrible time for us all.'

'I can imagine.'

'This is their farmhouse,' I say, pointing out the front windscreen. 'Do you want to have a look around?'

'Are we allowed? Does someone else live here?'

'No. Your grandparents left this place to your mother in their will.'

Christine hasn't been back since Ma's death, but she won't sell it. She was scarred by what happened that day, but this place was her home once. It's all she has left of her parents, and I know she'll never part with it.

I thought about asking Christine for the keys to get inside, but I didn't want to push my luck. Just having Jem here is a huge step. I tried for months to get Jemma to come back here after Ma's death, but she flat out refused.

We walk down the front path towards the house—her eyes are everywhere as we step onto the large wraparound verandah. Ma and Pa always sat out here of an evening. In the summer months, they would sit side by side drinking iced tea, and Ma would make homemade lemonade for me and Jem. On colder nights, they would sit under the multi-coloured blankets that Ma crocheted. Jem and I had our own blankets as well.

'They were Ma's and Pa's rocking chairs,' I say as she runs her hand over the back of one. 'We used to sit on that swinging chair down there.' I turn my body slightly and point to the far end of the verandah where the long wooden bench seat hangs from the roof by large chains. 'Or occasionally we'd lie out on the grass and look up at the stars.' I give her a moment to absorb it all before I speak again. 'Come check out the view from the back of the house. You can see over the entire orchard from up here.'

'Okay.'

She smiles when I place my hand on the small of her back and guide her in that direction. When we reach the rear of the house, she comes to a sudden stop.

'Wow.'

I'm pretty sure I wore that same look of amazement the first time I came here. She takes a few steps forward and her hands grip the rail as her eyes take it all in. Not only can you see the rows of perfectly aligned apple trees, but also the rolling green hills nestled behind them. The view from up here is nothing short of postcard-worthy. 'It's breathtaking.'

'It is,' I reply, but unlike her, I'm not talking about the landscape. My eyes are firmly fixed on her.

When I hear her stomach growl, I look down at my watch and see it's almost midday. 'Shall we have our picnic down by the river? It's only a five-minute walk from here, it'll be just like old times.'

She smiles. 'I'd like that. I was hoping we'd get to see the river.'

I have so much to show her. I'm going to drag this day out as long as I can. Who knows when I'll get this opportunity again?

I leave her standing on the back verandah while I collect the picnic basket and a blanket from the car.

As we head across the grassed area towards the apple trees, she points to the large wooden barn. 'What's in there?'

'That's where Pa used to store his machinery and the apples after harvest.'

'It's big.'

Although the trees haven't been tended to for some years now, they're in surprisingly good condition. I'm saddened to see all the rotten apples scattered on the ground beneath the trees though, it's such a waste.

'What was that?' Jemma asks, grabbing hold of my arm.

'What was what?'

'That rustling noise.' Coming to an abrupt stop, I listen. When I hear the noise she's referring to, I turn my head in that direction. 'Do you think it's a snake?' she asks, moving closer to my side.

'Not this time of year, it's not warm enough' I say, chuckling. 'Stay here. I'll go check it out.'

'I'm coming with you.' The way she latches onto my arm tells me she's frightened.

'There's nothing to be afraid of.'

'I'm not afraid,' she says, straightening her shoulders.

'Right.' I chuckle again because I know damn well she is.

We make our way down a few rows and the noise gets louder. Placing my hand out, I halt her. Crouching down slightly, I smile when I see a baby goat feasting on the apples that have fallen from a tree.

'Shh.' I place my finger against my mouth, and gesture for Jemma to follow me with my other hand. 'Come,' I whisper.

All sign of fear disappears the moment the baby goat comes into view. 'Oh my god, it's so cute,' she says in a soft voice. 'It's so tiny.'

A loud bleating sound comes from behind us, making Jemma scream and jump behind me. I throw back my head and laugh when I see two larger goats standing a few metres away.

'It's not funny,' she says, slapping my arm. I beg to differ; I find it hilarious. When the larger goat takes a step closer and releases another bleating sound, Jemma's fingers dig into my flesh. 'Shoo them away. Please shoo them away.'

'You're not afraid of goats, are you?'

'No! Umm, yes. Crap, Braxton, do they bite?'

'They must be wild goats. They're probably trying to get to their baby.'

She pops her head out from behind me. 'That one has horns.' We hear another bleating sound, and see a few more goats approaching from the other direction. 'Crap, there's more. They're surrounding us ready to attack.' I can hear the strain in her voice, but I still can't help but laugh.

'They're not going to attack us,' I say, trying to calm her.

'Get them away!' She's starting to panic now, so I snap into action.

'Scram!' I yell, taking a step forward and flicking my free hand out in front of me.

I expect them to run, but that's not what happens. Instead, to my amazement they all fall onto their sides like a pack of dominoes, their stiffened legs protruding from underneath them. It's such a comical sight, I have no control over the loud laugh that spills from my mouth. That is until Jemma speaks.

'Oh my god, you killed them,' she cries. For a split second I think I have as well, until a few of them move, thrashing their bodies around trying to stand. The rest quickly follow. It's the weirdest thing I've ever seen. Have I just been punked by a small tribe of goats?

'What the hell just happened?' I ask.

'I don't know.' I turn to face Jemma and see the same stunned look on her face.

'You saw that, right?' If she wasn't here to witness it, I could have sworn I was hallucinating. 'Did they fake their own deaths?'

'I think they fainted,' she says. A smile tugs at her lips moments before she covers her mouth with her hand and starts to laugh. It starts off as a giggle but soon turns into a full-on belly laugh. It's infectious. When she snorts, I lose it to the point that tears fill my eyes and my sides hurt. It feels so good to truly laugh again, but more importantly to hear Jem laugh.

We're both still chuckling as we continue down to the river and hear the trickling of the water as we approach.

'Wow,' she says when the river comes into view. 'It's even more beautiful than I imagined.'

'It's pretty special,' I agree as I lay out the blanket and picnic basket and follow her towards the water's edge.

'I love that about your letters,' she says as I stop beside her. 'The way you describe things ... I swear if I close my eyes, I can almost picture everything.'

'I'm glad you're enjoying them. Do you want to hear something interesting?'

'Sure.'

'I did some research on the human brain after the accident, and found out that we only remember twenty per cent of our lives. And out of that, it's usually the poignant moments from our past that stick with us ... things that stood out at the time. You've been such an important part of my life, Jem, so it's only natural that my poignant moments involved you.'

'Wow. Only twenty per cent? I thought it would've been more.'

'Me too.'

I bend down and pick up a pebble from near my feet, then skim it across the water. As kids, Jem and I had competitions to see who could get the most bounces. I usually won, but there were times I purposely threw a bad one so she could beat me. I would never admit that to her, though. She used to have a fierce competitive streak, and she would have hated it if she knew she hadn't won legitimately.

She bends down and picks up a pebble. 'Can you teach me how to do that?'

'Sure. Hold it in between your forefinger and thumb.' I try to ignore the feelings that well up when I wrap my fingers around her hand to reposition the pebble. My eyes flick to hers and I find her staring at me, but I look away. It's so easy for me to get lost in those big brown eyes of hers, and I'm worried I'll do something stupid, like try to kiss her. 'Try to keep it at that angle when you throw it, so it skims across the surface of the water, instead of sinking.'

Her first throw is a flop and the pebble sinks straight to the bottom, but the steely determination of my old Jem shines through as she picks up pebble after pebble until she masters it. I love that although she's a different person from the one she once was, there are still some characteristics of the old her present.

'Are you hungry?' she asks, leading me back to the picnic blanket.

'Starved.'

'Good. I've packed plenty.' She reaches into the picnic basket and pulls out a container that's filled to the brim with sandwiches cut into triangles. 'I wasn't sure what you liked, so I went with ham, cheese and lettuce.' I see a grin form on her face.

'I love that my letters have given you back a piece of your past.'

'I've read them so many times I've lost count.' She sighs as her gaze moves down to the container on her lap. 'I don't want them to be just words on a piece of paper . . . I want them to be memories so familiar they almost seem real.'

'They *are* real,' I say, reaching for her hand. When she lifts her face to meet mine again, the sadness I see in her eyes tugs at my heart. 'Everything we shared was real, Jem.' I blow out a long breath and force my voice to remain steady. 'It was real,' I repeat, squeezing her hand.

We eat our lunch in silence, just enjoying the scenery, the sunshine, and each other's company.

'I made you something special,' she says, when we've finished eating the sandwiches. She reaches into the basket again and pulls out a dish wrapped in a red-and-white cloth.

'I asked Christine for Ma's recipe . . .' She removes the cloth and reveals a delicious-looking apple pie.

'It's Ma's recipe?' I ask, sitting forward and rubbing my hands together.

'The apples might not be as good as the ones here on the farm, but I followed the recipe to a tee. Christine helped me with the pastry, though. I hope you like it.'

'I'm sure it's delicious.' I smile from the pie to her. 'Thank you for going to all this trouble.'

'You've been so good to me, I wanted to do something nice for you.'

I watch as she cuts a large piece and places it on one of the red plastic plates she's brought. 'Hold on, let me get you a fork,' she says, rummaging around in the bottom of the basket.

'Thank you.' I don't know if it's because it's Ma's recipe, or the fact that Jemma made it, but I find myself moaning as soon as the first bite is in my mouth. 'Mmm.'

A smile tugs at her lips as we eat, which makes me even happier.

Once I've had a second helping of pie, we pack everything back into the basket.

'Would you like to go for a walk along the river bank? Like we did when we were kids?'

'I'd like that.'

Standing, I help her to her feet.

'See that tyre on the ground under the tree?' I ask. 'That used to be our swing. The rope must've eroded in the weather.'

'That's a shame. It's a beautiful tree, though.'

'It's a willow.'

'It would be a great tree to climb . . . well, maybe not for you.' I can't help but chuckle at her comment, and at myself. 'I love that I know things about you that the old me didn't know.'

'It's a lot easier to confess your fears on a piece of paper, I suppose.'

She stops walking and points towards the water. 'I think I just saw a fish come up to the surface.' My eyes follow her hand. 'There it is again.'

The excitement in her voice has me grinning. A fish? That's a long way off from what she thought the first time she saw that when we were kids.

'It's a platypus, not a fish, or the Loch Ness Monster.' I smile to myself as I think back to that day, all those years ago.

Her eyes are trained on the river, waiting for it to reappear. 'The Loch Ness Monster?'

'Just a myth,' I reply with a smile. 'Keep your eye out along the water's edge and you may see one out of the water. They usually make their burrows along the water's edge.'

'Okay.' She looks at me and matches my smile before moving her gaze back to the river.

We walk along in silence for a few minutes, until she asks me the question I've been dreading. 'Braxton ... What happened to Ma?'

I know that my reply is going to upset her, but I have to tell her. 'Pa's death broke her.' I tug at the collar of my shirt just thinking about it. 'The funeral was the worst. Your father and I had to help her into the church, she could barely walk.'

'That's so sad,' Jemma says.

'It was. I'd never seen her so distraught. She was always such a happy person. At the burial, when it was time to lower the coffin into the ground . . .' I exhale a long breath before continuing. 'She threw herself on top of it, begging him to take her too.'

'Oh my god.'

'Your mum stayed with her on the farm for a while. She tried to get Ma to come back to the city and live with them, but she refused to leave. The farm was her home, and her connection to Pa.'

'That's so sad.'

'We travelled back to the city that night with your father. I held you in my arms while you cried yourself to sleep.' She stops walking and turns to face me, giving me her full attention. 'Later that week, we got a call from your mother.' I fall silent. That morning still haunts me.

Stephen was in a meeting at work, so Christine called us. Jem was in the shower, so I was the one who took the call. I'm grateful for that, because Christine was screaming hysterically into the phone. I could barely make out what she was saying. I'd never heard her so distressed. *She won't wake up . . . She won't wake up*, she'd cried into the phone. *Oh god! Somebody please help me . . . She won't wake up.*

I'd never felt as helpless as I did in that moment. We collected Stephen, and the three of us drove straight out to the farm.

'What did she say?'

'She'd gone in to wake Ma up that morning, and she'd . . .' Jem can already tell where I'm heading with this because her hand comes up to cover her mouth again. 'She'd . . . umm . . . passed away in her sleep. The coroner said she'd had a heart attack, just like Pa. She wanted to be with her husband, and she got her wish.' I swallow hard, and when I see Jemma wipe the tears from her eyes, I instinctively pull her into my arms, resting my chin on the top of her head. 'Your mum was never the same after that day.'

She doesn't reply but her grip on me tightens.

—

'I can't believe how many stars are in the sky tonight,' Jemma says as we lie on the blanket staring up into the darkness. She seems in no rush to leave, and I'm enjoying my time with her too much to even suggest it.

'I know. You never see this many stars in the city.'

The serene trickling sound of the running river fills my ears, and crickets chirp in the distance. This is the most relaxed I've felt in months.

'Oh, did you see that?' she says, pointing up above.

'A shooting star.' It's quickly followed by another one. 'You need to make a wish.'

'Why?'

'It's custom to wish on a shooting star.'

'Oh.'

I turn my face in her direction and in the moonlight I see her eyes clenched shut. It makes me think back to the first time she saw a shooting star when we were kids. The only difference is that she voiced her wish out loud that day—I'd give anything to know what she's wishing for now.

Sadness washes over me when we finally decide to pack up and head home. I've missed this place, and being back here with Jemma has given me some peace, and I think it has done the same for her. I can only hope she allows me to bring her back again one day. I know in my heart Ma and Pa would want us here.

'It's a good thing that it's a full moon tonight,' I say as we walk back up towards the farmhouse.

'Why?'

'Otherwise we wouldn't be able to see. I didn't even think to bring a torch. I wouldn't make a great boy scout.'

She doesn't even flinch at my response. The joke is totally lost on her, but maybe one day I can share it with her. One day.

———

'What are you doing?' she asks as I pull over to the side of the road and position the car so the headlights shine into the paddock ahead. I had hoped to bring her here before it got dark, but our time together by the river was too perfect to rush.

'I have one more thing to show you before we head out of town.'

She doesn't reply, but she climbs out of the car and allows me to lead her to the barbed-wire fence.

'What do you want to show me?'

It's dark out, but with the moonlight and the high beams we should be able to see. I hope this goes to plan.

'Can you do me a favour?'

'Sure . . .'

'Place your hands on either side of your mouth . . . like this.' I move my hands up towards my face mimicking what I want her to do. She hesitantly does exactly as I ask, but I can tell she's confused by my request. 'Perfect. Now, call out "Tilly-Girl" in the loudest voice you can.'

I find myself smiling when her eyes widen. 'She's still alive?' she asks as her head snaps in my direction. 'I've been too afraid to ask you what happened to her.'

'She's old, but most definitely alive. The couple who own this farm, Mr and Mrs Talbot, were friends of your grandparents. They offered to care for Tilly-Girl until you were ready to come back.'

Her hands drop down by her side. 'I abandoned her?'

'No, you didn't. You rang them almost daily to check on her. You had every intention of coming back for her when you were ready.'

Her gaze moves down to the grass below. 'I can't believe I did that to her.'

'Hey, it's okay.' I reach for her hand, giving it a comforting squeeze. Every fibre of my being wants to pull her into my arms again, but I don't. I don't want to risk spoiling her day by overstepping the mark. 'It wasn't like that. You never stopped loving her, Jem. There was no way we could've brought her back to our place. You did what was best for her, she has room to run around here.'

She shrugs, but I can tell she's not convinced. It was one of the hardest decisions she ever made.

'Call out to her,' I encourage.

She lifts her hands to her mouth again. 'Tilly-Girl!' she screams.

We hear her before we see her. The sound of hooves pounding against the hard ground fills the air. Moments later she comes bounding over a small hill, heading straight towards us. Jemma's eyes are fixed on the horse, and mine are fixed on her. I'm grinning from ear to ear at the delight I see on her face.

'My Tilly-Girl,' she whispers, her smile bright.

The horse comes to a stop a few metres away from us, and stares at Jemma briefly before reverting into her familiar dance of leaping and spinning around all at once. It's amusing to watch, and I hear Jemma giggle beside me. Tilly-Girl doesn't have the youthful energy she once had, but I love that she still does this.

Tilly-Girl finally stills before slowly walking towards the fence. Jemma does the same, that ever-present pull drawing them together. I hear her sweet laugh when the horse rubs her face up against the side of Jem's. When she's finished with her greeting, Jemma throws her arms around the horse's neck, kissing the side of her face. Just like she used to do.

'Tilly-Girl.' I see a lone tear roll down Jem's cheek. 'My Tilly-Girl.'

NINETEEN

Jemma

'Morning,' Christine says as I enter the kitchen and take a seat at the table.

'Morning.'

She leans down and kisses my head. 'That smile on your face makes me so happy.'

'I had a great time yesterday.' I'm still on a high from my day with Braxton on the farm.

Without replying, she turns and walks towards the stove and starts to make my breakfast. Even after all this time I can tell she's still hurting from her parents' death.

She reacted strangely when I first told her Braxton and I were going there, and I found her crying in the kitchen a few minutes later. After what Braxton shared with me yesterday, I understand why she would feel that way.

I hear my phone ding with a message and I can't help but smile. I get the occasional text from Rachel, or Stephen, but I'm already hoping it's from Braxton. A fluttery feeling settles in the pit of my stomach when I see his name on the screen.

Morning. Hope you slept well. I just wanted to thank you for yesterday. I had a great time.

I reply straightaway. *I had an amazing day. Thank you. I'm still smiling.*

My phone beeps again a few moments later. *I'm happy to hear that. I've always loved to see you smile.*

Christine interrupts my thoughts as she places a mug of coffee down in front of me.

Before I get a chance to reply, another message comes through. *I did some research when I got home last night, in regards to those crazy goats. They're called myotonic 'fainting' goats. Apparently, they have a hereditary mutant gene, and when they're excited or startled their muscles stiffen temporarily, causing them to fall over.*

Just thinking about that moment has me giggling. 'What's so funny?' Christine asks.

'Braxton,' I reply. 'He just reminded me of something funny that happened yesterday, that's all.'

I don't go into detail. Christine was very quiet when I got home last night. She usually asks me for the details of my day, but not about my trip to the farm. Clearly hearing anything about her parents is still too raw for her.

'It's good to see you two getting on again.'

I nod my head and sip my coffee. I *am* enjoying my time with him. We're still a long way from where we apparently used to be, but it's not hard to see how I once loved him.

Placing my mug down, I type my reply. *That must've been what happened yesterday when you scared them.*

I only scared them because you made me. His reply makes me laugh. I don't know why I was so scared of some silly goats, but I was.

Thank you for being my knight in shining armour.

His reply comes through almost instantly. *It was my pleasure.* It's quickly followed by another message. *I'm about to head out, I have plans. Enjoy your day.*

You too.

I place my phone back in the pocket of my jacket after replying, and although I'm still smiling, I find myself wondering what his plans are. Apart from the times he takes me to my appointments, or his occasional visits, I have no idea what he does in his own time.

Christine places two plates of scrambled eggs and toast on the table, before taking a seat beside me. 'It was late when you got home last night.'

'It was. It was already dark by the time we left the farm.' I see her squirm in her seat. 'The place looks great. Stephen ... I mean Dad, has been paying someone to look after it.' The way her eyes widen tells me she knew nothing of this. 'Braxton said Dad wants it to be perfect for you when you decide to go back.'

'That's nice of him,' she says, in a clipped tone, 'but he needn't have bothered. I have no intention of going back there.'

In light of what Braxton told me yesterday about Ma's death, I feel like I understand her so much better. *Especially the mood swings.*

'What happened between you and Dad?'

Christine exhales a long breath before standing. 'I don't want to talk about it,' she snaps as she collects her plate and walks towards the sink. She didn't even finish her breakfast.

Although her back is to me, I see her raise her hand to wipe her eyes, and I know she's crying. It's obvious that whatever happened between my parents, she's still hurting because of it.

Rising from my chair, I make my way towards her. Her body stiffens when I slide my arms around her waist from behind.

'Whatever it was, I'm sorry, Mum.' I feel her relax when I rest my cheek against her back. 'And I'm sorry about Ma and Pa.' I feel a lump rise to my throat as I speak, I'm struggling to comprehend it all. I wish I could remember them; well, maybe not those parts, but the good times.

'The past is in the past, and that's where it needs to stay,' she whispers.

I sit out on the back patio enjoying the sunshine for much of the morning. There's been a definite shift in me, and I actually feel gratitude for being alive. I no longer want to lock myself away and hide from the world.

It's Sunday, so I have no place to be. It's weird no longer having a career at my age. I often wonder about it, and what my life was like prior to the accident.

I have left Christine to herself; it's clear she needs some time alone. Braxton had plans, so I will be on my own until Rachel visits this afternoon.

My mind drifts to Braxton. He occupies my thoughts a lot lately. I was surprised at my need to drag out our visit to the farm for as long as I could. I definitely felt a connection to that place, it was beautiful, but I think it had more to do with the company.

Placing my coffee cup down on the small table beside me, I pick up the pile of Braxton's letters and remove the elastic band I've been using to keep them together. I open the first one, starting at the very beginning. I reread them every chance I get. It's all that I have left of my past, and I'm hoping if I read them enough, the memories will become permanently engrained in my mind. They have become my lifeline.

Once the last letter is read, I carefully fold it and place it back in the envelope. A contented sigh falls from my lips as I settle back into my chair. My eyes are focused on the large tree in the yard. It's the only one, so it must be the one that Braxton fell out of. Suddenly I'm curious.

I walk towards it and look up into the branches above. It's far too high for me to climb. Without thinking, I turn and head straight for the garage. I remember seeing a large extendable ladder resting up against the wall one day when I wandered in there. I carefully lift it and lay it down on the concrete floor. It's much heavier than I anticipated. I try to be quiet as I pick it up and carry it to the yard. If Christine discovers what I'm doing, she's likely to blow a gasket. Her overprotectiveness isn't lost on me. In all fairness, I'd probably be the same if it was my child.

Laying it out on the grass, it takes me a few minutes to figure out how to extend it to full height, before locking it into place. A small groan escapes me as I haul it up and manoeuvre it against the trunk of the tree.

I make sure it's securely fixed in place before I start to climb. I feel none of the crippling fear that Braxton mentioned in his letter. Heights obviously aren't something I'm afraid of. The higher I get, the more disappointed I become. So far I've seen nothing engraved into the trunk. There's still a lot of tree above, and I've almost reached the top of the ladder.

That's when I notice the broken branch. It's about a metre above my head. Butterflies flutter in my stomach as I climb one more step and slowly make the transition from the ladder to the large branch that sits below the broken one. I hope it can hold my weight.

It would have made more sense to just ask Braxton what he carved into the tree, but I feel compelled to see it with my own eyes. *I was carving my heart into that trunk. My deepest, darkest secret.* I need to know what that was.

My fingernails dig into the bark as I get my footing right before stretching my body upwards. At first I don't see it, but then I notice a heart that has blended into the bark over the years. Engraved within this heart are letters and a word: *BS loves JR.* The sight of it touches me deeply.

He voiced it out loud not long after I got out of hospital, which made me feel extremely uncomfortable, but things have changed between us since then. Our renewed friendship is starting to blossom.

I'm not sure if it's because the young Braxton took the time to do this despite his crippling fear of heights. Or maybe I'm just scared that I'll never feel the things I once did, and won't get to experience that once-in-a-lifetime love again. Nevertheless, I'm completely overcome by my emotions. I slide my arms around the tree, hugging it with all my might, and I do something I haven't done since I woke from my coma. I sob my heart out.

———

'Hi, Dad,' I say when he rises from his chair and kisses my cheek. He called me last night and invited me to lunch. It worked out well, because Braxton dropped me off after my physio and I didn't have to hurt Stephen's feelings by telling him Christine doesn't want him anywhere near the house.

'Hi, pumpkin. You look well.'

I find myself smiling at his pet name for me. I wouldn't have known that if it wasn't for the letters.

'Thank you. I feel great.'

Well, a lot better than I used to feel, anyway. I have the will to live now, and as much as I yearn to be the person I once was, I'm beginning to come to terms with the fact that may never happen. But it doesn't mean I have to stop living, or that I can't enjoy the future that lies ahead. I'm already starting to make new memories.

'How's rehab going?'

'Really well. Starting next week, I only have to go two days instead of five.'

'That's wonderful news.'

It *is* wonderful news, but there is a part of me that's disappointed, because it means I might not get to see Braxton every day.

'How are things going at the bank?'

'Great . . . busy.'

I smile before speaking again. 'Can I ask you a favour?'

'Sure. Anything,' he replies.

I reach into my bag and pull out the envelope that contains my memory bracelet and charms. 'Could you attach these for me?' I open the flap and tip them out into the palm of my hand to show him. 'I don't have the tools to do it myself.'

'I can certainly do that for you,' he says.

I had thought about asking Braxton to do it, but I want to see the look on his face when he notices it on my wrist.

'There's a list inside the envelope with the order I need them in. Hopefully I'll have more to add to it. Can we leave room for them?'

'Anything you want, pumpkin.' Again, I smile when he calls me that. 'Where are these charms from?'

'Braxton.'

He nods his head as he takes the envelope from me, placing it in the pocket of his suit jacket. 'Are you ready to order?'

'I am. I'm starved.'

'Me too,' he says smiling. 'I've taken an extended lunch break, so there's no rush. Spending time with my little girl is more important.'

I pick up the menu off the table, and suddenly the number of choices makes me anxious.

'The club sandwiches here are delicious,' Stephen says in a kind voice.

'That sounds great.' I place the menu down on the table. 'I'll have one of those.' I have no idea what a club sandwich is, but I'll take my chances.

'Braxton took me out to the farm on the weekend,' I say once our order is placed. 'Thank you for keeping up with the maintenance on the property, that's really nice of you.'

'There's nothing I wouldn't do for your mother,' he says simply. 'Or for you.'

I look down at the white linen tablecloth as I ponder my next words. This seems like the perfect opportunity to ask what I've been dying to know. 'You can tell me to mind my own business, but what happened between you two?'

My father clears his throat, as his gaze moves down to the table. I'm suddenly unsure if I'm ready for his response, but there's a part of me that needs to know. I don't understand how all this bitterness can have come from what was once a wonderful marriage.

'There's no easy way to say it, I suppose.' He pauses, then sighs. 'I cheated on your mother.'

I have no control over the gasp that falls from my lips. 'You *what*?' I feel my eyes widen as I speak.

'I'm sorry you have to go through all this again. It was bad enough I broke your mother's heart, but I broke yours as well. You didn't speak to me for more than a month afterwards. The past few years have been tough on us all.'

'What happened?'

'I have no excuse for what I did, but for you to fully understand, it's best I start at the beginning.'

My head is spinning as I wait for him to continue. *Poor Christine.*

He tugs at the tie around his neck, loosening it slightly. 'Your mum was devastated after her father died, and rightly so, but to lose both her parents in such a close proximity was unimaginable.' I slide my hands off the table and place them on my lap. 'When we arrived at the farm after her mother's death, she was inconsolable. To the point she was admitted into hospital and sedated.'

I watch him, unsure what I can say.

'Seeing the woman I love like that was hard,' he continued. 'So hard.'

'If you loved her so much, how could you cheat on her?'

He bows his head before answering. 'The weeks, months—and *year* that followed were hard. The death of your grandparents changed your mother. She fell into a deep depression. She no longer smiled, she hardly ate, or slept for that matter, and over time she totally shut me out. She shut us all out.' He pauses and runs his hand over his face. 'She refused to get help. I never stopped loving her, but you need to understand that it was hard for me too. You were already living with Braxton. I felt incredibly alone.'

'So, you found someone else to give you what you weren't getting at home?' My words come out more aggressively than intended, but it appears he abandoned my mother when she needed him most.

'No. It wasn't like that. Karen was my secretary. She'd been working for me for over fifteen years. She noticed the shift in me . . . I think everyone did, I was miserable. After a lot of persuasion, she finally convinced me to open up. Truth is, I needed someone to talk to . . . I certainly couldn't talk to your mother. We ended up developing a close friendship. That's all it was. That is until one night we went out for drinks after work.' He exhales, and I don't like where this is heading. 'We shared a cab home. The driver dropped her off first, so I walked her to the door . . . I ended up kissing her goodnight. It wasn't just a peck, either.'

'I see.' I can't seem to hide my disappointment. 'And?'

'And that's it. She invited me in, and I told her no. That kiss was a mistake. I loved your mother, I still do. I left immediately and the guilt I felt on the way home ate away at me. Your mother had moved out of our bedroom a few months earlier. She'd been sleeping in your old room. That night I tossed and turned, and in the morning I confessed everything. Your mother was upset, with good reason. She slapped me across the face and then told me to leave.'

I take a few moments to let his words settle in. 'So, you only kissed her? It never went further than that?'

'No. But that was bad enough.' When his voice cracks it makes my heart hurt. I don't condone what he did, but in a way I understand it. 'I made the biggest mistake of my life, and lost the best thing that had ever happened to me in the process.'

'Oh, Dad.' Reaching across the table, I cover his hand with mine.

'I miss her so much,' he confesses, bowing his head and wiping his eyes with the back of his hand.

He's hurting just as much as she is. I may not know a lot about either of them, but any fool can see that they're miserable without each other.

My father offers to drive me home after our long lunch, but I opt to take the bus. One, because I don't want to upset Christine by having him near the house, and two, because I need time to digest everything he told me. I don't know how, but I'm going to find a way for my parents to at least communicate. Stephen said after she kicked him out she refused to talk to him. I'm not taking sides—I sympathise with them both—but I think it's time for them to forgive and move forward. Life is too short.

By the time I step off the bus, I decide not to say anything yet. I need time to think it through and come up with a plan.

'You're home late,' Christine says when I walk through the front door.

'I decided to stay in town for a while.'

'That's good. Would you like a sandwich?'

'No, I've already eaten,' I reply as I follow her into the kitchen.

'This came for you earlier,' she says with a smile, picking up a letter and passing it to me.

Leaning forward, I kiss her cheek. Surprise lights her eyes. I feel for her even more after my lunch with Stephen today.

She's been through some hard times. First losing her parents, then her husband . . . in a way she probably feels like she's lost her only child as well.

'Thank you,' I say, holding up the letter, but my gratitude for her runs far deeper than just that.

LETTER SIX . . .

Dearest Jemma,

The fourth of July 2004. It was school holidays, and this would mark our last extended stay at your grandparents' house. By the time the next school holidays rolled around later that year, you would be working in your first part-time job. But we didn't know that then.

July meant it was winter, and the first few days of our holiday at the farm brought rain. We spent it mostly playing board games and helping Ma bake sweets. She made us her official taste testers, and she had no complaints from me. You could say I've always had a sweet tooth.

The rain finally eased by day three, so we got up early and spent an hour out in the garden catching worms. When we were done, we grabbed our fishing rods—Ma and Pa had given them to us the previous Christmas—and headed to the river. I always loved that you weren't afraid to pick up the worms and bait your own hook, like most girls were. Actually, there wasn't much that frightened you.

The ground was muddy that day from all the rain, so Pa advised us not to take Tilly-Girl with us. You were disappointed because you'd been eager to ride her, so we took the long way down to the river, via her paddock, so you could see her.

Pa would leave his white wooden rowboat down by the bank for us during our stay. It was far too cold to swim, so we got plenty of use out of it during the winter months. You would help me overturn it and push it into the river. I would roll up my pants before stepping into the near-freezing water, and piggyback you from the shore to the boat so you didn't get wet.

We would row to our usual spot and drop the anchor. Some days we sat there for hours and didn't catch a thing, but other times we did really well. If we managed to bring home some trout, Pa would clean up our catch, and Ma would cook them up in a scrumptious lemon butter sauce for our dinner.

This particular day proved to be one of the slower ones. We'd been down there for a few hours and hadn't even got a bite.

'Holy crap,' you blurted out suddenly, jumping to your feet. 'Did you see that?'

'Easy there,' I replied, trying to settle the boat as it rocked violently from side to side.

'Pass me the net!'

'Have you caught something?'

'No, but I think I just saw the Loch Ness Monster.'

I laughed when you squealed with excitement. 'You're crazy. There's no such thing.'

'I'm not lying, Braxton. I just saw it.'

'You might have seen something, but it wasn't that.'

'I saw it, goddamn you,' you snapped, flicking your foot out, connecting it with my shin. Your tone made me chuckle, which only seemed to annoy you more. 'Oh my god, we're going to be famous. We'll be on the news and everything.'

I hadn't doubted that you saw something, but I knew it wasn't what you thought.

'There it is again!' you squealed. This time you didn't bother asking me for the net, you turned in haste and grabbed it for yourself. How you possibly thought you could catch a giant creature of the deep in such a small net was beyond me, but I let you go. You were as stubborn as hell when you set your mind to something, and you wouldn't have listened to me anyway.

I stuck my head over the side of the boat and saw that your so-called monster was actually a platypus skimming along the surface of the water.

You lunged forward in an attempt to scoop it into your net. It wasn't your wisest move. It not only sent the boat toppling over, it threw us both into the freezing water.

I broke the surface first, and my head darted from side to side as I searched for you.

'Jemma!' I called out at the top of my voice. 'Jemma, where are you?'

I was about to dive back under to search for you when you emerged. You were gasping for air and your lips had already turned a light shade of blue.

I swam the few strokes to reach you, sliding my arm around your waist. 'The rods!' you cried as I manoeuvred you towards the bank.

'I'll go back for them.' My first priority was you. Your entire body was shivering when we finally made it to dry land. I'm sure I was as well, but I can't remember because I was too worried about you. 'You need to get up to the house and out of these wet clothes. I'll come back for the rods.'

'Okay.' Your teeth were chattering and your movements were slow, so I scooped you into my arms and started to jog. I only made it a few metres when I slipped in some mud, sending us both tumbling to the ground.

Under any other circumstances, we both would have laughed our heads off, but the cold wind wasn't doing us any favours. My concern for you was only escalating.

Surprisingly, there was no stern lecture from your grandparents when we finally made it back to the farmhouse. Only concern. They took us into separate rooms and ordered us to strip out of our wet, muddy clothes before wrapping us up in blankets. Pa sat us down in front of the open fireplace in the main room, while Ma rushed to the kitchen to make us large mugs of hot cocoa.

Pa went down to the river and retrieved the boat and fished out our rods, which he found further downstream.

Not a word was spoken about it again, but Ma made us stay indoors for the next few days to make sure we hadn't caught a cold from our misadventure. My admiration for them only grew stronger after that day. They really were amazing people.

The night before we were due to go home, Ma cooked us up a huge feast. I could tell she loved having us stay there. She always got a little teary when it was time for us to go home.

Afterwards, we moved out to the front verandah. Ma placed Pa's colourful crocheted blanket over his lap before taking a seat beside him. I watched on with a smile as he reached for her hand and wrapped it in his own. When she smiled back at him, I could clearly see the love reflecting in her eyes.

It was a chilly night, but there wasn't a cloud in the sky, so we opted to lie on the grass instead. Well, actually, in winter we lay on a tarp because the ground was cold and damp. You had your pink crocheted blanket, and I had my blue one.

'There's so many stars in the sky tonight,' you said.

'Mmm. You don't see this many in the city.'

'Oh my god, did you see that light that just flashed across the sky?' you said, suddenly more alert.

'Yep, a shooting star.'

'Oh. I always wondered what a shooting star would look like.'

'You need to make a wish,' I said. 'You always wish on a shooting star.'

'I wish . . .' You paused briefly and I wanted to tell you that you couldn't say aloud what you wish for, otherwise it won't come true. At the time I didn't believe that anyway, but now I'm not so sure. 'I wish that you were my forever boy, Braxton Spencer.'

You slid your hand under my blanket and laced your fingers through mine. When you turned your face in my direction, our eyes locked, and the way you looked at me was different from all the *other times. It made my heart race, because if I wasn't mistaken, it was the exact same look that Ma had given Pa minutes earlier.*

For me, it was a moment that held more questions than answers. Was it possible that we could ever be more than just best friends? I knew you loved me, because you'd told me, but it gave me hope that maybe, just maybe, you loved me in the way I secretly loved you.

I tightened my grip on your hand, as a ray of hope ignited within me. 'I wish that too, Jem.'

What we had is far too beautiful to be forgotten.

Your forever boy,

Braxton

I sigh as I clutch the letter to my chest. Does he even realise how wonderful these letters are? I love how he signed this one with, *your forever boy*. I'm not sure what lies ahead for us, but I do know I need him to be a part of my life.

My wish may have ignited a ray of hope in his heart on that day, and that's exactly what his words seem to be doing for me. My wish on my first falling star had similarities to my most recent one. You'd think I would have wished for my memory to return, but I didn't. I wished that I could love Braxton again, as deeply as I once did.

I pull out my phone and search for Stephen's number, so I can send him a text. *Can we meet for lunch again tomorrow, or one day this week? I have two more charms for you to add to my bracelet.*

I open my palm and smile down at the tiny fisherman in a boat, and the silver shooting star.

TWENTY

Braxton

Bella-Rose is absolutely not what I expect when I walk into the animal shelter. I tell Diane, the manager, that I want a male, a bigger dog, easy to train. Maybe something with short hair, low maintenance. A good companion to keep me company on those lonely nights.

The dog cowering before me is none of these things. She is a small white Jack Russell with tanned patches and large, brown, pleading eyes. She looks frightened, confused, and alone—just like Jemma the day she woke from her coma.

As soon as I see her in the kennels, my heart tells me she's the one. I have never been an impulsive person, but this dog looks lonely and afraid, which is exactly how I feel.

'Hey girl,' I say, crouching down so as not to intimidate her. 'There's nothing to be afraid of. I won't hurt you.' I speak in a soft soothing tone as I extend my arm towards her. She's hesitant at first, but then to my surprise she takes a few steps towards me, sniffing my outstretched hand and then licking one of my fingers. 'That's a good girl,' I say as I stroke my hand gently across the top of her head, making her tail wag.

'We got her yesterday,' Diane tells me. 'Her owner passed away and there was nobody else to take her. Poor little girl.

She's been like that ever since she arrived. She probably doesn't know what's going on. But,' she adds with a hopeful smile, 'maybe now she's found a new home?'

I smile in return.

When we arrive back at the house, I place her down on the front lawn and give her a few minutes to explore. At least we have a fence out here, so she can spend her days outside when I'm at work.

Bella-Rose barks at Samson when we move inside and I introduce them. She hovers under my feet from the moment I put her down. It'll probably take her some time to settle in, but I have every confidence that she will.

I set up her bed near the back glass windows that overlook the ocean, and fill her bowl with water. There's some leftover barbecue chicken in the fridge, so I chop it up and make myself a chicken sandwich for lunch, and give the rest to Bella-Rose. She practically inhales it, and I'm so pleased to see her eat. It gives me hope that she's as happy to be here as I am to have her.

'Do you want to go for a walk along the beach, girl?' I ask, holding out the hot-pink lead I bought her. The way she bounces around with excitement makes me laugh. It looks like she has springs in her feet.

As ever, my thoughts are on Jemma. I miss her, and I wish I had an excuse to go over and visit. My feet are propped on the coffee table, and Bella-Rose has perched herself on my lap. The television is on, but I'm not really watching it.

I'm happy that Jemma's trips to the rehab will be less frequent—that means she's improving—but at the same time I'm gutted, because it means I will see her just a few times a week. I don't see enough of her as it is. There's a gaping hole in my heart that only she can fill. Part of me is missing . . . the best part . . . *her*.

I would love to call or go around to Christine's and see Jemma face to face, but at the same time I want to give her the space she needs, so I send her a text.

Hi.

It's such a lame message. I have so much I want to say—I always do—but I force myself to continue with baby steps. When she's ready for more she'll let me know.

I don't expect a reply, but that doesn't stop me from hoping for one. My wish is granted a few seconds later when my phone dings. *Hi. How are you?*

I'm good. How are you?

I'm good too. I've just bitten the bullet and found the courage to ask Christine if she has any photos of Ma and Pa.

And?

I wait for her reply, but instead of a text, my phone starts to ring. I'm smiling like a fool when I answer it. 'Hey.'

'Hi,' she replies in the sweet voice I miss so much. 'I thought it would be easier if I just called you. It takes me forever to type a response.' She pauses and I hear her let out an exasperated breath. 'I'm still trying to get used to this damn thing. You don't mind me calling, do you?'

'Not at all. You can call me anytime, you know that. So, what did Christine say?'

'She's gone upstairs to get them.' I can hear the excitement in her voice. 'After everything you told me the other day, I was hesitant to ask. I understand now why there's no photos of them in the house. It's obviously a painful reminder for her.'

'Yeah. It's a shame, but we all do what we need to do to cope, I suppose.'

'What are you doing now?' she asks. 'Rachel bailed on me. She had to go back to the hotel for a video conference with a client in New York.'

'Nothing much, why?' I inwardly hope her question is leading to an invitation to come over.

'You should come over and look at them with us. Christine said she has a box of stuff upstairs. Umm ... that's only if you want to. No pressure. I'm sure you're busy. I just ... umm ... I know how much you cared for them.'

Her nervous babble makes me smile. Doesn't she realise wild horses couldn't keep me away? Not only do I get to see her, but I would love to reminisce about Ma and Pa. They were like grandparents to me as well, and I hate how taboo this subject has been since their deaths.

'I'd love to.'

'Really?'

'Yes.' *I'd do anything to see you*, I want to add, but I don't. Not expressing how we truly feel is something we haven't done since we were kids, so it's taking some getting used to.

'Great. We'll wait until you get here before we start. I'm a little worried how Christine is going to take it all.'

I agree, it could go either way, but it's time she started to remember the good times and stop focusing on the bad. That's the only way I'm surviving my situation with Jem.

I leave Bella-Rose happily munching on a rawhide bone, and within half an hour I pull into Christine's driveway.

'Hi,' Jemma whispers when she answers the door.

'Hi.' God, it's good to see her.

She moves to the side allowing me to enter. 'Christine's in the lounge room.'

'Why are we whispering?' I ask with a curious smirk.

She shrugs before answering. 'I'm not sure if this is a good idea. She's gone really quiet, and is just staring at the box on the table like it's about to jump out and bite her.'

'This is a good thing, Jem. Yes, she might get upset, but I think it will do her the world of good to remember the positive times, and stop focusing on the negative ones.'

'You know, you're right.' The corners of her lips curve up into a smile. 'I'm glad you're here.'

She reaches out and places her hand on my arm. One simple touch from her has the ability to awaken every last nerve ending in my body.

'Hi, Christine,' I say as I enter the lounge room, making my way towards her. Jemma was right, she does look frightened.

'Hi.'

She remains seated when I come to a stop in front of her, so I lean down and kiss her cheek.

'I might make us all a coffee before we start,' Jemma says, rubbing her hands together nervously.

'Sounds great. Do you want a hand?'

'No. I can manage.' She gives me a tight smile before turning and leaving the room.

'How are you?' I ask Christine, taking a seat beside her.

'I'm not sure if I can do this,' she says quietly.

'You know you can.' I place my hand over the top of hers. 'It's time. Your parents wouldn't want this. They'd want you to remember the good times, and there were so many good times.'

She turns her face towards me and I see the tears glistening in her eyes. I can sympathise with what she's going through, I lost a parent as well. In a way, I've lost them both. I don't think I'll ever truly get over my mother's death, but trying not to focus on that dreadful day, and instead remembering all that we were, has helped me live on.

'There were so many good times,' she agrees, with the beginnings of a smile.

'Don't just do this for Jem, do it for yourself. Hold onto those wonderful memories because that's all you have now. It helps . . . I know.'

'You're right.'

I remove my hand from hers, and she leans forward, reaching for the large chocolate-coloured, leather-bound box on the table. She takes a deep breath, as she slowly removes the lid.

'My mother gave me this box the night before she died. I think she already knew that she was leaving us to be with my father. She handed it to me just before she went to bed. *I want you to have this,* was all she said. She hugged me so tight and told me how much she loved me. I didn't suspect for a moment it would be the last time I'd ever hear her say those words to me.' She places the lid down beside the box, and wipes the tears from her eyes. 'I have no idea what's in here. I've never looked inside.'

'Well, maybe it's time that you did. She gave it to you for a reason.'

'You've started without me?' Jemma says, entering the room carrying a large wooden tray with the coffees and a plate of biscuits on board.

'Let me help you.' Standing, I meet her halfway and take the tray out of her hands.

'I baked the cookies last night. They probably don't hold a candle to Mrs Gardener's, but I hope you like them.'

I'm so touched I barely manage to sound normal when I reply. 'I'm sure they'll be delicious.'

I carefully place the tray on the table, and Jemma passes one of the coffees to Christine. 'Here you go, Mum.' I notice mine has milk in it as well, but again I don't have the heart to tell her. 'This one is yours,' she says to me.

'Thank you.' I reach for a cookie before taking my seat beside Christine, and Jemma moves around to the other side of her. I dunk the cookie in the coffee for a few seconds before bringing it to my mouth. 'Mmm.' When my gaze moves to Jemma, I find her watching me intently. 'They're yum.'

She gives me a bashful smile before taking a sip of her coffee. 'Do you always dunk your food into your drinks?' She pulls a funny face, like it's a weird habit to have. Little does she know she was the one who taught me that trick.

'Don't knock it until you try it.' They were the exact same words she said to me all those years ago.

She shrugs before leaning forward and picking up a cookie. She was never one to shy away from trying new things. I loved that about her.

I forget to mention the part about not leaving the cookie in for too long. I can't help but laugh when she pulls it out and half of it is missing. The look on her face is priceless. Her eyes widen and her forehead scrunches up and she looks down into the coffee mug.

'There's a two-second rule. Any longer and you run the risk of having it turn to a gooey mush and sink to the bottom of the cup.'

'Oh.'

The sweet giggle that falls from her mouth is like music to my ears. She always had a great sense of humour.

Christine finally makes the move and lifts out a pile of photographs from the box. The one on top is a black-and-white image of a younger Ma and Pa. They're holding a baby in their arms; presumably Christine. A small strangled sob escapes Christine, as her finger lightly runs over the image. It's the first time I've seen a picture of Ma and Pa in their youth. They're a handsome couple. Jemma leans forward and gives me a small smile when we both automatically place a hand on each of Christine's legs for comfort.

'Tell me about them,' Jemma says as Christine flips through the images before passing them on to us. 'What was your life like growing up?'

'I have very fond memories of my childhood.'

Again, Jemma leans forward and looks at me. I wonder if she's thinking about our childhood memories—the ones I've written about in the letters.

'This is your grandfather,' Christine says, holding up a picture of a young Pa in his army uniform. 'He served in World War Two. That's where he met my mother. There should be a photo of her in here. I remember seeing it when I was young.' She shuffles through the images until she finds what she's looking for. 'Here it is. She was a nurse with the Red Cross.'

'I know her,' Jemma says, taking it out of Christine's hand before I get a chance to see it. 'I remember her from the hospital.'

'That's impossible. This photo was taken more than forty years before you were even born.' She leans over and takes the image from her daughter's hand. I see a smile cross her face as she stares down at the photograph. 'She had a smile that would light up a room . . . I miss her so much.' She passes the photo to me. 'Here's another one of her during wartime.'

'It's her, it's definitely her,' Jemma whispers.

'Impossible,' Christine replies in a dismissive tone. 'As I said, you weren't even born when these were taken. This was during the Second World War.'

Ignoring her mother, Jemma turns her attention to me. 'Can you remember ever seeing this nurse at the hospital?' She passes me the other photograph. 'She worked the nightshift, and she'd hold my hand and sing to me. You remember her, don't you?'

The hopeful look on her face tugs at my heart, but I have to tell her the truth. 'No. I can't honestly say I do.'

'Of course you don't,' Christine snaps, standing and leaving the room. My eyes move back to Jemma and I see her bite her bottom lip to try and hide the quiver.

Reaching out, I grab hold of her hand.

'I'm not lying,' she whispers.

TWENTY-ONE

Jemma

The moment I'm seated in Braxton's car, I pull out the diary that I stashed in my handbag. I sat up half the night going through the rest of the box. It all became a bit too much for Christine in the end, so she went to bed and left me to it.

'What's that?' Braxton asks.

'Ma's diary. She wrote it during the war.'

'Wow.'

'I want to read you a small passage from it. It's from the day she met Pa—May seventeenth, 1941. It just proves I'm not imagining things.

> *It has been over a week since I've had a chance to sit down and write. I am both physically and mentally exhausted. The days seem to be getting longer, and the casualties are growing at an alarming rate. One thing I've learned from my time here in England is that war is senseless. Beds line the corridors due to the lack of space in the wards, and if this continues it won't be long until we're completely out of room. I pray this never happens.*

I've made it my mission not to become attached to my patients, but in one particular case I'm afraid I have failed.

Private Albert Griggs was unconscious when he arrived three days ago, and I was assigned to help one of the doctors attend to his wounds. I was putting pressure on the large gash in his forehead when he first opened his eyes.

'Are you an angel?' he asked as his large brown eyes focused on me. 'You are so beautiful, just how I imagined an angel would look.'

'I'm a nurse at the hospital.'

'Then I'm not dead?'

'No, you're very much alive. You were injured in a mortar attack, but you're in good hands. Doctor Adams is one of the best.'

His face lit up as he reached for my hand, moments before losing consciousness again.

His isn't the first hand I have held. There have been many occasions where I have tried to comfort soldiers when they were afraid or in pain, or those dreadful moments when I know they won't survive their injuries. Holding someone's hand when they take their last breath is a feeling I don't think I will ever fully recover from.

There's something different about Private Griggs. A light flutter settled in the pit of my stomach as he gripped my hand. That has never happened to me before.

In the days that followed, I felt drawn to him. Some of my quieter moments were spent by his bedside. He was still unconscious, but I held his hand, just like that first day, and sang to him; and as he gripped my hand that same flutter returned.

'That's exactly what she did with me, Braxton,' I say, looking up from the dairy. 'She held my hand and sang to me. You believe me, don't you?'

Braxton's eyes widen slightly before he speaks. 'Do you think there's a chance that you dreamed it? I dreamed about my mum once, years after she died.'

'I don't know. Maybe. But it felt so real.' In my heart I want to believe it was more than just that. I feel like I got to know a part of my grandparents that even the old me didn't, and it brings me a sense of peace. 'How would I know she used to sing to Pa?'

'I have no explanation for that, Jem. Maybe it's a story you were told as a child.'

I shrug. 'Possibly.'

'If it's any consolation, the dream I had about my mum seemed realistic. And it comforted me.'

'Believing that Ma came to me gives me comfort too.'

He reaches across the centre console and places his hand on my leg, which reassures me. 'Then that's all that matters, Jem.'

His words make me smile, though just moments later my mood sours when Braxton's phone rings and I listen to the message played back via voicemail.

'Hi, Braxton. It's Diane.' Right away I find myself wondering who she is. 'I'm just checking in to see how things are going with Bella-Rose. You two really seemed to hit it off the other day. If you could call me back when you get a chance, that'd be great.'

'Bella-Rose?' I have so many questions, but that's all I manage to say.

His eyes dart to me briefly before focusing back on the road. 'I've been lonely without you,' he says quietly, and my heart sinks.

I know I am the one who has kept him at arm's length, but hearing his words hurts so much. I have an immediate dislike for Bella-Rose, whoever she is.

I'm thankful when we pull into the car park at the rehabilitation centre a few minutes later, because I feel like I'm on the verge of tears, which is stupid. I've been wondering what he does in his spare time; now I know.

The logical side of me knows it's unfair of me to expect him to wait around until I'm ready. I don't even know if I'll ever be ready, but right now I can't even process all the emotions I'm experiencing: hurt, sadness, jealousy, disappointment and confusion. In one tiny moment my entire world has come crashing in around me.

'There's no point in you hanging around,' I say, when he turns off the ignition and unbuckles his seatbelt. 'I have plans this afternoon anyway.'

His brow furrows at my response. 'That's fine. I can take you wherever you need to go when we're done here.'

'There's no need.' I can't even make eye contact with him as I reach for the door handle. 'Thanks for the lift, though. Have a great day.'

'Hey.' He reaches out and wraps his hand around my elbow. 'Is everything okay, Jemma?'

I glance at him over my shoulder and see the confusion on his face.

'Everything is fine,' I lie, forcing out a smile. 'I'll see you later, okay?'

'Okay. I'll pick you up Friday morning, but hopefully I'll see you before then.' *I doubt it*, is my first thought. 'If you need anything in the meantime, just call.'

I nod and then quickly climb out of the car and hurry towards the building. I'll text him tonight and let him know I'll catch a bus to my appointments from now on.

Two days pass, and I've had no contact with Braxton. Well, he has called and texted me a few times—he even came to the house yesterday, but I pretended I was asleep when Christine came up to my room—but I have ignored him at all costs. I feel dreadful for it, but it's just easier this way.

He has more than done his part in helping me on my road to recovery. It's time I cut him loose and let him live the life he deserves. *A life without me.* Why does the thought of that make me want to cry?

I hear footsteps coming up the stairs, so I quickly lie down and turn my back to the door. Christine has noticed the change in me, and I can tell she's worried. I've reverted back to my old way of coping . . . hiding away from the rest of the world. Things were just moving too fast, I guess. I got swept up in the whirlwind of it all before coming crashing back down to reality, and suffering a massive blow to the heart in the process.

'Jemma, it's me,' I hear Rachel say from the other side of the door. 'Are you awake?'

I roll over onto my back before finally sitting up. I have been avoiding her as well, but I can't continue like this. I need to talk to someone, and she's all I really have. Burdening Christine with my problems isn't an option. She's going through far too much of her own at the moment.

'Yes, I'm awake. Come in.'

'Hey,' she says, opening the door and popping her head in. 'I was beginning to think you were avoiding me.'

I shrug as I cross my legs in front of me. 'I've been avoiding everyone.'

She sits down on the edge of the bed. 'Is everything okay?' When she places her hand on my leg, I raise my gaze to meet hers. 'Jesus,' she says when she sees the tears in my eyes. Without hesitating, she pulls me into her arms. 'What's going on? Talk to me.'

I'm not about to admit that I am devastated by the thought of Braxton and what's-her-face . . . Bella-Rose. What sort of a name is that anyway? Pulling back, I wipe my eyes. 'I guess everything is getting a bit too much. I thought I was doing fine, but it's obvious I'm not.'

'I understand this is hard for you, but you were really starting to make some progress. Don't take a step back ... you need to keep moving forward.'

'Easier said than done.' I sigh before continuing. 'I don't even know who I am anymore.'

'And you're never going to find that out while you're locked away in this room sulking.' Her words sometimes come out harsh, but she's straight to the point and that's what I love about her, and it's what I need right now. 'The Jemma I know is a fighter. She's kick-arse. She never lets anything pull her down.'

'You say that like it's not a big thing. How would you feel if you lost everything? Not just your memory, but your entire life. Your husband, your parents, your friends, your home, your career ... *everything*. I've lost it all.'

'That's the thing. You haven't lost any of that. Your memory, yes ... and your job, but that's no great loss, your boss was an arsehole. But as for the rest, we're all still here. And we're not going anywhere. I know this is huge. I do. Just give it some time, it will all eventually work itself out.'

'I hope so.'

Rachel leans back and looks me over with a burgeoning smile. 'You know what you need?'

'What?'

'A girls' night out. Just the two of us. It'll be like old times. We can do dinner, and maybe go dancing afterwards. You love to dance.'

'Do I?' It feels weird that I don't know this.

'Yes. You kind of suck at it, but you love it nevertheless.'

'I don't suck,' I say, slapping her leg, and she laughs. 'Do I really suck?'

'Well, put it this way: the first time we went out dancing together, I actually thought you were having a seizure.'

'What?' I screech.

'I'm kidding,' she replies as she grabs hold of her stomach and falls back on the bed. When a loud boisterous laugh erupts from deep in her throat, I reach out and slap her again.

'You bitch.'

My comment only makes her laugh harder, and as much as I try not to join her, it's infectious.

When we finally get our emotions under control, she assures me my dancing isn't as bad as she made out—though the fact that she seems to be suppressing a smile when she says this makes me sceptical.

'So, Saturday night . . . it's a date, right? Dinner, dancing and lots of fun.'

'The jury is still out on the dancing part, but yes, I'd love to come.'

'I almost forgot, Christine asked me to give you this.' She pulls a letter out of the back pocket of her jeans, and I recognise Braxton's handwriting straightaway. The usual excitement I feel when I get one of his letters isn't present this time round. Maybe because I'm still hurting, or maybe it's because this time I'm unsure what it's going to contain. Is it about my past—our past—or is it a letter wishing me a nice life so he can run off into the sunset with Bella-Rose?

'Thanks,' I say, taking it from her and placing it on my bedside table. I'm certainly not going to open it in front of her . . . I'm not sure if I'm going to open it at all.

LETTER SEVEN . . .

Dearest Jemma,

The seventeenth of September 2004. It was a day of mixed emotions for me. There was a bounce in my step as we climbed off the school bus that afternoon. It was a Friday afternoon, after all, and that meant I had you to myself for the entire weekend. Since you'd become my neighbour, they were my favourite days of the week.

Your mum had drinks and snacks waiting for us when we arrived home. I was old enough to look after myself by now—I was almost sixteen—but I still went to your house every day after school. My father was still working late, so I would also stay for dinner, and Christine would make him up a plate for when he got home. Four years had passed since my mother's death, yet your mum still looked after us both.

You and I were sitting at the kitchen table getting our homework out of the way when the call came in. Your mother answered it.

'It's for you,' she whispered, placing her hand over the receiver. 'I think it's him.'

That immediately got my attention.

'Oh my god!' you squealed, jumping up from your chair and hurrying to take the phone. Who the hell was 'him'? I was totally confused, and I'll admit, a little angry. If I was honest, though, it was more jealousy than anything. I wasn't prepared to share you with another guy. 'Hello? . . . Yes, this is Jemma . . . Uh huh . . . Really? . . . Yes, I'd love that.' The one-sided conversation was doing nothing for my rising blood pressure. 'Okay, of course . . . No, I'm free tomorrow.'

Your eyes darted to me, and I am pretty sure I was scowling.

The smile on your pretty face was huge as your gaze moved back to your mother, I'm surprised it didn't split in two. Seeing you happy was one of my favourite things, but I was learning fast that this wasn't the case if the cause of your happiness involved a male other than me. Well, unless it was your father, or mine, or Pa, or even old man Jenkins from the newsagent . . . he was funny and always made us laugh with his wacky sense of humour.

I didn't mind seeing any of these men in your life make you smile, but this . . . this I minded, a lot.

I stop reading, and rest the letter on my lap. I can relate to everything he was feeling in that moment, because that's exactly how I felt listening to his message from Diane. There's a part of me that doesn't want to hear what happens next, or who I'm talking to on the phone. I don't want it to be a boy. I don't want anyone to come between our friendship, which is crazy. This letter was about our past, so whoever it was, it has already happened. There's not a damn thing I can do to change it.

You hung up the phone and squealed so loudly my ears rang. 'He wants to see me tomorrow.'

I sat there stunned when you leaped into your mother's arms. 'That's wonderful news, sweetheart,' she said. 'I'm so happy for you.'

'Who wants to see you tomorrow?'

I have never been a violent person, but I was already gearing up to rip him apart.

'Mr Jefferies,' you replied. 'He owns the ice-cream parlour in town.'

'What! He's old. Like, pushing fifty.' My tone was abrupt.

'Fifty isn't old,' Christine piped in, but neither of us paid her any attention.

'So! What does his age have to do with it?'

I had no answer for that. To be honest, I was confused. I was certain you were going to mention one of the guys from school, or at the very least, someone our age. So, Mr Jefferies kind of threw me.

I couldn't blame other guys for wanting you. You were beautiful—to me you were the prettiest girl in the school, and I knew I wasn't the only one who thought that.

'I applied for a job there. Just over the summer . . . and I got it. He wants me to come in for training tomorrow.'

You scrunched your hands up in front of you as your body bounced with excitement, and my anger was quickly replaced by hurt. I couldn't wrap my head around the fact that you had kept this from me. We used to tell each other everything.

'You what?'

'I got a job. Aren't you happy for me?'

Happy is not the word I would have used. Hurt, pissed off maybe, but definitely not happy. I slammed my textbook shut and rose from the table in such a hurry, my chair toppled over and fell to the floor.

'Braxton, wait up!' *you called as I walked out of the room, but I didn't stop. My head was spinning.* 'Braxton.' *I'd already made it to my front yard by the time you caught up to me.* 'Braxton, stop.' *You reached out to me, but I shrugged your hand away.*

'Leave me alone, Jemma.'

'What in the hell is your problem all of a sudden? You were fine a few minutes ago.'

I stopped walking and spun around to face you. 'Why didn't you tell me you applied for this job?'

The look on your face was a mixture of hurt and annoyance. 'Because I wanted to surprise you. To be honest I didn't even think I'd get it.'

'Well, surprise,' *I said with sarcasm dripping from my voice.*

'Why are you acting like such a jerk?'

I wanted to tell you that I was hurt that you didn't tell me, and upset that I wasn't going to get to be with you on the weekends anymore. Those two days were the highlight of my week. I was being selfish, I know, but I had no control over my emotions. So, I just stood there, and said nothing.

'Fuck you, Braxton Spencer.'

I don't know what hurt most—the sadness I saw on your face or the anger when you pushed against my chest.

It was the first time I'd ever heard you really swear. It was also the closest we'd ever come to a fight. I didn't know what to say or do, so I turned away from you and stormed into my house.

Slamming the front door behind me, I headed straight to my room. I'd never felt anything like this before. I sat on the edge of my bed and buried my face in my trembling hands.

That night I hardly slept. I was laden with guilt. I knew I had acted like a total arse. I should have been happy for you, but instead I was miserable—I couldn't even fathom what my weekends would be like without you.

When morning finally rolled around, I sat by my bedroom window and watched you leave for your first day on the job. Your dad was driving you, and as you made your way to the car you turned and stared at my house. You should have been happy, excited even, but because of me you looked really sad. I knew it was all my fault, yet I still couldn't find it in me to go outside and wish you luck. It's stupid, but in that moment it felt like this was the end of us. Like things were changing and you were slipping through my fingers. I loved things just the way they were, and I didn't want to lose you . . . or what we had.

Hours later—it was around midday, and I was still moping around—there was a knock on the door. 'Can I talk to you for a minute?' your mother asked.

I moved aside so she could enter. 'I brought you over some lunch. I thought you might be hungry.' She handed me a plate containing a wrapped sandwich as she passed.

'Thank you.'

I had no appetite, but I appreciated the gesture.

'You're welcome, but that's not why I'm here.' I took a seat on the sofa, and your mother sat beside me. 'I know you're upset about Jemma getting a job, but I wanted you to know that I held her while she cried herself to sleep last night.' I bowed my head. Knowing I was the cause of those tears was hard for me to swallow. Hurting you was the last thing I ever wanted to do. 'Do you know why she took this job?'

'No.'

I still couldn't bring myself to look at her, so my focus remained on the carpet below.

'She wanted money so she could buy you a Christmas present. She wanted to buy you something special, with her own money. That's the only reason. It's only a temporary position, just over the summer.'

'I didn't know that,' I whispered.

'To be frank, Stephen and I aren't overly happy about her working; we both think she's a bit too young, and we'd much prefer she concentrated on her studies for now. But this was important to her . . . you are important to her.' She placed her hand on my leg and gave it a gentle squeeze before she stood. 'I just thought you'd like to know that.'

I'm glad she told me, but it made me feel lower than I ever had in my life.

After she left, I set off on the long walk to town. I had no money for the bus, but that didn't bother me—I would have walked to the ends of the earth for you.

You were busy serving when I got there, so I stood out on the street and watched you through the large window. You looked cute in your uniform: tiny hot-pink shorts, a white polo with matching hot-pink dots, and a white hat. Your beautiful brown hair was pulled back into a high ponytail.

I tried hard not to focus on your long, lean legs, but it was impossible. You've always had the most amazing legs.

I stop reading again, and stare down at my legs. He wouldn't say that now. I may have had amazing legs once, but not anymore. They're horribly disfigured by the huge ugly scars that will forever remind me of the accident.

The older we got, the harder it became for me to hide my true feelings for you. You were no longer the little girl with the missing front teeth who stole my heart; you had grown into a beautiful young woman who owned me completely.

I must have stood out there for about fifteen minutes until all the customers had left. You were wiping down the counters when I entered. Your eyes widened in surprise when you noticed me standing just inside the doorway. I was worried about how you'd react to seeing me, but I needn't have been. Moments later your face broke out into a beautiful smile, and it made my heart race.

'Braxton,' you said as I stepped towards the counter. 'What are you doing here?'

'I've come to apologise. I acted like a jerk yesterday.'

'You did,' you said, as your gaze moved back down to the countertop, 'but I forgive you.'

I can't even put into words how relieved I felt when you said that.

'Would you like an ice cream?'

'I don't have any money on me,' I replied.

'That's okay. I have some change left over from my lunch. Actually, I didn't even eat lunch. I wasn't hungry.'

I saw sadness flash through your eyes, and the guilt I had been burdened down with all day quickly returned. I knew exactly how you felt, because I hadn't eaten anything either.

'I'm sorry, Jem.'

'It's okay. You're here now. That's all that matters.'

You moved over to the display cabinet that held all the different ice-cream flavours. 'I want you to try the new creation I invented today, it's called The Braxton.'

'You named it after me?'

'I did. I was going to call it The Triple-Decker-Jerkoff, but I didn't think my new boss would appreciate that.'

I laughed as you picked up the metal scoop and rolled the first flavour into a neat ball. 'This one is Apple Pie Delight. I know how much you love Ma's apple pie.' You placed it on the cone and rinsed the scoop before moving to the next flavour. 'Vanilla

Dream, because you can't have apple pie without vanilla ice cream. They're made for each other.'

'Exactly,' I replied as my smile grew wider. They were made for each other, just like we were.

'And lastly, Wicked Chocolate, because I know how much you love chocolate.' You grinned proudly as you held the cone out to me. 'Ta da . . . behold The Braxton.'

A way to a man's heart is through his stomach so they say, but in that moment I didn't fall head-over-heels in love with you, because I'd been hopelessly in love with you for years.

What we had is far too beautiful to be forgotten.

Yours always,

Braxton

I look down at the tiny ice-cream charm in my hand, and I do something I haven't done all week . . . *I smile.*

TWENTY-TWO

Jemma

I look over at the clock next to my bed and see it's only 5.15am. I hardly slept last night. My head is all over the place. I'm restless and can't seem to find peace.

Throwing back the covers, I get up and head to the bathroom. I can't stand being cooped up in this house anymore. I need to get out, and get some fresh air into my lungs.

Leaning over the vanity, I splash water onto my face. When I look in the mirror, I see dark circles under my eyes.

After brushing my teeth and running a comb through my hair, I head back into my room. Pulling my nightgown over my head, I toss it on the bed. I'm getting out of here for the day, and I know exactly where to go. The place I feel most at peace . . . the beach.

The sun hasn't even risen by the time I leave a note on the kitchen table for Christine and then close the front door behind me. It's starting to get a little light, though, as I make my way to the bus stop.

The bus pulls up as I approach the stop, and I have to jog the last ten metres so I don't miss it. I still have a slight limp, but I can live with that.

I hope to be at the beach before the sun rises. According to my phone, today's sunrise should be around 6.30am. I should make it in time.

I zip up the front of my jacket and pull the hood over my head as I make my way across the sand. There's a nip in the air this morning.

The bus stops further down the beach, but just like my last visit I find myself drawn towards my favourite house; the pretty white one with the sky-blue shutters and trim around the windows.

Once I reach my destination, I stand and stare at the house for a few seconds, before turning to face the ocean. I'm just in time: the sun is starting to rise. I fill my lungs with the fresh sea air and sit down on the sand.

I pull out my phone when the sun appears on the horizon and snap a few shots. It's just as beautiful as I imagined it would be.

I pull my hood further down over my head and sigh as I stare out at the ocean. I knew coming here was what I needed; I'm already starting to feel calmer. I draw my legs towards my chest and wrap my arms around them, resting my chin on my knees. I close my eyes, letting the sound of the waves soothe my soul. I'm so lost in the moment I don't even hear the footsteps approach until I'm almost barrelled over. My eyes spring open when a cute little dog jumps onto my lap and starts to lick the side of my face.

'Hello there,' I say, giggling at its excitement.

'Bella-Rose!' I hear someone call from the distance, and my body instantly tenses up. I not only recognise that name, but the voice as well.

I quickly stand up and reach for my bag just as the dog starts jumping up my leg.

'Bella-Rose,' he says again in a breathless tone. The voice is coming from behind me now, but I can't bring myself to turn around. 'Come here, girl.' He reaches down and scoops up the dog and I want to turn and run. 'I'm so sorry about my dog, she's never done that before.'

My hood is up and my back is to him, so he can't see my face. But it's no use, there's no escape.

When I turn, the first thing I see is the surprise on his face. 'Jemma.'

'Hey.' My gaze moves to the left of him, and then the right. He's on his own. Then I look at the dog in his arms and it dawns on me. *I feel like such an idiot.*

'What are you doing here?' he asks as a smile spreads across his face.

'I just needed some air. I've been cooped up in Christine's place all week.'

'I know. I came around the other day. You haven't been answering my calls or texts. I was starting to worry. I thought maybe you were avoiding me.'

I shrug. I'm certainly not going to admit that I thought his dog was his damn girlfriend. 'I just needed some space from the world for a while. I was starting to feel overwhelmed by it all.'

'That's understandable,' he says, reaching out and rubbing his hand down my arm. It leaves a tingly feeling in its wake. Why does he have to be so understanding?

'I'm sorry I didn't return your messages.'

'You don't need to apologise.'

'So, is this your dog?' I ask, trying to sound casual but probably failing. 'I remember you mentioning you wanted to get one.'

'Yes, this is Bella-Rose.' He runs his hand affectionately over her fur. 'I'd originally planned to get a puppy, but when I saw her, I knew she'd be coming home with me.'

'Love at first sight, hey?'

He smiles before answering. 'Not exactly.' He tells me how he felt when he learned that Bella-Rose's owner had died; he couldn't not take her home.

I reach out to scratch Bella-Rose under the chin. 'Poor girl.' I move my gaze back to Braxton. 'You're a good guy, Braxton Spencer.'

'I have my faults,' he admits, with a shrug.

'Well, I'm yet to see any of them.'

This brings a smile to his face. 'I was just about to grab a coffee. Would you like to join me?'

'I should get going. I left Christine a note to say I'd be home in time for breakfast, and my bus will probably be here shortly.'

'Just a quick one, then I'll drop you home on my way to see my dad.'

'Okay.' The truth is, I've missed him.

He turns and gestures for me to follow, but to my surprise he doesn't head in the direction I expected. He walks straight towards my favourite house.

'Where are you going?'

'To my house. This is where I live . . . where you used to live.'

'This is our house? I lived here?'

'Yep. I built it for you.'

'You built this house?' I stop walking and stare at him in wonderment.

'Well, not technically, I designed it. It was your dream house when you were a kid.'

'Wow,' I whisper as my gaze moves down to the sand around my feet. No wonder I felt so drawn to this place.

We climb the steps that lead to the back deck, and suddenly I'm feeling anxious about being here. It's too soon. I'm not ready. I pause when he wipes his bare feet on the mat by the large glass sliding doors.

'Are you coming in?'

I shake my head. His shoulders slump slightly, but he tries to cover it up with a smile. 'Well . . . umm . . . make yourself comfortable out here, I'll just go grab the coffee.' He gestures towards the outdoor setting, before disappearing inside. There's a part of me that wants to go in and look around, but I'm scared to do that. I feel weird about all these things that should be familiar to me but aren't.

I walk across the deck, towards the long white wooden bench seat. It holds a mixture of cushions: some are blue-and-white striped, the blue the same shade as the window trim, and some are plain blue with white piping around the edges. I like them. It helps tie this space in with the rest of the house. Taking in my surroundings has me pondering my old career. It makes me wonder if that passion I once held for design will ever return.

The bench seat has been placed close to the house, under the only covered part of the deck. It makes sense, I suppose, because it's sheltered from the weather there. Off to the left is a large white six-seater wooden table; in the centre are three white box lanterns, each containing a half-burned candle. My eyes are then drawn to the string of fairy lights that span the perimeter of the deck. I find myself wishing it was dark so I could see what they looked like when turned on, imagining how lovely it would be to dine out here by candlelight.

On the far right-hand side of the deck sits a barbecue, complete with a small outdoor kitchen, bordered on either side by palms in tall sky-blue pots. I see a large decorative anchor mounted on the wall.

As I sit, I take in the small white coffee table in front of me. There's a rectangular wicker basket as a centrepiece, and within it sits a blue candle surrounded by shells and ornamental blue starfish. I love the attention to detail everywhere I look; it's all very simple, yet effective. Did I decorate it? The thought has my stomach flipping. I wish I could remember.

I settle back in the chair and try not to over-analyse everything. I still can't believe this is my home, or was my home. The fact that I was drawn to it from the moment I first saw it gives me hope. I pray that one day it will all come back. I'm not sure how I'll cope if it doesn't. Apart from Braxton's letters, there's a huge chunk of my life missing.

'Here you go,' Braxton says, breaking my train of thought. He places a tray down on the coffee table, and my gaze gravitates towards his hands. He has beautiful hands, so strong and masculine. I find myself wondering what they would feel like against my body, and that thought shocks me.

My eyes quickly dart up to his face, and I find him grinning. I love it when he smiles like that, because it shows off his cute dimple. His blue eyes sparkle in the morning sunlight as he passes me my coffee.

'I made it just the way you like it.'

'Thanks.' I take a sip of my coffee, and it tastes amazing. 'What's in this?' I ask.

'Caramel syrup. You usually used it instead of sugar.'

'It tastes divine. I must get some of this for Christine's.'

'You can take the bottle I have here. I can buy some more.'

He picks up his own coffee and takes the seat beside me, and Bella-Rose comes and lies by his feet. I try to ignore the fact that he's so close I can feel the heat generating off his body. I also try to ignore how good he smells.

'It's so pretty here,' I say.

'It is. We used to sit out here every morning and have our coffee.' I don't reply because again, I hate that I don't remember any of this. My old life seems like a good life, but it's worlds away.

'Are you hungry?' He leans forward and picks up a plate that has two muffins on it. 'They're blueberry, one of your favourites.'

'Did you make these?'

'Hardly,' he scoffs. 'Unless you count defrosting them in the microwave. I couldn't cook to save my life. You were

199

the chef in this house. I'd sometimes help with the prep, but basically I was the washer-upper. I always left the cooking to you . . . it was safer.'

I find myself wondering how he gets by now that I'm not here to look after him. This situation is totally out of my control, but it doesn't stop me from feeling bad for him.

My eyes flicker to the mug in his hand. The one he gave me looks new and stylish, but his is clearly old. There's writing on it, but I can't make out what it says, because his hand is in the way.

'Your coffee is black. Did I get the last of the milk?'

'This is how I usually have my coffee,' he says, chuckling.

'I put milk in your coffee at Christine's.'

'I know.'

'You should have said something.'

'I didn't want to hurt your feelings.'

'You wouldn't have, silly,' I say, bumping my leg with his. 'At least now I know for next time.'

We sit in silence and drink. It's not awkward or uncomfortable—surprisingly, it feels . . . *right*.

I'm not sure how much time passes, but Braxton eventually looks down at his watch. 'Well, as much as I'm enjoying having you here, I guess I better get you home. I have a meeting at ten, and I still need to go and see my dad.'

An idea pops into my head and words are out of my mouth before I even realise. 'Can I come with you?'

'To see my dad?'

'Yes, I'd love to see him again.'

His face lights up. 'Of course. I'd like that.'

We're both smiling as we leave.

———

'Let me take those,' I say to Christine as we unload the shopping bags from the taxi.

We had a nice morning together. After we shopped, we had lunch at a cafe, where I ordered caramel syrup in my coffee. I feel like we need to start doing normal things like this. Christine has helped me start to live again, and I want to help her do the same.

Christine checks the mailbox as I walk towards the house and place the groceries down on the front porch. 'I must get you a key cut for the front door,' she says, climbing the stairs.

'I'd like that.'

It would be nice to be able to come and go as I please. Now that my rehab is only a couple of days a week, I have so much spare time on my hands. I no longer have a job, and with no memory of my design skills or tastes, there's no way I could go back to doing that. Maybe I should think about finding a new career.

Christine unlocks the door, and I gather the grocery bags and carry them into the kitchen.

'This came for you,' she says, passing me a letter and a small parcel. My pulse quickens. They're from Braxton.

I place them down beside me, and quickly unpack the groceries, eager to get this done so I can read my letter.

'Let me do that,' Christine says. 'Go read your letter.'

'Are you sure?'

'Yes.'

I slide my arms around her waist, hugging her tight. 'Thank you for today . . . it was nice.'

'It was just like old times,' Christine smiles.

LETTER EIGHT . . .

Dearest Jemma,

The twenty-fourth of December 2004. The ice-cream parlour was closed over the Christmas period, so I was looking forward to spending the next two days with you. You'd worked almost every day of the school holidays leading up to Christmas, and I was missing you so much. I spent a lot of time at the hardware store helping my dad. He didn't expect me to do it, but I was happy to be able to help him, and to be honest, I was completely lost without you around.

Your shift finished at 4pm, so I made sure I left the hardware store in plenty of time to pick you up. I did this every day, and we'd catch the bus home together. It was summer, so the ice-cream business was booming and you were run off your feet. You always looked so tired when I'd collect you from work, which I hated, but the way your face would light up as soon as you saw me melted my heart.

'Promise me you won't leave my side for the next two days,' you said once we'd taken our seats on the bus. 'I've missed you so much.'

'I've missed you too.' If only you knew how much.

'Promise me, Braxton.'

'I promise I won't leave your side,' I used my finger to cross my heart for added effect, 'except when I go to the bathroom, of course. Unless you insist on coming in there with me as well.'

'Eww, gross. No way!' you screeched, bumping your shoulder with mine. 'Bathroom breaks are definitely allowed.'

Ma and Pa had arrived at your place by the time we got home. They'd always come down at Christmas time. We'd spend Christmas Eve decorating your tree, while your mother and Ma were busy in the kitchen getting a start on our Christmas feast for the next day.

Christmas was no longer celebrated in our house. Since my mother's death, my father had lost interest. He always had a wrapped gift for me on Christmas morning, and joined us at your place for Christmas lunch—your parents insisted on it—but that was the extent of it. For him, it wasn't Christmas without her.

It was around 10pm when we finished decorating the tree. Your parents and grandparents gathered in the main room for the official turning-on of the Christmas lights. It's a job that your father usually did, being the man of the house, but this particular year I was bestowed with the honours. You have no idea how much that meant to me.

I stood beside the tree while Christmas carols played softly in the background. The moment your father gave me the nod, I flicked the switch and watched as all your faces lit up with smiles. I loved my time with your family, I truly did, but it was also a constant reminder of everything I'd lost.

I smiled along with you all, but the entire time I was fighting back tears. Seeing you all together and so happy made me think of my mum, and how much I missed her. It also made my heart ache for my dad. We both lost so much the day she died.

My mum loved Christmas; it was her favourite time of the year. My dad's store would close for a few days, and we would be together as a family. She would decorate the entire house in the weeks leading up to it, and when she was home she would play Christmas carols and sing along. If I happened to be in close proximity, she would grab me and make me dance with her.

I can still picture the smile on her face as we waltzed around the room. I loved seeing her smile like that. On Christmas Eve, she would stay up late making Christmas cake for the following day, along with her special custard; she'd make it from scratch, she hated that powdered stuff. Her honey-glazed ham was to die for.

'I can't wait to give you your present in the morning,' you said, linking your arm through mine as you walked me to the door. You were practically bouncing with excitement. 'I hope you like it.'

'I'll love it.' You'd worked hard to earn the money for that gift, and that alone was enough. It meant so much that you'd go to such lengths for me.

Christmas morning I woke to a loud banging on my front door. 'Braxton,' I heard my father call out a few minutes later. 'Jemma's here.'

Jumping out of bed I rummaged through my top drawer for the small wrapped present I'd stowed inside. My father had given me fifty dollars for all the work I'd done at the hardware store in the weeks prior. I didn't want his money, but he insisted.

I used it to buy you a gift.

My father was standing at the base of the staircase as I descended, but my gaze was firmly fixed on you. You were standing just inside the doorway, still dressed in your pink pyjamas. Your hair was sticking up all over the place, but to me you'd never looked more beautiful.

'Merry Christmas, Pop,' I said to him when he pulled me into a one-armed hug.

'Merry Christmas, son.'

The smile on your face grew as I walked towards you. I was only wearing a pair of pyjama bottoms, and I had to suppress my grin when your eyes slowly travelled the length of my body before making their way back to my face.

I'd grown a lot in the nine years we'd been friends. I was now tall and buff, and I liked the idea that you'd just unashamedly checked me out.

'Merry Christmas, Brax,' you said as you revealed the small square wrapped box from behind your back.

'Merry Christmas, Jem.' I too held my present for you out in front of me.

My stomach did a flip-flop when your face lit up.

'You got me a gift?'

'Uh huh.'

'Open yours first.' I could hear the excitement in your voice as you spoke. I held my breath as I tore into the paper, revealing a black box. I slowly opened the lid and couldn't believe my eyes.

'A watch?' I'd never owned a watch before.

'Yes. Do you like it?'

'I love it,' I replied, pulling you into my arms. 'I love it so much, Jem. Thank you.'

I could tell you were happy that I liked my gift by the huge smile I saw on your face when I finally released you.

I wasted no time strapping it to my wrist. It was perfect, and not only the best present I'd ever received, but the most valuable—and I don't mean in monetary terms. It was a gift given by you, a gift from the heart, and one you'd worked hard to buy. It's something I still treasure to this day.

'Open your gift.'

I stood and watched you unwrap it. Unlike me, you took your sweet time, taking great care not to tear the paper. I was eager for you to see what I'd bought for you, and the suspense was killing me.

You gasped as soon as you removed the lid from the small pink box. 'Oh my god, Braxton.' When your eyes moved back to me, I was surprised to see they were brimming with tears. I watched as you ran your fingertip over the tiny silver shell-shaped earrings. 'They're so beautiful.'

'As soon as I saw the shells, they reminded me of you.'

'I love them,' you whispered as you wiped your eyes. 'Thank you.'

Later that day, my father and I joined your family for lunch. Ma and your mum always went over the top, but they got no complaints from me. I stuffed myself until I was so full I felt sick. My favourite part of the day, though, was seeing the shift in my father. Once he and your father got stuck into the port after lunch, a different side to him emerged. He relaxed, and seemed no longer burdened by his circumstances. I loved seeing him so carefree and happy, even if it was only for just that one day a year.

Boxing Day was usually spent at the beach, and this year was no different. Your dad dropped us off midmorning, with strict instructions that he would pick us up at 2pm. I had my new watch with me. I'd even slept in it on Christmas night ... I didn't want to take it off.

We were older now, so we didn't require a chaperone wherever we went. Not only were we sensible, but your parents knew I would look after you, just like I always had.

With you working, it had been weeks since we'd come here, and as we walked towards our usual spot, you pointed towards the row of houses that lined the beach.

'Oh look, they've knocked down that old house.'

I headed in that direction to get a closer look. There was something about buildings that fascinated me. The different shapes, sizes and designs. The framework for a new house was already erected, and I tried to imagine what it would look like when it was completed.

I knew that, when I left school, I was either going to build or design houses, but I was yet to decide which.

'How nice would it be to live this close to the beach,' you said. 'I wish I was rich.'

'If I ever win the lottery I'll buy you one of these houses.'

'That's sweet.' You bumped my shoulder as a smile spread across your pretty face.

'Which one would you prefer?'

'None of these,' you replied. 'I'd build my dream house.'

'You have a dream house?'

'I do.' You linked your arm through mine as we continued down to the beach. 'I even drew a picture of it. I'll show you when we get home.'

We spent most of the morning swimming, and when we were done, we built a snowman out of wet sand—complete with seaweed hair, twig arms and shell eyes. We'd been doing this for so many years it had become a Christmas tradition.

Later that afternoon, as my dad lay on our sofa sleeping off the effects of his big day on the drink with your father, I lazed around your lounge room in front of your television. When I asked to see your drawing you seemed pleased, and raced off to collect it from your room.

'I'm going to live in a house exactly like that one day,' you announced as you handed it over for me to study. It was a white weatherboard two-storey house, complete with a white picket fence out front. The drawing was so detailed, right down to the blue shutters and trim around the windows. You had even added a colourful garden that ran the length of the front porch.

'I love this,' I said.

'A girl can dream,' you replied with a sigh, but I didn't doubt it for a second. 'Dreams are free, you know.' I handed the drawing back to you, and I'm pretty sure that's the exact moment my future was confirmed. I was going to become an architect. You wanted that house, and I was going to make sure you got it. There was nothing I wouldn't do to make your dreams come true. 'You can buy the house next door, and we can be neighbours just like we are now.'

I smiled and nodded, but there was no way I was going to settle for being your neighbour. I was going to marry you one day and we were going to live in that house together.

A boy can dream too . . .

What we had is far too beautiful to be forgotten.

Yours always,

Braxton

I place the letter down beside me and pick up the small parcel. As soon as I see the pink box, I'm smiling. I know what's inside: the shell earrings he bought me when we were teenagers.

They're beautiful, and a similar shape to the shell charm on my memory bracelet. I remove them from the box and slide them into my ears, then search in the envelope for my charm.

I find three: a house, a wrapped gift and a snowman.

Also in the envelope is a folded piece of paper. When I open it I can't contain my smile. It's the picture I drew of my dream house. It's not just a square with a triangle on top for the roof, like I imagined it would be. There's so much detail in it. But the biggest surprise for me is that it's almost identical to the house where Braxton lives.

He really did build me my dream house.

TWENTY-THREE

Braxton

'Hey, Pop,' I say, entering his room. I love the smile that appears on his face as soon as he sees me. More often than not I just get a blank stare.

'Hi, son.' The moment those words are out of his mouth I find myself grinning. Today is a good day; today he remembers me. He leans forward in his chair and looks behind me. My first thought is he's looking for Jem, but sadly she isn't with me today.

I've waited on the back deck every morning since I last saw her. I even resorted to taking Bella-Rose for walks along the beach just in case I ran into her, but there has been no sign of her. 'Where's your mum? She's not with you.'

My heart sinks. He doesn't ask for her often, but when he does, it always ends badly.

'No, she's not,' I say as he stands and hugs me.

'Oh. Where is she? Is she coming to see me later?'

I briefly think about making up some elaborate story, but I've never lied to him and I'm not about to start. 'She's ... umm ... not coming, Pop.'

I feel terrible when I see his face drop.

'Why?' he asks.

I scratch my head as I think of the best way to put this, but there really isn't a good way to tell him he lost his wife.

'She passed away a long time ago.'

His whole body sinks, and I hate the look of confusion I see on his face. 'What? How? Why didn't you tell me? I would've gone to the funeral.'

I take a seat beside him and place my hand on his shoulder. 'I'm sorry, Pop.'

A lump rises to my throat when he covers his face with his hands and starts to weep. It was hard enough seeing him going through this when he first lost her. I hate that he has to relive it all these years later.

'I can't believe she's gone. Not my Grace. How am I supposed to go on without her?'

I don't know what to say to that, so I rub his back instead. Again that nagging guilt I've carried around all this time comes flooding to the surface.

'It's all my fault,' I whisper.

He stops crying and looks up at me. His tear-stained face does nothing to ease my pain. 'What do you mean it's all your fault?'

We've never discussed this before, but maybe it's time we did. 'You woke me in the middle of the night because you needed to take her to the hospital. I was supposed to get up, but I fell back asleep . . .' I pause, then force myself to keep going. 'Her appendix burst on the way to the hospital, and she died a little while later on the operating table. If only I'd got out of bed straightaway, and hadn't held you up . . .'

He stares out the window for the longest time, and I'd love to know what is going through his mind. He probably doesn't understand anything I've just said. I wish we'd had this conversation before he got sick.

'That's right . . . I remember,' I hear him whisper. Minutes pass before he makes eye contact with me again. 'Braxton.'

It's been so long since I've heard him say my name. 'Do you really think it's your fault?'

'It's what I know.'

He straightens his posture and clears his throat before answering. 'Well, you're wrong. Your mother had those pains for two days. I kept telling her to go to the doctor, but she refused. She was stubborn like that. She hated doctors. The only time she went without a fight is when it was for you.'

'You remember?'

'Of course I do,' he says, flicking his hand. It almost makes me want to laugh. He's obviously forgotten he has Alzheimer's and doesn't even remember his own name most days. I don't know what to make of all this because he gets so confused, but I do remember her not liking doctors. 'She died because she left it too late. It had nothing to do with you.'

'I feel responsible, Pop.'

'Well, don't. Have you been carrying this around with you all these years?' He sighs when he looks at me. 'I wish you'd talked to me. I could've set you straight.' He drapes his arm around my shoulder, pulling my body towards his. 'I'm so sorry you felt that way, son. It wasn't your fault.'

He speaks with such confidence, and there's a huge part of me that yearns for his words to be true. But at the end of the day it's irrelevant, it's still not going to lessen my feeling of loss, or bring my mother back.

I stay a little longer than usual, and I'm pleased that by the time I leave he has reverted to no memory of me—because that also means he's forgotten our conversation. It would have been impossible for me to walk away if he was still upset.

As soon as I arrive at the office, Lucas notices. 'Hey, buddy,' he says, following me into my office. 'Wanna talk about it?'

'Talk about what?' I stow my briefcase beside my desk and take a seat in the leather chair.

'Whatever it is that's got you looking so sullen. Is it Jemma?'

I can't help but give him a half-smile; he can read me like a book. 'No . . . my dad.'

There's no point in denying it, he won't let it go until I talk to him.

'Shit.' He plonks down on the corner of my desk. 'He didn't have another fall, did he?'

I scrub my hand over my face. 'No. He just . . . he asked where my mum was this morning. It's just hard watching everything he's gone through. He lost his wife in her prime, and worked his whole damn life in a job he pretty much hated. He shouldn't have to live out the rest of his days like this.'

'Life can be a real bitch sometimes.'

'Don't I know it.' I feel him watching me as I boot up my laptop. After a few moments of silence he finally speaks again. 'I think Saturday-night drinks are in order.'

'I don't really feel like going out.'

'Well, start feeling like it. I'll pick you up at seven.' He slaps his hand against the desk before standing. 'I won't take no for an answer, Spencer.'

With that he turns and leaves. I settle back into my chair and find myself smiling. A night out on the town with him might actually do me good.

⏤

When I arrive home later that evening, I'm surprised to find a visitor waiting on my front porch. 'Rach. What are you doing here? Is everything okay?'

She stands and walks towards me. 'Everything's fine,' she says, kissing me on the cheek. 'I'm here to raid Jemma's wardrobe. I'm taking her out Saturday night and I want her to look nice.' My face must betray my feeling of trepidation, because she quickly adds, 'It's a girls' night. She needs this, Braxton.'

Breathing suddenly feels difficult, so I loosen my tie. I agree she needs it, but it still makes me feel uneasy. I never experienced these insecurities when she was mine, but she isn't mine anymore; well, not in her eyes. What if she meets someone else?

I reach into the back seat to grab my briefcase. 'Lucas and I are going out Saturday night as well. We should organise to meet up later on.'

Her face immediately darkens. 'If Lucas is going to be there, then no.'

I stop and look at her. 'What the hell happened between you two? You used to be friends.'

I still can't wrap my head around this one. My last memory of them together is at our wedding, laughing and dancing.

'I'd rather not talk about it,' she says as we climb the front steps. Before I get a chance to respond, Bella-Rose comes barrelling out of the doggy door I had installed.

'Hey, girl,' I say as she jumps against my leg with excitement.

'Oh my god. You have a dog? When did you get her?'

'I do.' I reach down and scoop her into my arms. I chuckle when she licks my cheek. 'This is Bella-Rose. I got her from the animal shelter.'

'Aww. She's so cute!' Rachel beams as she scratches Bella-Rose under the chin.

'She's my new companion. It gets lonely in this big house all by myself.'

Rachel's smile softens as she looks at me. 'I'm sorry.' That's all she says, and I appreciate that she doesn't fill me with false hope. Like me, she knows there's no guarantee that Jemma and I will ever get back what we once had.

'I don't want to go to our usual haunt,' I say to Lucas as he backs out of my driveway. My bet is that's where Jemma and Rachel will go, and as much as I'd like to see her, I don't want Lucas's attitude towards Rachel to ruin their night—or ours.

'No problem. We can go to that place I took you last time.'

'Sounds good.'

I don't bother telling him why, because I don't want to sour his mood. I wish I knew what the hell was going on with those two, but neither of them will talk about it, so for now I'll butt out.

We take a seat in one of the booths off to the side, and after ordering a couple of Coronas and some dinner, Lucas sits back and looks at me.

'So, how are things going with you and Jemma?' he asks.

'Still the same, really. We've made some progress, I guess.' I exhale. 'But I feel like every time we take a step forward, it's followed by two steps back.'

'Hang in there, mate.'

'I'll wait forever if I have to.'

'What about your dad?'

I shrug. 'Same. He has his good days, and not so good.'

The waitress brings our drinks over, and Lucas raises his in the air. 'To better times ahead,' he says, clinking his bottle with mine.

'To better times.'

We're a few beers in when the food finally arrives. Thankfully the conversation has turned lighter, to sports and work.

'Can I get you something else to drink?' the waitress asks when she places the food down in front of us.

'Just a beer for him,' Lucas says, gesturing towards me. 'I'm driving.'

I'm laughing at something Lucas said, as we eat, when I see his fork pause mid-air. His mouth is still open, but his expression turns from shocked to angry in a millisecond. 'What the fuck is she doing here?' he snaps, dropping his cutlery down onto his plate. I don't even need to ask who it is.

Although I'm still perplexed by his behaviour towards Rachel, my heart starts to race because if Rachel is here, that means Jemma is as well.

Looking over my shoulder, I see them both approach the bar and take a seat on the stools that Lucas and I sat at the first time we were here. My gaze zeros in on Jemma; she looks so beautiful in that electric-blue dress. It was a gift from Rachel for her birthday, and was designed especially for her. She wore it that night when I took her out for dinner. I bought her a necklace that year to go with it – a heart-shaped sapphire pendant that was surrounded by small diamonds.

My gaze follows her every move as she takes in the space around her. The look of wonderment in her eyes tells me she loves this place, just like I knew she would. I find myself smiling as I watch her. There's no doubt in my mind that the designer is still in there somewhere.

I'm taken aback when Lucas stands, and for a minute I think he's going to approach them and make a scene. But he pulls two fifty-dollar notes out of his pocket and throws them down on the table.

'You're not leaving, are you?'

'Yep. That's exactly what I'm doing.'

'Sit down and finish your dinner. They haven't even noticed we're here.'

'I've suddenly lost my appetite,' he says, reaching for his jacket. 'I'm sorry, man, but I just can't be near her anymore.'

He doesn't even wait for me to stand before he stalks to the exit. I quickly place my cutlery down and take a swig of my beer before following him out. My eyes are focused on Jemma as I pass. I'm glad she appears to be having a nice time tonight.

I smile when Jemma laughs at something Rachel says, but it's wiped from my face when I see the bartender's flirtatious grin as he places a glass of red wine in front of her.

My thoughts revert back to the first time she drank wine, not long after she moved in with Rachel. It was a Friday night and Lucas and I were hanging out at the girls' apartment. Back then the four of us did everything together. Jemma and Rachel managed to consume two and a half bottles between them. It wasn't a pretty sight, and it resulted in me holding Jemma's hair back while she hugged the toilet bowl for the rest of the evening.

I'd love to go over and say hello to the girls—and give the bartender the message to back off—but I need to find out what the hell is going on with my best mate.

'Lucas wait up,' I call out as I step out into the crisp air. He doesn't stop, so I jog to catch up to him. 'What's got into you tonight?'

'Leave me alone,' he grumbles.

'Wait *up*.' I reach for his elbow, pulling him to a stop. I'm not letting this go until I get to the bottom of it. In all the years we've been friends, I've never seen him act like this. 'What's going on with you two?'

He tugs his arm out of my grip, spinning around to face me. 'It's just . . . Ugh!' He runs his hands roughly through his hair in frustration. 'I can't be around her anymore.'

Without another word he turns again, heading towards his car.

'Hey,' I say, following him. 'Talk to me, man.'

'There's nothing to say.'

'Lucas, don't do this.' He takes a few more steps before grinding to a halt.

'Do what?'

'Don't shut me out.'

This time when he turns to face me, I'm taken aback to find him on the verge of tears. 'What do you want me to tell you? That I'm madly in love with her, and she doesn't feel the same way about me? That she played me? That she ripped my fucking heart out and stomped on it like a cold-hearted bitch? Is that what you want me to say?'

His revelation floors me. 'If that's the truth, then yes.'

I can already tell by the look on his face that it is. I stand there dumbfounded, at a loss for words. It's true what they say: there's a fine line between love and hate. I've never seen him so angry.

TWENTY-FOUR

Jemma

'Are you up, honey?' Christine asks, softly knocking on my door.

'Yes. Come in.'

I've been awake for a while, but just lazing around in bed. It was after one in the morning when the taxi dropped me off. I had such a good night with Rachel—she's fun, and I've become very fond of her.

She hugged me so tightly last night, and told me how much she's missed me.

'How was your night out?' Christine asks, placing a cup of coffee on my bedside table.

'I had a great time.'

'I'm glad. You two always had fun together.'

'Rachel told me last night she's going back to New York.' I sit up, and reach for my coffee.

'Really, when?'

'In a few days. She said she has some things to sort out. I'm not sure when she'll be back.'

Christine sits down on the edge of my bed. 'I knew it would only be a matter of time. She loves her job in New York.'

'I know. I'm going to miss her.'

'She'll come back. She always does.'

I smile, trying to mask my true feelings. The thought of her leaving makes me sad; I've become accustomed to having her around.

'We'll make her a special dinner before she leaves,' Christine suggests.

'That'll be nice, she'd like that.'

Christine places her hand briefly on my knee and smiles, before standing. 'This came for you earlier.' Excitement bubbles inside me as she holds up a letter, along with a pink sports bag. 'Braxton dropped it off, as well as this bag.'

'What's in the bag?' I ask, reaching for it.

'Your running gear.'

'I run?'

'You used to. You loved it. You even did it competitively for a while when you were younger.' She stands and walks towards my desk and returns with three medals. 'You won these when you were in high school.' I'd noticed them hanging on a hook below the shelf that houses a few trophies and ornaments, when I first came to live here, but I've never inspected them closely.

I take them out of her hand and study them. One has an inscription engraved on the back: *Jemma Robinson—2005 cross-country state champion.*

'You were so fast. You could have made a career out of running if you'd wanted to.'

'Why didn't I?'

'You ran for fun. The competitive side was something that never interested you.'

'So I just gave up?' I unzip the sports bag and see that she was right: it contains shorts, tights, singlets and a pair of brightly coloured sneakers.

'You gave up competing, but you still ran every day, right up until the accident.'

'Wow.' There's still so much of me I don't know.

She stands and walks towards the door. 'Read your letter, and when you're ready, come downstairs and I'll make you some breakfast.'

LETTER NINE . . .

Dearest Jemma,

The twelfth of February 2005. It was a Saturday, and the day of the cross-country state championships. I'd always known you were a fast runner; you beat me in races when we were kids, and you won most of the events at all the school sports carnivals. Long-distance events were your favourite, but you never pursued athletics outside of school until one of the teachers suggested that you enter a local cross-country event. It took a bit of persuasion from me and your parents, but you eventually filled out the forms and started training for it.

You ran a few kilometres every morning and afternoon. On the weekends, your father would drop us at the beach so you could run along the sand. It was soft and a great way to strengthen your legs.

You ended up winning both the local and regional events, and even managed to break the state record previously held by a girl by the name of Natasha Wilkinson. You'd never competed against her before but would be up against her in the state championships.

We were all up early that morning and travelled the long distance to the event. Your parents and grandparents took their seats in the grandstand, and I was sitting on the fence by the grassed area while you warmed up.

You were stretching when a blonde girl approached. You immediately smiled—nothing unusual, you were friendly to everybody—and didn't hesitate in extending your hand to her. She didn't take it. I couldn't hear what she was saying from where I sat, but by the look on your face, I could tell it wasn't good.

Jumping down off the fence, I headed towards you both. But when she saw me approaching, she quickly turned and walked away.

'What was that all about?' I asked.

'That was Natasha Wilkinson,' you answered, with an eye roll.

'Who?'

'The girl who held the state record. Well, she did, until I broke it.' I could tell by the scowl on your face that she had made you angry. 'She told me to watch my back, and that she hoped I like the taste of dust because I'd be eating hers very shortly.'

'What?'

'I know, right?'

You went back to your stretches, and appeared undeterred by what she'd said. I, on the other hand, was furious. I scanned the area, looking to see what direction she'd headed in.

'She better not do anything to you during the race.'

'I'm not scared of her. She's just trying to put me off my game. Little does she know her words spur me on ... I'll take great pleasure in beating her now.'

You were always so driven, so I didn't doubt it for a second, but I still had an uneasy feeling in my gut.

When the contestants were called to the starting line I took my place with your family in the grandstand. You'd swear I was the one about to compete, judging by the butterflies in my stomach.

We had a great view of the start and finish lines from where we sat, but for the rest of the race you would be out of sight. It was a four-kilometre open-air course that consisted of hills, valleys and flat terrain, with a variety of surfaces including grass, dirt and gravel.

Nasty Natasha, as we eventually dubbed her, was giving you the evil eye as you all stood in a diagonal line, waiting for the starter to sound his pistol. I saw you glance at her briefly, and a proud smile burst onto my face when you gave her a cheeky wink. You didn't seem to be threatened by her at all.

The next twenty or so minutes were an agonising wait for us all, and when the first cheers were heard, we knew that someone had entered the stadium and we all jumped to our feet.

I was so proud when I saw you powering to the line. Nasty Natasha was a good five-to-ten metres behind you, with tears streaming down her face.

'She's in the lead, Stephen!' your mother squealed with excitement as she jumped up and down.

'Go, Jemma!' I called out.

'Go, Jem-Jem! Go, you good thing!' I heard Pa scream a few seconds later.

'That's my granddaughter,' Ma said proudly, turning to tell the people behind us.

We all hugged each other when you finally crossed the line, and I'm pretty sure he'll never admit to this, but I swear there were tears in your father's eyes.

You were bent over with your hands on your knees as you tried to catch your breath, and Natasha had collapsed onto the ground in a sobbing mess.

A few minutes later, I watched in awe as you approached her and offered your hand. Again she refused to take it, but this time she took it a step further by slapping your hand away. I heard a few people in the crowd gasp, including your mother and Ma.

On our drive home later that day, we stopped off at a nice restaurant for a celebratory dinner. Ma and Pa didn't join us because they had a long drive back to the farm.

I remember watching you as we sat at a table in the small Italian restaurant you'd chosen. You'd been quiet since we left the track. Your eyes kept moving between your parents and me as you ate. The look on your face was so humbling. The three of us were beaming, still riding the high of your win. But your joy seemed to come from somewhere else—from seeing the people you loved happy. I knew you well, and it made me wonder if you were doing this more for our benefit than your own. You'd only agreed to compete because we practically begged you.

A month later, the Australian championships were held interstate. Your mother hated flying, so we left a few days earlier and drove the twelve-hour trip with your parents.

First, second and third place from each state's championships qualified to compete in this event, so that meant Nasty Natasha would be there.

When it was time for the race to start, I went through all the emotions I had at the previous event. And like the previous event, we all jumped to our feet when the first runner entered the stadium for the final leg of the race. But this time it wasn't you in the lead. It was a girl I hadn't seen before, neck and neck with Natasha.

I didn't even see who crossed the line first, my focus was on the tunnel they had emerged from moments before. Competitor after competitor appeared, but there was still no sign of you.

'Where is she?' I heard your mother say. I couldn't answer that, but I felt uneasy. I was about to go in search of you, when you suddenly appeared. You were limping, with blood trickling down your leg and one of your running shoes clutched tightly in your hand. I had a gut feeling that Nasty Natasha was behind this.

The entire crowd stood and cheered you on as you hobbled to the line. Unlike Natasha, there were no tears streaming down your face, but I could tell you were devastated, and my heart hurt for you.

After the first-aid officer cleaned you up, an official came and spoke with you. As I suspected, Natasha was behind it. A couple of the other runners had witnessed her push you down into a small ravine.

She won the race in a photo finish, but later that day she was disqualified and stripped of her medal. She also had to face a judiciary a few weeks later, and was suspended from competing for a year.

What made me proudest was learning that when the officials tried to pull you from the race because of your injuries, you refused. I love how you always fought for what you wanted, and despite the odds you never gave up.

That night as we lay in bed at the hotel, you whispered into the darkness. 'Braxton, are you awake?'

We were in single beds, and your parents were sharing a double bed just a few metres away.

'Yeah, I'm awake,' I whispered back.

I rolled onto my side to face you, and you did the same. I couldn't see your face, but I could make out your silhouette in the moonlight that was shining through the window.

'I don't want to do this anymore.'

'Do what?' I asked.

'Compete. I still want to run, I love it, but only for fun.'

'Don't let Natasha's actions turn you off doing something you love.'

'That's just it. I love the running part, but the competing not so much.'

'In my heart I suspected that,' I confessed.

'Because you get me, Brax. Nobody knows me like you do.'

Your words made me smile. 'You can still run without competing.'

'Did you hear Mum and Dad on the drive back to the hotel?' You sighed before continuing. 'They kept saying how next year I'll show them. Next year will be my year.'

'Yeah, I heard them.'

'I'm worried I'll disappoint them, but I really don't want to compete next year.'

'Just tell them the truth, Jem, they'll understand. We can tell them together if you like.'

'I'm so glad I have you on my side,' you said, stretching your hand out towards me. I reached for you, interlacing my fingers with yours.

'Always.'

'Night, Brax.'

'Night, Jem.'

Our fingers remained entwined as we both fell asleep.

What we had is far too beautiful to be forgotten.

Yours always,

Braxton

The running gear Braxton sent over now makes sense. I can't help but wonder: is he trying to merely share a memory, or rekindle my passion? Either way, he has me thinking that if I loved to run so much before the accident, maybe it's something I should get back into. It's not like I have much else to do. I could run through the neighbourhood, or on the beach.

Although I still have a slight limp when I walk, I've been doing small sprints on the treadmill during my rehab sessions, to help strengthen my legs. Maybe I could try running on the beach next time I'm there. I should probably check with my physiotherapist first.

I smile when I see the small running-shoe charm in the bottom of the envelope. I look down at the memory bracelet on my wrist. It's so full with memories of my past, but there's still room for many more.

I don't want these letters to ever stop.

⁓

'You're up early,' Christine says, coming into the kitchen and rubbing her eyes.

'I'm sorry if I woke you. I was just writing you a note.'

She eyes me up and down, and I see a smile form on her face. 'You're going for a run?'

'I am.' I originally put on the shorts, but the horrible red scars on my leg were visible, so I opted for the three-quarter tights instead. 'There's a bus due in fifteen minutes.'

'A bus?'

'Yes, I want to run on the beach.'

'That was always your favourite place. It's still dark outside, are you going to be okay?'

'The sun should be coming up by the time I arrive.'

'It's times like this I wish I had a driver's licence,' she says.

'I wondered about that. Why don't you?'

'I'm a shocking driver.' She laughs, shaking her head. 'There wasn't much need for a car growing up in the country. I'd ride my horse everywhere.'

'You had a horse as well?'

'Yes, her name was Frostie,' she says, her smile widening. 'I loved that horse. My father bought her for me one Christmas.'

I release a contented sigh. 'Pa sounds like he was a good man.'

'He was.'

'It still doesn't explain why you're a bad driver. If you've never driven, how would you know?'

'Your dad thought it would be a good idea for me to have my licence when we found out I was expecting you. I had a few lessons, but I was dreadful. Nobody wanted to get in the car with me. Even the instructor your father hired to teach me quit after the first lesson.'

'Oh my god,' I say, giggling. 'You must've been bad.'

'Well, the apple doesn't fall far from the tree, I'm afraid: you weren't much better when you first got behind the wheel.'

'Really?'

'Yes, really. You're lucky your father has the patience of a saint, otherwise you may never have got your licence either.'

As I head out the front door my smile fades as a thought occurs: was my poor driving the reason I had my accident? Nobody has ever told me what really happened that day.

The sun is rising by the time I arrive at the beach. I pause as soon as my feet hit the sand, inhaling the fresh salty air.

I set off down the beach at a slow pace—even though apparently I have done this a thousand times before, it's a new sensation and it takes a bit of getting used to. A few minutes in, I can already feel the muscles in my legs burning. My heart is racing and my breathing laboured, but I feel wonderful. My eyes are focused on Braxton's house as I draw nearer, and I feel the sting of disappointment when I don't see him sitting on the back deck.

It takes me about twenty minutes to reach the end of the beach. I contemplate stopping to catch my breath, but I'm on a high. I completely understand now why I always loved to run, and I'm grateful to Braxton for reminding me.

I steal a glance towards his place again as I make my way back down the beach. There's still no sign of him. I try not to dwell on it, but as I get closer my heart skips a beat when I see the glass sliding door open. Bella-Rose appears on the deck first, closely followed by Braxton. Butterflies erupt in my stomach the moment my eyes land on him. I can't explain all these feelings I get when I'm around him, but I like them. I like them a lot.

As if lured by a magnetic force, his attention is immediately drawn in my direction. Without thinking, I raise my hand and wave, and he reciprocates. It's hard to tell from this far away, but I think he's smiling. I know I am.

The moment Bella-Rose spots me, she comes bounding down the stairs and sprints across the sand towards me.

I stop running and crouch down. 'Hey, girl,' I say, trying to catch my breath as she licks the side of my face.

I'm busy giggling and patting her when a shadow falls over me. Looking up, I see Braxton's handsome face smiling down at me.

'Good morning.'

'Morning,' I reply, and my voice sounds a little strange to me. Standing, I wipe my palms nervously down the side of my tights. Although I was hoping to see him this morning, I suddenly feel self-conscious about my appearance. I'm sweating and must look a mess. I brush away the damp hair that has been glued to my forehead, tucking the loose strands behind my ears.

'It's good to see you running again.'

I smile, my nerves fading. 'Your letter inspired me.'

'I'm glad. You used to run this beach every morning.'

'Really?'

'Yep. Every day, except if it was raining heavily. You'd say it was the perfect way to start the day.'

'Did you ever come with me?'

'Never. I couldn't keep up with you,' he chuckles.

Is it crazy that I miss my old life, a life I don't even remember? Things just seem to have been much simpler back then.

'Do you have time for a coffee?' His question has me beaming. I was hoping he'd invite me up. 'I was just about to make myself one.'

'I'd love one.'

'Shall we?' He gestures towards the house, then holds his elbow out towards me. I slide my arm through his, trying not to blush at the look he gives me when I do.

We walk in silence, with Bella-Rose following closely behind. I'm immensely aware of my skin against his, but again I'm mortified that I'm so gross and sweaty. God, I hope I don't smell.

This time he doesn't invite me inside, and I'm glad. I hope one day I'll be ready, but for now I'm happy to just sit on the back deck and enjoy the view, and of course the company.

I sit on the bench seat, and my eyes flit around the space. I really love it out here.

I eye him as he settles back into the seat and takes a sip of his coffee; he has beautiful full lips. He's drinking out of that old cup again, and today I can see the writing on it. *You're cute, can I keep you?* I know there's a story behind that, and I hope that he will share it with me one day.

'What?' he says, when he notices me watching him.

'Nothing.' I bring my coffee cup to my lips to avoid saying more.

‑

'Can I ask you something?'

His eyes leave the road briefly, landing on me. 'Sure. You can ask me anything.'

'Did my poor driving have anything to do with my accident?'

'Your poor driving?'

'Yes, Christine said I was a terrible driver, like her.'

I see him trying to suppress a smile as he speaks. 'In the beginning, you were pretty bad, but you got better over time.'

'So, my accident had nothing to do with my driving ability?'

He exhales a large breath before he answers. 'You ran a stop sign, but the weather was really bad that day, and visibility was poor.'

'The accident was my fault?' My eyes widen and my mouth gapes open.

'Yes.' His gaze darts in my direction, before focusing back on the road. 'Yes, it was.'

'Was anyone else injured?' I feel incredibly selfish for not knowing this, or asking before now.

'The other driver suffered minor injuries, but basically walked away from it unscathed.'

'I see.'

'His car T-boned the side of yours, so you took most of the impact.' He reaches across the centre console, and grabs hold of my hand. 'It was an accident, Jem. You were a good driver.'

We're silent for the remainder of the drive. He doesn't let go of my hand, and I'm thankful.

TWENTY-FIVE

Braxton

'You made me breakfast?' Jemma asks with surprise the next morning as she climbs the back steps that lead onto the deck.

When I dropped her off yesterday, after visiting my dad, she said she would probably see me this morning after her run. So, I took the chance and bought a few of her favourite things, just in case. I set the table the way she used to like it. I miss sharing my mornings with her. I miss sharing everything with her. The nights are the hardest; I still have trouble sleeping without her beside me.

'I sure did. Muesli, yoghurt and fresh fruit. The breakfast of champions is what you used to call it.'

'Wow. I never eat like this at Christine's. She usually makes me toast and eggs.'

'Sometimes we'd have eggs on the weekend, but you would cook them.' I pull out her chair for her.

'It looks delicious. And really healthy.'

'You were always the healthy one in this family.'

'I don't doubt that,' she says, laughing. 'I know all about your sweet tooth, Mr Spencer.'

'Guilty as charged,' I say, smiling.

'How do you stay so . . . umm . . . trim?' I see a slight blush cross her cheeks as she speaks.

'Weights. I usually work out most days. I use the gym I set up in the garage.' She smiles before staring down at the food in front of her. 'You used to love pouring the yoghurt over your muesli, but I can grab you some milk if you prefer.'

'No. The yoghurt sounds good.'

'Well, eat up. I'll just go grab the coffee.'

I watch her through the kitchen window as I wait for the coffee to brew. She's smiling as she takes a slice of melon and a few strawberries off the platter, placing them on the small plate beside her cereal. I just want to pretend for the next half-hour that nothing has changed between us, and things are the way they've always been—her loving me just as much as I love her.

'Thank you,' she says, when I place the coffee down in front of her. 'This is delicious.'

'I'm glad you're enjoying it. I'd be happy to make breakfast for you every day if you wanted me to.'

'That's sweet, but I wouldn't expect you to go to all this trouble.'

'You're worth it,' is all I say, taking the seat opposite her.

I lather my toast in butter and strawberry jam, and when I look up I find her watching me. 'What? Jam is healthy—it's made from strawberries.'

'And a tonne of sugar too, I bet,' she says, laughing in the way that always makes me smile.

Shrugging, I take a bite. 'I've been meaning to ask you, has Rachel said anything to you about Lucas?'

'No, why?'

'Never mind.'

'Oh my god. You can't just say that and not tell me, Braxton!'

My smile widens. She was always nosy; I could never keep a secret from her. 'It was just something Lucas said the other night.'

'What did he say?' She leans forward in her chair as she awaits my reply.

'I think something was going on between him and Rachel behind our backs.'

Her eyes widen with shock. 'No *way*. Really? Why would you think that? Rachel hasn't even mentioned him to me.'

'You might not have noticed, but he's been really aggressive towards her lately. It's totally out of character for him. They always got on well.'

'And?'

'And, when I called him out on it the other night, he confessed to being in love with her.'

'Get *out*.'

The way she says that makes me chuckle. 'He said she didn't feel the same.'

'I'm going to ask her. She's coming over for a farewell dinner tomorrow night.'

'A farewell dinner?' Her comment surprises me.

'Yes. She's going back to New York.'

I can tell by her expression that she's saddened by this. She always got a little low when Rachel came home for the holidays and then left again. She hated her being so far away, but she also understood that New York was where Rachel needed to be for her career.

'Don't tell her what I told you though. Jesus, Lucas would kill me if he knew.'

'I won't, but I'll definitely see what I can find out. Women have a way with things like that.'

'Don't I know it,' I say, snickering.

As I clear away the breakfast dishes and stack the dishwasher, I slide my next letter into my back pocket, to give her when I drop her off. I was inspired to write it after our conversation in the car yesterday morning. I ducked out yesterday when I was at work, picking up a tiny car charm to accompany it.

LETTER TEN . . .

Dearest Jemma,

Late August, 2005. I'm not sure of the exact date, but this was the month you got your learner's permit. A month that I not only worried for your safety, but that of everyone else on the road . . . including the pedestrians. Okay, that may be a slight exaggeration, but let's just say you didn't get off to the best start.

We both sat on your front steps as you waited for your dad to arrive home from work. You and I had caught the bus into town after school so you could sit your theory test at the motor registry. You hadn't expected to pass on your first attempt, but you did. As we would find out later that day, the actual driving wasn't so easy.

The moment your father pulled into the driveway, you leaped up and ran to him. 'I got my learner's!' you screamed, waving your L-plates around in the air.

'That's wonderful, pumpkin,' he said, pulling you into an embrace and kissing your forehead. 'I'm so proud of you.'

'Can you take me for a drive . . . please?' You held your hands up in prayer position for added effect.

He laughed at your antics. 'After dinner.'

'Oh please, Daddy,' you begged. Like me, your father was powerless to your pleas. 'Just one lap around the block.'

'Okay, one lap.'

'I love you, Daddy,' you squealed, leaping into his arms.

He went inside to drop off his briefcase and say hello to your mum before showing you how to secure your L-plates to the front and back of the vehicle.

'Come on, Brax,' you called out when it was time to get into the car. We sat in the driveway for a good twenty minutes while your father went over all the gadgets with you. Finally, you turned the key in the ignition and shrieked with excitement as the car roared to life.

'Place your foot down firmly on the brake pedal,' your dad said, 'and release the handbrake. Good girl. Leave your foot on the brake, and move the gearstick into reverse ... Right, now remove your foot from the brake and place it down lightly on the accelerator.'

I'm not sure if you didn't hear the lightly part, or whether you had lead in your shoes that day, but the car went flying backwards so fast it catapulted our bodies forward. Lucky we had buckled up, or I'm certain we all would have flown through the windscreen.

'Braaake! Jesus Christ! I said lightly,' your father scolded. You did as he asked, but you slammed your foot down so hard that we were all pushed back into our seats.

'I'm sorry, Daddy.'

Your father pinched the bridge of his nose while releasing a long drawn-out breath. 'It's okay, pumpkin. Let's try this again. Put the car in reverse and ease out gently. Gently!' He made sure to accentuate the word gently this time. 'Use the mirrors to guide you.'

The car moved about a metre, and then jerked when you put your foot back on the brake. You did this all the way down the driveway. By this stage I was pretty certain I was going to end up with whiplash.

'Watch the letterbox,' your father warned, but it was too late. There was a sickening crunch as you ran straight over the top of it.

'Shit,' you said as you continued backward. I placed my hand over my mouth to muffle my laugh.

You missed the driveway completely, and our bodies were thrown around when the car drove over the gutter one wheel at a *time. From the street I could now see the poor flattened letterbox in a crumpled mess on the footpath.*

'I'm sorry, Daddy,' you said again. I'm pretty sure you muttered those exact words a hundred times over the coming days.

'I hated that letterbox anyway,' he replied, but you could tell by the tone of his voice he wasn't impressed. Your mum had bought it at a craft fair. It was shaped like a bird house, and had fake birds sitting on top. 'Go back a little further,' he instructed. 'Then straighten up.' You went back further all right, but a little too much. It was garbage night and bins lined the footpath on both sides of the street. You reversed straight into Mr Drake's, knocking it over and spilling rubbish all over the place.

'Put the car in park,' your father said with frustration, before removing his seatbelt and exiting the vehicle. You and I both followed. 'I think that's enough driving for one day.' I again had to stifle my laugh. I felt bad for finding this situation humorous as soon as I saw you were on the verge of tears. 'We need to clean this mess up.'

The following afternoon, your father let you have another crack at it. He was a braver man than me, because I was already thinking of excuses as to why I couldn't come. But in the end I decided I'd risk my life, if it meant supporting you. Love can make you do crazy things sometimes.

'I've just got to duck home and grab something,' I said as you placed your L-plates on the car.

When you saw my bike helmet on my head, your eyes widened before narrowing into slits. 'Very funny, arsehole,' you snapped, playfully punching me in the arm.

Your dad laughed as I climbed into the back seat. 'Smart man,' he whispered before you reached the driver's side.

This time it was impossible for you to take out the letterbox, because it was gone. My fingers dug painfully into the leather lining in the back seat as the car jolted down the street, but I started to relax a little when I noticed you could actually drive okay in a straight line. It didn't last long, though.

'Put your right indicator on,' your father said as we neared the end of the street. 'Brake slightly,' which was more of a sudden jerk, 'then turn the wheel to the right as you round the corner.'

You didn't turn it enough, and we mounted the kerb and almost ran down a pedestrian, and the small dog she was walking.

It's safe to say that after one trip around the block with you, your father and I were a collective nervous wreck. 'I'm going to need to invest in one of those helmets,' your father whispered to me while you removed the L-plates from the car.

When we entered the house, you looked completely deflated and headed straight for your bedroom.

'You two are as white as ghosts,' your mother said when we walked into the kitchen.

'She's definitely your daughter,' your father replied with a sigh, as he headed straight for the fridge to grab a beer. I was nearly seventeen, and underage, but boy could I have done with one of them as well.

For the interim, your dad banned you from driving on the road. Instead, for the next four weeks he took you to the local oval, or at night to an empty car park. It wasn't until he was certain you were fit to drive on the road again that the proper lessons recommenced.

The more you drove, the more confident you became, and before long we were all comfortable getting in the car when you were behind the wheel.

A year later, on the eleventh of August 2006, it was time for you to take your driving exam. Your father had no idea you'd booked in for it; you told me you were scared of letting him down if you didn't pass. He had dedicated so much time to making sure your driving was up to scratch.

I came with you, and I saw how badly your hands shook when the instructor called your name. 'Good luck, Jem,' I said, hugging you briefly. 'You've got this in the bag.'

I paced back and forth in the motor registry as I awaited your return. Thirty minutes later you walked through the door with a huge smile on your face.

'I passed!' you said, leaping into my arms.

'I'm so proud of you.' I wrapped my arms around your waist, swinging you in a circle.

That night your parents took us out to dinner to celebrate. They let you drive. You couldn't have wiped the smile off your father's face if you tried.

The following Saturday morning, you woke to find a small red second-hand car sitting in your driveway. It was a 1999 Ford Laser, wrapped in a huge white bow.

'Be safe,' your father said, handing you the keys. 'Always remember everything I taught you.'

'I promise, Daddy,' you said, wiping a tear from your eye.

That weekend we drove anywhere and everywhere. You even let me drive some of the time. My father couldn't afford to buy me a car, but I was okay with that. I didn't need one now anyway—wherever you went, I was right beside you. Just the way it had always been.

What we had is far too beautiful to be forgotten.

Yours always,

Braxton

TWENTY-SIX

Braxton

Now that Jemma has started running again, I get to see her almost every day. The best part is having her at our home, even if it's only for a short time. In those moments I can pretend we are everything we once were. And it gives me hope that one day we will be that again.

Today at the end of her physiotherapy we received the best possible news: no more sessions.

'I guess those morning runs along the beach have done me wonders,' Jemma says with a sweet smile as we leave the rehab centre for the last time.

They've done me wonders as well. They've done *us* wonders; I feel we have taken a huge step forward.

'I can't believe this is my last time here. I can finally try to put this all behind me and move on with my life,' she says as we head towards the car.

All I can think is: *Please don't let that be a life without me.*

'We should celebrate,' I suggest, all the while expecting her to shut me down.

'Celebrate how?'

'I could take you out for dinner tonight.'

When her brow furrows, I already know what the answer is. 'I'm sorry, I can't.'

'Oh.' Just as I suspected. 'Never mind, it was just an idea.'

I break away from her, heading towards the passenger side to open her door.

'Braxton, wait.' She grabs hold of my elbow.

'It's okay, Jemma.' I turn to face her, and force out a smile. 'Forget I even mentioned it.'

'I don't want to forget it,' she says. 'Tonight we're having a farewell dinner for Rachel at Christine's, you're welcome to come if you like . . . or we can go out to dinner tomorrow night.'

'Really?'

'Yes, really.'

I try not to show how happy this makes me, but I fail miserably.

I help her in, before walking around the front of the car towards the driver's side. I'm whistling as I go.

'Braxton,' Jemma says shyly, picking at an imaginary piece of lint on her pants. 'Christine told me that you didn't leave my side when I was in a coma, and, well . . . you've helped me every step of the way since. If I haven't already said it, I just want to say thank you.'

Her eyes finally meet mine. 'You don't have to thank me, Jem. I promised to love you in sickness and in health, and I meant every word.'

She smiles before reaching for her seatbelt. 'Just so you know, if I had to choose one person to celebrate with, it would be you.'

Her words are spoken with such sincerity.

'What are you looking so cheery about?' Lucas asks when I waltz into his office.

'I'll be leaving early today.'

'Okay . . . The reason?'

'I have a date. Well, technically it's not a date, but I'm taking Jemma out to dinner tonight. She's finally finished with her rehab, so we're going to celebrate.'

His face lights up. 'No shit? I'm happy to hear that, buddy.'

I plonk myself down in the leather chair opposite his desk. 'I really feel like we're making progress.'

'For your sake, I hope you're right. Just don't go getting your hopes up. I'd hate for you to be let down again.'

'I know. But as long as she's still willing to have me in her life, I'm not giving up on us.'

'I wouldn't expect anything less.'

'So, how are you?' I ask.

'I'm super, why?' The way he squirms in his seat tells me he knows where I'm going with this question.

'Are you just going to pretend you didn't tell me you were in love with Rachel the other night?'

He shrugs. 'It was just stupid drunk talk. I didn't know what I was saying.'

'Right. You had what—two beers? I know you, man—even drunk-arse Lucas doesn't say things he doesn't mean.'

His body stiffens as his pleading eyes meet mine. 'Can we just drop it?'

'Okay. Just tell me one thing: how long has this been going on?'

'I don't know. Five or six years, I guess,' he says, slumping back into his seat.

'Five or six *years*? Shit. How did I not see this?'

'Because you were always too busy following Jemma around like a lost puppy.' I smile; he's probably right. 'At first it was a bit of fun. I mean, she's hot, she's funny . . . what's not to like? We'd hook up every now and then. After she moved to New York I missed her, and that's when I realised I'd developed real feelings for her.'

'And those feelings weren't reciprocated?'

'I thought we were going to drop this,' he snaps, running his fingers through his hair as he huffs out a breath.

'I'm sorry, mate.'

'Shit happens. She's not the first, and she certainly won't be the last.' He tries to brush it off with a casual flick of his hand.

Why do I get the feeling he doesn't mean that?

It's around four when I leave the office. I'm not picking Jem up until six, but I have a few things to do before then. The first thing on my agenda is to pick up my dry-cleaning, then head to the florist to buy flowers for Jemma. Not just any old flowers, her favourite kind.

I've made a reservation at our favourite restaurant, The Sea Shanty. It's where I took her on our first date. She won't remember that, of course, but I can only hope it will spark some kind of recognition, especially considering she designed the interior.

The food has always been amazing—the best seafood in town—but when we first started going there the décor was dated and mismatched. It used to drive Jemma insane, so when the new management took over four years ago, she was delighted when they hired her to redesign the place.

I can't wait for her reaction when she sees it. I made sure to tell the owners, Matt and Trish, about Jemma's memory loss when I made the reservation. I don't want them to be offended by Jemma's aloofness, nor do I want them to say anything that might upset her. I need tonight to be perfect.

I take Bella-Rose for a walk along the beach when I get home from work, before jumping in the shower. I'm standing in front of the sink in the bathroom, shaving, when I hear my phone ding in the bedroom, alerting me I have a message.

After washing my face, I head into my room. My towel is hung low around my waist. My black trousers and the blue shirt Jemma bought me when we were on our honeymoon in Hawaii are laid out on the bed. She said it reminded her of my eyes. It will be the first chance I've had to wear it.

When I see Jemma's name on the screen, I get a sinking feeling in my stomach at the thought that she might be cancelling.

I'm excited about tonight. Rachel and I went shopping yesterday afternoon. I bought a new dress. I hope you like it.

I'm smiling as I type my reply. The fact that she even cares if I like it makes me happy. I don't want to get my hopes up, because technically this is just a celebration dinner, but I have a good feeling about tonight.

I'm looking forward to tonight too, I reply. *I can't wait to see your new dress. I don't doubt for a second that you'll look beautiful.*

My stomach flutters with both excitement and nerves when I pull into Christine's driveway. I wasn't even this nervous when I took her out on our very first date, but things are very different now.

The young, naïve Braxton took everything for granted. Back then, I presumed she would be mine forever, but now I know better.

I tell myself I'm being stupid. It's just dinner with Jem, there's nothing to be nervous about. We've dined together thousands of times over the years.

When the door opens and I'm greeted by Jem's smiling face, all my nerves vanish. I take a step back, as my eyes travel down the length of her body. The sight of her literally takes my breath away.

She's wearing a red silk sleeveless dress that stops just above her knees. It's simple, yet incredibly sexy, accentuating her luscious lean body perfectly. I've always loved her in red. It stands out beautifully against her dark hair and olive complexion.

'Wow!'

'You like?' she says, placing her hand over the scar on her arm. I hate that it makes her feel self-conscious.

'I love,' I reply, using my free hand to gently remove hers. Those scars will be a permanent reminder to us both, but they're a part of her now. 'You don't have to hide from me, Jem.'

She gives me a tight smile. 'I love your shirt,' she says. 'It makes your blue eyes pop.'

'You bought this for me on our honeymoon.'

Her smile is worth the time it took to iron. 'I have good taste.'

'Of course you do: you married me, didn't you?' She laughs as she playfully slaps my arm. 'Oh, I almost forgot,' I say, holding the flowers out to her. 'These are for you.'

When her face lights up, my heart sings. That's exactly the look I was hoping for; it confirms my old Jem is still in there somewhere.

'They're beautiful, thank you.' I'm transfixed as she brings them to her nose and closes her eyes. My lips curve up when she inhales deeply. 'Mmm. They smell divine. And I love the purple and yellow together.'

'They have always been your favourite.'

She smiles and moves to the side so I can enter. 'Come in, I'll just put these in water before we go.'

When she turns and walks towards the kitchen, I start to follow, but I'm instantly stopped in my tracks. The red dress she's wearing is backless. *Completely backless.* The base stops just above the curve of her perfect round arse. I inwardly groan as I shove my hands in my pockets. Everything in me wants to reach out and touch her—if I can get through the night without doing exactly that, it will be a damn miracle.

We fall into easy conversation on the way to the restaurant, but my mind is consumed by that dress. If she wore it to drive me crazy, she succeeded.

As we walk from the car I instinctively move to place my hand on the small of her back, but I quickly rethink that move; touching her silky soft skin will do me no favours.

I already feel utterly frustrated . . . I have been aching for her for months.

'Wow, this place is beautiful,' she says as soon as we step inside The Sea Shanty. 'Oh, look at that row of round windows. They look like they're off a ship.'

'They actually are.'

'What a neat idea . . . such a great touch.' Her comment makes me smile.

Trish, the owner, walks into the reception area a minute later.

'Braxton, it's so good to see you again.' She pulls me into a hug, before moving her attention to Jemma. She's smiling, but I can also see a hint of sadness in her expression; she knows about Jemma's accident, about what she has lost. 'Hi, I'm Trish.'

'Hi. It's lovely to meet you,' Jemma says, extending her hand, but Trish ignores it, opting to pull her into an embrace instead. I'm pleased to see Jemma smiling when Trish lets her go. 'You have a lovely place here.'

'We have you and your amazing eye for detail to thank for that.'

Jemma's eyes, clearly confused, briefly dart towards me. I feel for her; I can only imagine how it must feel to be thrust into a world you no longer remember. I've learned over the past few months to ease into things gently with Jemma, otherwise she becomes overwhelmed. 'Matthew, get your sexy butt out here,' Trish calls out over her shoulder, 'Braxton and Jemma are here.'

Her comment makes me laugh, and I notice that even Jemma smiles. I love these two, and Jemma did too.

'Where are my two favourite people?' he bellows from somewhere in the back of the restaurant.

His face lights up as soon as he steps into the reception area. He vigorously shakes my hand before pulling Jemma into a crushing hug. When he finally lets her go, he cups her face in his hands.

'How have you been, sweet girl? We heard about what happened, and the missus and I were really shaken by the news.'

Jemma smiles awkwardly and takes a step back. I see Trish elbow him in the side and I have to suppress my laugh. 'I'm doing okay,' she says, tucking a strand of hair behind her ear. That's when I notice she's not only wearing her memory bracelet on her wrist, but also the shell earrings I gave her when we were kids.

'Come on, Matthew,' says Trish, 'leave them be. I have your table ready,' she finishes, turning to me.

'Only the best table in the house for our favourite customers,' Matt says.

They lead us out to their private dining area on the balcony, overlooking a clear, uninterrupted view of the ocean. She wasn't kidding about the best seats in the house.

I had booked this same table for our nineteen-day anniversary, the day of Jemma's accident. It has taken us longer than I planned to make it here, but finally the night has come.

I pull Jemma's chair out for her.

'Always such a gentleman,' Trish says, elbowing Matt in the ribs. 'You could learn a thing or two from him, Matthew Sutherland.'

'Do we know these people well?' Jemma asks, when we're finally alone.

'We used to dine here often.'

'Oh. Okay. I really like them.'

'Me too. They're good people.'

I watch her as her eyes move around the space. The old Jem would do that everywhere we went. 'The view from here is spectacular.'

'It's breathtaking,' I reply, looking straight at her.

'I love the way this place is decorated.'

'Would you be surprised if I told you that you decorated it?'

Her eyes widen. 'No way. Really?'

'Uh huh.'

She looks around in wonderment. 'I'm impressed that I did this. It has a very nautical feel to it. The perfect décor for a seafood restaurant.'

'That's the look you were going for.' She had decorated it in a similar colour scheme to our own place: whites, blues, and a hint of yellow here and there. She draped white fishing nets from the ceiling and handpicked a variety of nautical memorabilia.

'You have an amazing talent for interior design.'

She goes quiet and I notice her gaze moves down to her lap, so I reach for her hand across the table.

'I secretly knew you'd been dying to get your hands on this place when Trish and Matt took over. You hated how mismatched the old décor was.'

She giggles before squeezing my hand. 'Thank you.'

'For what?'

'For everything. I'm not sure where I'd be right now if it wasn't for you. You keep me sane.'

I let go of her hand and sit back in my chair when the waitress approaches. She places a Corona with a wedge of lime in front of me, and to Jemma she presents a tall glass that contains ice and a dark orange liquid. It's garnished with a piece of lemon and one of those tiny umbrellas. We both thank her before she turns and leaves.

'Did we order these?' Jemma asks.

'No. We're here a lot and Trish knows what we like, so they never bother taking our order.'

She picks up her glass and takes a sip of her drink. 'Yum. What is this?'

'Vodka, lemon, lime and bitters.'

'It has alcohol in it?'

'It does.'

'It tastes better than that awful wine Rachel had me drinking the other night.'

'Wine doesn't really agree with you,' I chuckle. I don't bother elaborating, because it will only embarrass her. I'll save that story for another time.

The entrees come out, followed by the mains a while later. 'Wow, what is that?' Jem whispers to me across the table when the waitress leaves.

'Lobster mornay. It's your favourite dish.'

Her head lowers as she studies the shell of the lobster.

'You just eat the lobster meat and sauce inside it,' I say as I watch her.

A playful smile tugs at her lips as her eyes move back to mine. 'Did you seriously think I was going to try to eat the shell?'

Shrugging my shoulders, I smile as I pick up my beer and take a swig.

Music is playing softly in the background as we talk about everything and nothing, just like we always did. Though so much of our time was spent together, there was always so much to say.

'I feel like I need to go for a run now to burn off some of that food,' she says contentedly.

Running wasn't the way we had burned off food before the accident, but I already know that's not how this night will end. Instead, I ask her to dance. Not because I enjoy dancing, but there is nothing I love more than to hold Jemma in my arms.

Her face illuminates with a smile. 'Okay.'

Removing the napkin from my lap, I stand and move around to her side of the table to pull out her chair. I can't take my eyes off her back as I follow her onto the dance floor. It's driving me crazy. This dress is almost my undoing; I've always loved her long, lean back. There's not a single part of her that I don't love. Her eyes, her lips, her perfect little nose, her pretty face, her long legs, her dainty hands, her soft skin . . . I could go on forever. I remember all too well the feeling of her beneath the weight of my fingertips, and the sensation of our naked bodies meshed together, connected as one.

I yearn for that again. *Every damn inch.*

She comes to a stop in the middle of the dance floor, and turns to face me. When I see a nervous smile tug at her lips I don't hesitate to pull her into my arms. Her breath hitches and I have to suppress the groan that bubbles in the back of my throat as my hands slide around her waist, coming to rest on her bare back.

Her arms encircle my neck, and her body instantly melts into mine. I close my eyes and savour this moment. She feels like home when she's in my arms.

She starts to sway to the music, and my body can't help but react to her. I find myself willing my erection to stay down, but I should know by now that I have no control over this. When it comes to her I never have. I clench my eyes tighter but it's no use, there's no sign of retreat. *Please don't let her notice.*

My eyes spring open when I hear her gasp a few seconds later. *Shit, she noticed.*

'I'm sorry,' I whisper into her hair. 'It's been so long since I've held you like this.'

She tilts her head back as her eyes lock with mine. The sadness I see on her face tugs at my heart. Asking her to dance was a mistake; she's not ready. I've been selfish, but only because I'm desperate.

My arms drop down by my side, but as I start to take a step back, she stops me. 'Don't. It's okay.' I feel my body relax as I reach for her again. 'Oh Braxton,' she says a moment later, burying her face in my chest. When I hear her muffled giggle, I draw my face back.

'Are you laughing at me?'

'No.' But then she loses it. I feel her body convulsing against mine as she laughs. When she snorts, I find myself laughing along with her. 'Talk about an awkward first date,' she says, removing one of her arms from around my neck, so she can wipe the tears from her eyes.

'Awkward doesn't quite cover it,' I mumble.

This moment is like deja vu, because the same thing happened to us the first time we danced together, back in high school. I consider throwing in the boy scout torch excuse that I used back then, but she won't get it. I still cringe when I think about that night, but it's also the moment that propelled our relationship out of the friend zone for good.

'Do you want to sit down?' I ask.

'Not yet. Besides, I don't think it would be wise if we were to part right now.'

I can still hear the amusement in her voice. The old Jem would have reacted the same way, but things are different now, and I'm constantly scared I'm going to do something that will drive her further away.

'True. Someone could lose an eye,' I reply.

She throws back her head and laughs.

I tighten my grip, and let out a contented sigh. 'Thanks for coming here with me tonight, Jem. You have no idea how much it means to me.'

She doesn't reply, but I'm okay with that. Instead she rests the side of her face against my erratically beating heart.

The song finishes, but she holds tight. 'One more song.' She'll get no complaints from me. 'I'm enjoying dancing with you.'

'Me too, Jem.'

We used to dance like this at home. If there was music playing, I would pull her into my arms, or vice-versa.

Our song comes on next, and it makes me wonder if Trish is behind this, or if it's fate. Either way, I take it as a sign. 'The First Time Ever I Saw Your Face' is the song that came on the radio the first time we danced, and the song we danced to on our wedding day.

It is the perfect song for us. It describes everything I've felt from the first time I laid eyes on her, our first kiss, the first time we made love, and everything in between.

Tonight I'm filled with mixed emotions, and listening to the lyrics is bittersweet. My love for her since the accident hasn't diminished one bit, but things are very different between us now.

When the last notes of the song play, she lifts her head off my chest and looks up at me, and I'm surprised to see tears falling down her beautiful face.

'Jem, what's wrong?'

She releases a nervous laugh before she speaks. 'That song . . . it was so beautiful. Those words really touched my heart.'

I smile as I run the pad of my thumb across her cheek. I have no idea why I don't tell her that this is our song, but I don't.

Everything in me wants to kiss her beautiful mouth as she stares up at me with those haunting brown eyes of hers, but instead I lean forward and simply place my lips on her forehead. It is enough.

TWENTY-SEVEN

Jemma

I find myself smiling as I stare out into the night on our drive home. I feel so happy, and I'm sad that it's coming to an end. It was a perfect first date.

When we pull into Christine's driveway I already know that Braxton will open my door for me by the time I've undone my seatbelt. I love how he always takes care of me.

Butterflies flutter in my stomach as he holds out his hand to me. 'I had such a nice time,' I say as he walks me to the door.

'Me too.' He slides his hands into the pockets of his trousers as we stop at the base of the stairs. 'Hopefully we can do it again sometime.'

'I'd like that.'

Things feel a little awkward as we stand and silently look at each other. I'd love to know what's going through his head right now. I know exactly what's going through mine: I want him to kiss me. I felt the same way when he stared down at me after our last dance at the restaurant. I don't entirely understand all these feelings I have when I'm around him . . . all I know is that he makes me *feel*.

I reach up to nervously tuck my hair behind my ears. His eyes follow my every move, before focusing on my memory bracelet.

'I love that you wore that tonight,' he says, reaching out to touch it.

'I love it.' I look down at my wrist as my fingers move over the charms. They touch the tiny bike, then the shell, before settling on the tree. 'This is for the day you fell out of the tree trying to rescue my kite.' My eyes dart up to him, and though he's smiling I see sadness in his eyes, which in turn makes tears cloud mine. 'I used Stephen's ladder to climb the tree in the backyard. I wanted to see the message you'd carved into the tree.'

'You did? But it was so high up.'

'Heights don't bother me.'

'Was it still there?'

'Yes. *BS loves JR*, inside a heart.'

A lone tear escapes, cascading down my cheek. Braxton's hand quickly moves to the side of my face, and his thumb gently swipes across my cheek, catching it.

'Can I kiss you, Jem?'

'Yes,' I reply without hesitation. In this moment there's nothing I want more.

My heart thumps furiously in my chest as he takes a step towards me, closing the gap between us. His fingers slide into my hair as he gently tilts my head back. His face inches forward, and the moment his lips meet mine the world around me stops. My hands fist in his shirt as my body instinctively melts into his.

He opens his mouth slightly and deepens the kiss, and I have no control over the soft moan that falls from my lips. His kiss awakens my entire body, making me feel so . . . *alive*.

I immediately feel the loss when he draws back. 'Wow,' I breathe. He rests his forehead against mine, and although I can't see his mouth, I know he's smiling.

Goosebumps pebble my skin as his thumb tenderly caresses my cheek. 'Goodnight, Jem.'

'Goodnight.'

When I close the front door behind me, I lean back into it and sigh. I feel my lips curve into a smile as my fingertips brush across them. Things are definitely changing between us, and surprisingly, that doesn't scare me in the slightest . . . it excites me.

I can't wait to see him in the morning.

My eyes spring open and then immediately close again as I'm almost blinded by the light flooding into my bedroom. Sitting up, I rub my eyes—and my heart sinks when I see it's 9.34am. I missed my run, but more importantly I missed breakfast with Braxton.

Throwing back the covers, I leap out of bed. I jump when I fling my bedroom door open and find Christine standing a few feet away.

'God,' I say, clutching my chest. 'I wasn't expecting to see you standing there.'

'Sorry, sweetheart. I was just coming up to check on you.'

'I slept in . . . I missed my run.'

My disappointment is quickly replaced with happiness when I see a letter in her hand. 'It appears you two had a great time last night. Braxton couldn't stop smiling when he dropped this off. His face looked a lot like yours does.'

'Thanks,' I say, taking it from her. 'We had an amazing time.'

'That makes me so happy.' She reaches for my hand, giving it a squeeze. 'You two were made for each other.'

I'm starting to believe that.

From what I've learned of my past, I think my parents were made for each other as well. 'Do you think you'll ever be able to forgive Dad for everything that happened?'

My question surprises her. She's silent for a brief time before finally answering with a very firm, 'No.' I sigh when she turns and heads towards the staircase. I refuse to believe that.

Closing my bedroom door, I look down at the letter in my hand and quickly find myself smiling again. I'm eager to find out about another adventure from my life.

LETTER ELEVEN . . .

Dearest Jemma,

The tenth of November 2006. It was a Friday, and two weeks before my high-school formal. The following year I would head off to university. You still had one more year of high school, and as excited as I was to embark on this new journey in my life, there was one major hurdle standing in my way: I was going to be an hour-and-a-half's drive from you. That thought made me sick to the stomach.

'I've got a fitting tomorrow morning for my tux for the formal, do you want to come with me?' I asked as we drove home from school in your red rocket. That's what you had affectionately named your car.

'Hell, yes. I need to come to make sure you actually get one.'

You were the one who talked me into going in the first place. You said one day I'd regret it if I didn't, but I doubted that.

Our school had a stupid rule that if you wanted to take a date, it could only be someone from your year, which meant I couldn't take you.

The next morning after breakfast we headed into town.

'Do I really have to go through with this?'

'Yes, you do.' I heard the tailor snicker when you said that.

'It seems like I'm going to an awful lot of trouble to just stand around and have a miserable time.'

'You're not going to stand around, mister. You're going to dance and have a wonderful time.'

'I'm not dancing.'

'Yes, you are.'

'I'll look pretty silly dancing on my own.'

'You're not going on your own, you can dance with your date.' This was news to me. 'It's your school formal. One you'll look back on in years to come with fond memories.'

'No, I won't. I'll look back and curse you for making me go.'

When the fitting was finished, I paid my deposit and was told I could pick the tux up on the Wednesday before the formal.

I was thankful that you didn't mention it for the rest of the weekend, but the following Tuesday, you sought me out at lunchtime. 'I compiled this list for you,' you said, handing it to me.

I looked down and saw a list of names. All girls from my year. I didn't even need to ask, I already had a fair idea what this was about.

'I asked around and none of these girls has a date for the formal.'

'I told you I don't want to go with anyone.'

I shoved the list back into your hands, but you promptly thrust it straight back into mine. 'You have to take a date. You're going to look silly turning up on your own. All your mates have dates.'

'I don't care if I look silly.'

'Come on, Braxton, humour me here, will you?'

I blew out an exasperated breath before scrunching the list up and shoving it into my pocket. 'I'll think about it.'

For the next two days you pestered me to the point where I ended up asking Samantha Murphy. It turned out to be a huge mistake. Not only did she squeal when I asked her, she followed me around like a lost puppy for the next week and a half. She sat next to me in class, and became my permanent shadow at recess and lunch. She somehow even got hold of my phone number. All I will say is, thank god for caller ID.

The day of the formal, my father closed the shop early—which was a rarity—so he could be home in time to see me before I left. He was also lending me his car for the night. I couldn't really expect Samantha to catch a bus with me to the formal, and it's not like my father had the money for me to hire a fancy car like some of my mates had.

When I was ready I stood in front of the mirror, and was surprised by how good I actually looked in my tux. Dressing up like this was something I didn't do often. Actually, my mum's funeral, and your thirteenth birthday were the only other times I'd worn a suit.

'You look great, son,' my father said when I headed downstairs. 'My boy is now a man. Where has all this time gone? It feels like only yesterday I was bouncing you on my knee.' I was taken aback when he pulled me into a crushing hug. 'I'm so proud of you, and if your mother was here she would be too.'

'Thanks, Pop,' was all the reply I could manage.

When my father finally drew back, he turned his face away from me and wiped his eyes. My dad never showed his emotions, and my heart hurt for him as I swallowed hard, trying to get rid of the lump that had now formed in my throat.

'I called into the florist on my way home to get this for you.' He turned and picked up a clear plastic display box from the side table. There was a small white flower arrangement inside. 'It's a corsage for your date. I don't know what colour her dress is, so I went with white to be safe. I bought one for your mother when we went to our school formal.'

'Thanks, Pop,' I said again.

'I also wanted to give you this.' He then pulled a cheque out of his back pocket and handed it to me.

'What's this?' I looked down and had to blink a few times when I saw all those zeros.

'It's to pay your university fees.'

'You can't afford this kind of money.' I extended it back towards him. 'I can't take this from you.'

'You can accept this, and you will,' he said, pushing my hand away. 'Your mother and I used to put a few dollars away each week for your education, but then . . .' His words drifted off, but I knew what he was going to say. 'I ended up having to use that money for her funeral.' My gaze moved down to the carpet, and the lump in the back of my throat grew bigger. 'Life can be unfair sometimes, son, but you just make the best of what you've got.'

'But this is money you don't have.'

'I took a small mortgage out on the store. I don't want you to start your adult life with a huge student loan hanging over your head.'

'Pop . . .'

'Please. It would mean a lot to me if you'd accept this. I want you to have all the opportunities I didn't. I want you to do something you're passionate about, and have a successful career, a career you love. Be somebody, son . . . be the man you were destined to be.'

I sighed deeply before nodding my head. 'I won't let you down, Pop. I'm going to be the best damn architect this town has ever seen.'

'That's my boy,' he said, patting my shoulder.

I only agreed to take the money because I knew how much it meant to him, but I felt horrible doing it. It was something that would weigh heavily on my mind for a long time to come. I knew how hard things were for him, and this extra loan to pay off would only make things even harder.

'I took the car through a car wash earlier today so she was clean for you,' he added, grabbing the keys off the small table by the door and handing them to me. 'Let me just get the camera. I'd like to take a few photos of you before you leave.'

I pulled out my phone and sent you a text; I didn't want to go without seeing you. You'd been a little distant with me the past few days, which concerned me, but I thought you might have come over to see me before I left.

My father got me to stand in front of the large green bush in the front yard while he snapped a few pictures. I kept looking down at my phone, but you still hadn't replied. As I was about to say goodbye to Pop, your reply came through—and my heart sank. You were busy, you said, and couldn't come outside. It was *unlike you, and as I drove to Samantha's house I replayed the past few days in my mind. I knew that you must have been upset with me, because you'd never acted like that towards me before. Maybe I was clueless, but I had no idea what I'd done wrong.*

At the dance I forced out a smile and pretended I was having a great time, but the truth was I was miserable. All I could think about was you.

While Samantha was on the dance floor with her friends, I ducked out for some fresh air. The first thing I did was pull out my phone to see if you had sent me any messages. You hadn't. Leaning up against a brick wall, I closed my eyes and sighed.

'Braxton.'

My eyes sprang open when I heard my name. Standing a few metres away, like some beautiful apparition, was you. You were casually dressed in a pair of jeans and a white jumper. Your attire was in stark contrast to the ball gowns the other girls were wearing inside, but I remember thinking how beautiful you looked.

'Jem. What are you doing here?' Pushing off the wall, I closed the distance between us.

'I wanted to apologise for the way I've been acting these past few days.'

'You should've just texted me. How did you even get here?'

'I caught a bus.'

'In the dark . . . by yourself.'

'I knew I wouldn't be able to sleep until I saw you. I had to come.' You sighed as your gaze moved down to the ground.

'What's going on, Jem?'

'I don't know,' you replied, shrugging your shoulders.

'Hey.' I placed my finger under your chin, lifting your face to mine. The last thing I expected was to see tears in your eyes. 'Talk to me.'

My mind swam as I tried to make sense of all this. I knew that things were changing for us, with me going away to uni, but this seemed like something more.

'I heard Samantha tell some of the girls at school that she was going to have sex with you after the formal.'

'What?' That was so ridiculous I almost laughed. I hadn't even planned on kissing her.

Before you got a chance to say anything else, Samantha appeared at my side. 'Braxton,' she said, linking her arm with mine, 'are you coming back in?'

My attention was still focused on you, but yours was now on her. The look you were giving her confused me. Was it possible you were jealous?

'I shouldn't have come,' you said as your eyes moved back to me. 'Enjoy the rest of your night.'

Samantha tugged on my arm, but I gently shrugged her away. There was no way I was going to let you get back on a bus alone at that time of night.

'I'm sorry,' I said to Samantha. 'I need to go after her.' She looked sad as she turned and walked back inside. I felt bad that I had ruined her night, but my first priority was, and always will be, you.

'Jemma, wait.'

I needed to know why you were so upset about this. I grabbed hold of your arm, pulling you to a stop. When you swung around to face me, tears were streaming down your face.

'Leave me alone.'

'No, I want to know why you're so upset about what Samantha said.'

'Because.'

'Because why?'

'Because I don't want you to have sex with her.' You reached out, pushing me in the chest.

'Enough,' I said, grabbing hold of both of your wrists. 'Talk to me, Jem. Help me understand, because I have no idea what's going on.'

There was a pained look on your face when you finally confessed. 'I thought I was okay with you bringing a date tonight ... turns out I'm not. I don't want to lose you to her ... to anybody.'

'You're never going to lose me. Never. You'll always be my best friend.'

'Don't you get it? I don't want to be just friends anymore,' you whispered. 'I want to be the person you dance with, the one you kiss ... the one you have sex with.'

I could only stare at you, not quite believing your words. You were everything I had ever wanted, and all I could manage was: 'What?'

'I'm in love with you, Braxton. Not just friend love. Love, love. I think I have been for years, I just didn't know it. When I heard Samantha say she was going to have sex with you, I honestly felt like I couldn't breathe. I couldn't stand the thought of you being with anyone but me.'

I stood there for the longest time. I so wanted it to be true but I couldn't quite believe what I was hearing.

'Say something,' you pleaded as your eyes scanned my face.

But suddenly everything clicked into place. I knew that this was no time for words, it was time for action. I was about to do something I'd wanted to do for years.

I cupped your face in my hands and tilted your head back slightly, placing my lips against yours. I can't tell you how many times I'd stared at your beautiful lips over the years and wondered what they would taste like.

They tasted sweet, like honey, just like I knew they would.

I finally drew back, resting my forehead against yours. 'Wow,' I heard you whisper, and even though I think I was still in shock that we'd actually just kissed, a huge smile exploded onto my face—and I saw it reflected in yours.

'Do you want to get out of here?'

'What about the formal?'

'I didn't want to come anyway, remember? You made me.'

My hands were still cupping your face, and yours were resting on my hips. 'Next time I try to make you do something you don't want to do, ignore me.'

'I'll hold you to that.'

You linked your arm through mine and rested your head on my shoulder as we walked towards my father's car. I'll admit that there was a small part of me that was worried this was going to ruin our friendship, but I was willing to take a chance on love, because you were all I had ever wanted.

'I'm not ready to go home yet,' you said as we pulled out of the car park. 'Can we just drive around for a while?'

We ended up driving to the lookout. As kids we'd ride our bikes up there, but it was the first time we'd ever been there at night.

'Wow, the city looks so beautiful all lit up,' you said.

'It does.' But all I could think was that it didn't look half as beautiful as you.

I reached across the centre console for your hand, lacing our fingers together. 'Are you sure this is what you want?'

'A hundred per cent,' you answered. 'And you?'

'A hundred and fifty per cent.'

You were smiling as your body gravitated towards mine. 'Kiss me again.'

You didn't need to ask me twice.

When we finally came up for air, I reached over, flicking through the radio stations.

'Oh, this one, leave this on,' you said. 'Love song dedications.'

'What?'

'It's where people ring up on a Friday or Saturday night and dedicate a song to the person they love. I listen to it all the time.' You slapped my arm when I laughed at you. 'It's really sweet.'

I opened my door and climbed out of the car.

'Where are you going?' you asked.

I didn't reply.

Walking around the front of the car, I moved towards your side. I opened the door and extended my hand to you. 'Dance with me, Jem.' You looked at me like I'd lost my mind. 'You said you wanted to be the one I danced with, so let's dance.'

I slid my arms around your waist, and you wrapped yours around my neck. The song that was playing soon came to an end, but neither of us let go.

'I want to dedicate this next song to the love of my life,' a man's voice said over the radio. 'We've been best friends since we were kids, and in a few short weeks she'll become my wife. I know she's listening tonight, and I just want to say, I love you, Boo-Boo.'

'This could be our song too,' you said. 'Apart from the getting married part, they sound exactly like us'.

'I need to hear the words first,' I replied.

The song was called, 'The First Time Ever I Saw Your Face'. And you were right, it was the perfect song for us.

I drop my arms, resting the letter in my lap. I can't believe that was the same song we danced to last night. It touched something deep inside me when I heard it, and now I know why.

Your body moved slowly against mine as our lips connected. When I started to get a sensation down below, I clenched my eyes shut. I knew what was about to happen, but no matter how hard I tried to stop my body reacting to you, there was no use.

I wanted the ground to open up and swallow me whole, and I prayed you wouldn't notice. But even I knew that was impossible; our bodies were pressed tightly against each other.

A few seconds later you pulled out of the kiss and gazed up at me. I knew my face was as red as a beetroot.

'Is that a dagger in your pocket, Mr Spencer?' You were supressing a smile as you spoke. 'Or are you just pleased to see me?'

I buried my face into the crook of your neck as humiliation consumed me. 'No, it's a torch.' It was the first thing that came to mind. 'You never know when you're going to need one. I learned to always be prepared when I was a boy scout.'

You tossed your head back and laughed. 'You were never a boy scout.'

I pulled away from you, mortified. I'd never experienced anything like this before—you were the first person I'd ever held like that, the first person I'd ever kissed.

'It's getting late, I should get you home.'

'Braxton.' You reached for me when I turned and started heading back to the car. 'Don't walk away from me.'

'Just drop it, Jem.'

'Please.' You slid your arms around my waist from behind, halting me. I let out a sigh when you rested the side of your face against my back. 'It's a natural reaction. I'm sorry for laughing. I actually like that it was me who did that to you.' I inhaled a sharp breath when your hand moved down below my waist.

I liked this brazen side of you.

'You do?' I asked, turning in your arms to face you.

'Yes.' You manoeuvred your arms around my neck. 'You make me feel like that too, but unlike you, I don't have a torch to prove it. They don't teach you those kinds of things in the girl guides.'

This time I laughed. Leaning forward, I planted a soft kiss on your nose. You always knew the right thing to say to make me feel better.

'This is a learning curve for us both, but you're the only person I want to experience this with, Jem.'

You smiled, and suddenly everything was perfect again. 'Great, now that we've got that sorted, we need to finish our first dance. Our song isn't over yet.'

And that's exactly what we did. A few minutes later the heavens opened up, but even that wasn't enough to pull us apart.

We were just content being in each other's arms despite the fact that we were getting soaked.

When your body started to shiver, I bundled you into the car.

'I need to get you home and into some dry clothes. I can't have my girlfriend getting sick.' I winked at you as I closed the passenger door before running around to the driver's side.

We were both drenched, but I was more concerned about you than me. Grabbing my suit jacket off the back of my seat, I draped it over you, before cranking the heater up to high.

You placed your hand on my leg, which made me smile. I still couldn't believe this was actually happening. Yesterday we were best friends, but now we were so much more than that.

'Am I really your girlfriend now?' You were beaming as you spoke.

'I hope so. I let you feel my torch, remember? I don't let just anyone feel my torch.'

You pushed your head back into the seat and laughed. 'That's right, you did. And I sincerely hope that you don't go around letting just anyone feel your torch, especially now that you're my boyfriend.'

I cleared my throat before reaching over to turn the radio up. All this talk about torches was dangerous.

I held your hand all the way home, and kissed you goodnight when I walked you to your door. 'Sweet dreams, Jem,' I said, brushing my lips against yours one more time. I could have stood there and kissed you until the sun came up, but you were cold and wet, so I let you go.

'I'll dream of you,' you whispered.

That night had started out pretty crappy for me, but it ended up being one of the best nights of my life.

What we had is far too beautiful to be forgotten.

Yours always,

Braxton

These letters tell me so much about myself, but they also let me get to know Braxton. I've learned just as much about him from reading these—things I'm sure the old me didn't even know.

Placing the letter down beside me, I search in the bottom of the envelope for my charm. I find a small piece of paper instead.

I didn't have time to buy the charms to go with this letter, because I wrote it last night after dropping you off. I'll give them to you when I see you tomorrow morning at breakfast. x

TWENTY-EIGHT

Braxton

I pace back and forth on the deck as I wait for a glimpse of Jemma. Christine told me she was still asleep when I dropped the letter off yesterday morning, but I can't help but wonder. Was she really asleep? Or was she just hiding up in her room to avoid me? Did I overstep the mark by kissing her? She said yes when I asked her permission, and she did kiss me back.

I run my hands through my hair as uncertainty clouds my mind. Things were never this difficult before. I always knew where I stood with her.

I went into a panic yesterday when I woke and saw it was almost nine. I thought I'd missed her, that she'd come for breakfast only to find me not there.

I couldn't sleep after dropping her off the night before. After tossing and turning for a few hours, I eventually got up and wrote her another letter. It was some ungodly hour by the time I finally crawled back into bed and hugged her pillow, just like I've done every night since the accident. I've washed and changed the sheets numerous times since then, but not her pillowcase. It still smells of her. It's the only thing that helps me sleep.

When I jumped out of bed yesterday, I threw on a T-shirt and a pair of sweats before walking the length of the beach with Bella-Rose. Jemma was nowhere to be seen. I ran back to the house and showered and changed in record time, before rushing to Christine's.

That kiss ... even today, it's still in the forefront of my mind. She kissed me just like she used to. It's been two days, and I'm still smiling about it.

I'm pulled from my thoughts when I hear someone speak. 'Good morning.'

I swing around and relief washes over me when I see Jemma standing on the sand at the bottom of the steps.

She came.

'Morning.' I walk towards the edge of the deck. She's not dressed in her running gear today. 'I wasn't sure if you were going to come.'

'I'm sorry I didn't make it yesterday morning, I slept in.'

'Me too.'

I must remember to give her the charms before she leaves. I bought a boy and girl kissing, and a tiny umbrella to symbolise the rain. I even considered buying a torch charm as a joke, but that's a moment I'm okay with her not remembering.

'Are you hungry?' I ask, reaching for her hand.

'Starved.'

I don't know what to do. Do I kiss her? The morning after our very first kiss, there was no confusion on how to act. Things are so different now. Back then I knew she was mine, but now I'm not so sure.

In that split second, I decide not to. Although I want to kiss her badly, I don't want to push her. Our kiss the other night propelled our somewhat strained relationship to a whole other level, and I'm not going to do anything to jeopardise that.

I do, however, keep her hand clasped in mine as I lead her towards the table on the deck. 'Sit,' I say, letting go of her hand and pulling her chair out. 'I'll go and make us a coffee.'

'Thank you,' she replies, smiling up at me.

We fall into easy conversation as we eat. She listens as I talk about my work, the small everyday things that make up my life. It's just the type of easy breakfast chat we used to have.

'Speaking of work, I better clean up this mess so we can get going.' I would much rather spend my day out here with her curled up on the bench seat like we used to on weekends, but I force myself to stand and collect the dishes.

'Let me help you,' she says.

'You don't have to.'

'I want to.'

I stand to the side so she can enter the house first, and I smile when she does exactly that. She pauses just inside the doorway as she takes in the large space before her. This house was once so alive with laughter and happiness, now it just seems far too big and quiet.

When we designed the interior, we wanted plenty of room, not only for our friends to stay over, but for the family we planned to have in the future—but I push those thoughts out of my mind. I'm just so happy she has finally found the courage to come into the house.

'Wow,' she says softly. 'It's so beautiful in here.'

The windows that run along the back of the house let in an abundance of natural light, which makes the room appear larger and illuminates the interior, increasing the overall beauty of the space. Working together on the plans for this place is one of my most precious memories of us.

I unload the dishes onto the breakfast bar and join Jemma. 'Let me take those,' I say, reaching out for the coffee mugs she's holding. 'Feel free to have a look around if you'd like.'

She keeps hold of the mugs. 'Let me help you with the dishes.'

I think that's her polite way of saying thanks-but-no-thanks, and I'm okay with that. *Baby steps.*

'You can rinse.'

'Okay.'

I can tell she's a little overwhelmed by all this, but she's smiling. Smiling is good.

We set to work, and I can't help but watch her as she stops to gaze out the window. Seeing her like this—relaxed, rinsing breakfast dishes at the sink—is such a familiar sight, and something I once took for granted. But not anymore.

'The view from here is breathtaking. I'd be happy to wash dishes every day if I could do it from here.'

I pack the dishwasher as she rinses, and we have it done in no time.

'I'll just run upstairs and grab my keys, and we'll be off,' I say.

'Could I use the bathroom before we go?'

'Of course.'

I lead her across the living room, and again I see her eyes everywhere, taking it all in. Then she spots Samson.

'Oh, is this the bird you mentioned? The one that belonged to your father?'

'Yes. Samson.'

'Come say hello. He misses his pretty girl.'

'His what?'

'That's what he calls you, *Pretty Girl.*'

'He does not,' she says with a smile.

'Come see.'

As soon as he sees us, he flies towards the front of the cage, latching his clawed feet around the wire. His eyes are firmly fixed on Jemma, and he starts to bounce up and down as we get closer. '*Squawk* . . . Pretty Girl.'

'See, I told you.'

'Pretty Girl ... Pretty Girl ... who's my Pretty Girl ... *squawk.*'

'Oh my god,' she says, covering her mouth and giggling.

'Yes, your Pretty Girl is here,' I say to Samson, sliding my finger in between the bars of the cage and scratching his neck.

'I can't believe he calls me that.'

'I might have taught him to say it.'

She laughs as she sticks her finger inside the cage. Samson moves along a few bars, until he can rub his face against her finger. 'He's so colourful.'

'He's a rainbow lorikeet.'

'You're such a pretty boy, Samson,' she whispers.

That's exactly what she has always said to him.

'The bathroom is the second door on the right,' I say, pointing her in that direction. 'I won't be long.'

When I return a few minutes later I freeze on the bottom step when I see her standing in front of the stone fireplace, staring up at the large canvas on the wall. It's my favourite picture of us on our wedding day. It captured the essence of us. We look so in love—because we were. It's hard for me to look at it every day and be reminded of everything I've lost, but I feel compelled to keep it up. Whether or not she decides to come home, this place will always be ours. It's a part of her, just as much as it's a part of me.

I watch her for a moment before speaking. I would give anything to know what she's thinking. 'Are you ready?'

She swings around to face me before tucking a stray piece of hair behind her ear; it's a habit she's retained from before. 'Sure.'

Up until now we have used the side access, but this time we leave through the front door, past the garden.

'It's so lovely out here,' she says as I lock the front door.

'You used to spend hours out here on the weekends, tending to all the flower beds. I should probably think about hiring someone to maintain it. I wouldn't know the first thing about pruning roses, or distinguishing a weed from a plant.'

'Maybe if you're free one weekend, I could come over and do them for you.'

I smile. 'I'd really like that.' *Boy, would I like that.*

The hope I've been carrying around inside me is burning so bright. What we have now is nothing compared to what we once had, but it's far better than how things were in the weeks after the accident.

'Oh, before I forget,' I say, digging into my pocket, 'here are the charms that were missing from the last letter.'

She holds out her hand, and I see the corners of her lips turn up as she looks down at them. 'They're perfect.'

'I also have this.' I pull another letter out of my back pocket, passing it to her. There's a charm that says *I love you* inside. She will understand why when she reads my words.

'Thank you. I really look forward to receiving your letters.'

'I've enjoyed writing them. Reliving the past with you has been nice.'

I reach for her hand as we walk down the front steps towards the car. That crushing feeling I've been walking around with on my chest since her accident is so light in this moment I can barely even feel it.

LETTER TWELVE . . .

Dearest Jemma,

The twenty-fifth of November 2006. It was a Saturday, and the morning after my formal. I had lain awake for most of the night. I was on such a high, but again there was that niggling feeling inside that things would be different between us. I needn't have worried.

Around 6am I woke to my phone ringing. I jolted upright. My curtains were drawn, so with the screen lit up it was easy for me to locate my phone in the darkness. I smiled as soon as I saw your number.

'Good morning, boyfriend,' *you said as soon as I answered. Your raspy voice told me you'd just woken up, but your words had me feeling immediate relief.*

'Good morning, girlfriend,' *I replied rubbing my eyes. There was something special about our conversation in the darkness. It reminded me of all the times we'd shared a room together when we were kids. We would talk for hours until eventually falling asleep.*

'So, it's true, I didn't dream it.'

'Well, if you did I must have had the same dream.'

'So, we really kissed, danced in the rain, and I felt your torch.'

Your reply made me laugh, but I was cringing on the inside.

'We definitely kissed, and danced in the rain, but the torch part never happened; you must have dreamed that.' *I heard you giggle on the other end of the line, and it made me smile.* 'So, what do you want to do today?'

'Make out.'

My smile grew. 'Okay, we can definitely do that. What else?'

'We could go to the beach.'

I had a feeling you would say that. You always wanted to go to the beach. 'Sounds great. Let me have some breakfast and I'll come over.'

'Brax?' *you said before I hung up.*

'What?'

'Eat really fast, I can't wait to kiss you again.'

'Okay,' *I said chuckling. The feeling was definitely mutual.*

Twenty minutes later I knocked on your front door. You were already dressed in your bikini and a white sundress. Your long brown hair was pulled back into a high ponytail. You looked beautiful—for once I didn't feel guilty for thinking that. You were my girlfriend now, so I was allowed to think those kinds of things.

You glanced over your shoulder to make sure your parents weren't nearby, then you grabbed the front of my T-shirt and pulled me in for a scorching-hot kiss. You tasted like a combination of mint and sweetness.

I sat at the kitchen table with you and your father while your mother cooked your breakfast. 'Have you eaten, Braxton?' she asked, placing a coffee down in front of your father.

'Thanks, love,' he said, smiling up at her from behind his newspaper.

'Yes, I've already eaten,' I replied, without taking my eyes off you. You were staring at me too, and I'm pretty sure we were both wearing dreamy smiles on our faces.

'What are you two up to?' your mother asked as her eyes darted between us. Your father folded down the front of his paper to study us both as well.

'Nothing,' you quickly said, looking down into your orange juice.

'You both look like the cat who ate the canary.'

'Nope, wasn't me,' I said. 'What about you, Jem—did you eat the canary?'

'Definitely not,' you answered, vigorously shaking your head. 'I don't like canary, it tastes too . . . feathery.'

I couldn't help but laugh. Your father just shook his head and smiled before going back to his paper. Your mother, however, continued to eye us both sceptically.

When you'd finished breakfast, you packed sunscreen, snacks and cold drinks into a bag for us.

You handed me the keys to your car as we walked across the front lawn. You used to prefer me driving. Even though you had improved, I must admit I felt safer being the one behind the wheel.

I reached for your hand as soon as I reversed out into the street. Being able to touch you was going to take some getting used to, but I was happy, and I could tell you were as well.

'Pull over,' you said as I turned the corner.

'Why? Did you forget something?'

'Just pull over,' you demanded.

As soon as we stopped, you removed your seatbelt and leaned over towards me. 'I just want to kiss you.'

We did a lot of kissing that day . . . a lot. And I'd be lying if I said I didn't love every minute of it.

After our incredibly hot make-out session in the car, we eventually arrived at the beach. We walked hand in hand to our usual spot before laying our towels down on the sand. You removed your sundress, while I pulled my T-shirt over my head.

We usually applied our own sunscreen to our arms, legs and face, but then I would do your back and you would do mine. Usually I would be quick—I didn't want you to know how much I enjoyed having my hands on your skin—but things were different now. I no longer had to hide my feelings.

I took my sweet time as I slowly massaged the cream into your silky smooth skin. You knew exactly what I was doing.

You had a cheeky smile on your face as you held your ponytail to the side and glanced at me over your shoulder. Our eyes were locked as I moved my hands to your sides, splaying my fingers over your stomach. Your pretty brown eyes fluttered shut and a soft moan fell from your lips as I slowly and meticulously ran my hands up and down your torso.

It was at that stage I knew I needed to stop, so I dropped my hands down by my side. I knew that if I didn't, I would end up with a tent in my pants, just like the night before. As much as I longed for the day I could explore your body the way I wanted to, this wasn't the time or the place.

I chuckled when you pouted.

Reaching for your hand, I laced my fingers through yours as we ran down to the water. When we were about waist deep, I let go and we both dived under an incoming wave. You surfaced right in front of me.

You positioned your arms around my neck as your lips connected with mine. This situation was new to us, but we seemed to make the transition from best friends to lovers effortlessly. One thing I'd learned since last night was that you liked to kiss.

When my arms slid around your middle, pulling your body flush with mine, you wrapped your legs around my waist under the water. I groaned into your mouth when you started to grind yourself against me. The devious smile on your face as you pulled out of the kiss told me you knew exactly what you were doing.

Your hands moved to the sides of my face, and your eyes locked with mine. 'I want you to be my first. I want to experience everything with you.'

'I want that too, Jem, but not here. Not with an audience. I want our first time to be special.'

You smiled before brushing your lips against mine. 'I love you, Braxton Spencer.' Your face dropped as you waited for my reply. It never came. 'Don't you love me too?'

'Of course I do.'

'Then why don't you say it? You've never told me you love me.'

'Just because I don't say it, doesn't mean I don't.'

You looked hurt as you untangled your legs from my waist and stood in the shallows, your arms dropping by your side. 'Well, it would be nice to hear it.'

You tried to pull away from me, but my arms were still around your waist, and I wasn't letting go anytime soon. 'The last person I said those words to . . . died.'

You frowned, trying to make sense of what I was saying, then realisation hit.

'Your mum?'

'Yes.' Bowing my head, I focused on the water around us as I tried not to let the memories of that night take over.

'Oh Braxton,' you said, sliding your arms underneath mine. You held me tight as you rested the side of your face against my chest. 'You don't ever have to say those words to me if it makes you feel uncomfortable. As long as I know you love me, that's all that matters.'

*I placed a soft kiss on your hair. 'Just know that I do, Jem . . .
I always have . . . and I always will.'*

What we had is far too beautiful to be forgotten.

Yours always,

Braxton

TWENTY-NINE

Jemma

'The taxi should be here in about fifteen minutes, Mum,' I say, popping my head into the bathroom as she puts the finishing touches to her make-up.

'Thanks, sweetheart.' She places the top back on her lipstick before turning to face me. 'Does this look okay?'

'You look beautiful.'

'It's been so long since I've been anywhere nice, or had someone else cook for me.' I smile at her comment, but inside my stomach knots. I feel awful for deceiving her, but it was my only option. 'We're going to have such fun. I might even let my hair down and have a glass of wine.'

Half an hour later, my leg bounces and my hands twist together nervously in my lap on the drive to the restaurant. 'Are you okay?' Christine asks, reaching for my hand.

'I'm fine, Mum,' I lie, forcing out a smile. This seemed like such a good idea at the time, but now I'm rethinking my devious plan.

Christine reaches into the front seat, passing the driver a twenty-dollar note. 'Keep the change,' she says.

There's a huge smile on her face and her arm slips through mine as we walk down the concrete path.

'Good evening,' the maître d' says, when we enter the restaurant.

'We have a reservation under Robinson,' I reply.

'Yes, here we go,' he says as his finger runs down the list in front of him. 'Party of three. Your other guest is waiting.'

'Other guest?' Christine asks quizzically as I reach for her hand, following the maître d' towards our table.

The moment she stops walking, grinding us both to a halt, I know she has seen him.

'What's he doing here?' she snaps. The look she gives me is equal parts hurt and anger.

'I'm sorry, Mum.'

'Why would you do this to me?' she says as tears rise to her eyes.

She spins around and starts to walk towards the exit.

'Please,' I say and reach for her elbow. 'I just wanted to have dinner with my parents together. I want to hear stories about my life when I was a child, when we were a family.' She stops walking, but doesn't turn around. 'Please, Mum, it would mean so much to me.' I feel horrible and completely selfish for pulling that card on her, but there's some truth to my plea.

She finally turns to face me. 'Fine, but don't expect me to converse with that man. As soon as we've eaten I want to leave.'

'Okay.' I reach for her, wrapping her in my arms. 'Thank you.'

We continue towards the table, and Stephen stands. His confused gaze moves between me and my mother. Technically I didn't lie to him, I just asked him to have dinner with me and left out the part about her coming.

'Pumpkin,' he says, leaning forward to place a soft kiss on my cheek.

'Hi, Dad.' His attention then moves to my mother. 'Christine, you look lovely.'

'Huh,' she huffs, grabbing hold of the back of a chair.

'Let me,' my father says.

'I can seat myself, thank you very much.'

I cringe when she flicks his hand away. I lock eyes with him. Seeing his pained look makes me realise I was stupid to think this would work. I haven't even eaten yet and I'm already suffering from indigestion.

When the waiter approaches the table, he directs his attention to Stephen. 'Would you like to start off with some drinks, sir?'

'That would be great.' He looks to Christine, but she dips her face down and stares into her lap. 'Do you still love sav blanc?'

'Possibly,' she says, without making eye contact.

'What about you, pumpkin?'

'I'll have a vodka, lemon, lime and bitters, please . . . Actually, make it a double.' I need it. The waiter nods before jotting my order down on his notepad.

'And a bottle of your best sauvignon blanc,' Stephen says, eyeing the waiter. 'And two glasses, please.'

Hooray, they both like the same wine. That's a start, I guess.

The three of us sit in silence until the alcohol arrives. I proceed to down my drink like a parched man in the desert; anything to take the edge off. I hope my parents will do the same, but the waiter pours just a small amount of wine into their glasses. I raise my own glass, signalling for another vodka. I'll be finished this by the time the next one arrives.

Stephen takes a small sip compared to Christine's gulp.

'So,' I say, trying to get this show on the road. 'I brought you both here tonight because you're my parents—obviously— and we were a family once.' My gaze moves down to the crisp white tablecloth, suddenly realising I should have planned this better. When I raise my eyes again, I see I have their complete attention. 'As you both know, Braxton has been writing me letters about my past, things we both experienced growing up.

What I was hoping to get out of tonight was some insight on my life before we moved here.'

If this doesn't work, I'm not sure where to go next.

A genuine smile forms on Stephen's face before he speaks. 'You were such a happy baby . . . Wasn't she, Chris?'

My mum glares at him, before looking at me. 'You were,' she says as her scowl turns into a smile. 'You were a good sleeper, and eater. You never gave us any trouble.'

'You loved your dummy when you were little.'

'Didn't she ever,' Christine chimes in.

'Remember those little noises she used to make when she'd suck on it?' Stephen says as his eyes move back to her. I'm waiting for her scowl again, but instead I see a smile tug at her lips.

'I do. It was so cute.'

'Your mother and I would stand there for hours just watching you sleep.'

'We did,' she agrees. 'We ended up taking it away from you just before your second birthday because it was starting to make your front teeth protrude.'

'God, she cried, didn't she, Chris?'

'For three long, agonising days,' she says, looking at him.

'My heart broke for both my girls. You couldn't bear to see her so upset. By day three you were begging me to buy a replacement dummy on my way home from work.'

'I remember,' she says, with a small laugh. 'Instead you brought her home a baby doll and told her since she was a big girl now she could take care of her own baby.'

A huge smile breaks out onto my face as I watch them.

'She loved that baby doll,' Stephen says.

'She did. She took it everywhere.'

'What was her name again?'

'Annabelle,' Christine says, nodding at the memory. 'She named the doll Annabelle.'

The conversation is completely between these two now, it's like I'm not even sitting at the table, and my heart is smiling as I watch on.

'That's right, Annabelle. Remember when the doll got lost?'

'How could I forget? She cried herself to sleep that night, sobbed in my arms.'

'I felt so bad for her,' Stephen replies.

The conversation then moves onto a funny story about when I was being toilet trained. They're both laughing. They look so happy, and it's just like the way Braxton described my parents in the letters, not how I've seen them recently.

They're so engrossed in their conversation, I take the chance to slip away from the table. 'I'm just going to use the ladies,' I say.

'Okay, pumpkin.'

Instead of heading to the bathroom, I walk towards the exit and out into the crisp evening air. My plan has worked out even better than I could have hoped.

It's completely dark outside now, and chilly. I rub my hands down my arms because I left my jacket hanging over the back of my chair in the restaurant—but I'm not going back inside to get it.

I'm not even sure where the bus stop is from here, so I reach into my pocket and pull out my phone.

'Jemma,' Braxton says as soon as he answers. 'Is everything okay?' Just hearing his voice has me smiling.

'Everything's fine. I was just wondering if you were busy.'

'I was just about to order a pizza for dinner.'

'Oh. Never mind then, I can catch a bus home. There has to be a stop around here somewhere.'

'Where are you?'

'In town.'

'I'll come get you. I don't want you catching a bus on your own at this time of night.'

Ten minutes later, I spot his car coming towards me. I step out to the kerb, waving my hand above my head so he can see me.

'Hey,' he says, when I climb into the passenger seat.

'Hi.'

'You look nice.'

'Thanks, so do you.' He's still in his work suit; he looks so handsome in a suit.

'Can I ask why you're in town alone, at night?' His eyes meet mine momentarily as he pulls away from the kerb.

'Actually, I wasn't alone.'

'Oh.' I can hear shock in his tone.

'I was dining with my parents.'

'Christine and Stephen . . . together?' His gaze leaves the road briefly, darting in my direction.

'I tricked them both into coming. Neither of them knew the other was going to be there.'

'Ouch,' he says, scrunching up his face. 'I bet that didn't go down well.'

'Surprisingly, when I left the restaurant to call you, they were both talking and laughing.'

'No way.'

'Yes way.'

'Did you spike their drinks or something? Your mum can't even stand being in the same room as him.'

'I know. She was pretty pissed with me when we first got there, but then they started reminiscing about stories from my childhood.'

'Well, I hope for your sake that this devious plan of yours works.'

'Me too,' I say as I text Stephen. *Hi Dad, it's Jemma. I'm not in the bathroom, I snuck out. You two seemed to be getting on okay, so I wanted you to have some time alone, to hopefully sort things out. Mum would never admit it, but*

I know she still loves you. Don't worry about me, I'm in the car with Braxton, he's driving me home. I'm sorry for deceiving you both, and I hope you're not angry with me. Can you please make sure Mum gets home safely?

A few minutes later I get a reply. *Your mother has just gone to look for you. And I'm not angry. I'm grateful, extremely grateful. You've pulled off the impossible tonight, kiddo. I can't thank you enough. I'm not going to get my hopes up, but this is the first time your mother has spoken to me in years. Thank you, pumpkin. I'll make sure she gets home okay. Love Dad.*

'What did he say?' Braxton asks.

'Things are going well.'

I see him smile as he watches the road. 'I'm proud of you for doing this.' He reaches across the centre console and grabs my hand. Butterflies flutter in my stomach when he laces his fingers through mine.

'So, I snuck out before we even ordered . . . Can I share that pizza with you? I'm starved.'

'Absolutely,' he says, his face lighting up. 'Do you want to come to the beach house, or would you prefer to go to Christine's?'

I find myself beaming. I'd like nothing more than to spend the remainder of my evening with him. 'The beach house is fine.'

It's close to midnight when Braxton pulls into Christine's driveway. The house is bathed in darkness, so she's either still out with my father, or in bed. I'm fine with either one—I don't want to face her tonight, just in case she's angry with me.

At the beach house I finally got to see the back deck lit up by the lanterns and fairy lights. It was just as beautiful as I imagined it would be.

We ordered a pizza and ate outside by candlelight. We stayed out there until the wind whipped up, and Braxton suggested we move inside. We ended up watching a movie together on the sofa. It was nice—there was no kissing or making out, but I was okay with that. I was acutely aware of his leg touching mine the whole time, though.

'Thanks for coming to rescue me tonight, and for the pizza and the movie,' I say, when we reach the front door.

'It was my pleasure. Thank you for the company.'

Leaning forward, he places a soft kiss on my cheek. It's sweet, but I really wouldn't have minded if he kissed my lips instead. 'Sweet dreams, Jem.'

'Goodnight.'

'Sweetheart,' Christine says, stroking my long brown hair as I sob into my pillow. 'We'll find Annabelle, she's probably packed inside one of the boxes.'

'Daddy said he looked inside the boxes and Annabelle wasn't there.'

'She'll turn up.'

'She won't . . . she's gone forever. Who am I going to play with now?'

'What about Bradley next door, he seemed like a nice boy,' she says in a soft voice. 'I bet you two will end up being the best of friends.'

I raise my head from the pillow, turning my face towards her, but my vision is clouded by tears. 'His name is Braxton,' I reply. 'Not Bradley.'

'Sorry. Braxton.' Christine wraps my small body in her arms, rocking me gently.

'Found her!'

I pull back to see a breathless Stephen standing in the doorway of my bedroom. He's holding Annabelle in the air, with a huge smile on his face. 'She was lodged under the seat in the car.'

'Annabelle!' I cry out joyfully, leaping off the bed.

———

When I reach the hallway, a smile tugs at my lips as I hear Christine humming in the kitchen. That's a good sign . . . *I hope.*

'Morning,' I say, poking my head around the corner.

'Morning, sweetheart. Come sit, I was just about to make some toast.'

I smile when she pulls out a chair for me. 'You're not angry at me?'

'A little.' Christine tries to look stern, but it's not very convincing. 'I don't like being misled.'

'I'm sorry. Dad still loves you, and I know that you're hurt by what he did, but if you're honest with yourself you'd have to admit that you still care about him too.'

She sighs as she takes the seat beside me. 'You're right, I do. He was the love of my life, and feelings that intense don't just disappear overnight. But I'm not sure if I'll ever be able to get past the betrayal.'

I want to remind her it was just a kiss, but I don't. I'm pretty sure I'd be pissed off if my husband kissed another woman. Instead, I place my hand on top of hers. 'I understand why you did the things you did, I do, but you played your part in this too. You neglected him. You shut him out when you needed him most.'

She sighs. 'I know, but I was in a bad place. I lost both my parents in the space of a week.'

'I get that, I really do. And I'm sorry you went through that. From what Braxton's told me you had good reason for being depressed, but Dad loves you; you should have let him help you through that. Shutting him out only made matters worse. Can't you see that?'

'I . . .'

When tears rise to her eyes, I pull her into my arms. 'It's okay, Mum. Everything is going to be okay. I just wish you would let go of the anger and hurt. It's destroying you.'

Within seconds, her tears manifest into racking sobs, but I don't let her go. I don't try to stop them either. She needs to get them out, and finally grieve so she can move forward.

A long time passes before they finally stop. 'I'm sorry for making you cry, but I bet you feel better for it.' I reach for the tissue box that's sitting in the centre of the table, passing it to her. 'As much as I'd love to see you two back together, I'd settle for just friends.'

She gives me a hopeful smile. 'Friends I can do. We actually had a really nice time last night.'

'I'm happy to hear that.'

When she goes to stand, I stop her. 'You sit, let me make you breakfast.'

'Thank you,' she says tenderly, and I know she's thanking me for more than breakfast. These people are my family and have done so much for me. I want to give something back. Just because I don't remember my life with them, doesn't mean I haven't developed true feelings for them.

Memories of my dream last night flutter around in my head. Was it just a coincidence? My parents had talked about Annabelle last night at dinner. They never mentioned how she got lost, though.

'Can I ask you a question?' I say as I wait for the toast to pop up.

'Sure.'

'Did you ever find out what happened to Annabelle?'

'Your doll?'

'Yes.'

'Your father found her in the car, if my memory serves me correctly . . . I think she'd fallen under the back seat.'

I can't stop the smile that spreads across my face as I turn my back on her. I don't want her to see it. I'm not going to get my hopes up, or anyone else's for that matter. But maybe, just maybe . . . Could this be the first sign?

THIRTY

Braxton

'I'm heading home,' Lucas says, popping his head into my office.

'I'm not far off leaving as well.' I look up, meeting his gaze. 'I just want to finish this letter to Jemma.'

He gives me a thoughtful smile. 'How are you two going?'

'We're going okay.' I feel myself grinning just thinking about her.

'I'm glad.' He pushes off the doorframe. 'I'll see you in the morning.'

'Night, buddy.'

I pull up the calendar for the year 2006 on my laptop, so I can find the exact dates I'll need for this letter.

LETTER THIRTEEN . . .

Dearest Jemma,

The first of December 2006. We'd managed to keep our relationship a secret for a week, but we were making out every chance we got. It was only a matter of time before we got caught. Looking back on that day now, I'm thankful it was your mum who caught us, and not your dad.

It was a Friday. I'd been waiting all day for you to get home. I was sitting on my front verandah when I noticed you coming down the street, and I ran to meet you halfway. I wanted to kiss you so badly, but I couldn't risk any of the neighbours seeing us.

As we approached your place, you grabbed my hand and pulled me down the side of your house, behind the bins.

I pushed you up against the wall, crashing my lips into yours. My actions were that of a desperate man. We hadn't taken our relationship any further than kissing, but my torch seemed to be a constant fixture in my pocket. We were both more than ready to take the next step, but we still lived with our parents, so it was impossible. And there was no way I was going to let our first time be in the back seat of your car.

I'd taken a part-time job mowing lawns, without your knowledge. I was trying to earn enough money to take you away somewhere nice, and I wanted it to be a surprise. I scheduled my clients during school hours, and I planned to spend the holidays working while you did your shifts at the ice-cream parlour.

My hand slid underneath your top as our kisses became hot and heavy.

'Oh my god! What the hell are you two doing?' we heard your mother screech.

I pulled away from you, but it was too late: we'd been caught. I still remember the look on your mother's face. She was as white as a ghost, her eyes were wide with shock, and her mouth was gaping open.

'Let me explain, Mum,' you said, taking a few steps in her direction.

You stood before her, but said nothing. I'm not sure if you were thinking of an excuse, but unless you were going to tell her you'd been choking and I was using my tongue to dislodge the food stuck in the back of your throat, then the truth was the best way to go.

'I'm waiting,' she replied, tapping her foot impatiently on the concrete.

You still couldn't seem to find the words, so I stepped forward. 'Jemma is my girlfriend,' I said. 'She has been for a week now. We both realised that our feelings for each other ran far deeper than friendship. I'm sorry we kept this from you, but we had planned on telling you, Mrs Robinson. We both just wanted to get used to the idea of being a couple before sharing our news with the rest of the world.'

'I see.' She paused briefly as her eyes moved back and forth between us. 'Well, I suppose I knew this would happen sooner or later. You're just lucky it was me who caught you, and not my husband. I suggest you both tell him your news tonight when he gets home from work. If he walks in on what I just did, it's not going to end so well.'

With that, she turned and walked back into the house.

'Shit,' you said as soon as she was out of sight. 'I guess the cat's out of the bag.'

'I guess it is. I'm not looking forward to telling your dad, though.'

'Why? He loves you.'

'I'm just not,' I said, shrugging my shoulders. You were his little girl, and he was very protective of you.

'He'll be fine.' You slid your arms around my waist and gave me a devious smile. 'Now, where were we?'

I was no longer in the mood. 'No more kissing until we've spoken to your dad.'

You lifted my arm, looking down at the watch on my wrist. 'That's over two hours away,' you said, pouting. 'I'm not sure if I can survive that long.'

Leaning forward, I sucked your bottom lip into my mouth. 'I'm pretty sure you will.'

———

My leg bounded nervously under the table as we sat in the kitchen and waited for your dad to arrive home from work. Your mother was behind us, busily stirring dinner on the stovetop.

I felt sick in the stomach when we heard your father's car pull up in the driveway. The moment he entered the kitchen, you reached for my hand, giving it a comforting squeeze.

He kissed the top of your head. 'Hey, pumpkin.'

'Hi, Daddy.'

'Brax, my boy,' he added as he passed me, ruffling my hair.

'Mr Robinson.'

'Hi, sweetheart,' he said when he reached your mum, planting a soft kiss on her lips. 'Dinner smells delicious. We were busy at the bank today, so I didn't get time for lunch. I'm starved.'

'It will be ready in about ten minutes,' she replied.

That was my cue; it was now or never. 'Mr Robinson,' I said, inhaling a large breath as I stood. 'Could I have a word with you?'

My eyes briefly met yours. I love you, you mouthed, and it was in that moment I knew that whatever punishment I was about to receive from your father was worth it.

'Sure.' He gave me an inquisitive look as he followed me into the lounge room. 'Is everything okay, son?'

'There's something I need to tell you.'

'Shoot.' He eyed me sceptically and he slid his hands into the pockets of his trousers.

'Jemma and I recently realised that our feelings for each other go beyond friendship.'

His expression turned serious. 'I see.'

'We've decided to enter into a relationship.'

He took time to ponder my words. He wore a stoic look the entire time, so I was unable to gauge how he truly felt.

'Do you love her?' he asked eventually.

'Very much.'

'Jemma, can you come in here, please?' he called out. I wasn't sure if that was a good sign or not.

'Has there been any funny business going on?' he asked as we waited for you.

'No, sir, but we've kissed.'

He cleared his throat, but didn't reply.

'Yes, Daddy,' you said, coming to stand beside me. Your father's gaze moved down to our hands when you laced your fingers through mine.

'I'd like to hear your take on this . . . relationship.'

You looked at me as you spoke. 'I love him, and he loves me. I'm not sure what else you want me to say,' you replied.

'That's enough,' he said, nodding his head. He took a few steps towards me. 'As long as you treat my daughter with respect, and don't break her heart, we won't have a problem. Understand?'

'Yes, sir.'

'Good.' He extended his arm, and we shook hands. 'I'd welcome you to the family, but you've been a part of the family for years.'

———

The nineteenth of December 2006. That was our first official date. It was either coincidence or fate that it happened to be on the nineteenth. The restaurant was booked out weeks in advance, and this was the only day I could get. It was a Tuesday, but you were on school holidays, and I didn't have to start uni for another few months. It also happened to be the day before my eighteenth birthday.

I'd made reservations for us at The Sea Shanty. It had been my mother's favourite restaurant. My father would take us there on special occasions. It was also the fanciest place I knew.

After dropping you at work that morning, I headed to the shops to buy a new shirt and some flowers.

That afternoon when we pulled into your driveway, I turned off the car. 'Can I take you out on a date, Jem? A proper one.'

'Really?'

'Yes.'

We'd been a couple for almost a month and although we'd spent every day together, I'd never taken you anywhere nice.

'Okay, I'll run inside and change.'

'I don't think you understand. This is a date date. I'm taking you out to a fancy restaurant. You need to dress up.'

'Okay,' you said as your face lit up.

I unbuckled my seatbelt and leaned across to brush my lips against yours. 'I'll pick you up at seven.'

There was a huge smile on your face as I helped you out of the car. 'I'm so excited,' you squealed. 'Our first official date.'

I showered and shaved before dressing in my new clothes. I wanted to look nice for you. I even snuck into my dad's room and used his cologne.

It was just before seven when I knocked on your front door. Surprisingly, I wasn't nervous. Like you, I was excited, and eager to see you all dressed up.

Your father answered the door.

'Come in,' he said. 'They're upstairs. Christine's been helping Jemma get ready. You know what women are like.' I chuckled when he rolled his eyes.

'Jemma, Braxton's here,' he called out from the base of the stairs.

Tingles ran the length of my spine as you made your way down the stairs a few minutes later. I can't even put into words how beautiful you looked. The first time I'd seen you all dressed up was on your thirteenth birthday, but tonight you didn't look like a beautiful young girl, you looked like a sexy-as-hell woman.

Your mum had curled your long brown hair and pinned one side back with a yellow flower. There was a hint of make-up on your face, which made you look so much older than your seventeen years. The sexy yellow dress hugged your body perfectly and stopped mid-thigh, accentuating your long tanned legs. My eyes slowly travelled down your body, drinking in every inch of you.

I swallowed hard before finally releasing the breath I'd been holding. 'You can close your mouth now, son,' your dad murmured as he stalked into the kitchen.

'You look stunning,' I said as you came to a stop in front of me. 'These are for you.' Even the flowers I bought you matched your dress.

'I love them.' Your face lit up as you gazed down at the bouquet, and it made my heart race. 'They're the most beautiful flowers I've ever seen.'

But those flowers didn't hold a candle to your beauty. After bringing them to your nose and inhaling their fragrance, you leaned forward and placed a soft kiss on my lips.

As we walked towards your car, you rummaged around inside your bag.

'Did you forget something?'

'No, I'm just searching for a tissue so I can wipe my lipstick off. I'm dying to kiss you properly.'

Your comment made me laugh. I was starting to believe that if you could be permanently attached to my lips, you would.

'Wow, this place looks busy.'

Once we were seated at the restaurant, I watched you as your eyes scanned our surroundings. You always did that wherever you went; you'd been doing it since we were kids.

'Have you noticed nothing matches in here?'

I hadn't, but it was evident that the interior designer was already burning brightly inside you, even though you had yet to make a career choice.

The waitress brought our menus over and we ordered two Cokes. 'You should try the lobster mornay,' I suggested. 'My mum always ordered that. She said it was the best she'd ever had.'

'Mmm yummy,' you replied as you scanned the menu. 'Ugh. It's fifty-nine dollars. I might just stick with the fish and chips.'

'You love lobster.'

'I know, but it's too expensive.'

'This is a date, Jem, I'm paying. Order the lobster.'

'Brax,' you said, reaching for my hand across the table. 'You don't have that kind of money to throw away. What I eat isn't important. I'd settle for a slice of bread and a glass of water, as long as you're the one I'm dining with.' I pulled your hand up to my mouth, placing a soft kiss on your knuckles. You always said the sweetest things, but I'd already decided that you were having the lobster whether you wanted it or not. I would have given you the world if I could.

The twentieth of December 2006. It was the following day, and also my birthday. When I walked you to the door the night before, after the best first date anyone could ask for, you had a surprise for me as well.

'I need you to meet me out here at 5am,' you said.

'5am? That's only six hours away. Why so early?'

'Because it's my boyfriend's birthday, and I have a special day planned.'

It was 4.55am when I quietly closed the front door of my house, careful not to wake my dad. Your place was bathed in darkness, but I could see the light was on in your bedroom, so I knew you were awake.

I leaned up against your car and waited, all the time wondering what your plans were. Thinking back, if I'd known what you had in store for me, I would have run back into the house and barricaded all the doors. I still get a sick feeling in my stomach just thinking about it.

A few minutes later you ran out of your house and threw yourself into my arms. 'Happy birthday!'

You tasted of mint when your lips met mine. It was the perfect way to start my birthday.

'So, are you going to tell me where we're going?' I asked as you reversed out of the driveway in the darkness.

'Nope. You'll see when we get there.'

When you headed towards the freeway, I thought we were going to Ma and Pa's, but then you took the on-ramp in the opposite direction.

The sun had risen by the time we neared our destination. We were in an area I'd never been before—a lot of farm land around—so I still had no clue where we were going. You put your indicator on and pulled over to the side of the road in front of a large paddock.

'Surprise!' you said, pointing towards the passenger-side window. I turned my head, and my heart dropped into the pit of my stomach. There, lying on the grass, was a giant hot air balloon, yet to be inflated. 'Are you excited? It's going to be epic.'

I wanted to tell you there was no way in hell I was going up in that thing, but I just couldn't bring myself to burst your bubble.

'Wow,' was all I could manage to get out. But then I turned my head to look at you, and your face was glowing. I knew you would have saved hard for this surprise. 'It's going to be amazing,' I lied.

As we walked across the grassed area, I felt physically sick inside, but I tried my best not to show it.

'You must be Jemma,' the balloon boy said, offering his hand to you. He didn't look much older than us, which did nothing to ease my concerns.

'Yes, and this is Braxton, my boyfriend. It's his birthday today.'

'Hey,' he said, looking at me briefly before focusing his attention back on you. The way his eyes moved down your body instantly got my back up. I'd seen plenty of guys look at you that way in the past, but that didn't mean I had to like it.

Balloon boy started going over the do's and don'ts, and the procedures we needed to follow in case of an in-air emergency, but the only thing I could hear was the thundering beat of my pulse in my ears.

My knuckles turned white as I gripped the side of the basket. You stood beside me leaning over the side as you watched the ground below disappear. I willed my hands to release themselves from the death grip I had on the basket, pulling you into the safety of my arms.

'This is the best thing ever.'

I forced out a smile, but I wholeheartedly disagreed.

You glanced at balloon boy over your shoulder. 'How high will we go?'

'We have perfect conditions . . . light winds and good visibility, so we can get up to around two thousand feet if you like.'

I had issues with being a few metres off the ground, so it was a miracle I didn't pass out, or keel over and die from heart failure.

I needed a distraction, fast. I grabbed hold of your face, crashing my lips to yours. Our mouths stayed locked together for a long time, but unfortunately not long enough. We were still in the air and climbing at an alarming rate.

'Don't move,' I whispered when you tried to pull away.

'Why?'

'Two words: boy scout.'

You buried your face in my chest and giggled.

Turning you in my arms, my front was now pressed against your back, as I reached for the edge of the basket and held on for dear life.

I can't put into words how relieved I felt when we finally landed. I climbed out of that basket at lightning speed before reaching for you. What I really wanted to do was get down on my hands and knees and kiss the damn ground, but that would have been a dead giveaway, so instead I grabbed hold of your face and planted a chaste kiss on your lips.

'That was amazing . . . simply amazing,' you squealed, leaping into my arms. 'I'm on such a high.'

'Me too.' That wasn't a lie, I was. But my high was from being back on the ground.

'We need to do that again someday . . . no actually, we need to go on a plane next.' The excitement in your voice made me smile despite everything. 'I've always wanted to fly away to some exotic beachside destination with you.'

I had no reply for that. I would have been happy to get on board a plane with you—if it just sat on the tarmac and didn't take off.

But in my heart, I already knew we would jet off somewhere one day. Especially now that I knew it was something you had always wanted. Being with you, even if it was at thirty thousand terrifying feet in the air, was better than not being near you at all.

There's nothing I wouldn't do to make you happy.

What we had is far too beautiful to be forgotten.

Yours always,

Braxton

I place the charms inside the envelope before sealing it. A rose to symbolise the flowers I gave her on our first date. And a hot air balloon; my birthday gift from hell.

THIRTY-ONE

Braxton

It's Sunday, and although it's my day off, I'm up at the crack of dawn. I'm too worked up to sleep. Jemma's coming over today to work in the garden.

Last night we talked on the phone for almost two hours. It reminded me of old times. When I went away to university, we'd do this every night. She'd give me a blow-by-blow account of her day, and I'd tell her about mine. Although I was an hour-and-a-half's drive from her, we didn't miss a minute of each other's day. It helped keep us connected. It didn't stop me from missing her, though.

The hardest part of our conversation last night was saying goodbye, and then trying to fall asleep without her wrapped in my arms. At least there was a smile on my face as I lay there thinking about her. Until there's reason not to, I'm going to remain positive. Every step forward is a step closer to getting her back.

After a long walk on the beach with Bella-Rose, I wear a path in the hardwood floors waiting for Jemma to arrive. Poor Bella-Rose paces along with me, but eventually she gives up and curls up on her bed.

Looking down at my watch, I see it's almost eleven. I want to call her, but I don't want to seem too eager. We didn't agree on an exact time, but she said midmorning.

A few minutes later there's a knock on the door, and my worry that she might have changed her mind soon turns into elation. 'Hey,' I say when I open the front door. She's dressed ready to work, in a pair of tights and T-shirt. Her hair is tied back in a low ponytail. I've noticed since the accident that she has a side fringe instead of having it all pulled back from her face. My guess is it's to hide the scars.

'I'm sorry I'm late. I just had to swing past the shops and grab some things.'

She lifts up her arm that's holding her shopping bags.

'Let me take those.' I reach for them. 'You didn't need to bring anything. I've already organised lunch.'

'This is dinner,' she says with a smile. 'In one of your letters you mentioned how your mum would cook a roast on Sundays. It's Sunday, so I thought I'd cook one for you . . . that's if you want me to, of course.'

My smile is as bright as hers. 'I'd love that.' Leaning forward, I place a soft kiss on the side of her face. 'Thank you.'

Once the groceries are packed away, we head out into the yard, where I have her gardening tools and bucket waiting.

Gardening is not something I ever enjoyed, but Jemma loved being out here; she found it therapeutic. 'I might get started on the lawns then if that's okay.'

'Go. I'm fine. This is actually very relaxing.'

I duck into the house quickly, grabbing her iPod from our room. She used to love listening to music while she gardened.

'What's that?' she asks when I hand it to her.

'Your iPod. It has all your favourite songs on it. You used to listen to music while you were out here. Sometimes you'd even take it when you went for a run. I've been meaning to give it to you.' There're so many of her things still here at the house, but I've been reluctant to let them go. 'You can choose what playlist you want to listen to by scrolling up and down. Then just press play. You can attach the iPod to your clothes . . . here.' I take it from her hand, and clip it onto her T-shirt. 'That way your hands are free.'

'Thanks,' she says, smiling.

She goes back to her gardening, and I retrieve the mower and edger from the garage. I have never looked forward to doing the lawn so much in my life.

—

'That looks scrumptious,' she says when I place the prawn-and-avocado salad in the middle of the table. It looks more like rabbit food to me—I bought some crusty rolls to go with it—but Jemma used to love it.

'It's one of your favourites.'

The gardens and lawn are all done, and everything looks great again, just like it used to.

Jemma puts the plates and cutlery on the table before taking a seat.

'I Skyped with Rachel this morning.'

'That's nice. I'm glad you two are doing that again. You used to Skype all the time before the . . .' I let my words drift off. Picking up the tongs, I scoop some salad onto her plate.

She pops a prawn into her mouth before continuing. 'Anyway, I mentioned Lucas. I never got a chance to bring it up when she came over for the farewell dinner.'

That comment gets my attention. 'And?'

'She burst into tears. Oh Braxton, it was awful,' she says with a sigh.

'Shit. You didn't tell her what Lucas told me, did you?'

'No. I'd never do that. I brought up the shopping centre you guys designed. But as soon as I mentioned his name she lost it. When she finally stopped crying, she told me everything.'

I wait for her to elaborate, but she doesn't.

'You don't have to tell me what she said if you don't want.' As much as I'm curious to know, I don't want to put her in an awkward position.

'I trust you won't relay any of it to Lucas.'

'You know I'd never do that. Whatever we discuss has always stayed between us. I'd never do anything to jeopardise your friendship with Rachel.'

'I'd never do anything to jeopardise your friendship with Lucas either.'

'I know you wouldn't.'

She smiles, before continuing. 'She told me they've been secretly hooking up for years. Did you know that?'

'Until Lucas's confession, I had no idea.'

'Basically, things started to get serious between them after our engagement party.'

'It's been going on that long?'

'Yes. He spent the night at her hotel, and when he drove her to the airport the next day, he asked if he could call her. She said that at first he didn't call often, but over time the calls became more frequent. Sometimes they'd talk for hours. Apparently they made a pact not to tell us.'

'Why?'

'She said we were always trying to set them up, and they were just having fun.'

'We were,' I chuckle. 'They always got on so well.'

'Anyway, to cut a long story short, after our wedding he took her back to his place. That night he told her he loved her, and she told him she loved him too. He begged her not to go back to New York.'

'That wouldn't have gone down well—she loves that job.'

'I know. She said at the time she panicked. She waited until he fell asleep and snuck out.'

'Ouch!'

'He turned up at the airport the next day, and she told him she wasn't prepared to give up her job. And he told her he wasn't interested in a long-distance relationship. They got into a big fight, and haven't spoken since.'

Sitting back in my chair, I ponder her words as I take a swig of my beer. 'It all makes sense now.'

'We need to do something, Braxton. If they love each other, they shouldn't be apart.'

I try not to show how much her comment stings. *We* love each other, but we're apart. Well, I love her; she just doesn't remember that she loves me just as much.

'I'm not sure if there's anything we can do.'

'We need to try to get them to talk. I really felt for her this morning.'

'I feel for Lucas as well, but I don't know how we can fix this when she's on the other side of the world.'

'That's the thing: she told me she's thinking of quitting her job and moving back to Australia.'

I certainly wasn't expecting her to say that. 'Well, I guess that changes everything.'

———

'I should think about getting this roast in the oven,' Jemma says as she rinses the lunch dishes and passes them to me to stack in the dishwasher. 'Christine said it takes about three hours to cook.'

'That sounds about right. I'll help you with the prep when we're done here, I'm an expert potato peeler.'

'Is that so?' she says, laughing. 'You're a man of many talents.'

Once upon a time I would have thrown her over my shoulder and carried her upstairs to show her just how talented I was, but those days are long gone. It's funny, because when we were younger I was content with being friends, but now I'm not sure I will ever adjust to being just that—not after everything we've shared. I'm trying, I really am, but the closer we become, the harder it gets.

I switch on the oven while she grabs everything from the fridge. This is only her second time in the house since the accident, but she already seems at home.

She sets the timer once the roast is in the oven, before we head outside to take the dog for a walk along the beach.

'She seems to love living with you,' Jemma says as I pick up the stick Bella-Rose drops at my feet.

'Yes, she does. It works both ways, I'm thankful for the company.'

Jemma doesn't reply; instead, I'm pleasantly surprised when she reaches for my hand. We walk the rest of the beach in silence, but her hand remains firmly clasped in mine. The only time she lets go is when I bend down to pick up a shell.

'For your collection,' I say, passing it to her.

'It's pretty, thank you.'

We spend the rest of the afternoon enjoying the sunshine on the back deck, while we wait for the roast to cook. The house smells divine. Today has been perfect. My only gripe is that it's going too fast. Soon she'll have to leave, and my full heart will feel empty once more.

A southerly wind whips up after dinner, so we move inside to the lounge room where it's warmer. She doesn't appear to be in a rush to leave.

I choose not to turn the television on, preferring to just talk instead.

Although Jemma's attention is solely on me, I notice her gaze occasionally flicker to the canvas of us above the fireplace. She hasn't seen the wedding album yet—it arrived after the accident—and I'm torn about whether to show her. I'm not sure why I'm so scared to see her reaction, but I am. Maybe I'll send it with one of the letters.

'Do you have any pictures of your mum?' Jemma asks, out of the blue. 'I'd love to see one if you do.'

Rising, I walk towards the long low-line entertainment unit, where Jemma kept our albums.

Many years ago, I confessed to her that I was frightened that memories of my mum were fading, and how guilty it made me feel. How could I possibly forget her? I could vaguely remember the scent of her perfume, and picture her smiling face in my head, but over time her image had become clouded, and I hated that.

About a week later, Jemma presented me with an album filled with pictures of my mum she had got from my father.

'If you ever feel like your memory of her is slipping, just look through this,' was all she said when she passed it to me.

When I opened it, the first picture I saw was of my mum holding me minutes after my birth. She had a huge smile on her face, and a look of love in her eyes. I immediately closed it when a lump rose to my throat, and I pulled Jemma into a tight embrace.

'Thank you,' I'd whispered as I fought back the tears.

My eyes flicker now to the wedding album when I open the drawer. It's sitting right on top. I have looked through it so many times, and on each occasion my heart broke a little more.

Moving it to the side, I take out the album of my mother and pass it to Jemma.

The first time I looked through it was the day Jemma gave it to me. I locked myself away in my room and wiped the tears from my eyes as I turned each page. All the happy memories that had been overshadowed by her death came flooding back.

That night I dreamed of her. She came to me in my sleep and asked me to dance with her, just like she'd done when

I was a child. But I was no longer a small boy; this time I towered over her small frame. There was no music, but she hummed a tune that was unfamiliar to me. Although I knew it was just a dream, in that moment I felt at peace.

'Oh wow, she looks so much like you,' Jemma says, opening the album to the first page.

I have my father's build and jawline, but my mother's nose, eyes and hair colouring. I don't always get upset like I did the first time I looked through these photos; sometimes I smile and feel grateful for the time we had together. I'm hoping this is one of those times.

My heart feels heavy as I tell Jemma the stories that go along with the images. Over time I have learned to live with my loss, but the longing to be with my mother again never lessens.

Finally we come to the last page. The photograph shows our last Christmas together. I'm sitting on the floor surrounded by presents and discarded wrapping paper. My mum is wearing a Santa hat and holding a piece of mistletoe above my head as she kisses my cheek. I'm scowling, and now I hate myself for it. I was only eleven, at that awkward age, but I would give anything to have her do that to me now.

'Hey,' Jemma says placing her hand on my leg as I stare down at the image.

'I took everything for granted,' I whisper. 'I had no idea at the time that this would be our last Christmas together.'

'You weren't to know . . . none of us knows what lies around the corner, Braxton. That's life, it's so unpredictable.'

Tears rise to my eyes as they meet hers. 'Ain't that the truth?'

If you told me a few months ago that my wife and I would be living in separate houses, I wouldn't have believed it. I thought nothing would ever pull us apart, our connection was too strong.

She lifts her hand off my leg and places it on the side of my face. When her gaze flickers down to my mouth, I don't hesitate to bring my lips to hers. This time I don't ask permission, I need to seek solace in her. She has always been my comfort, my happy place.

I'm taken aback when she shifts her body before climbing onto my lap and straddling me. It's hard for me to hold back and not take the lead, but I know I have to let her move things at her own pace.

When her lips meet mine again, my fingers slide into her hair as I tilt her head back slightly, deepening the kiss.

'Braxton,' she breathes into my mouth.

The restraint I'm forced to show makes me feel like I'm a kid again, not an adult who has been deeply intimate with his wife too many times to count. She's even harder to resist now because I know what I'm missing.

I groan when she pushes her hips forward, seeking the friction. My hands move down to her waist as I slowly rock her body against mine. I already know I'll be having another cold shower tonight, but this isn't about me, it's about her. I want her to experience this. It's something the old Jem couldn't get enough of.

'Braxton.' Her fingernails dig painfully into my shoulders as she picks up the pace on her own. When she pulls out of the kiss and tilts her head back, a perfect little 'O' forms on her lips. I know what's about to happen, because I've seen that expression so many times over the years. 'Oh god,' she moans as she continues to move against me. 'Mmm,' she practically whimpers as another wave hits. It takes every ounce of strength I have not to stand and carry her up to our room.

Her body goes limp and collapses against mine. 'What just happened?'

This moment is like deja vu.

'You had an orgasm.'

I can tell she's mortified when she buries her face further into my chest. 'You must think I'm such an idiot.'

'Far from it.' I place my finger under her chin and lift her face so I can see her. 'Your very first orgasm happened in the exact same way.'

'Really?'

'Yes. We were making out in the back of your car. You were straddling my lap, just like you are now.'

'Did I know what was happening?'

'Nope. You asked me the exact same question.'

'I'm sorry.' Her expression shows genuine concern.

'Sorry for what?'

'For what just happened.'

'Don't ever be sorry for that. Watching you come undone is still one of my favourite things. The look of ecstasy on your face,' I say as I tuck a stray piece of hair behind her ear. 'The way you'd bite your bottom lip between your teeth. Those sexy little noises you make.' I run my thumb gently over her lips as I speak. 'The sweet blush that spreads across your cheeks. The look of pure lust in your eyes. You have no idea what it does to me.'

'Did I get embarrassed back then too?'

I lift her off my lap and seat her beside me. I can't have this conversation with her while she's straddling me.

'Hardly,' I chuckle. 'You asked me if we could do it again.'

'Geez, I was forward,' she says, turning a deeper shade of red.

Her comment makes me laugh. 'Not at all. We were young and still experimenting. I loved the way you were. I loved everything about you.' I want to add *I still do*, but I don't. 'We'd never been with anyone else, only each other.'

Her eyes meet mine, and she smiles. 'I like that.'

'You're all I ever wanted, Jem. Nobody could ever hold a candle to you.'

She tucks her legs up under her chin, and I settle back into the lounge and cross my legs, trying to hide my raging hard-on.

'Did we . . . you know . . . have sex often?'

I have to suppress my smile, because I can tell she's uncomfortable asking. It's very sweet.

'Yes. About twenty times a day,' I reply, trying my hardest to keep a straight face.

'We did *not*,' she says, nudging me with her shoulder, making me laugh.

'Okay, maybe twenty is a slight exaggeration.'

'A slight exaggeration. I doubt I'd be able to walk if I had sex that much every day, let alone be able to function throughout the day . . . or hold down a job. I would have been permanently on my back.'

'When we were younger we went at it like rabbits.'

'Oh my god, Braxton,' she squeals, covering her face. 'Stop it!'

It's times like this that I notice the real change in her. We had a very open relationship, and the old Jem knew she could talk to me about anything.

'Well it's the truth, we did,' I say. 'We waited for months before we took the plunge, but once we did, there was no stopping us. Every chance we got, it's what we did. We couldn't get enough of each other.'

That's the way it stayed, right up to the accident.

'Did I . . . umm . . . enjoy it?' she asks as her face turns a beautiful shade of pink.

'Of course. I'm an exceptional lover.'

'Of course you are,' she says, giggling.

'You always found me irresistible, you couldn't keep your hands off this fine specimen of a man.' I run my hand down the front of my body as I speak.

With that statement, she completely loses it, and seconds later I do as well. When she wipes tears from her eyes, it only makes me laugh more.

This is the old us, the way we've always been—fun, easygoing, completely ridiculous . . . always down for a good laugh.

It's the perfect end to a perfect day.

THIRTY-TWO

Jemma

It was late when Braxton dropped me off last night, so I told him I wouldn't make breakfast this morning. I am now regretting that decision; I had such an amazing time with him yesterday, and I want to see him again.

When I don't find my mum in the kitchen—and it's not lost on me that I now think of her as my mother and not Christine—I go in search of her. I'm surprised to find her curled up on the sofa with a box of tissues beside her. My first thought is that she is sick, then I notice Ma's diary in her hand. It brings an instant smile to my face.

'Morning,' I say as I walk into the room and sit down beside her.

Instinctively, I snuggle into her. It doesn't feel weird or forced, it feels like a natural thing a mother and daughter would do.

'Morning, sweetheart,' she replies, placing a soft kiss on the side of my head.

'You're reading Ma's diary?'

'I am. I'm so grateful you encouraged me to do this. I'm learning so much about my parents. It's helping . . .' She pauses briefly before finishing her sentence. 'It's helping me forget the bad memories and focus more on the good ones.'

'I'm glad. I'm sorry for what you had to go through, but Ma wouldn't want you to remember her in that way. She loved Pa, and just wanted to be with him. I can understand that.'

'You're right. They loved each other very much.'

I slide my arm through hers, resting my head on her shoulder. 'Just like you and Dad once did ... and me and Braxton.'

'It's sad how life's circumstances can change.'

'It is. As long as you don't lose hope, I believe anything is possible.'

'It's been wonderful having you here,' she says, placing her hand on my leg. 'When you first had your accident, I thought I'd lose you, just like I'd lost everyone—my parents, my husband. I don't think I could have gone on if that happened. But I should never have underestimated you. You were always so strong. You fought hard to not only live again, but to find some kind of normality. I'm so proud of you for not giving up.'

'There were times I wanted to give up,' I admit.

'But you didn't. Witnessing your strength has helped me in ways I could never have even imagined.'

A lump rises to my throat and without even thinking the words just fall from my mouth. 'I love you, Mum.'

'Oh, sweetheart,' she says as tears fill her eyes. 'I wasn't sure if I'd ever get to hear those words again. I love you too.'

I sit there for the longest time, just enjoying being near her.

'Do you want a cuppa?' I ask eventually.

'I'd love one. Oh, I almost forgot, a letter came for you earlier.'

She points to the envelope sitting on the coffee table, and I snatch it up on my way to the kitchen.

Dearest Jemma,

The thirteenth of January 2007. It's hard for me to forget this day, I was so nervous. It was the day I had to ask your father if I could take his little girl away for the weekend.

I'd been saving hard, and I just needed your parents' blessing so I could book the flights.

It was a Saturday, you were at work, but both your parents were home. My stomach churned as I walked across your front lawn.

'Braxton,' your mum said with surprise when she opened the front door.

'I was wondering if you and Mr Robinson had a few minutes. There's something I'd like to ask you.'

'Of course, sweetheart, come in.' I followed her into the lounge room. 'Stephen's out the back, I'll go and get him.'

'Thank you.' I rubbed my hands together nervously as I sat on the sofa.

'Are you okay?' she asked, frowning.

'Yes,' I lied.

A few minutes later she came back into the room, your dad by her side. I stood and shook his hand, before we all sat. They were on the sofa opposite me, and I was grateful for the distance.

'Christine said you want to talk to us about something,' he said, opening up the lines of communication.

'Yes . . . I umm . . . want to take Jemma away next weekend.'

'Just the two of you?'

'Yes. I've been saving for the past few months. I'd like to surprise her and take her to Queensland.'

'Will you be staying in the same room?'

'Yes,' I replied, swallowing hard. I wasn't going to lie to him.

'Not happening,' your father said, standing. 'She's only seventeen and too young to go away . . . alone . . . with you.'

'Hold on,' your mother chimed in as he went to leave the room.

'I said no, Christine,' he snapped. 'I don't want to hear another word about it.'

'She's my daughter as well, or have you forgotten that?'

'No, I haven't forgotten that,' he said, turning to face her, but his shoulders slumped a little. 'She's just a baby.'

'She's almost eighteen,' she retorted, rolling her eyes. 'We knew this was going to come sooner or later, we were their age once too.'

Your mother had taken you to the doctor a month prior and got you started on birth control, so I already knew how she felt about this.

'But she's my little girl.'

'And I was my father's little girl when you and I . . .' Her eyes darted to me, and I was thankful she didn't finish that sentence. As much as I loved your parents, there were certain things I didn't want, or need, to know about them.

With that, your dad turned and stormed from the room, and my heart sank. There was no way I was going to defy him and go through with this without his blessing.

I stood. 'Thanks for trying, Mrs Robinson.'

'Leave it with me,' she replied, walking me to the door.

I felt like all hope was lost as I flopped down onto my sofa, burying my head in my hands. I sat there for the longest time, trying to come up with another way; I wanted so badly to do this for you.

I was pulled from my thoughts when I heard my name. When I looked up, I was both surprised and a little worried to see your father standing at my front door.

'Mr Robinson. Come in.' I opened the screen to let him in, even though I wasn't sure if that was a wise move.

'I'm not staying. What I need to say can be said from out here.'

'Okay.' That didn't sound good.

He cleared his throat and shoved his hands into his pockets before he spoke again. 'You have my blessing.' With that, he turned and walked down the front stairs.

'Thank you,' I called out as he stalked back to your place, but he didn't reply.

Although I rushed out and booked everything straightaway in case your father changed his mind, it would still be another five days before I told you. I hated keeping secrets from you, but your reaction was worth it.

It was a Wednesday afternoon, and I'd just picked you up from work. 'I have to work again tomorrow,' you said with a huge sigh, as you climbed into the passenger seat of my dad's car. 'That makes six days in a row.'

I'd spoken with your boss, Mr Jefferies, the previous Saturday while you were in the staffroom retrieving your bag. He'd swapped your shifts around so you could have the end of the week off.

'At least you don't have work Friday, Saturday and Sunday,' I replied. 'We'll have three whole days together.'

'That's if he doesn't call me in.'

I was grinning to myself because I knew that wasn't going to happen. 'We can do something nice if he doesn't,' I said, reaching for your hand.

'I'd like that.' You looked over at me and smiled. 'Can we go to the lookout for a little while? I'm not ready to go home yet.'

'Sure.'

'I just want to kiss you for a couple of hours ... or maybe forever.'

'Okay,' I chuckled. You were always great for my ego. 'You'll get no complaints from me. I don't have to pick my dad up until six.'

'We have five days to make up for. Five long days. That's a lot of kisses, you know.'

———

I'd barely put the car into park before your lips were on me.

'Can we move into the back seat?' you asked a few minutes later.

'Why?'

315

I was waiting for you to bring up sex again. It had become a touchy subject. You'd been mentioning it a lot, and I'd been avoiding it like the plague. In your defence, you had no idea of the plans I'd been working towards.

'Don't worry, I'm not going to pressure you into having sex with me, I just want to be able to kiss you without the gearstick digging into my side.'

'Jem, you don't need to pressure me to have sex with you. You know I want this as much as you do, I just want it . . .'

'To be perfect,' you said, finishing my sentence. 'As much as I want this, I love that you care enough about me to want it to be special.'

You leaned forward and brushed your lips against mine, before climbing between the seats into the back of the car.

Once I joined you, I lifted you onto my lap so you were straddling me. 'Now, where were we?'

'Right here,' you answered, placing your lips against mine.

It didn't take long for our kiss to become heated, even the windows in my father's car had fogged up. You were grinding yourself against me. Usually I wouldn't let it go this far, because it was getting tougher for us both to deny ourselves, but we were only a few days away from going all the way, so this time I didn't fight it.

Your movements quickened and you moaned into my mouth. Although, like you, I was a virgin, I was far from naïve about what was happening. I had friends who'd had sex, and they talked about their conquests a lot, and in great detail.

Your fingers were digging into my shoulders when you pulled out of the kiss. Your bottom lip was between your teeth, and I saw your eyes roll back in your head as you tilted your face towards the roof of the car.

'Oh god, Braxton,' you whimpered. 'This feels so good.' You released a long drawn-out moan before stilling. Your cheeks

were flushed and there was a glazed look in your eyes when they finally met mine. 'I don't know what just happened, but I want to do that again.'

I couldn't help but laugh. 'If I'm not mistaken, I'm pretty sure you just orgasmed.'

Your face was lit up with amazement. 'Wow . . . just wow. That was incredible. I've never felt anything like it before. If sex feels that good, I want to do it right now.'

I lifted you off my lap. Two more days, I kept telling myself. Two more days.

Leaning forward, I reached across the passenger seat and took the plane tickets from the glovebox. I'd planned to surprise you the following day when I picked you up from work, but this moment seemed like the perfect time.

'What's that?' you asked, when I passed you the envelope.

'A surprise.'

A huge smile broke out on your face and you tore into the envelope. 'Oh my god! We're going on a plane?'

Even the mere mention of that word made me feel sick. I could have easily taken you somewhere within driving distance, but your dream was to fly to an exotic beachside location, so I wanted this for you.

'Yes, we leave Friday, just the two of us. We're flying to the Gold Coast and staying in a hotel on the beach until Sunday.'

Squealing, you threw yourself into my arms and squeezed me tight. 'I can't believe I'm finally going to get to go on a plane!' You drew back so you could see me, and the look on your face turned serious. 'We're going to have sex, right?'

I smiled. 'Yes, we're going to have sex.'

The nineteenth of January 2007. Eleven years to the day since we first met.

'You look nervous,' you said on the elevator ride to our room. It surprised me that you could tell now, yet you failed to see it on the flight.

'I am.'

Thankfully, I was now of legal drinking age, so I ordered a beer before boarding, and another one on the flight. It helped calm me somewhat.

The night before we left, my father had given me a man-to-man talk before presenting me with a box of condoms and a lecture on safe sex. The next morning your father had done the exact same thing. I found out on the plane that your mother had given you a box of condoms as well. As awkward as all three conversations had been, we both found it amusing that we now had three boxes of condoms between us. How much sex did they think we were going to have?

'I'm nervous too, Brax, but I'm so ready for this ... we're ready for this. Aren't we?'

'I want this more than I've wanted anything in my life.' And that was the truth. I wanted to show you how much I loved you, since I was incapable of expressing it with words.

'It's going to be beautiful,' you said, reaching for my hand and lacing your fingers through mine. I had no doubt it would be, but there was still a part of me that worried I'd let you down.

I brought our linked hands up towards my face, placing a kiss on your fingers.

We arrived on our floor and I let go of your hand, picking up both our suitcases. I'd called the hotel during the week and organised a surprise to be waiting for you in the room. I also made sure that we had a room with a view of the ocean.

'Oh my god! You can see the ocean from here,' you said as soon as we entered our suite. I placed the bags down just inside the door and watched you as you rushed towards the floor-to-ceiling windows to take in the view. 'I love it here already.'

As I crossed the room, I smiled when I saw the surprise awaiting you on the bed. You'd been so preoccupied with the view, you hadn't even noticed.

Opening the glass sliding doors, we both stepped out onto the small balcony. You could smell the sea from where we stood. 'It's breathtaking.'

When you turned to face me, I could see tears glistening in your eyes. 'I love you so much, Braxton Spencer,' you said as you slid your arms around my waist. I wanted to tell you how much I loved you too, but again the words failed me.

'Let's check out the room.' I reached for your hand as we walked back inside.

You froze just inside the doorway, and I heard you gasp the moment you saw the bed. 'Braxton,' you whispered. 'Did you organise this?'

'I wanted it to be special . . . something you'd always remember.'

You walked towards the king-size bed and picked up one of the blood-red rose petals that were spread over the white linen. The hotel staff had placed lit candles on the bedside tables, and on the rich dark brown ottoman at the foot of the bed sat a rectangular white ceramic plate holding chocolate-dipped strawberries.

Your eyes met mine, and you smiled. 'I'm glad we waited now. Thank you for going to so much trouble to make my first time everything a girl could wish for.' I watched in silence as you picked up one of the strawberries. 'Mmm,' you moaned as you took a bite.

Walking towards me, you held the other half up to my mouth. I took a bite, before drawing your body flush with mine, and placing my lips on yours. Our kiss tasted of chocolate and strawberries.

'Do you want to go for a walk along the beach, or maybe get some lunch?'

'Later,' you replied. 'Right now, I want to get naked.'

My aspirations for this trip were huge—it was all I'd thought about in the previous weeks—but now that the big moment had arrived, I was frozen with fear. I didn't want to disappoint you.

I stood there as you took a step back and started to unbutton your blouse, one agonising button at a time. When you were done, you pushed it over your shoulders and down your arms. It fell to the floor, pooling around your feet. My eyes moved down to the swell of your breasts that were covered by the pink lace of your bra. I swallowed hard when your hands moved around to your back, as you unclasped it.

'You're wearing too many clothes,' you said, dropping it to the floor beside your shirt. I had to swallow down my groan as I took in the sight of your naked breasts. They were perfect, just how I imagined they would be.

Reaching up, I started to undo the buttons of my shirt. I moved a little faster than you. My movements were more desperate, because I was now itching to touch you.

When you moved your hands to your waist, undoing the button on your jeans, I followed suit. A few seconds later I was standing there in my boxer shorts, and the only thing you were wearing was your pink lace panties.

We stood there and stared at each other for a few moments, before you hooked your thumbs into the sides of your underwear. This time I couldn't hide the groan as you dragged them down your long, lean legs.

'You're so beautiful,' I whispered as my eyes drank you in.

When your gaze moved down to my boxers, and one of your eyebrows raised, I chuckled. You were always impatient when you wanted something.

I bent over slightly as I removed them, and the smile on your pretty face grew when I stood to full height. The gig was up. My lie had been revealed. There wasn't a pocket in sight, yet here I was with my torch shining bright. I wasn't the always-prepared boy scout I claimed to be. I was a young man who was utterly

*besotted by the exquisite beauty that stood before him. My forever
girl. The person who completely owned my body, my heart and
my soul.*

*I took a few steps towards you, closing the distance between
us. I lightly ran my trembling fingertips down the side of your
face, across your collarbone, and down your arm, before lacing
my fingers through yours.*

*You sucked in a sharp breath as your eyes fluttered shut.
'Braxton,' you whimpered as my lips softly connected with yours.
I slid my other hand around your waist, pulling your body flush
with mine. Skin against skin.*

*Deepening the kiss, I slowly walked you backwards towards
the bed, never once taking my lips from yours. When the back
of your legs connected with the mattress, I gently laid you down,
before settling over the top of you. As I gazed deeply into your
big brown eyes, all my indecision vanished.*

'I love you, Jemma Isabella Rosalie Robinson.'

*'I love you too,' you replied as tears filled your eyes. 'I love
you so much sometimes my heart aches.'*

*That day we gave ourselves to each other completely. Our
bodies and hearts became one.*

What we had is far too beautiful to be forgotten.

Yours always,

Braxton

I release a contented sigh as I refold the letter. I'm grateful
that he was my first, and for all the trouble he went to making
it so special. These letters make me see just how lucky I've
been to have his love.

Taking the charms out of the envelope, I lay them out on
the palm of my hand. Two hearts linked together, and a tiny
plane. A smile forms on my lips as I stare down at them.
Although we no longer live together as husband and wife,
there's a part of me that knows my heart still belongs to him.

THIRTY-THREE

Braxton

'He seems happy here,' Jemma says, linking her arm through mine as we leave the nursing home and walk to my car. 'But do you feel sad leaving him? Because I do.'

'All the time,' I admit. 'Some days are harder than others, but it's never easy.'

'How come he never came to live with us?'

'We both had jobs and a mortgage to pay. And as much as we would have liked to have him with us rather than in a home, neither of us could afford to give up work and give him the full-time care he needed.'

'Life can be so unfair at times.'

'It can, but you need to make the most of what you've got, I suppose.'

'True.'

'Are you coping all right with the mortgage repayments without my income?'

'I'm doing okay.' I smile as I open her door. It was sweet of her to ask, but since our shopping-centre deal, money no longer seems an issue. 'That reminds me, the insurance cheque came for your car a few days ago. I put it into your bank account, but it probably won't clear until the end of the week.'

'Okay.'

'I'm not sure if you ever want to drive again, but the money is there if you want to buy another car.'

'Am I still able to drive with my memory loss?'

'It's something we'd have to look into. You may need to sit another test, or do some lessons.'

'I'm not sure if I'm ready for anything like that yet. I'm happy catching the bus. Besides, if I have to start from scratch, it could be dangerous.'

'Fair enough,' I say, chuckling. 'You have me to chauffeur you around.'

'I do.' She looks over at me and smiles. 'Do you have any plans this weekend?'

'No. Why?'

'Please don't feel you have to say yes, but I'd love to go and visit Tilly-Girl on Saturday.'

'Consider it done.'

'And maybe I could come over on Sunday and cook you another roast. We could bring your dad to the house for the day.'

'He'd like that . . . so would I.'

I reach for her hand, and she lets me hold it all the way back to Christine's. When I pull into the driveway, she stays seated, showing no indication of wanting to leave. I take that as a sign; I won't put pressure on her, but I'm going to take every opportunity I can to try to win her back.

Leaning over, I cup the side of her face as my lips gently meet hers. I don't know what we are, but we've definitely moved past the friend zone. It's another step forward, and as long as we're moving in the right direction, I'm happy.

My forehead rests against hers when I finally pull out of the kiss. 'I have another letter for you.'

Her lips curve into a smile when I retrieve it from the glovebox. I've enclosed a small coffee mug charm inside.

Dearest Jemma,

The ninth of February 2007. Even though you were putting on a brave face, I saw you wipe the tears from your eyes a number of times throughout the day. We were packing up my father's car ready for me to head to university. My heart was heavy, and like you, I struggled to remain composed.

There was a huge part of me that was excited to embark on this new adventure, but it was overshadowed by the pain of leaving you behind. Even though I would be just an hour-and-a-half's drive away, I would only get to see you on the weekends, and that didn't sit well with me at all. You'd been a part of my everyday life for the past eleven years. I wasn't sure how I would survive without my daily dose of your pretty face.

My father had taken us and your parents out for my farewell dinner at The Sea Shanty, the night before. You kept your head bowed, pushing the food around on your plate. I'd occasionally see you wipe your eyes, and it broke my heart.

My hand clutched yours tightly, under the table. Seeing you like this did nothing to ease my sense of foreboding about leaving. I was grateful, however, that your parents agreed to let you spend the night at my house. We hardly slept; instead we talked, we made love, and I held you while you cried. Although I was still physically there, I was already missing you.

I had already decided to make the trip on my own. Having both my father and you at the other end would do nothing to help me settle. My dad had insisted I take his car for that week. He told me it was his way of guaranteeing I would come home the following weekend, which was ironic because nothing could have kept me from coming home to see you. I was already doubting I would last a week.

I left around 1pm after a lunch your mother had made but neither you or I had eaten.

The four of you stood by the car, and I said goodbye to your parents first. Your mum got all teary as she hugged me tight. 'Can you keep an eye on my dad while I'm gone?' I whispered to her.

I knew she would, she always did, but I felt compelled to ask her. I was worried about leaving him alone.

Your father shook my hand and told me how proud he was, which meant a lot. Saying goodbye to them was hard, but my next two goodbyes were what I dreaded the most. I silently prayed that I'd be able to hold it all together.

'Bye, Pop,' I said, extending my hand to him, but he pulled me into an embrace instead.

'Make me proud, son.'

'I will.' Tears stung my eyes as he held me. 'I love you, Pop.' I hadn't said those words to him since my mother's death. I'd been too scared to.

'I love you too, son.'

He released me and took a step back, then reached into his pocket and pulled out a wad of notes and shoved them into my hand. 'No, Pop,' I said, trying to give the money back to him. 'I still have money I saved from my lawn-mowing jobs.' Plus I'd lined up a few interviews for part-time work to keep me going once I got there.

'Take it . . . please.'

The tortured look on your face as I moved towards you only served to make the lump that had formed in my throat grow bigger.

I pulled you into my arms, squeezing you tight, and the tears you'd been fighting all day came flooding to the surface as you sobbed into my chest. I clenched my eyes shut, fighting back my own.

'I'm going to miss you so much,' I whispered into your hair.

'I'll miss you too.'

When I finally let you go, I cupped your face in my hands, using the pad of my thumbs to wipe your tears away. 'I'll call you when I get there, and we can Skype every night.'

'Okay,' you said as more tears leaked from your eyes.

I placed my lips against yours and held them there for the longest time. How was I going to survive a whole week without your kisses?

'I love you, Jem.' Expressing my love to you came easy now.

'I love you too.'

'I'll be back Friday afternoon.'

'I'll be waiting.'

I looked at the four of you as I started the car. The four most important people in my life . . . my family. It was incredibly hard for me to drive away from you all that day. I wound down my window as I reversed out of the driveway. My dad's arm was draped over your shoulder, and your head was resting on his chest.

I waved goodbye once I reached the street. 'Drive safely,' your mum called out as she wiped a tear from her eye.

'I love you,' you mouthed when my gaze moved to you. I blew you a kiss, and you pretended to catch it, before placing your clenched hand over your heart.

I put my foot down and drove away. It was only then that I let my emotions go. I wiped the tears from my eyes with the back of my hand as I set off down the street, ready to embark on this new chapter in my life.

—

The fourteenth of February 2007. It was a Wednesday. I said I wouldn't be back until Friday, but there was no way I could miss seeing you on our very first Valentine's Day.

I had secured a job working nights in a small pub not far from the university. I had been training all week, ready for my first shift the following Monday, so I would have to drive home and back in the one day.

I sat on the bonnet of your car when I reached the school. You had no idea I was coming. Excitement grew within me when the bell sounded, marking the end of your day. There was a bunch of red roses in my hand, and under my arm was tucked a white *teddy bear with a big red bow around its neck. It played 'You Are My Sunshine' when you pressed its tummy.*

You've always been my sunshine, Jem. The mere sight of you brightens my day.

It had only been five days since I'd seen you, but it felt like a lifetime. You were walking with a few of your girlfriends when one of them elbowed you, pointing in my direction. I inhaled a sharp breath, because your beauty has always managed to leave me breathless. You froze the second your eyes landed on me. You just stood there for a brief time staring, and for a split second I was unsure if you were happy that I was here.

Relief flooded through me when a huge smile broke out on your face, and you dropped your backpack and ran to me.

'Braxton,' you said, leaping into my arms. 'What are you doing here?' I buried my face in your hair and inhaled your sweet scent.

There were tears glistening in your eyes when you drew back to look at me.

'It's our first Valentine's Day,' I said, 'and I needed to see my girl.'

You crashed your mouth against mine. Christ, how I'd missed the feel of your soft lips. A few of the other students cheered and whistled as they passed, but it didn't deter us in the slightest. We had five days worth of kisses to make up for.

Once we left the school, you asked me to take you home so you could give me my gift. You had bought me a mug that said, 'You're cute, can I keep you?'

To this day, it's still my favourite mug, and I drink out of it every day.

What we had is far too beautiful to be forgotten.

Yours always,

Braxton

———

The weekend rolls around fast. I called over to Stephen's apartment last night and took the spare keys to Ma and Pa's house, just in case Jemma wants to go inside. I also packed Tilly-Girl's saddle into the trunk of the car.

It's a beautiful autumn day, perfect for a ride.

I arrive at Christine's house just after eight. The earlier we leave, the longer I get to spend with her.

Before I even make it to the front porch, Jemma leaves the house. My eyes drink her in. Her jade green top hangs off to one side, revealing a slender shoulder. I can't recall seeing her in this top before, it must be new. She's wearing knee-high tan boots over a pair of skinny jeans that perfectly showcase her long legs. Legs that she once willingly wrapped around me. The recent memory of her straddling my lap floods my mind.

'You look beautiful,' I say.

'Thank you. You look rather dashing yourself.'

I extend my hand to her when she reaches the bottom step, pulling her into my arms. 'Good morning.' Bringing my face forward, I brush my lips against hers. I kiss her hello and goodbye every time we're together now. As long as she's okay with that, I'm not about to stop.

'Good morning,' she replies, sliding her arms around my waist.

'Are you ready to go and see Tilly-Girl?'

'I can't wait to see her. I could hardly sleep last night I was so excited.'

I place a soft kiss on her forehead before drawing back, and a movement in the window catches my eye. It's Christine. She's watching us with a huge grin on her face. I give her a quick wave before reaching for Jemma's hand.

'I brought Tilly-Girl's saddle with me in case you feel up to riding her.'

'I'd love to ride her.'

As we make our way onto the freeway, my eyes leave the road briefly, and I see her smiling as she relaxes back into the seat. She reaches across and places her hand on my thigh. It seems like such a natural reaction, it's something she always did. Turning her head slightly, she gazes out her window. She seems so content.

'Did I go to the same university as you?'

'You did. You started the year after me.'

'Did we live together?'

'No. Well, not officially, anyway. Your parents set you up in shared accommodation off campus. Your apartment wasn't far from mine. That's how you and Rachel became such good friends, she was your roommate.'

She turns her face in my direction. 'Why didn't I live with you?'

'Your parents thought we were too young for that kind of commitment, but we spent almost every night together. If you didn't sleep at my apartment, I slept at yours.'

Her lips break into a smile as she turns her head to gaze back out the window.

We spend over an hour at Ma and Pa's. Jemma is eager to go inside and have a look around. It's still exactly the same as I remember it, albeit a little dustier.

I stand back and observe Jemma as she walks from room to room, answering all the questions she asks. 'I'm really grateful that you brought me back here. It's nice to have an actual visual of the inside of the house, instead of trying to conjure one up in my mind,' she glances at me over her shoulder as she speaks. 'The kitchen where we helped Ma bake treats, the fireplace we sat in front of after our misadventure with the Loch Ness Monster, and the bedroom that you and I shared when we were kids . . .'

Her words tug at my heart. These were all moments from our past that I have included in my letters. It's just another example of how difficult life has become for her. The accident may have stolen her away from me, but what she lost that day was far greater. My stories can give her back snippets of her past, but the visions, emotions and feelings that she once associated with those times are lost forever.

She picks up ornaments, runs her hands over the rich wooden furniture, and studies the framed pictures on the mantelpiece, as well as the ones hanging on the wall.

'Do you think it would be okay if I took a few of these pictures home?' she asked as she stands in front of the old fireplace. 'It seems so wasteful just having them sitting here with nobody to look at them.'

'I don't think your mother would mind. If she does, we can always bring them back.'

Out of the ten or so pictures, she chooses three: one of her sitting on Pa's lap while he's driving the tractor, one of her parents on their wedding day, and one of the two of us as kids with Ma.

She hugs the three framed pictures to her chest as I lock up the farmhouse. 'Next time we come back, I'd like to give the place a good clean,' she says. 'Maybe vacuum and dust, and open some windows to let the fresh air in. It's very stuffy in there.'

I called Mr Talbot yesterday, informing him that we would be dropping by to visit Tilly-Girl. There is a part of me that's concerned about Jemma riding again, but it's something she always loved and I want her to experience it again. Since the accident she seems fragile, but in reality she's anything but. She's one of the strongest, most courageous people I know.

After saddling the horse, I help her up, before climbing on behind her. I want to make sure she's comfortable before letting her ride Tilly-Girl on her own. It's been years since I've sat behind her on this horse.

After we do a few laps around the paddock, I hop down, giving her the reins, and I spend the next few hours leaning on the fence post, smiling the entire time as I watch her. It's a beautiful sight seeing her so happy and carefree. The bond between Jemma and the horse is as strong as ever, even if she doesn't remember it.

I can tell it is hard for her to say goodbye, but I promise to bring her back every weekend if that's what she wants.

'I've had the most amazing day,' she says as we head down the long driveway, towards the main road.

'I meant what I said, we can come back every weekend if you like.'

She places her hand on my leg again. 'Thank you for today . . . thank you for everything.'

It starts to sprinkle as we drive out of town. 'Are you hungry, or would you prefer to head back to Christine's?'

I still can't bring myself to refer to that house as her home.

'I'm starved. Riding Tilly-Girl really worked up my appetite.'

'There's a place not far from here . . . Mama's Country Kitchen. Ma and Pa used to take us there as a treat when we were kids. All their meals come with a side of sweet potato. They're cooked whole in the skin, and served topped with whipped cinnamon butter. You used to love them.'

She loved them so much she used to steal mine sometimes too.

'That sounds perfect.'

She not only ate all of her sweet potato, she polished off half of mine, just like old times. She may not realise it, but there are parts of her that are still the same.

By the time I pay the bill and we leave the restaurant, it's pouring with rain. 'Wait here,' I say. 'I'll bring the car around so you don't get wet.'

Pulling the back of my jacket over my head, I make a dash for the car. I'm halfway across the car park when someone grabs hold of my arm. Suddenly I find Jemma standing beside me. The rain has already drenched her hair, and she squints as the heavy drops pound against her face.

'Dance with me?'

There's a part of me that wants to just keep her dry and warm, but how can I say no? It's been almost ten years since we've done this, and if she wants to dance with me in the rain, then that's exactly what I'll do. Giving her back pieces of her past in the letters I've written is nothing like letting her experience those moments firsthand.

Turning, I reach for her and pull her body against mine. 'We don't have any music,' I say, matching her smile.

'We don't need music.'

The side of her face rests against my chest, as she holds me tight.

Memories of our very first dance in the rain come flooding to the surface. Everything was so new to us back then, and in a way, it's the same now. It's a new beginning. A chance to relive all the magic we once shared.

THIRTY-FOUR

Jemma

It's just after seven when I climb out of bed. I'm tired, but excited. Braxton is picking me up at nine and we're heading to the shops to get what we need for the roast lunch I'm cooking, and then we'll collect his father on our way back.

It was late when we got home last night. The house was in darkness, so I snuck upstairs and had a warm shower before climbing into bed. As tired as I was, it took me ages to fall asleep. I was still on a high from the day I'd spent with Braxton and Tilly-Girl.

I'm eager to tell my mum about yesterday. She's coming along in leaps and bounds, and finally starting to deal with the death of her parents. It's like a part of her died when they did, and she stopped living. I'm sure it's something she'll never get over, but at least she's talking about them again.

I'm smiling as I round the corner to enter the kitchen, but then I stop dead in my tracks. 'Dad?' I say.

He's standing with his back to me, over by the sink, wearing my mum's pink robe. It's way too small, and looks ridiculous. I place my hand over my mouth to muffle my giggle.

He turns to face me, and I'm pretty sure the surprised look on his face is mirrored on my own. 'Pumpkin!'

'What are you doing here?'

'I . . . umm . . . spent the night. I hope you're okay with that.' He takes a few steps towards me. 'I took your mother out for dinner last night, and . . .'

I hold my hands in the air as I close the distance between us, before wrapping my arms around him; I don't need details. 'I'm more than okay with it,' I say. 'I'm so happy to see you here.'

'I'm happy to be here . . . you have no idea how much. We have you to thank for giving us the push we both needed.'

'I would have been okay just to have you both talking again, but this . . .' I draw back from him and wipe my eyes.

'I know, pumpkin . . . I know.'

'You look ridiculous in that robe, by the way.'

He clears his throat, and I giggle when he tries to adjust the front of it. 'I wanted to make your mum a cup of coffee. I used to take one into her every morning when I lived here.'

'Well, maybe you need to bring your own robe with you next time.'

He chuckles as he leans forward, placing a soft kiss on my forehead. 'That's a good idea.'

———

When Braxton picks me up later he can't believe my father spent the night, but he is just as happy about it as I am. As we leave, my parents are making plans to spend the day together.

My high from yesterday continues, and over the next few hours my cheeks start to ache from smiling so much. My family is well on its way to becoming a real family once more. What I love most is that they actually feel like a family to me now.

Although I still have no memory of my past life with them, in my heart they belong to me, and I belong to them. That empty feeling of not belonging that I felt when I first woke from my coma seems a distant memory now.

'That smells and looks delicious,' John says as I place his dinner down in front of him. I roasted pork today. 'It reminds me of the Sunday roasts my Grace used to make.'

Today's a good day for him memory wise, which only heightens my good mood. I move around to Braxton next, placing his plate down in front of him. 'I gave you extra crackling, since I know how much you love it.'

His eyes widen as he looks up at me. 'You remember that?'

I don't know. Did he tell me that, or do I remember? I can't answer that honestly. It wasn't mentioned in the letters because I know them off by heart. 'I must,' I say with a shrug. I don't have an actual memory of it; it's just something that felt familiar as I dished up his dinner.

The hopeful smile I see on Braxton's face as he reaches for my hand tugs at my heart. I'm not sure if my memory will ever return, but I'll never stop hoping.

John appears to enjoy his day with us, but as the afternoon wears on he becomes tired and confused, and we take him back to the nursing home around seven. We stay for a while, until he's settled. As I observe Braxton fussing over him, trying to make him as comfortable as possible, I can tell he loved having his father at the house. He's a great son, and an exceptional human being. It warms my heart to watch them.

My father's car is in the driveway when Braxton pulls up outside Christine's. It brings an instant smile to my face. I glance over at Braxton, and I see him smiling as well. 'Do you want to come in and say hello?'

'Maybe another time.'

'Okay.' I try to mask my disappointment as I remove my seatbelt. I think it's more that my time with him has come to an end, rather than the fact that he doesn't want to see my parents.

He removes his own seatbelt, reaching for me. 'Let them have their time together. This is all new to them . . . kind of like us. Who knows, he may even move back in.'

'I hope so.'

He doesn't mention anything about us moving back in together, but I get the feeling that's what he's implying. There's definitely a part of me that would entertain the idea. But like he just said, this is all new to us, and it's far too soon to make any big decisions.

He kisses me lightly, then draws back. 'I've been dying to do that all day,' he admits before kissing me again. Minutes pass, possibly longer, before we finally come up for air, and I immediately feel the loss when he removes his lips from mine.

Reaching forward, he opens the glovebox. 'I have another letter for you,' he says, passing it to me, and my smile returns.

'Thank you.'

I give him one last kiss before exiting the car, and he stays in the driveway until I'm safely inside.

I come to a stop in the doorway of the lounge room and see my parents sitting side by side, with their hands locked together, as they watch television. It's an image I feel I've seen a thousand times, and again I wonder if it's a real memory.

'Come sit with us, pumpkin,' my dad says, tapping the spot beside him.

I think back to what Braxton just said in the car, and although there's a part of me that wants to join them, I decide against it.

'I'm tired. I've had a big day. I think I'll just turn in for the night.'

'Okay. Goodnight, sweetheart,' my mum says.

'Night, pumpkin.'

'Goodnight.'

I jog up the stairs towards my bedroom, busting to read Braxton's letter.

Dearest Jemma,

The fourteenth of December 2009. It was a Monday, and six days before my twenty-first birthday. You'd spent the night at my apartment but had left early because you had classes. I didn't have to be at the university until midday.

I smiled when I walked out into the kitchen and found the note you'd left for me on the fridge. You did this often.

Morning, my handsome boyfriend,

I didn't wake you, because you looked so peaceful. I lay there and stared at your gorgeous face for the longest time before finally dragging my arse out of bed. Text me when you get to campus. Rach and I are going to cook tonight, so bring Lucas with you.

Love you.

See you later,

Jem xx

I still have that note, along with every other one you left me. I couldn't bring myself to throw them away.

I had errands to run before my first class, so I got ready to head out. I grabbed my wallet from my bedside table, but my watch wasn't there. After searching the drawers, under the bed, and the surrounding area with no luck, I flew into a panic. I turned the entire apartment upside down, but still my watch was nowhere to be found. I tried to retrace my steps from the night before—I was sure I'd left it where I always did—but, nothing.

I woke Lucas, who wasn't impressed. He'd been out with some girl and hadn't gotten home until the early hours of the morning.

'Have you seen my watch?'

'What?'

'My watch.'

'That old-looking thing with the cracked screen?' he mumbled.

'Yes. I love that watch . . . Jem gave it to me. Have you seen it?'

'Nope,' he answered, rolling onto his side and covering his face with a pillow.

I grabbed the spare key to your apartment and headed over there—and felt utterly disillusioned when I left empty-handed. This was the first time in five years that my watch hadn't been strapped to my wrist, and I felt totally lost without it.

As soon as I got to campus, I searched my locker before heading to lost property. I didn't text you at all that day. I felt sick inside, and didn't know how to tell you I'd misplaced the watch.

As the days passed, I started to doubt I would ever see it again. A few times you asked me if everything was okay, or why I was acting weird. I'd smile and play it down. I knew I couldn't keep it from you forever. I'd even considered trying to buy a replacement, but I wanted the one you gave me, not an imitation.

The night before my birthday, Rachel went out with some friends, so you cooked a romantic dinner for the two of us at your apartment. It was also the night I had planned to come clean. I rubbed my hand over my wrist as I tried to think of the best way to say it, but there was no good way.

'Jem,' I said, reaching for your hand across the table. 'I have a confession to make.'

'A confession?' You screwed up your forehead as you spoke.

'I . . . I umm . . .'

'Jesus, Braxton, you're scaring me. What have you done?'

There was no easy way to say it. 'I lost my watch . . . the one you gave me.'

'Oh thank god,' you said, breathing a sigh of relief. 'I thought you were going to say something far worse than that.'

'I'm not sure it could get any worse. I love that watch.'

You giggled as you stood, which only confused me. There was nothing humorous about this. You'd worked hard to save the money to buy me that watch.

My eyes followed your every move as you disappeared into your room and then emerged a few moments later with a small wrapped box in your hand.

'This is only a small part of your present. You have to wait until tomorrow for the rest.'

I was perplexed. I'd lost the watch, and you were giving me a present?

Reality dawned as soon as I opened the box. I couldn't believe my eyes. I was filled with mixed emotions: relief, confusion and anger.

'That's my watch!' The screen had been replaced, and it sported a shiny new band.

'It is,' you replied, your face lighting up. 'Surprise.'

'You had it all along?'

'Yeah, I wanted to surprise you.'

All I could think of was the stress I'd lived through that past week. 'Did you think I wouldn't notice it was missing? I've worn it every day since you gave it to me.'

'Are you mad at me?' You pouted your bottom lip.

'Yes . . . no.' I sighed, pinching the bridge of my nose. 'I understand you were doing a nice thing, but I love this watch and everything it represents. This week was a total nightmare. I was devastated thinking I'd lost it.'

'I'm sorry.' You closed the distance between us, and enveloped me in your arms. 'Do you forgive me?'

'Of course.' It was impossible to stay mad at you. 'I'm just glad to have it back.'

'They did a great job with it.'

'They did.' It looked just as shiny and new as the first day you'd given it to me.

'I had a message engraved on the back.'

A smile tugged at my lips when I turned it over and read the inscription on the back.

'I love it . . . thank you.' I already treasured this watch, but it meant even more now.

'Happy birthday eve, Brax.'

I couldn't stop smiling as I strapped it to my wrist. I'd felt like a piece of me had been missing, but now I was whole again.

'Don't forget tomorrow night you're all mine, I'm taking you out for your birthday.' I couldn't think of a more perfect way to spend my twenty-first birthday, although I would have liked to be able to see my dad too. I'd spoken to him on the phone earlier that day, but it had been a few weeks since I'd seen him. I was missing him. 'You can pick me up at six.'

'It's a date.'

I arrived at your apartment at 5.56pm. I know that because I looked down at my shiny watch before knocking. I'd even slept in it the previous night, I was so glad to have it back.

I had no idea where you were taking me for dinner, but I dressed in my best jeans and a nice button-down shirt you'd bought me. Although you were the one taking me out, I still brought you flowers—your favourite kind, the yellow roses and purple irises.

'Come in, it's open,' you called out from inside.

I opened the door, and walked into complete darkness.

'Surprise!'

The sudden loud noise made me jump, then the lights came on, practically blinding me. The first person I saw was my dad. He was wearing a ridiculous smile on his face, and it matched the ridiculous party hat on his head. The entire room was decorated with streamers and balloons. There was also a pile of wrapped presents sitting on the coffee table.

I felt emotion well up as my eyes moved around the room. All the important people in my life were there: you, my dad, Lucas, Rachel, your parents, even Ma and Pa.

'Happy Birthday, Brax,' you said, coming to stand with me. 'I hope you're okay with this. I wanted to do something special for your twenty-first.'

'It's more than okay,' I replied, bending to kiss your lips. I'd never been thrown a birthday party before, and it meant the world to me.

What we had is far too beautiful to be forgotten.

Yours always,

Braxton

There's a huge smile on my face as I refold the letter. I can't believe it took twenty-one years for someone to throw him a birthday party. I'm so glad I did that for him.

I pull the little watch charm out of the envelope, and I find myself wishing he had included the inscription I had engraved in the letter.

I take my memory bracelet and run my fingers over the charms. It is almost full, which saddens me a little. The letters are going to have to stop sooner or later, when Braxton runs out of things to say. I will miss them when that happens—they have been my lifeline.

THIRTY-FIVE

Braxton

I see her staring at my watch as we eat breakfast at our home. 'Is that the watch you mentioned in the letter?' she finally asks.

'The one and only,' I answer, beaming. I love this watch. 'Not a single day has passed that I haven't worn it . . . except that week you stole it.'

'Yeah, sorry about that,' she says with a cheeky smile, and I know she's not sorry at all. Then she falls silent, shifting slightly in her seat. 'What did I have engraved on the back? You never mentioned that part in the letter and I'm dying to know.'

Her question has me grinning. I was hoping she'd ask. 'You want to see it?'

'Please.' The hopeful look on her face tugs at my heart-strings. As much as I hate what has become of us, reliving our past with her, and experiencing her reactions as she rediscovers everything for the first time, is priceless.

I unbuckle the watch from my wrist and pass it to her. She groans when she reads the inscription. *You are the tic in my toc.*

'Oh god, that's so cheesy. Did I really write that crap?'

I have to stifle my laugh when her face turns bright red. 'I think it's sweet.'

'You do not. You're just being polite. I'm surprised you even married me . . . I'm so lame.'

'You're far from lame. Every morning when I read it, it brings a smile to my face.' I chuckle as she passes the watch back to me, and I strap it to my wrist.

'Probably a humorous smile.'

'Not at all . . . I love being the tic in your toc.'

'Somebody kill me now,' she says, covering her face with her hands.

'Hey.' Reaching out, I remove her hands from her pretty face. 'If it's any consolation, you're the tic in my toc too. Always have been, and always will be.'

I see the beginnings of a smile as she picks up her spoon.

'So, my father ended up staying over again last night.' I'm pretty sure she's telling me this to change the subject. 'There's no talk of him moving in yet, but I think it's on the cards.'

'I hope so.'

'My mum has been practically floating around the house.' She giggles as she pops a spoonful of cereal into her mouth. But what stands out for me is that she said *mum*, not Christine. 'I've never seen her so happy.'

'Love will do that to you.'

———

It's around midday when I fold the piece of paper and place it in the envelope. I'm still in two minds about what I've included in the latter part of this letter, but in my heart I think it's something Jem would want to know. It was a terrible time for us both, but also a poignant moment in our relationship. I only hope that this memory doesn't devastate her like it did in the past.

I add the small jewellery box and the tiny ring charm, and then carefully slide the image in alongside the letter.

LETTER SEVENTEEN . . .

Dearest Jemma,

The sixth of July 2012. It was a Friday, and we'd both come home for the weekend. I kissed you goodbye in the driveway, as you headed inside to your parents, and I went to my place to see my dad.

'I'm home, Pop!' I called out, walking through the door.

A few seconds later, he came down the stairs and pulled me into a hug. 'It's good to see you, son. I wasn't expecting you this weekend.'

'Jem and I thought we'd surprise you guys. I've missed you.'

'I've missed you too. Come on, let me put the kettle on.'

'How have you been?' I asked as I sat at the kitchen table.

'I'm good. Really good. How's school?'

'Great. I can't believe I only have a few more months before I graduate.'

'Have you given any thought to where you want to work?'

'Yeah. I've put in a few job applications already.'

I was torn. There was a huge part of me that wanted to work in my home town, but that meant I would have to leave you behind. You still had one more year of study to go.

'That's great. I'm proud of how well you're doing. I don't think you'll have any trouble finding a job.'

'How's the shop going, Pop?' I asked as he placed a cup of coffee down in front of me, before taking a seat.

He runs his fingers over his chin before he speaks. 'Actually, I wanted to talk to you about that. The council has rezoned the area as R4.'

'Oh, really? High-density residential.'

'I've already been approached by a few developers.'

'And what do you think? Are you interested in selling?'
Personally, I thought he'd given enough of his life to that store, but I knew that I would support him if he decided not to sell.

'At first I wasn't, but the more I think about it, the more I've warmed to the idea. Mario's already decided to sell the mechanic shop next door, and the garage across the road put a For Sale sign up a few days ago. And I've got a lot more competition now, since that Bunnings went up in town.'

'What kind of money are you looking at? Have they made you an offer?'

He watched me take a sip of my coffee before he replied. 'That's the thing, they've offered me one-point-five million.'

I inhaled so sharply my coffee went down the wrong pipe and made me cough so heavily it sprayed all over the table—and on my father. 'Dollars?' I asked, when I finally caught my breath.

He chuckled as he wiped the coffee from his face. 'I know. I think I'd be stupid not to consider it. That's more money than I could earn in a lifetime.'

'Well, if it's something you want to do, you know I'll support you all the way. That kind of money could set you up for life.'

'It could set us both up. I'd like to give half to you.'

My eyes widen in disbelief. 'No, Pop. It's your money, you earned it. I'll be out in the workforce soon, I can forge my own living.'

He had that determined look in his eyes when he replied. It was a look I knew well. 'My mind's made up, son. I'm going to call the developers in the morning.'

———

The tenth of September 2012. My father was a stubborn man. No amount of protest from me could stop him from doing what he wanted. Once he paid off the loan on the house, and the business, he walked away with eight hundred thousand dollars, *half of which he gave to me. It still didn't sit well with me, but he insisted.*

I kept this from you, but not because I didn't want you to know about the money. I had big plans for it, and I wanted to surprise you.

We'd been home visiting for the weekend, and I had no classes that Monday, so when you headed back to uni on the Sunday night, I stayed behind. I told you I was helping my dad move the last of his things out of the store. It was a lie. We'd finished doing that the previous day.

Instead, my father and I went house hunting. Beachside house hunting, to be precise. It was your dream to live by the beach, and I was determined to see that happen. Or at the very least, die trying.

The first few beachfront properties the real estate agent showed us were well out of my price range. I was a student, and although I had a huge chunk of the deposit, I only had a part-time job. Even with your father being the bank manager, I knew there was no chance of me getting finance.

The agent and my father tried to talk me into looking at property away from the ocean, but I was insistent. I didn't want the beach to be five minutes away, or something glimpsed in the distance. I wanted it to be smack bang in your face. A place where you could step out of your back door, and be on the sand.

By the end of the day, I was feeling disillusioned. I headed back to my father's place to pack up my things. It appeared my surprise for you would have to wait.

As I loaded my backpack into the car, and shook my father's hand, my phone rang in my pocket. I'd expected to see your name on the screen, but instead it was the real estate agent.

'I think I've found your beachside property. Mind you, the house is small, more like a shack, but the location is perfect and in your price range ... it's exactly what you were looking for.'

'When can I come and look at it?' I asked in an excited voice.

'The property is vacant, so right now if you like.'

My pulse was racing as I jotted down the address. As soon as she mentioned the house was situated at number nineteen, in my heart I knew it was a sign ... it was destined to become ours.

I bundled my dad into the car, and off we went. She wasn't lying when she said it was a shack. It was a one-bedroom fibro house that had been built in the early forties. It was in desperate need of some TLC, but in a way it was perfect. It meant when we could afford to, we'd be able to knock it down and build your dream house. I had already started drawing the plans for it.

Apparently, the old man who'd lived there had recently passed away and his two sons were looking for a quick sale. The asking price was more than the four hundred thousand I had, but my father agreed to give me an interest-free loan for the rest, until I got on my feet.

Apart from planning to go on a brief cruise, he was just going to bank his money. I guess when you've struggled financially for as long as he had, you don't part with your fortune easily.

It was further down the beach than I originally would have liked, but that view ... it was breathtaking. My heart raced just thinking about your reaction. I knew you were going to love it.

———

The twenty-ninth of November 2012. I'd now graduated, and uni was over for you for the year. With my new purchase in mind, I had moved back home temporarily, and was putting all my efforts into finding local employment.

You cried when I told you of my plans, because it meant that we would be separated again. 'I thought you were going to look for work closer to campus so we could still see each other every day.'

'This wasn't an easy decision for me, Jem, but it makes sense. I don't want to get settled in a job and have to leave in a year's *time when you graduate. I want us both to eventually settle back home. I want our kids to grow up in that area, just like we did.'*

'Our kids?'

As soon as I mentioned kids the tears stopped, and your face lit up with a huge smile.

I pulled you into my arms. 'Yes, our kids. You're my forever girl, Jem, of course there's kids in our future.'

For the time being I seemed to have dodged a bullet, but I knew once you found out the real reason you would forgive me completely.

You'd spent the morning at the beautician with your mother, which gave me time to set everything up. Of course, your parents and my father were all in on this. They'd helped me immensely over the past few weeks.

Later that afternoon, I asked you if you wanted to go for a walk along the beach. I held your hand as we walked along the shore.

'There's something I want to show you,' I said, once we were close.

I led you across the sand towards the shack. Your parents and my father had helped me clean the place up. We'd given the interior and exterior a fresh coat of paint; the outside was now white, with blue trim around the windowsills. It was a long way from your dream house, but at least the colours and the location weren't.

My dad had sanded back the wooden floors inside, before re-staining them. He'd even retiled some of the bathroom. He no longer had the store to go to, so he was grateful for something to do.

Your parents bought us a small sofa, a television, a bedroom suite, and all new appliances for our kitchen. Your mum had taken you shopping a few weeks earlier, under the false pretence of redecorating your bedroom at their house. She got you to pick out the colour scheme, as well as a rug, new linen and curtains.

'What are you doing?' you asked as we reached the back door.

'I said I had something to show you.'

'I know, but you can't just break into somebody's house.'

'I have a key,' I said, pulling it out of my pocket and dangling it in front of you. 'So, technically I'm not breaking in.' Your face screwed up into a cute little frown as I unlocked the door. 'Ladies first.'

Your head darted around to see if anyone was watching us, and I chuckled at the fact that you thought we were doing something illegal. I reached for your hand, guiding you through the doorway.

The place was tiny, so we only had to take a few steps down the hallway, past the kitchen on the right and laundry on the left, before entering the small lounge room. I'd organised for your mum to come to the house as soon as we'd left to go for our walk, to light the thirty-odd candles I'd placed strategically throughout the room.

'Braxton,' you gasped, halting. 'What's all this?'

'This is our new home. I bought it for you, Jem. It's not much, but I promise you when I can afford it, I'll build you your dream house.'

Your eyes widened, and your mouth gaped open, but before you had a chance to reply, I got down on one knee. 'Almost seventeen years ago, an angel walked into my life . . . you. Over the months and years that followed you not only became a big part of my life . . . you became my life . . . the reason I look forward to waking up every day. I love you. I always have, and I always will. You own my heart, my body and my soul . . . I wouldn't be complete if you weren't by my side. Say you'll be my forever girl, Jem . . . marry me?'

You didn't answer straightaway, and although there were tears streaming down your face, you were smiling. I saw you pinch yourself a few times as I waited for your reply.

'What are you doing?'

'I'm making sure I'm not dreaming.'

I chuckled. 'You're not dreaming Jem. This is all real. Now are you going to answer me, or leave me hanging?'

You leaped towards me with such enthusiasm, you knocked me off balance and sent me tumbling to the floor. You landed on top of me, and started raining kisses all over my face. 'Of course I'll marry you! There's nobody else . . . there'll never be anyone else.'

We spent our first night in the house together. I gave you a key but told you there was no pressure for you to move in straightaway.

'Are you going to live here?' you asked.

'Yes.'

'Then so am I. I want to be wherever my fiancé is.'

My heart swelled when you said that.

The next morning we sat on the back step drinking our coffees. 'I can't believe this will be my view for the rest of my life,' you said.

'When I have enough money, I'm going to put a big deck off the back. We can sit out here every morning and have breakfast together.'

'That sounds magical,' you replied, resting your head on my shoulder. 'I can't believe you did all this for me.'

'There's nothing I wouldn't do to make you happy, Jem.'

———

The eleventh of January 2013. I debated about whether to add this into the letter, but it's a moment in your life that, although tragic, I'm pretty sure you'd want to know about.

It's something you didn't talk about a lot, but I found the image that I've enclosed with this letter taped inside the lid of the treasure box I made you, so I know you looked at it often.

The previous six weeks had been perfect. We'd done more work to the interior, and fixed up the yard. You'd added a small garden out the front. The place wasn't much, but it was ours, and we loved it.

You still had another month before uni started back, and I'd finally landed a job—it was with a small architectural firm just outside of town—which I would start the following week.

I'd woken up this particular morning, to find you vomiting in the bathroom. 'Jem. Are you okay?'

'Urgh, I feel dreadful,' you replied.

You had a strong immune system and rarely got sick, so I was immediately concerned. When I found you like this, again, the following morning, I put you in the shower and once you were dressed, I took you straight to the doctor.

He said you'd probably picked up a virus, but took some blood just to be sure.

By the time we arrived back home, you said you were feeling a lot better, but I still made you go back to bed.

The next morning I found you vomiting again. I called the doctor and he said the results of your bloodwork should be back later that morning, and he would call us as soon as he had them.

The call came in just before midday. I sat on the side of the bed while you spoke with the doctor. I knew it wasn't just a virus when I saw all the colour drain out of your face.

'What did he say?' I asked the minute you'd ended the call.

Your stunned eyes met mine. 'He said I'm pregnant.'

I don't know how long I sat there and stared at you, unable to speak, but I eventually reached out, pulling you into my arms. 'You're pregnant?' I could hear the shock in my voice when I spoke.

'It appears so.'

I pulled back so I could see your face. 'How do you feel about that?'

'Shocked . . . Happy . . . Shocked.'

When I saw a smile tug at your lips, I smiled too. 'We're going to be parents.'

'Yes,' you whispered as your smile widened. We wanted this child because it was a product of our love.

The next day, we went back in to see the doctor. He gave us our options, but we assured him we wanted this baby, so he booked you in for an ultrasound later that afternoon to find out how far along you were.

You were almost seven weeks. They even gave us a small printout of the baby, which was more like a tiny dot at that stage. There was a huge smile on your face as you stared at that image all the way home.

We decided to keep the news between us for a while, as we adjusted to the thought of becoming parents. I started looking around for weekend work, because we were going to need the extra money.

Five days later, you woke me in the middle of the night. 'Braxton, I don't feel so good. I have bad cramps in my stomach.'

I sat up, turning on the lamp beside my bed. 'What do you mean you have cramps? Is that normal?'

'No. I think I need to go to the hospital.'

I jumped up and threw on a T-shirt and some sweatpants, before moving to your side of the bed. When I pulled back the covers to help you up, I froze when I saw that you were lying in a pool of blood.

I scooped you into my arms and practically ran to the car. You moaned loudly as I placed you down gently in the passenger seat. 'You're going to be okay, Jem,' I said. 'I've got you.'

I tried to remain strong, but inside I was anything but. All I could think about was my mum, and how she'd gone to the hospital and never returned. I was scared for our baby, but I was terrified I was going to lose you.

When we arrived at emergency, they performed another ultrasound, and then gave us the devastating news: you had miscarried. An hour later they wheeled you down the long corridor, towards the operating theatre for a curette.

I held myself together right until the very end, but the moment you disappeared through those doors, I completely broke down.

The next day the doctor discharged you. You didn't speak a single word from the time you woke that morning, nor on the drive home. I was so concerned, it was like a part of you had died along with our child. In a way, I guess it had.

You didn't even protest when I carried you from the car into the house. There was no fight left in you, which only served to worry me more.

When we reached the bathroom, I helped you undress, then turned on the shower. I left you in there while I stripped and remade the bed. I put your bloodied pyjamas and the sheets straight into the washing machine.

You were out of the shower by the time I came back, so I helped dry you before slipping a nightgown over your head. I pulled back the covers on our bed, and you climbed in. You still hadn't spoken a word, and I didn't know what to say to you.

'Is there anything I can get you, Jem?'

'No,' you whispered.

I sat down on the side of the bed. 'Are you sure you're okay?' It was a stupid question, of course you weren't.

You just shook your head, and as soon as I saw the tears rise to your eyes, I pulled my T-shirt over my head, slipped out of my sweats and climbed in beside you.

I pulled you into my arms. 'When you're ready, we can try again.'

The moment those words were out of my mouth, you started to sob. It made my already broken heart break a little more.

We stayed in that position for the rest of the day. We cried, we talked, and we cried some more. We shed tears for our loss, and for our child. For the first breath they would never take. For the long, full life they would never get to live. For the undying love we had to offer that they would never get to feel.

What we had is far too beautiful to be forgotten.

Yours always,

Braxton

THIRTY-SIX

Jemma

Tears trickle down my face as I sit on the edge of my bed and stare down at the ultrasound image in my hand. The picture of my baby, a baby I can't remember.

There's a tightness in my chest, and the loss is heartbreakingly painful.

I reach for my phone. I feel compelled to call Braxton, but I know he's at work and I don't want to disturb him. He's the only one who can understand what I'm feeling in this moment.

Hi, I type. *I just wanted to say thank you for telling me.*

A few minutes pass before I get a reply. *It's something I thought you'd want to know. Are you okay?*

No. I feel like my heart is breaking all over again.

A few seconds later I jump when my phone rings. 'I'm sorry, Jem,' is the first thing he says. 'I should have waited until I was around to give you the letter. I'm stuck in a meeting and I can't leave.'

'It's okay,' I say, sniffling. 'I didn't expect you to. I just wanted to say thank you. I'll be all right, honestly.'

'I should be finished here in about half an hour. I'll come straight over when I'm done. We can talk then.'

'You don't have to come, Braxton, but thanks for offering.'

After ending the call, I wipe the tears from my face before opening the lid of my treasure box and tucking the ultrasound picture safely inside. I pick up the smaller envelope that housed the letter and find a small engagement-ring charm inside. Although my heart is still hurting, I smile. He also included a box in the parcel, which I take out next.

I draw in a sharp breath once I open the lid of the white velvet box and see my engagement ring. It looks shiny, like new, which makes me wonder if he had it cleaned before sending it to me.

I slide it onto my finger and admire my hand. It's not overly big, but it's beautiful. *Exquisitely beautiful.* Though I'm pretty sure I would have loved a piece of wire if it was from him.

I leave the ring on my finger for the time being, and lie down on my bed. Closing my eyes, I will my mind to remember ...

'Did you remember to grab the tomatoes, babe?' I call out when I hear a door close in the distance.

I'm standing in a tiny kitchen I don't recognise, stirring something on the stove. I peer into the pot ... it looks like spaghetti sauce. Looking out towards the window on my right, I see a row of shells along the windowsill above the kitchen sink. I find myself smiling as I get lost in the ocean view beyond.

'Yes, I got the tomatoes.' I jump when a pair of strong hands slide around my waist.

Glancing over my shoulder, I see Braxton's handsome face smiling back at me. He plants a chaste kiss on my lips before letting me go. I continue to stir the sauce as I watch him unpack the groceries onto the countertop.

'Lettuce, cucumber, tomatoes, red onion and an avocado. Is that everything?'

There's a sweet grin on his face as he turns towards me. My eyes zero in on his cute little dimple. I love that dimple.

'Yes, that's everything.'

He looks down into the bag he's still holding. 'I also got these.'

He reaches in and pulls out a pair of tiny white socks with a pink trim around the band. Tears rise to my eyes when I read the inscription on them: *I love my mummy.*

'Braxton, they're beautiful,' I say, taking them out of his hands.

'And these,' he adds, pulling out another pair. They have a blue trim and say: *I love my daddy.*

I sniffle as I take both pairs of socks in my hands. 'I love them so much. I still can't believe we're going to be parents.'

'You're going to make the best mum,' he says, his eyes shining.

As he inches his face towards mine, I feel a hand softly run over my hair. I open my eyes and I'm no longer in the small kitchen, wrapped in his arms. I'm lying on my bed in my room at my parents' house, and Braxton is sitting on the edge of the mattress looking down at me. There's a sweet smile on his face, and again I gravitate towards his dimple.

'I'm sorry. I didn't mean to wake you.'

'I didn't realise I'd fallen asleep.'

'You must have been having a nice dream, because you kept smiling.' I sit up, but don't reply. 'I've missed watching you sleep, Jem.'

His gaze flickers down to my hand, to the engagement ring.

'I was just trying it on. It's so pretty.'

When I go to remove it, he places his hand over mine. 'Please don't take it off, Jem.'

'I . . .'

'Please. I'm not trying to pressure you, and don't worry, I won't get the wrong idea about you wearing it. I just want to see it on your hand. Whether or not we live together as husband and wife again, I bought it for you to wear . . . it's yours.'

He looks away, down to his lap, and the sadness I see on his face hurts my heart. I raise my hand and run it down the side of his face. 'I'll leave it on,' I whisper.

Braxton's eyes keep moving between my face and the ring on my finger as I eat breakfast. I'm glad I kept it on, because I can see how happy it makes him. There was a part of me that didn't want to take it off, but I worry that he will get the wrong idea. There's no denying that I have feelings for him, that he's on my mind all the time. When we're together I feel so happy, and when we're apart I miss him. But I still have a long way to go before I'm ready for anything like that. What I feel is not enough. I want to be able to feel the way I did before the accident.

He was so sweet when he came to my house last night. He asked me how I was feeling and when I said sad, he told me to scoot over and then lay down beside me. We stayed there, me wrapped in his arms, and it made me wonder if this was how he'd held me the first time I went through the loss.

I ended up falling asleep again, but this time there were no dreams. I desperately wanted to ask him whether he had given me those baby socks, but I'm not ready to disclose that information. A scattered dream here and there isn't enough to warrant that. I don't want to get anybody's hopes up until I'm sure.

After I help him clean up, and we visit his father, he drops me back at my mum's. 'I have another letter for you,' he says as we sit in the driveway. 'There's nothing sad in this one, I promise,' he adds with a gentle smile.

Sliding his hand into my hair, he pulls my face towards his. I part my lips when his mouth meets mine. I can see why the old me wanted to kiss him so much. I'm officially addicted to his kisses.

He draws back slightly. 'I hope you have a nice day. Call me if you need anything.'

'I will,' I whisper.

Neither of us moves. It's getting harder and harder to leave him.

LETTER EIGHTEEN . . .

Dearest Jemma,

The thirty-first of December 2014, and the clock had just struck midnight. I slid my arms around your waist from behind. 'Happy New Year, Jem,' I said as I planted a soft kiss on your cheek. We were standing on our back deck, watching the fireworks in the distance. I loved how the neon colours in the sky reflected back in the water.

'Happy New Year, Brax,' you replied as you turned your head and brushed your lips against mine.

We'd been living in our dream house for almost six months. We loved it, but there was a part of us that missed our tiny shack. You cried your eyes out the day it was demolished.

We ended up moving in with your mother for five months, while the new house was being built. It was trying at times, because she was in the depths of depression. Her parents had long since passed away, and your father had moved out. It was incredibly hard to watch the shell of a person she had become.

'This year is going to be an amazing year,' you said, turning in my arms. 'Just think, in nineteen days I'm going to be Mrs Braxton Spencer.'

'Say that again.'

'Mrs Braxton Spencer.'

'It has a nice ring to it,' I said, gently brushing your hair back from your face. 'I can't wait for you to be my wife.'

'I can't wait for you to be my husband.'

We had only one more week of work, then we were off for an entire month. I couldn't wait to spend every second of that time with you.

Life was good . . . it was perfect, actually. Sometimes I worried it was too perfect. My parents had been happy, right up until the moment my mother died. Your parents had been happy too, until everything fell apart.

Even though our future looked bright, something niggled deep inside me. It was concern for what possibly lay ahead. It seems so ironic now.

———

The nineteenth of January 2015. Lucas placed his hand on my leg as we sat in the front pew at the church. 'Will you stop that,' he complained. 'That bouncing is making me edgy.'

I wasn't nervous, I was excited. In a matter of minutes, you would arrive. I looked down at my watch, and smiled. Two minutes, to be precise. You'd promised me the day before that you wouldn't be late, and you'd never broken a promise.

When the priest took his place in front of the altar, he signalled for Lucas and me to stand. 'Good luck, son,' my father said as I passed him. I didn't need luck, I was already the luckiest man on earth, because I had you.

Chills ran up my spine as the music started to play. 'Endless Love', sung by Stan Walker and Dami Im. You told me that you'd heard it on the radio, and it made you cry. 'It's like it was written for us,' you said.

Rachel appeared in the doorway first. She looked beautiful in a jade-green dress that she had designed herself; she designed your wedding dress too. I was yet to see it, but you'd told me how much you loved it.

I leaned slightly to the left, trying to catch a glimpse of you, but all I could see was a flash of white.

I smiled at Rachel as she slowly walked down the aisle towards me. She was a quarter of the way down before you came into full view. My heart skipped a beat as soon as my eyes locked with yours.

Even though the veil was over your face, I could see that your eyes were trained on me as well. I'll never forget the look on your face as you made your way down the aisle. You looked so happy, as happy as I felt.

My gaze didn't leave you until you were standing before me.

'Who gives this woman's hand in marriage today?' the priest asked.

'I do,' your father replied.

He reached out and shook my hand, before taking a seat beside my dad. Your mother had put up quite a fuss about him attending the wedding. She insisted that we keep him as far away from her as possible. You were still hurting from the break-up, but there was no way you were getting married without him present, so we compromised.

I reached for your hand, lightly tugging you towards me. 'You look beautiful,' I whispered.

'So do you,' you replied.

I helped you pull your veil back, and then interlaced your fingers through mine. I wanted to kiss you badly in that moment, but I knew I had to wait.

Surprisingly, we both held it together as we exchanged vows and rings.

'I love you, Mr Spencer,' you whispered as I pulled you into my arms on the dance floor at the reception for our first dance as husband and wife.

'I love you too, Mrs Spencer,' I replied, placing my lips on yours.

———

The twenty-first of January 2015. It was the day we arrived in Kauai, on the shores of Tunnels Beach in Hawaii, and took refuge in our beautiful ocean villa.

We made the most of our honeymoon, enjoying every moment of our time together. We took long walks on the beach, and ate exquisite food that was brought to our villa every day via a canoe. We swam in our private ocean pool, and we made love into the early hours of the morning. We were so far removed from the rest of the world, and neither of us wanted it to end. If I'd known the horrors that awaited us after our return, I would have kept you on that island forever.

They say that after you marry someone things don't really change, that it's just a piece of paper. I don't agree, because things were definitely different for me. I felt closer to you than I ever had, if that were even possible. You were no longer just an extension of me, you were a part of me.

What we had is far too beautiful to be forgotten.

Yours always,

Braxton

I find two things inside the envelope: a small car charm that has the words *Just Married* on the back, and my wedding band. I slide it onto my finger next to my engagement ring. Braxton said that there was nothing sad in this letter, but sad would be the best way to describe how I'm feeling in this moment.

THIRTY-SEVEN

Jemma

I've pulled up Braxton's number numerous times throughout the day, but I've chickened out from calling him each time. It's been three whole days since I've seen him, and he's made no contact with me. It has rained since Wednesday, so I haven't been able to go for my run along the beach, which means I've missed breakfast with him too.

The longer I don't hear from him, the more I worry. I miss him so much. I miss him to the point that I think I'm actually pining for him.

I stand and start to pace back and forth in my room. I just can't settle. I open the laptop sitting on my desk. It's almost 7pm here, so that would make it 5am in New York. I know Rachel gets up early to go to yoga before work, so I take the chance and Skype her.

'Jesus, Jem, it's five o'clock in the morning here,' she says as her face comes into view on the screen. Her eyes are squinting from the bright light of the monitor, and her hair is sticking up all over the place. I have to stifle my laugh. She looks like a hot mess.

'I'm sorry. I just . . . I don't know . . . needed to talk to you.'

'Hey, what's up? Is everything okay?'

'Yes . . . no. I haven't heard from Braxton in three days.'

'Oh. Did you two have a fight? Things seemed to be going so well.'

'That's the thing, it's been wonderful . . . he's been wonderful.'

'Well, maybe he's just busy with work. You said yourself they were doing really well.'

'Maybe. Seeing him every day, and then not seeing him at all . . . it's hard. I miss him.'

'Is he still writing you letters?'

'I'm not sure. The one he gave me three days ago was about our wedding day, and our honeymoon . . . that was just before the accident, so maybe it was the last letter.'

'I see.' She ponders this briefly, then continues. 'Maybe he's feeling disillusioned.'

I never thought about it like that. Could he be giving up on us? 'Possibly,' I say, suddenly feeling deflated.

'Call him, Jem. Ever since the accident he's fought hard to try to win you back. He's been so patient, and he gave you the distance you needed. Throw him a bone, he at least deserves that after all the effort he's put in.'

'You're right,' I say, looking down at the carpet. He's done all the chasing, it's about time I did some of my own. 'I'm going to call him. Thanks, Rach. I'm sorry if I woke you . . . go back to sleep.'

'Yeah right, I'm wide awake now.'

'I'm sorry.'

'That's okay. I can call you back on my lunch break . . . what time will it be there? Oh that's right, 2am.'

'Don't you dare,' I say, giggling.

'At least I got you smiling, pretty girl.'

'Thank you.'

'I'll see you in ten days.'

'I can't wait.'

She has finally made the decision to come home. She's already given notice at her work, and has started to pack up her apartment. I'm looking forward to having her back here. With Braxton's help, I'm going to try to work out this thing between her and Lucas.

After we say our goodbyes, I log off and pick up my phone. This time I don't hesitate pressing the call button.

'Jem. Is everything okay?' he says as soon as he answers my call.

'Hi. Everything's fine. I haven't spoken to you in a few days ... three actually ... I just, umm, wanted to see how you were doing.'

'I'm okay. How about you?' To me, the tone of his voice doesn't appear to match his words.

'I'm doing okay.'

'I'm glad.'

Even though he's being polite, he seems distant. Or maybe that's just my paranoia. 'So, what have you been up to?'

'Working. Same old same old.'

'What about tonight? Do you have any plans?' I chew nervously on one of my fingernails as I wait for his reply.

'I do actually.'

'Oh. Okay.'

'I'm going out with Lucas. It's been a while since we've had a boys' night out.'

'That's great. You deserve it.' I really mean it, but I'm still fighting back tears. 'Well, have a good night.'

'I will. You too.'

I want to tell him how much I've missed him, but the words won't come. 'Bye.'

'Goodbye, Jem.' I hear his voice crack slightly as he speaks. Why did that goodbye seem so final?

I head downstairs, my stomach churning. I feel panicked—
I don't want to lose him.

My parents have gone out to dinner. They invited me to
come along, but I said no. They need their time alone; they
have so much making up to do. My dad has been coming over
every night for dinner, but only stays over on the weekends.
I'm expecting an announcement any day, saying he's moving
back in. It's plain to see how smitten they are, and it makes
me so happy seeing them together again.

I enter the kitchen and head straight for the fridge. I'm
not even hungry, but I poke around inside. I end up making
a coffee and settling on the sofa in front of the television.
The dreaded feeling of loneliness, the one I felt when I first
woke from my coma, settles deep in my gut. I don't like this
feeling one bit.

It's around ten when I hear a car pull up outside, followed
by a door closing. I walk towards the window to see who it
is. I hope it's Braxton, but I don't think he'd turn up unan-
nounced at this time of night. It's probably just my parents
returning from dinner.

I pull the curtain to the side and peer out into the night.
I see a dark figure run across the front lawn towards the kerb,
and hop into the passenger side of a car that's parked there.
A few moments later it drives away, disappearing into the night,
and suddenly I feel uneasy, because I don't recognise the car.

I head out into the hallway, to check the front door is
locked, and that's when I notice the envelope on the floor.
Someone has slipped it under the door.

As soon as I pick it up and turn it over, I see Braxton's
handwriting. The fact that he didn't knock, or want to say
hello, does nothing to lift my mood.

After turning off the television, and rinsing my mug in the
sink, I head up to my room.

Dearest Jemma,

As I sit here and ponder everything we once were, and everything we are today, I suddenly realise that this is not only the nineteenth letter, but also the last.

It's uncanny that they'd end on this number. There's no denying the number nineteen holds a special significance for us.

It was the nineteenth the day we met. A day that would change my life forever.

It was the nineteenth when we went on our first official date.

It was the nineteenth when we took our relationship to the next level, the day our bodies and hearts connected as one.

Our home, the place I proposed to you and promised to love you until I took my very last breath, whether by fate or pure coincidence is the number nineteen. I'd like to believe it was fate.

It was not only nineteen years to the day we met that you gave me your hand in marriage, making me the happiest man in the world, it was also the nineteenth.

That's why I gave you this necklace nineteen days later, with the number nineteen on it. I thought that nineteen was the number that symbolised everything we were. Every important milestone we'd experienced together. The number that not only brought us together, but bonded us forever. But I was wrong.

It would also be the number that played a hand in snatching you away from me, shattering my world and everything I held dear. You were my life and without you by my side, I could no longer breathe.

If nineteen years is all I'm allowed, then I'll take it. Meeting you enriched my life in so many ways, and I'll forever cherish every second you were mine.

Never in my wildest dreams did I think the day would come that I would no longer be your forever boy.

Braxton

I look at the necklace in my hand, and the beautiful diamond-encrusted number-nineteen pendant that hangs from it. I'm not sure if I would be able to stop the tears that now leak from my eyes, even if I tried.

My heart feels like it's in a thousand tiny pieces. I hate that he thinks he's no longer my forever boy, that this is the end of us.

All the anger I felt when I first woke from my coma comes flooding back to the surface. The unfairness of life consumes every inch of me until it's seeping out of my pores.

I want my old life back. I want to remember every beautiful second . . . but more than anything, I want to feel it. I want to feel that all-consuming love I once had for him. I want it all, but I can't have it. Life's a bitch, and in this moment, I hate her. I hate her so much I want to scream. But instead, I bury my face in my pillow and I cry. I cry for me. I cry for Braxton. But more than anything, I cry for us—for what has been so cruelly taken away. That's the true injustice here. I cry until the exhaustion consumes me. It's not until I fall asleep that the tears finally stop . . .

I'm suddenly thrust into a place that seems familiar, yet I've never seen it before. I'm in a large bathroom. I'm surrounded by sky-blue walls and shiny white tiles. There's a long, white vanity in front of me. My eyes focus on the beautiful white shell that sits in between the double sink.

I don't know where I am, but I feel panicked as I rummage through the make-up bag in front of me. I can't seem to find what I'm looking for. I open the drawer below the vanity and move a pink brush to the side. 'There you are,' I whisper as I grab the lip gloss that was hiding underneath it.

My eyes move back to the long rectangular mirror in front of me. It has recessed lights around the perimeter, illuminating my reflection. I'm rushing now, as I put the finishing touches to my make-up.

That's when I catch a glimpse of someone else in the mirror. It's Braxton. He's leaning up against the doorframe watching me. He's shirtless and wearing a pair of grey sweats that hang low on his hips. I feel my pulse quicken as my eyes rake over his bare chest, and the definition of each delicious muscle. From the perfect V just above the waistband, right up to his washboard abs, and his strong chest. He has a beautiful body, like a sculptured Greek god.

Only then do my eyes move back to his, and the adoring look on his face sends my heart into a flutter. The sheer love I feel for him in that moment consumes every fibre of my being. I've never felt anything like it. It almost takes my breath away.

'How long have you been standing there?' I ask as my mouth curves into a smile.

'I'm just admiring my beautiful wife.'

He pushes off the doorframe and stalks towards me. When his arms encircle my waist, he pulls me back into him. A soft moan falls from my mouth as his lips trail a path up my neck. I tilt my head to the side, allowing him better access.

'I'm already running late,' I breathe.

'I wish you didn't have to go.' His warm breath on my skin leaves goosebumps in its wake.

'Me either.'

'The next eight hours are going to feel like an eternity.'

I sigh in agreement. 'I know.'

His tongue glides over the sensitive spot behind my ear, sending shivers down my spine. He did that on purpose. 'Don't make any plans for tonight, because I'm taking you out to dinner.'

'You're taking me out? Where?'

'The Sea Shanty.' He groans as he sucks my earlobe into his mouth.

'What's the special occasion?'

'Our anniversary.'

My eyes fly open to meet his in the mirror. 'Our what?' My mind starts to race. *What anniversary?*

He turns me in his arms so I'm facing him, and pulls a small black box from his pocket. 'I was going to give this to you tonight, but I want you to have it now. Happy nineteenth anniversary, sweetheart.'

My hands tremble slightly as I take hold of the box. That's when I realise that today we have been married for nineteen days, and a huge smile breaks out on my face. The number nineteen has always held special significance for us.

Tears of happiness pool in my eyes as I open the lid. Inside I find a white-gold necklace holding a diamond-encrusted number-nineteen pendant.

'Oh Braxton, it's beautiful. I love it ... I love you.'

He smiles as his hand tucks a lock of hair behind my ear. 'I can't wait to spend the rest of my life with you, Jem.'

'Same.'

A lump forms in my throat and I feel like I'm choking back the tears. I use my hand to fan my eyes; I don't have time to redo my make-up.

Taking the box out of my hand, he removes the necklace. 'Turn around, and hold up your hair.' I do as he asks, gathering my long brown hair on top of my head so he can fasten the necklace. 'Perfect,' he says, planting a soft kiss at the base of my neck.

My fingertips glide over the pendant as I admire it in the mirror. 'Thank you ... I'll treasure it.'

Sliding his arms around my waist again, he rests his chin on my shoulder, and his eyes meet mine in the mirror. 'You know, I've been thinking ...'

'That could be dangerous.'

I laugh when he pokes my side.

'I want you to stop taking the pill.'

I feel my heartbeat accelerate as I swing around to face him. 'You do?'

'Yes. It's time we gave it another try, Jem. I want to see our baby growing inside you.'

Opening my eyes, I bolt upright. *I remember.* Flicking back the covers, I jump out of bed and scamper around in the dark, looking for my phone. My head is spinning. I need to call Braxton. I need to know if that's really what happened that morning, or if it was just a dream.

When I finally find my phone, I turn it on and the brightness of the screen hurts my eyes. I see that the time is 1.19am. There's the number nineteen again. I feel breathless as I find his number. I probably shouldn't ring him at this hour, but I'm desperate for answers. There's no way I can go back to sleep until I know.

'Hi, this is Braxton, I can't take your call at the moment, but if you leave your name and number, I'll get back to you as soon as possible . . .' My heart sinks.

I switch on the light and start to pace back and forth in my room and then decide screw it, I'm going over there.

I don't even bother to take off my pyjamas, I just slide into a pair of jeans and pull a jacket out of the wardrobe. I'm already dialling the taxi as I rush down the stairs and slip outside into the darkness. Twenty-five minutes later, the driver turns into Braxton's street. 'It's number nineteen,' I tell him, a smile creeping onto my face.

I pat down my pockets when we come to a stop outside his house. 'Shit!'

'That'll be nineteen dollars and five cents, but let's make it an even nineteen,' he says. Of course it's nineteen dollars. That only manages to make my smile grow. It's a sign, I know it.

'I've left my money at home, can you just give me a second. My husband will fix up the bill.' *My husband*, those words are not lost on me.

His house is in darkness when I reach the front door, and suddenly I'm second-guessing myself. It's the middle of the night. Nevertheless, I raise my hand and knock. I hear Bella-Rose bark from inside, and a few minutes later the porch light comes on.

The first thing I see is the surprise on Braxton's face when he opens the door. 'Jemma.' My eyes move down his body, he's shirtless and has a grey pair of sweats hanging low on his hips. He looks just as beautiful as he did in my dream. 'Jemma . . . is everything okay?'

My eyes snap back up to his face. 'I need money to pay the taxi driver.' I point over my shoulder. 'I can pay you back, I forgot to bring my purse.'

'Sure, give me a sec, I'll grab my wallet.' He steps back and opens the door further. 'Come in, it's cold out there.' A minute later he comes bounding back down the stairs, now wearing a T-shirt. 'Stay here. I'll be right back.'

Braxton closes the front door behind him when he returns, and comes to a stop in front of me, shoving his hands in his pockets.

It's so good to see him.

'Hi.'

'Hi,' he replies, smiling.

'I've missed you.'

'You have?'

'Very much.' His face lights up at my confession.

'I've missed you too, Jem, but it's a quarter to two in the morning. I'm sure you didn't come all this way to tell me that.'

'I didn't.' My gaze briefly moves down to the floor. 'I need to see the bathroom where I used to get ready in the mornings.'

'Our ensuite?' His brow furrows. 'Why?'

'Can I just see it?' I don't want to tell him why, just in case it's completely different from the one in my dream.

'Sure.'

He turns and walks towards the floating staircase. 'Is this the same bathroom I got ready in the morning you gave me the necklace?'

'Yes.'

My eyes are everywhere as I follow him into what I presume is our bedroom. There's a king-size bed, centred against the far wall. The covers are thrown back on one side, and I can see the indent in the pillow from where Braxton had been lying a few minutes earlier.

'This is our ensuite,' he says, gesturing with his hand for me to enter, while he remains in the doorway.

I gasp as soon as I step into the space. 'I remember the colour of the walls . . . and this vanity,' I say as I rush towards it. The mirror and the recessed lights are exactly the same as the ones in my dream. 'I remember this shell,' I whisper, picking it up. When I place it back down, I open the drawer and see the pink brush sitting on top.

I spin around to face him. 'The morning you gave me that necklace, you were standing in the doorway watching me put on my make-up. You were shirtless and wearing a pair of grey sweats, just like the ones you're wearing now. You looked so sexy, by the way.' The smile on his face grows as he takes a few steps towards me. 'You told me you wanted me to give up work so we could start a family, didn't you?'

'I did.'

'Braxton, I remember,' I say as I leap into his arms. 'I remember.' Tears of happiness are streaming down my face as he wraps me in his arms and swings me around.

When he finally puts me down, he lets me go to cup my face in his hands. 'Jem,' he whispers.

'I even remembered how much I loved you. The feeling was . . . euphoric.' I place my hand over my heart. 'It consumed me.'

'I love you so much, Jem,' he says as a lone tear leaks from one of his eyes.

'I love you too.'

His lips crash into mine and my body instinctively melts into his, as my arms slide around his waist. A soft moan falls from my lips when he deepens the kiss.

When he draws back and smiles, I'm smiling too.

'Do you still want to try for another baby?'

'Absolutely,' he says without hesitation. 'If that's what you want?'

'I'd love to have a baby with you, Braxton.'

'Well, when you're ready we can try.'

'Can I stay tonight? In our bed . . . with you?'

'Are you sure you're ready for that?'

'Yes.' My reply comes out almost desperate. 'I want everything we once had, and so much more. I've been thinking about it a lot since someone bragged about what an exceptional lover he was—I need to find out if he was telling the truth.'

He throws back his head and laughs before scooping me into his arms and carrying me back into the bedroom. 'He was telling the truth. Actually, I'm pretty sure he was playing it down.'

I giggle at his reply, but if he can make love anything like he can kiss, then I don't doubt it for a second.

He places me down gently, beside the bed.

'Let me be the judge of that,' I say.

'You're probably going to put him off his game now.'

'Really? Do you think maybe he's been talking himself up?'

'Not a chance in hell,' he replies, making me laugh. 'He's just a bit rusty, he hasn't done this in a while.'

'I'm sorry,' I say, running my hand down the side of his face. 'I'm sorry I hurt you . . . I'm sorry I couldn't remember how much I loved you.'

'It's okay, Jem. Even in the tough times, I never gave up hope that you'd find your way back to me.'

'Thank you for not giving up on me . . . on us.'

'That was never going to happen. We were meant to be.'

He places his lips on mine, before reaching for the zipper on my jacket. My body momentarily tenses, as he drags it open. 'Can we turn off the light?'

He draws back from me, studying my face. 'Why?'

'My scars,' I say, bowing my head.

He places a finger under my chin, raising my face to meet his. 'Your scars are a part of you, Jem, and there's nothing about you I don't love.'

He brushes the hair back from the side of my face, before planting a tender kiss on the scar beside my temple. Tilting my head back, I moan as his mouth softly trails a path across my jawline, and down my neck.

Gently pushing the fabric off my shoulder, he places another tender kiss on the scar that runs down my arm, where the surgeon made the incision so he could insert screws in my broken bones.

'You're perfect,' he whispers as his lips find their way back to mine.

And just like that all my insecurities vanish, because I know he means every word. His love for me is unconditional . . . *I feel it.*

EPILOGUE

Braxton

I lie perfectly still as she tips the last bucket of sand on my chest and pats it down tightly, just like I taught her. I'm buried right up to my neck. She's beaming as she stands and admires her handiwork. I find myself smiling at the joy I see reflected in her beautiful blue eyes. They're my mother's eyes, and every time I gaze into them I feel like a part of her is still with me. My beautiful daughter even bears her name . . . *Grace*. Grace Isabella Spencer.

The moment she was born was one of the happiest of my life. I can't even put into words how overwhelmed I felt looking down at my precious baby girl in my wife's arms. After losing our first child, and then almost losing Jemma, that moment seemed almost surreal.

'She looks just like you,' Jemma whispered. 'I know we already had a girl's name picked out, but would you mind if we called her Grace instead . . . after your mother.'

I remember wiping the tears from my eyes as I tried not to completely break down. 'I'd love that.'

'Daddy buried,' Grace says, pulling me back to reality.

The smile on her sweet face grows as she rubs her chubby little hands together to remove the sand that's stuck to them.

'You did a great job, princess.'

I turn my head slightly, and watch as she toddles over to her bucket, the one full of shells. Every weekend we walk along the beach together and collect them. It has become our ritual. Some mornings I wake and she's already standing beside my bed with her pink bucket in her hand.

She giggles as she pretends to sneak back to me. I quickly turn my head back, gazing up at the sky like I'm oblivious to what she's about to do. She does this to me every time. She saw Jem do it once, and squealed with delight when I broke free, tackling her mother to the sand.

'Hey, what are you doing?' I ask as she places two cone-shaped shells on my chest. She buries the base in the sand, so the pointed ends are facing upwards.

'Daddy boobies.' She covers her mouth with her hand to stifle her laugh.

'No! No boobies for Daddy.'

'Yes boobies,' she says as she starts to back away. She already knows what's coming.

'Roarrrr!' I bellow, breaking free from the sand.

She squeals as she scoops up her little pink bucket, and runs towards the house. She's only three, so her legs are tiny. It takes just a few steps for me to catch her. She squeals again when I scoop her into my arms.

Her body squirms when I bury my face in the crook of her neck and blow a raspberry against her soft skin. 'No, Daddy,' she cries out through her laughter.

We are still laughing as I brush the sand off her feet when we reach the back deck, before placing her down. 'Mummy, I have shells,' she calls out, running towards the sliding doors. I love that girl so much. I love both my girls.

After brushing my own sand off, I head into the house. I find Jem sitting at the kitchen table with my dad going through the memory book she made him. She does this every day. It's an album full of pictures of his life. His parents, my mother, me, Jemma and Grace. It even contains pictures of the store and Samson. Every day she sits with him, retelling him stories of his life, things he'll never be able to remember on his own.

His memory has almost totally gone now. There are no more good days, but he still seems happy, and I can't ask for more than that. He lives with us now. Jem never left after that night she spent here with me. We've been back together, in every sense of the word, ever since. A month later, we brought my dad home. Jem wasn't ready to go back to work, and she wanted him here, with us.

I hired a nurse to come in three times a day, to make things easier on her, but she still gave him all of her time. When she fell pregnant with Grace, we hired a full-time nurse. My father stays in the spare room downstairs, and I converted my office into a bedroom for his carer.

The bond that my wife has with my father is strong. Her memory has never fully returned, so she gets him.

I stand in the doorway and watch Grace climb onto my dad's lap. It's her favourite place to sit. They watch television together, and sometimes she reads to him. Well, she turns the pages and names all the pictures. Although he has no idea who she is most of the time, it's plain to see how much he adores her. His face lights up every time she enters the room.

'Morning, Pop.' I lean down and plant a kiss on his head. He just looks up at me with confusion in his eyes, but he still smiles. He's always smiling.

'That's me, Pa,' Grace says, pointing to the picture in the album on the table.

'It is,' he replies, smiling down at her.

I make my way around the table to Jemma. Bella-Rose is lying at her feet. 'Morning, babe.'

I bend down and brush my lips against hers, as my hand gently rubs over her very pregnant belly. Pregnancy suits her, I love seeing our baby growing inside her. We found out two weeks ago that she's carrying our son. His impending birth will complete our family perfectly.

'Morning, handsome,' she replies, eyeing me up and down.

'I'm just going to have a quick shower and wash the rest of this sand off, and then I'll help you organise breakfast.'

'Okay,' she says, smiling up at me. That sparkle that was always present in her eyes when she looked at me has returned.

⁓

'Hey, buddy,' I say, patting Lucas on the shoulder as he waltzes through the front door.

'Where's my little munchkin?' I should have known that would be his first question.

'Oh, hello to you too,' I say sarcastically, and he laughs. 'She's on the back deck with my dad, and Jemma's parents.' He heads in that direction, so I turn my attention to his wife. 'Hi, Rach.' I lean forward and kiss her cheek. 'Jem's in the kitchen.'

'Okay. How are you, Brax?'

'I'm fantastic.'

'You look happy.'

'I am.'

After Grace was born, Rachel's career took a turn away from women's fashion, when she started to design her own line of children's clothes. They really took off, and are now in all the major retail stores throughout Australia. She's happy, and doesn't seem to regret giving up her dream job in New York.

Jem and I tried every trick in the book to get Rachel and Lucas together when she first moved back to Australia. But they were both so stubborn, every attempt failed. In the end we got desperate.

We invited them both over one afternoon and locked them in one of the spare rooms upstairs. We told them we weren't going to let them out until they talked. It worked. They didn't emerge until the following morning, and they've been together ever since.

Jemma and Rachel are talking babies as they prepare the food in the kitchen, so after placing a soft kiss on my wife's cheek, I head out onto the deck.

I see that Lucas has already claimed Grace. They're walking hand-in-hand down to the water, Bella-Rose is trotting closely behind. He's going to make a wonderful father. He told me last week that he and Rachel are trying for a family of their own.

'Let me fill up your wine glasses,' I say to Jemma's parents. Stephen ended up moving back in with Christine a few days after Jem moved back in with me.

Jemma still makes her Sunday roasts, but instead of it just being us, we have our entire family over. The earth's axis finally aligned. Jem and I weren't the only ones to get our happily ever after. Lucas and Rachel, Christine and Stephen . . . and in a way, even my dad. He's out of the nursing home and surrounded by people who love him.

Jemma still wears the memory bracelet I gave her, and reads the letters often. I too have a letter. She gave it to me when we flew back to Kauai, in Hawaii, where we renewed our vows. She was three months' pregnant with Grace at the time. Rachel and Lucas came with us.

The morning of the accident I promised I would take her back there during the Christmas break, and I've never broken a promise to her.

Jem read it out as part of her vows. It choked me up then, and still does to this day.

Dearest Braxton,

The nineteenth of January 1996 was the day I was given the greatest gift I would ever receive . . . you.

On the nineteenth of January 2015, exactly nineteen years to the day after we met, we became one.

Nineteen days later I was in an accident, and I almost lost it all.

When I woke from my coma I felt empty inside, and now I know why—I had no memory of you, our love, or anything we had shared. Up until that fateful day, you had been my heart, and the air that I breathed. Without that, my life had no meaning. I felt completely lost.

You fought for us when I didn't have the will or strength to fight. You continued to love me, even when I didn't love you back. You never gave up on me, or on us, and for that I will be forever grateful. You proved yet again that you are, and always will be, my forever boy. I couldn't imagine my life without you in it, because you are my life.

The nineteen letters you sent became my lifeline. They helped remind me of everything we once shared, by giving me back pieces of our past. They gave my life meaning, a purpose, and the promise of a future. A future with you by my side. A second chance at life, and love. I will forever cherish what we once had, what we have now, and you . . . always.

What we have will never be forgotten.

Your forever girl,

Jemma

This renewed my faith in the number nineteen. It was our number, there was no denying it. Grace was even born a few minutes after midnight on the nineteenth of June. It was fate.

In the weeks and months that followed Jemma's accident, not only did I have to struggle to go on without my best friend, my soul mate, I had to fight tooth and nail to rekindle that magic we once shared. I was lucky enough to get her to love me once, and incredibly fortunate to get her to fall in love with me for a second time.

Things are different this time around, but with a lot of love, persistence and understanding, we have succeeded in building a better us ... a stronger us. We now know how fragile life can be. That's why we live for every second, every minute, every hour and every day.

Love with your entire heart while you have the chance, because life is far too precious to waste on any uncertainty.

This was our second chance at love. Our happily ever after.

Nineteen letters was all it took for her to realise we were meant to be.

Join us at

For competitions galore,
exclusive interviews with our lovely
Sphere authors, chat about
all the latest books
and much, much more.

Follow us on Twitter at
@littlebookcafe

Subscribe to our newsletter and
Like us at /thelittlebookcafe

Read. Love. Share.